SITUATION ROOM

(A LUKE STONE THRILLER—BOOK 3)

JACK

D0441448

ISBN: 978-1-63291-607-5

CHAPTER ONE

August 15th
7:07 a.m.
Black Rock Dam, Great Smoky Mountains, North Carolina

The dam sat there, immutable, gigantic, the one constant in Wes Yardley's life. The others who worked there called it "Mother." Built to generate hydroelectric power in 1943 during the height of World War Two, the dam was as tall as a fifty-story building. The power station that operated the dam was six stories high, and Mother loomed behind it like a fortress from some medieval nightmare.

Wes started his shift in the control room the same way he had for the last thirty-three years: he sat at the long half-circle desk, plunked his coffee mug down, and logged into the computer in front of him. He did this automatically, without thinking, still half-asleep. He was the only person in the control room, a place so antiquated it resembled a set from the old TV show *Space 1999*. It had last been remodeled sometime in the 1960s, and it was a 1960s version of what the future might look like. The walls were covered with dials and switches, many of which hadn't been touched in years. There were thick video screens which no one ever turned on. There were no windows at all.

Early morning was normally Wes's favorite part of the day. He had some time to himself to sip his coffee, go over the log from the night before, check the electricity generation figures, and then read the newspaper. Often enough, he would pour himself a second cup of coffee about halfway through the sports pages. He had no reason to do otherwise; after all, *nothing* ever happened here.

In the past couple of years, he had taken to reading the want ads as part of his morning ritual. For seventeen years, since computers had come in and the control room had gone automated, the big brains at the Tennessee Valley Authority had talked about controlling this dam from a remote location. Nothing had come of it so far, and maybe nothing ever would. Nothing had come of Wes's want ad perusals, either. This was a good job. He'd be happy to go out of here on a slab one day, hopefully in the distant future. He

1

absently reached for his coffee mug as he leafed through last night's reports.

Then he looked up—and everything changed.

Along the wall across from him, six red lights were blinking. It had been so long since they blinked, it took him a full minute to remember what those lights even meant. Each light was an indicator for one of the floodgates. Eleven years ago, during a week of torrential rains up north, they had opened one of the floodgates for the better part of three hours each day so the water up top didn't breach the walls. One of those lights blinked the entire time the gate was open.

But six lights blinking? All at the same time? That could only mean…

Wes squinted at the lights, as if that might help him see them better. "What the..?" he said in a quiet voice.

He picked up the phone on the desk and dialed three digits.

"Wes," a sleepy voice said. "How's your day going? Catch the Braves game last night?"

"Vince?" Wes said, ignoring the man's banter. "I'm down in the box, and I'm looking at the big board. I've got lights telling me that Floodgates One through Six are all open. I mean, right now, all six gates. It's an equipment malfunction, right? Some kind of gauge error, or a computer glitch. Right?"

"The floodgates are open?" Vince said. "That can't be. Nobody told me anything."

Wes stood and drifted slowly toward the board. The phone cord trailed behind him. He stared at the lights in awe. There was no readout. There was no data to explain anything. There was no view of anything. It was just those lights, blinking out of unison, some fast, some slow, like a Christmas tree gone a little bit insane.

"Well, that's what I'm looking at. Six lights, all at once. Tell me that we don't have six floodgates open, Vince."

Wes realized he didn't need Vince to tell him. Vince was in the middle of speaking, but Wes wasn't listening. He put the phone down and moved along a short narrow hallway to the observation room. It felt as if his feet were not attached to his body.

In the observation room, the entire south wall was rounded, reinforced glass. Normally, it looked out on a view of calm stream, flowing away from the building, turning right a few hundred yards away, and disappearing into the woods.

Not today.

Now, before him, was a raging torrent.

2

Wes stood there, mouth agape, frozen, numb, a cold tingle spreading across his arms. It was impossible to see what was happening. The foam sprayed a hundred feet into the air. Wes couldn't see the woods at all. He could hear a sound through the thick glass, too. It was the roar of water—more water than he could possibly imagine.

Ten million gallons of water per minute.

The sound, more than anything, made his heart thump in his chest.

Wes ran back to the telephone. He heard his own voice on the phone, breathless.

"Vince, listen to me. The gates are open! All of them! We've got a wall of water thirty feet high and two hundred feet wide coming through there! I can't see what the hell is going on. I don't know how it happened, but we need to shut it down again. NOW! You know the sequence?"

Vince sounded eerily calm; but then again, he hadn't seen all that water.

"I'll get my book out," he said.

Wes went to the control panel with the phone wedged in his ear.

"Come on, Vince. Come on!"

"Okay, I got it," Vince said.

Vince gave him a six-digit sequence of numbers, which Wes punched into the keypad.

He looked at the lights, expecting them to be off; but they were still blinking.

"No good. You got any other numbers?"

"Those are the numbers. Did you punch them in right?"

"I punched them in just like you said them." Wes's hands started to shake. Even so, he was starting to feel calm himself. In fact, more than calm. He felt *removed* from all this. He had once been in a car crash at night on a snowy mountain road, and as the car spun around and around, banging off the guardrails, Wes had felt a lot like he did at this moment. He felt asleep, like he was dreaming.

He had no idea how long those floodgates had been open, but six gates at once was a lot of water to release. Way too much water. That much water would overrun the river's banks. It would cause massive flooding downriver. Wes thought of that giant lake above their heads.

3

Then he thought of something else, something he didn't want to think of.

"Press cancel and we'll start over," Vince said.

"Vince, we got the resort three miles downstream from here. It's August, Vince. You know what I'm saying? It's the busy season, and they have no idea what's coming their way. We need to get these gates shut right this second, or we need to call somebody down there. They have to get their people out."

"Press cancel and we'll start over," Vince said again.

"Vince!"

"Wes, did you hear what I just said? We'll get the gates shut. If not, I'll call the resort in two minutes. Now press cancel and let's start over."

Dutifully, Wes did as he was told, fearing deep down that it would never work.

*

The telephone at the front desk rang incessantly.

Montgomery Jones sat in the cafeteria at the Black Rock Resort, trying to enjoy his breakfast. It was the same breakfast they served every day—scrambled eggs, sausages, pancakes, waffles— anything you wanted. But today, because the place was so busy, he was sitting in a corner of the cafeteria closest to the lobby. There were a hundred early-risers in here, taking up all the tables, gumming up the works at all the food stations. And that phone was starting to ruin Monty's morning.

He turned and glanced into the lobby. It was a rustic place, with wood paneling, a stone fireplace, and a battered front desk that hundreds of people had carved into over the long years. The desk was a mad intaglio of initials with hearts drawn around them, long-forgotten well wishes, and half-hearted attempts at line drawings.

No one was at the desk to answer the phone, and whoever was on the other end of the line was not getting the memo. Every time the phone stopped ringing, it paused just a few seconds, then started right up again. To Monty, this meant that every time the caller reached voice mail, he or she hung up and tried again. It was annoying. Someone must be desperate to make last-minute reservations.

"Call back, you idiot."

Monty was sixty-nine years old, and he'd been coming to Black Rock for at least twenty years, often two or three times a year. He loved it here. What he loved most of all was to get up early, have a nice hot breakfast, and get out on the scenic mountain roads on his Harley Davidson. He had his girlfriend Lena with him on this visit. She was almost thirty years his junior, but she was still up in the room. She was a late sleeper, that Lena. Which meant they would get a late start today. That was okay. Lena was worth it. Lena was proof that success had its rewards. He imagined her in the bed, her long brunette hair spread out across the pillows.

The phone stopped ringing. Five seconds passed before it started again.

All right. That's enough. Monty would answer the damn phone. He stood and creaked on stiff legs over to the desk. He hesitated just for a second before picking it up. The index finger of his right hand traced the carving of a heart with an arrow through the middle. Yes, he came here a lot. But he wasn't so familiar with the place that it was like he worked here. It wasn't like he could take a reservation, or even a message. So he would just tell the caller to try back later.

He picked up the receiver. "Hello?"

"This is Vincent Moore of the Tennessee Valley Authority. I'm at the control station of the Black Rock Dam, three miles north of you. This is an emergency. We have a problem with the floodgates, and request an immediate evacuation of your resort. Repeat, an immediate evacuation. There's a flood coming your way."

"What?" Monty said. Somebody must be putting him on. "I don't understand you."

Just then, a commotion started in the cafeteria. A strange hubbub of voices began, rising in pitch. Suddenly a woman screamed.

The man on the phone started again. "This is Vincent Moore of the Tennessee Valley..."

Someone else screamed, a male voice.

Monty held the phone to his ear but he was no longer listening. Just through the doorway, people in the cafeteria were getting up from their seats. Some were moving toward the doors. Then, in an instant, panic set in.

People were running, pushing, falling over each other. Monty watched it happen. A surge of people came toward him, eyes wide, mouths open in round O's of terror.

As Monty watched through the window, a wall of water three or four feet high swept over the grounds. A maintenance man in a golf cart driving by up a small hill from the main house was caught in the tide. The cart upended, flipping the man into the water and landing on top of him. The cart got caught for a moment, then slid down the hill on its side, pushed by all the water and gathering speed.

It slid right toward the windows, moving impossibly fast.

CRASH!

The cart slammed sideways into the window, shattering it—and a torrent of water followed.

It poured into the cafeteria through the smashed window. The golf cart came through the window, then slid across the room. A man tried to stop it, fell down in three feet of water, and didn't come back up again.

Everywhere, people were falling down into the rising water, unable to stand up again. Tables and chairs were sliding across the room and piling up against the far wall.

Monty got behind the desk. He looked down at his feet. The water was already up to his calves. Suddenly, across the way, the entire thirty-foot window of the cafeteria caved in, spraying great shards of glass.

It sounded like an explosion.

Monty prepared to run. But before his feet could take hold, before he could even scramble over the desk, all he could do was raise his arms and scream as the wall of water consumed him.

CHAPTER TWO

7:35 a.m.
United States Naval Observatory – Washington, DC

To Susan Hopkins, first female President of the United States, life couldn't be better. It was summer, so Michaela and Lauren were out of school. Pierre had brought them here once things had settled down, and finally, the whole family was staying here in the New White House. Michaela had bounced back from her kidnapping as if it had been a madcap adventure she chose to go on. She had even done a round of talk shows about her experience, and co-authored an article for a national magazine with Lauren.

Indeed, Susan and Pierre found themselves bending over backward so that Lauren didn't feel left out of the publicity. After the first TV interview, they insisted that the girls do the shows together. It was only right—while Michaela was trapped on top of a fifty-story tower guarded by terrorists, Lauren was home alone, her twin sister and lifelong companion ripped away from her.

Sometimes, Susan found her breath taken away at the thought of losing her daughter. She woke in the middle of the night from time to time, gasping for air, like a demon was sitting on her chest.

She had Luke Stone to thank for Michaela's return. Luke Stone had brought her back. He and his team had killed every single one of the kidnappers. He was a hard man to reconcile. Ruthless killer on the one hand, loving father on the other. Susan was convinced he had gone to that rooftop not because it was his job, but because he loved his own son so much he couldn't bear the thought of Susan losing her daughter.

In ten days, the whole family, minus Susan, would be heading back to California to get ready for the school year. She would lose them again, but it was only a temporary loss, and it had been great having them here. So great that she was almost afraid to ponder it.

"What are you thinking about?" Pierre said.

They were lying on the king-sized bed in the master bedroom. Morning light streamed in through the southeast-facing windows. Susan lay with her head resting on his bare chest and her arm around his waist. So what if he was gay? He was her husband, and the father of her two daughters. She loved him. They had shared so much together. And this, Sunday morning, was their quiet time.

7

The girls, being tweens, were moving into their sleeping late years. They would stay in bed until noon if Pierre and Susan let them. Heck, Susan might stay in bed too, if duty didn't call. President of the United States was a seven-day-a-week job, with a few hours of laziness on Sunday mornings.

"I'm thinking that I'm happy," she said. "For the first time since June sixth, I'm happy. It's been amazing having you guys here. Just like old times. And I feel like, with everything that's happened, I'm finally getting a handle on this President thing. I didn't think I would be able to, but I have."

"You've gotten tougher," Pierre said. "Meaner."

"Is it bad?" she said.

He shook his head. "No, not bad at all. You've matured a lot. You were still very much a girl when you were Vice President."

Susan nodded at the truth of that. "I was pretty girly."

"Sure," he said. "Remember how *Mademoiselle* had you out jogging in bright orange yoga pants? Very sexy. But you were Vice President of the United States at the time. It seemed a little… informal, shall we say?"

"It was fun being Vice President. I really loved it."

He nodded and laughed. "I know. I saw."

"But then things changed."

"Yes."

"And we can't go back," she said.

He looked down at her. "Would you want to, if you could?"

She thought about it, but only for a second. "If all those people could still be alive, the ones who lost their lives at Mount Weather, I would give this job back to Thomas Hayes in a heartbeat. But failing that, no. I wouldn't go back. I've got a couple more years to go before I need to decide about running for reelection. I feel like the people are starting to get behind me, and if I get another term, I think we'll do some great, great things."

He raised his eyebrows. "Another term?"

She laughed. "A conversation for another time."

Just then, the bedside telephone rang. Susan reached for it, hoping it was something insignificant.

It never was.

It was her new chief-of-staff, Kat Lopez. Susan could tell her voice right away. And already, she didn't like her tone.

"Susan?"

"Hi, Kat. You know it's not even eight a.m. on Sunday, right? Even God rested one day a week. You're allowed to do the same."

8

Kat's tone was serious. In general, Kat was nothing if not serious. She was a woman, she was Hispanic, and she had fought her way up the ladder from humble beginnings. She didn't get where she was by smiling. Susan thought that was too bad. Kat was super competent. But she also had a very pretty face. It wouldn't hurt her to smile once in a while.

"Susan, a large dam just broke in a remote area of far western North Carolina. Our analysts are saying it might be a terror attack."

Susan felt that familiar stab of dread. It was one thing about this job that she would never get used to. It was one thing about this new life of hers that she wouldn't wish on her worst enemy.

"Casualties?" she said.

She saw the look in Pierre's eyes. This was the job. This was the nightmare. Just a minute ago, she had breezily considered a run for another term in office.

"Yes," Kat said.

"How many?"

"No one knows yet. Possibly hundreds."

Susan felt the air go out of her as if she were a tire that had just been slashed.

"Susan, a group is gathering right now in the Situation Room."

Susan nodded. "I'll be down in fifteen minutes."

She hung up. Pierre was staring at her.

"Is it bad?" he said.

"When isn't it bad?"

"Okay," he said. "Do your thing. I'll handle the girls."

Susan was up and moving toward the shower almost before he finished speaking.

CHAPTER THREE

"How you holding up, Monster?"

"Fine, Dad."

Luke Stone and his son, Gunner, moved slowly up the steep, rough-hewn steps of the trail. It was a humid morning, hot and getting hotter, and Luke was mindful that Gunner was only ten years old. They took the mountain slowly, and Luke made sure they stopped for frequent rests and water breaks.

They moved higher and higher through the enormous boulder field. The massive stones were intricately laid to create a winding, almost Byzantine stairway, as if some Norse thunder god had come down from the skies and carved them with his own giant hands. Luke knew the stones had been placed by out-of-work young men plucked from East Coast cities by the Civilian Conservation Corps some eighty years before, during the depths of the Great Depression.

A little higher, and they came upon some iron rungs bolted into the stone face. They climbed the ladder, then meandered up a carved boulder switchback. Soon, the trail leveled off and they walked through some dense forest, before one final climb to the summit outlook. They climbed out onto the rocks.

Just in front of them was a steep drop-off, probably fifty stories down a sheer cliff to the large lake where they had parked. Further out, the spot offered a commanding view of the Atlantic Ocean, perhaps five miles away.

"What do you think, Monster?"

Gunner was sweaty from the heat of the day. He sat on a rock, unslung his backpack, and pulled out a water bottle. His black *Dawn of the Dead* T-shirt was drenched in sweat. His blond hair was matted. He took a swig from his bottle and handed it up to Luke. He was a self-assured kid.

"It's awesome, Dad. I really like it."

"I want to give you something," Luke said. "I decided to wait until we climbed the mountain. I'm not sure why. I just thought it would be a fun place to do it."

10

Gunner looked just slightly alarmed. He liked getting gifts, but generally speaking, he preferred ones that he had asked for.

Luke took the device out of his pocket. It was just a small piece of black plastic, about the size of a key fob. It didn't look like much. It could have been the clicker for an automatic garage.

"What is it?" Gunner said.

"It's a GPS unit. That means Global Positioning System." Luke pointed at the sky. "Up there in space, there are all these satellites…"

Gunner half-smiled. He shook his head. "I know what GPS is, Dad. Mom has one in her car. It's a good thing, too. She would get lost going around the corner without it. Why are you giving one to me?"

"See this clip it has in the back? I want you to clip it to your backpack and carry it with you wherever you go. I have an app on my cell phone that is set to track this unit. That way, even when we're separated, I'll always know where you are."

"Are you worried about me?"

Luke shook his head. "No. I'm not worried. I know you can handle yourself. It's just that we haven't been seeing much of each other recently, and if I can just look at my phone and see where you are, it's almost like being there with you."

"But I can't see where you are," Gunner said. "So how am I supposed to feel close?"

Luke reached into his pocket and came out with another GPS unit, this one bright blue. "See this? I'm going to put it on my key ring. When we get back to the hotel, I'll load the app into your phone, and then you can always know where I am."

Gunner smiled. "I like that idea, Dad. But you know we could always just text each other. Do you even text? I know that a lot of people your age don't."

Now Luke smiled. "Yeah. We can text. We can do both."

For Luke, it was a bittersweet feeling to be with Gunner up here. Luke had grown up without a father, and now Gunner was doing much the same. The divorce with Becca wasn't finalized, but that was coming. Luke hadn't worked for the government in two months, but Becca was adamant: she was going through with it anyway.

In the meantime, Luke had Gunner two weekends a month. He did everything in his power to make sure those weekends were chock-full of fun and adventure. He also did everything he could to

11

answer Gunner's questions in an even-handed, yet optimistic way. Questions like this one:

"Do you think we can do something like this with Mom one day?"

Luke stared out at the sea. Questions like that made him want to jump off this cliff. "I hope so."

Gunner perked up at the slightest hint of possibility. "When?"

"Well, you have to understand that your mom and I are having a little disagreement right now."

"I don't understand," Gunner said. "You love each other, right? And you promised you were going to quit your job, right? Did you really quit?"

Luke nodded. "I did quit."

"See, Mom doesn't believe that."

"I know it."

"But if you can make her believe it, then…"

Luke had quit, all right. He had quit and gone completely off radar. Susan Hopkins had promised to leave him alone, and she had honored that promise. He had also been out of touch with his old group at the Special Response Team.

The truth was, he was enjoying his time away. He had gone back to basics. He rented a cabin in the Adirondack Mountains for two weeks and spent nearly the entire time bow hunting and fishing. He bathed by jumping off the cabin's back dock each morning. He grew a beard.

After that, he spent ten days in the Caribbean, solo sailing through St. Vincent and the Grenadines, snorkeling with sea turtles, giant stingrays, and reef sharks, and diving a couple of shipwrecks from more than a hundred years ago.

At the end of each little trip, he would give himself a day to make it back to Washington, DC, and pick up Gunner for the next dad and son adventure. Luke had to admit, being retired agreed with him. A year from now, when he ran out of money, it wasn't going to be all that agreeable, but for now, he couldn't think of a bad word to say about it.

"Are you and Mom going to split up for good?"

Luke detected the slightest tremble in Gunner's voice when he asked that question. He got it, he really did. Gunner was afraid. Luke sat down on the rocks with him.

"Gunner, I love both you and your mom very much. The situation is complicated, and we're working through it the best we can."

12

That wasn't necessarily true. Becca was cold to Luke. She wanted a divorce. She wanted full custody of Gunner. She thought that Luke was a danger to Gunner and to her. She had practically threatened to get an order of protection against him. She was being unreasonable, and she came from a family with a lot of money. She could pay for a long and bitter custody battle, if need be.

"Do you want to be with her?"

"Yes, I do. Of course I do." It was the first lie Luke had told Gunner in this conversation. The truth was harder to ascertain. At first, he had. But as time passed, and Becca's position hardened, he became less sure.

"Then why don't you just come to the house and tell her? Send her roses or something, like every day?"

It was a good question. It didn't have a simple answer.

Inside Luke's backpack, a telephone started ringing. It was probably Becca, wanting to talk to Gunner. Luke reached inside the pack for the satellite phone he kept with him at all times. It was the only nod toward remaining on grid that he had made. Becca could always reach him. But she wasn't the only one. There was one other person on Earth who had access to this number.

He looked at who was calling. It was a number he didn't recognize, from the 202 area code. Washington, DC.

His heart dropped.

It was her. The other person.

"Is it Mom?" Gunner said.

"No."

"Is it the President?"

Luke nodded. "I think so."

"Don't you think you better answer it?" Gunner said.

"I don't work for her anymore," Luke said. "Remember?"

This morning, before they had left to come on this hike, they had watched TV news footage of the dam failure in North Carolina. More than a hundred confirmed dead, hundreds more missing. An entire mountain resort had been washed away by a wall of water. Towns downstream from there were being evacuated and sandbagged as fast as possible, but there were likely to be more casualties.

The incredible thing was a dam built in 1943 had simply malfunctioned after more than seventy years of nearly perfect operations. To Luke, that smelled like sabotage. But he couldn't imagine who would want to target a dam in such a remote area. Who would even know it was there? If it was sabotage, then it was likely a local issue, some group of militia members, or maybe environmentalists, or maybe even a disgruntled former employee, pulling a stunt that went horribly wrong, and with tragic consequences. The state police or North Carolina Bureau of Investigation would probably have the bad guys in custody by the end of the day.

But now the phone was ringing. So maybe there was more to it.

"Dad, it's okay. I don't want you to quit your job, even if Mom does."

"Is that so? What if I want to quit? Don't I get any say in the matter?"

Gunner shook his head. "I don't think so. I mean, a lot of people died in that flood, right? What if I was one of them? What if Mom and me both died? Wouldn't you want someone to figure out why it happened?"

The phone went on and on, ringing. When voice mail picked up, the phone stopped ringing for a few seconds, paused, and then started ringing again. They wanted to speak to Luke, and they weren't going to leave a message.

Luke, thinking of Gunner's words, pressed the green button on the phone. "Stone."

"Hold for the President of the United States," a male voice said.

There was a moment of silence, and then her voice came on the line. She sounded harder than before, someone older. The events of the past few months would age anyone.

"Luke?"

"Hi, Susan."

"Luke, I need you to come in for a meeting."

"Is this about the dam failure?"

"Yes."

"Susan, I'm retired, remember?"

Her voice lowered.

"Luke, the dam was hacked. Hundreds of people are dead, and all signs point to the Chinese. We are on the verge of World War Three."

Luke didn't know how to respond to that.

"What time will you be here?" she asked.

And he knew it was not a question.

14

CHAPTER FOUR

6:15 p.m.
United States Naval Observatory – Washington, DC

Luke rode in the back of the black SUV as it pulled into the circle in front of the stately, white-gabled 1850s Queen Anne–style residence that for many years had been the Vice President's official residence. Since the White House was destroyed two months before, this place had served as the New White House, which was fitting because the President had lived here for five years before taking on her new role.

The two months Luke had been away, he almost never thought about this place, or the people inside. He kept the satellite phone with him at the President's request, but for the first few weeks, he lived in dread of receiving a call. After that, he almost forgot he even had the phone.

A young woman met him on the walkway in front of the house. She was brunette, tall, very pretty. She wore a no-nonsense black skirt and jacket. Her hair was tied back in a tight bun. She carried a tablet computer in her left hand. She offered Luke the other hand. Her grip was firm, all business.

"Agent Stone? I'm Kathryn Lopez, Susan's chief-of-staff."

Luke was a little taken aback. "Are they recruiting chiefs-of-staff right out of high school these days?"

"Very kind of you," she said. Her voice was perfunctory. It told him she got that all the time, and most of the time it wasn't intended to be kind. "I'm thirty-seven years old. I've lived in Washington thirteen years, since right after I finished my master's degree. I've worked for a Representative, two Senators, and the former Director of Health and Human Services. I've been around the block a couple times."

"Okay," Luke said. "I'm not worried about you."

They moved through the front doors. Inside the doors, they were confronted by a checkpoint with three armed guards and a metal detector. Luke removed the Glock nine-millimeter from his shoulder holster and placed it on the conveyor belt. He reached down and unstrapped the small pocket pistol and the hunting knife taped to his calves and placed those on the belt as well. Finally, he took his keys from his pocket and dropped them on there with the weapons.

"Sorry," he said. "I don't remember there being a security checkpoint here."

"There wasn't," Kat Lopez said. "It's only been in for a few weeks. We've got more and more people coming here as Susan gets a grip on her duties, and security has formalized."

Luke remembered. When the attacks came, and Thomas Hayes died, Susan was suddenly elevated to the Presidency. The White House had been mostly destroyed, and everything—all arrangements, all logistics—had an ad hoc, almost desperate quality to them. Those had been crazy days. He was glad for the time off since then. It was a little amazing that Susan hadn't had any at all.

After the guards took Luke aside and gave him an extra pat-down and a quick skim with a metal-detecting wand, he and the chief-of-staff moved on.

The place was bustling. The foyer was crowded with people in suits, people in military uniforms, people with their sleeves rolled up, people walking fast through the hallways, trailing gaggles of assistants. One thing was obvious right away—there were a lot more women here than before.

"What happened to the last guy?" Luke said. "He used to be Susan's chief-of-staff. Richard…"

Kat Lopez nodded. "Yes, Richard Monk. Well, after the Ebola incident, both he and Susan agreed that it was a good time for him to move on. But even though he's out of here, he landed on his feet. He's working as chief-of-staff for the new United States Representative from Delaware, Paul Chipman."

Luke knew there were new Representatives and Senators coming in from thirty-nine states to replace the ones lost in the Mount Weather attack. It was a blizzard of people moving up from the minor leagues, or coming back from retirement. More than a few were the appointees of state governors with questionable ethics and long-established patronage systems. There were greasy palms all over the place.

He smiled. "Richard went from working directly with the President to working with a freshman rep from the second smallest state in the union? And you call that landing on his feet? It sounds like he landed on his head."

"No comment," Kat said, and almost smiled. It was the closest thing to humanity she had given him so far. She led him through the crowds to a double doorway at the end of the hall. Luke already knew the place. When Susan was Vice President, the large sunlit chamber had been her conference room. In the days after she took the oath of office, it rapidly transformed into an on-the-fly Situation Room.

It had been formalized, too. Modular walls ran the length of the room, covering the old windows. Giant flat-panel video screens had been mounted at five-foot intervals. A larger oak conference table had been brought in, and on the wall behind the head of it was the Seal of the President. There were about two dozen people inside when Luke and Kat walked in, a dozen at the conference table, and more in chairs lining the walls.

The gender change was evident here as well. Luke remembered sitting in here being briefed about the missing Ebola sample two months ago. Of the thirty people in the room at that time, Susan might have been the only woman. Twenty-nine men, half of them big and burly, and one small woman.

Now maybe half the people were women.

Susan rose from the head of the table when Luke walked in. She was different, too. Harder, perhaps. Thinner than before. She had been a fashion model in her earlier life, and she had carried baby fat on her cheeks right into middle age. That was gone now, and she seemed to have developed crow's feet around her eyes almost overnight. The bright eyes themselves seemed more focused, like laser beams. She had spent her entire life as the most beautiful woman in the room—by the time this presidency was over, that might no longer be the case.

"Agent Stone," she said. "I'm glad you could join us."

He smiled. "Madam President. Please. Call me Luke."

She didn't return the smile. "Thank you for coming."

Standing at one of the large screens was Kurt Kimball, Susan's National Security Advisor. Luke had met him once before. He was tall with broad shoulders. His head was perfectly bald.

Kimball offered him a handshake. If Kat Lopez's shake was firm, Kurt Kimball's was granite. "Luke, good to see you."

"Kurt, likewise."

The atmosphere was tense. These people hadn't spent the past two months camping and sailing. Even so, Luke had flown down here from Maine at a moment's notice, and dropped his son off with his angry, soon to be ex-wife, who saw all of this as reinforcement of the reasons she was divorcing him. You might think they'd offer him a little more warmth.

He decided to go with the flow. Hundreds of people had died this morning, and the people in this room, as least, thought it was a terrorist attack.

"Shall we get down to it?" he said.

"Please have a seat," Kimball said.

17

A seat at Susan's right flank had miraculously appeared, and Luke took it.

On the screen, a photo of a large dam appeared. Large wasn't quite the word. Massive was more to the point. A six-story building sat in front of the dam, the control center, with six partially open floodgates below it. The building was dwarfed by the dam rising behind it. Along the edge was a hydroelectric power generating station with row after row after row of transformers.

"Luke, this is Black Rock Dam," Kurt Kimball said. "It is approximately fifty stories tall and impounds Black Rock Lake, which is sixteen miles long, four hundred feet deep, and at any given time holds about ten billion cubic feet of water. As you probably saw on the news, just after seven a.m. this morning, the six floodgates you see along the bottom opened fully, and remained locked open for three and a half hours, until technicians could de-couple them from the computer system that operates them, and finally close them manually."

Kimball used a laser pointer to indicate the floodgates.

"If you look at the gates in relation to the building, you will see that they are quite large. Each one is ten meters tall, which means that six three-story-high jets of water were released all at once. The water pressure of Black Rock Lake sent the flood downstream at approximately twenty miles per hour, which doesn't sound all that fast until you're standing in front of it. Until this morning, the Black Rock Resort stood three miles south of the dam. The resort was made almost entirely of wood. The initial wall of water completely destroyed the resort, and as far as we know, the only survivors were a handful of people who left early to hike to the top of the dam, or to take drives on nearby scenic roads."

"How many people were staying at the resort?" Luke said.

"There were two hundred and eighty-one guests listed in their online reservations system. Perhaps twenty of them either left the resort before the flood, or never arrived there for one reason or another. All of the others were swept away and are assumed dead. Combined with other disasters downstream, it will be several days before we have any kind of accurate body count."

Luke got that odd familiar feeling. It returned like an old friend, one that you hadn't seen in a while and were hoping not to see anymore. It came as a sickness in the pit of his stomach. It was death, the deaths of innocent people, minding their own business. Luke had dealt with it for far too long.

"Did anyone try to warn them?" he said.

Kimball nodded. "Workers in the dam's control center called the resort on the phone as soon as they realized the floodgates were open, but apparently the flood had already reached there by the time they got in touch with anyone. Someone did pick up, but the conversation ended almost immediately."

"Jesus. And what were the disasters downstream you mentioned?"

A map appeared on the screen. It showed the lake, the dam, the resort, and additional towns nearby. Kimball indicated a town. "The town of Sargent lies another sixteen miles south of the resort. It's a town of twenty-three hundred people, and a gateway for visitors to the National Park. Most of Sargent is situated on a small hill, and the town received slightly more warning than the resort. They got enough warning, in fact, that the town emergency sirens sounded before the flood came. With an added sixteen miles to travel, the floodwaters hit with somewhat less force in Sargent, and many of the houses and buildings in town withstood the initial force of the flood and were not washed away. Many of the low-lying houses were, however, quickly inundated. More than four hundred people from Sargent are currently missing and presumed dead."

Luke stared at the screen as Kimball's laser pointer fell on the towns of Sapphire, Greenwood, and Kent, each one somewhat farther from the dam than the one before, and each one the site of a disaster in its own right. The scale of it was devastating, and although the floodgates were closed, the flood itself was going to continue traveling south and downhill for the next several days. Two dozen towns had been evacuated, but more fatalities were practically guaranteed. Some people in remote areas wouldn't leave, or couldn't.

"And you think hackers did this? How is that possible?"

Kimball glanced around the room. "Does everyone here have clearance to hear this next part? Can we please sweep anyone out who doesn't have clearance?"

Low murmuring went around the room, but no one moved. "Okay, I'm going to assume that anyone here belongs here. If not, it's your ass. Remember that."

He turned back to Luke.

"The dam was built in 1943 to generate much-needed electricity during the war. It was built and is operated to this day by the Tennessee Valley Authority. For most of the dam's life, the floodgates were operated by controls less sophisticated than your garage door opener. About twenty years ago, TVA started looking

19

at ways to save money by automating their dams. Control centers in old hydroelectric dams are incredibly inefficient by modern standards. You've basically got people there around the clock, and their jobs include reading and writing logbooks, and opening and closing the spillways from time to time. The floodgates are almost never opened.

"TVA was thinking they could aggregate ten or twenty dam control centers into one centrally located control center. So they retro-fitted several dams with computer software that can be operated remotely. Black Rock was one of them. We're talking about very simple software—yes means open the gates, no means close them. For one reason or another, they never did create the central control center, but they did make the software internet-based, in case they ever decided to do so. The final nail, so to speak, is that the science of encryption barely existed at that time, and the software has never been updated since it was first installed."

Luke stared, stunned.

"You're kidding."

He shook his head.

"It was easy to hijack this system. It's just that no one ever thought to do it before. What terrorist would even know this dam exists? It's in a remote corner of a rural state. You don't get a lot of style points for attacking Sargent, North Carolina. But as we've discovered, the results are as devastating as if they had attacked Chicago."

Susan spoke for the first time during Kimball's presentation. "And the worst thing about it is there are hundreds of dams like this across the United States. The truth is we don't even know how many there are, and how many are vulnerable."

"And why do we think the Chinese did it?" Luke said.

"Our own hackers at NSA traced the infiltration to a series of IP addresses in northern China. And we traced communication with those addresses to an internet account at a motel in Asheville, North Carolina, sixty miles east of the Black Rock Dam. The communications took place in the forty-eight hours before the attack. A SWAT team from the Bureau of Alcohol, Tobacco, and Firearms operates in that region, raiding unlicensed distilleries and breweries. That team was diverted to the motel, did a takedown of the room in question, and arrested a thirty-two-year-old Chinese national named Li Quiangguo."

An image of a Chinese man being led from a small nondescript motel by a group of tall and broad ATF officers appeared on the screen. Another image appeared of the same man standing on a narrow roadway across from a lake. He stood in front of a historic plaque that read *Black Rock Dam—1943*, with a couple of paragraphs of description below.

"Although he has travel documents including a passport under this name, we don't believe this is the man's real name. As you know, the sequence of names in China is reversed—the surname comes first, followed by the given name. Li is one of the most common surnames in China, practically a generic name, similar to Smith in the United States. And Quiangguo, in Mandarin Chinese, means *Strong Nation*. This was a name with militaristic connotations that was very common after the Chinese Revolution, but fell into disfavor probably forty years ago. Further, Li was found with a handgun in his possession, as well as a small vial of cyanide pills. We believe he is a Chinese government agent, operating under an alias, who was supposed to kill himself if he was about to get caught."

"So he got cold feet," Luke said.

"Either that, or he just didn't get to the pills in time."

Luke shook his head. "After an operation like this one, an agent willing to kill himself would be holding the pill bottle in his hand, or have it in his pocket, twenty-four hours a day. What were the communications?"

"They were a series of encrypted emails. We haven't broken the encryption yet, and it may be weeks before we do. It's one they haven't seen at NSA. Very complex, very tough to take down. So at this moment, we have no idea what the content of the emails is."

"Is the man talking?" Luke said.

Kimball shook his head. "He's being held in a cabin at a FEMA detention center in northern Georgia, about ninety miles southeast of the attack site. He insists he's simply a tourist who was in the wrong place at the wrong time."

"That's why we called you," Susan said. "We'd like you to go have a chat with him. We thought he might speak to you."

"Have a chat," Luke said.

Susan shrugged. "Yes."

"Get him to talk?"

"Yes."

"For that, I'll probably need my team with me," Luke said.

A look passed between Susan, Kurt Kimball, and Kat Lopez.

"Perhaps we'd better discuss that in private," Kimball said.

"Okay, Susan, so this is the part where you tell me again that the Special Response Team has been disbanded, right?"

"Luke..." she began.

They were sitting upstairs in Susan's study. The study was just as Luke remembered it. A large rectangular room with hardwood floors and a white carpet in the middle. The carpet served as the focal point for a sitting area with big comfortable upright chairs and a coffee table.

One entire wall of the study was a floor-to-ceiling bookcase. The bookcase reminded Luke of *The Great Gatsby*.

And then there were the windows. Giant, gracious, floor to ceiling windows which gave expansive views of the Naval Observatory's rolling grounds. The windows faced southwest and let in the afternoon light. The light was like something a master artist would try to capture.

The days were clearly getting shorter. Although it wasn't yet 7 p.m., early evening sunlight streamed through her windows. The day was already ending. Luke thought again briefly of his interaction with Becca when he dropped Gunner off. He shook the image away. It was too much to think about.

He sat on the opposite side of the coffee table from the President. Kurt Kimball sat at an angle to both of them. Kat Lopez stood behind Susan and to her right.

"Yes," Susan said. "There is no more Special Response Team. Most of the former staff have been absorbed into other roles within the FBI. At this point, it would be rather difficult to rebuild what you think of as your team."

"Susan," Luke said. "I'd like to remind you that you're asking me to come out of retirement again. You know what I've been doing for the past two months? I'll tell you. Camping, fishing, hiking, sailing. A little bit of hunting. A little bit of diving." He rubbed his beard. "Sleeping late."

"So you're fit for duty," Kurt Kimball said.

Luke shook his head. "I'm caked in rust. I need my team. I trust them. I can't really function without them."

"Luke, if you'd stuck around instead of disappearing, we might have been able to carve out a little agency for you..."

"I was trying to save my marriage," he said.

Susan stared right at him. "How did it go?"

He gave her a tiny head shake. "Not too well, so far."

22

"I'm sorry to hear that."

"So am I."

Susan glanced behind her. "Kat, can we have the status on Luke's former team members?"

Kat Lopez glanced down at the tablet in her hand. "Sure. That's easy enough. Mark Swann left the FBI for a job with the National Security Agency. He works at their headquarters here in suburban DC. He's been there three and a half weeks. He's moving through their classification system, and should begin work on the PRISM data mining project within another month.

"Edward Newsam is still with the FBI. He was out on medical leave for most of June and July. His hip rehabilitation is complete, and he's been reassigned to the Hostage Rescue Team. He is currently in training at Quantico for possible overseas intelligence work to begin later in the year. There's a note in his file that his employment status is likely to become classified in the coming weeks, at which point a Top Secret security clearance will be required to discuss his status or his whereabouts."

Luke nodded. Neither of these were much of a surprise. Swann and Newsam were among the best at what they did. "Can we get them on loan?" he said.

Kat Lopez nodded. "In all likelihood, if we request them, the agencies will honor our request."

"And Trudy?" Luke said. "I need her, too."

"Luke, Trudy Wellington is in jail," Susan said.

Luke felt his stomach drop at the words. He stared for a full five seconds, trying to process the words.

"What?" he finally said.

Susan shook her head.

"I can't believe you don't know. What have you been doing, hiding under a rock? Don't you look at the newspapers?"

He shrugged. "I told you what I was doing. I've been off the grid. They don't sell newspapers where I've been, and I've been leaving the computer at home."

Kat Lopez read from her tablet. Her voice was automatic, almost robotic. She had detached herself from what she was saying.

"Trudy Wellington, age thirty, was Don Morris's mistress for at least a year during the planning of the June sixth attacks. Email, telephone, text, and computer records suggest that as early as last March, she became aware of a plan to assassinate both the President and Vice President of the United States, and she was aware of who at least some of the conspirators were. She has been indicted on

23

charges of treason, conspiracy to commit treason, more than three hundred counts of conspiracy to commit murder, and a host of other charges. She's being held without bail at the Federal women's prison facility in Randal, Maryland. If convicted of the charges against her, she faces penalties starting with multiple life sentences, up to and including the death penalty."

Luke ran a hand through his hair. The news hit him like a punch in the head. He thought of Trudy, pictured her with her funny red glasses on, her eyes peeking over the top of her tablet computer. He thought of her on the night he went to her apartment at 3 a.m., opening the door with nothing on but a long, flimsy T-shirt, a gun in her hand. He thought of the two of them, and their bodies, together that night.

She was in prison? It couldn't be real.

"Trudy Wellington is facing the death penalty?" he said.

"In a word, yes."

"Basically, because she didn't turn Don in?"

Susan shook her head. "It's treason, no matter how you want to spin it. A lot of people died, including Thomas Hayes, who was both the President of the United States and a personal friend of mine. Wellington could possibly have prevented it, and chose not to. She chose to not even try. About the only way she can save herself at this point is to testify against the conspirators."

"I have trouble believing that she knew," Luke said. "Has she confessed?"

"She denies everything," Kat Lopez said.

"I would tend to believe her," Luke said.

Kat held out her tablet. "There's about two hundred pages of evidence. We have access to most of it, which you can review. You might feel differently after you do."

Luke shook his head. He looked at Susan. "So where does this leave us?"

She shrugged. "You can have Mark Swann and Ed Newsam for a couple days if you feel you need them. But you can't have Trudy Wellington."

She looked at him.

"And your chopper leaves in under an hour."

CHAPTER FIVE

August 16th
7:15 a.m.
Black Rock Dam, Great Smoky Mountains, North Carolina

From Luke's window, nothing seemed out of the ordinary as their sleek black helicopter flew low over the dam. They came in over Black Rock Lake, which was long, undulating, and picturesque, bordered on all sides by dense green wilderness and steep hillsides. A narrow roadway crossed the top of the dam. They flew past it, and the dam itself fell away, fifty stories down to the power house and the floodgates. The floodgates appeared to be operating normally, a small trickle of water flowing out from beneath them. About a quarter mile of electricity transformers, a spider web of steel towers and high tension wires, stretched away from the dam. They seemed to be intact.

"Not much to see," he said into his headset.

To his left sat big Ed Newsam, staring out the window on the opposite side. Ed's broken hip was mended, and it looked like he had been hitting the weight room. His python-like arms were more swollen than Luke remembered, his chest and shoulders were even broader, his legs even more like oak trees. He wore jeans, work boots, and a simple blue T-shirt.

In the row behind them sat Mark Swann. He was long and lean, his blue-jeaned legs jutting out in the aisle, his checkerboard Chuck Taylor sneakers crossed at the ankles in front of Luke. His sandy hair was longer than before, tied in a ponytail now, and he had swapped out his aviator-type glasses for the round John Lennon style at some point in the past two months. He wore a black T-shirt with the logo from the punk rock band The Ramones. The NSA offices must be quite the fashion show.

"The water went out the floodgates just like it's supposed to do," the chopper pilot said. He was a middle-aged man wearing a black nylon jacket with the capital letters FEMA in white on the back. "There was no damage to the dam or the dam facilities, and there were no casualties among dam personnel. The only thing that happened here was the access road got washed away. About three miles south is where the real action starts."

They had flown on a Secret Service jet from DC to a small municipal airport at the edge of the National Park. They had arrived just before sunrise, and this chopper was waiting for them. They didn't talk much on the flight down. The mood was somber, given the circumstances, and Trudy Wellington, as the intel officer, would normally have done most of the talking. Susan had offered Luke a different intel person, but Luke declined. They were coming down to brace a prisoner anyway. He could give them all the intel they needed.

Luke sensed they were all feeling the loss of Trudy, and a certain amount of shock at her situation. He also sensed, or thought he did, that both of these guys had moved on in their lives. New assignments, new training, new team members and co-workers, new challenges to look forward to. A lot could change in two months.

The Special Response Team was gone. Luke could have chosen to save it in some form—after the coup attempt and Ebola attacks he could write his own ticket and take them all with him—but instead he chose not to. Now the SRT was old news, and so was Luke Stone. He had retired, and that was one thing. But he had also disappeared, and he hadn't made much effort to keep in touch. Team cohesion was a big part of intelligence and special operations work. With no contact, there was no cohesion.

Which meant that right now, there was no team.

The chopper banked and headed south. Almost immediately, the devastation became clear. The entire area below the dam was flooded. Large trees were ripped out everywhere and tossed around like matchsticks. In a few minutes, they reached the site of the former Black Rock Resort. Parts of the upper floor of the main building were still intact, rising up out of the floodwaters. Cars were stacked up against the wrecked hotel, along with more trees, a few of which reached out of the water with arms to the sky, like religious converts imploring God for a miracle.

The effect of the cars and the trees and the various piles of flotsam was to build a mini-dam, behind which a wide lake had formed. About a dozen Zodiacs were parked on the lake, with teams of divers in full scuba gear either preparing to drop in, or climbing out, depending on the boat.

"They find any survivors here?" Luke said.

The pilot shook his head. "Not a one. At least that was the word as of this morning. They found about a hundred bodies in the resort cafeteria, though. They're bringing them up one by one. I don't think they've started the room to room search yet. They might even let the waters subside before they do that. Moving through corridors underwater is dangerous work, and probably unnecessary. Ain't nobody alive down there."

Ed Newsam, who had been sprawled out in his normal laid-back style, shifted in his seat and sat up just a touch. "How do you know that, man? Could be air pockets under that water. Could be people down there hanging on for a rescue."

"They've got underwater listening equipment on those boats," the pilot said. "If anybody's alive under that water, they didn't make a peep all day yesterday or last night."

"Even so, if I'm in charge, I've got my best divers going room to room right now. We already know the people in the cafeteria are dead. And the divers signed on for danger. The civilians didn't."

The pilot shrugged. "Well, son, they're working as fast as they can."

The chopper moved further south. The flood had cut a swath through the valley, ripping a path across the forest. It looked like a giant had blundered his way through here. There was water everywhere. Wherever the original riverbed had been was lost under all the water.

They passed over the town of Sargent, still four feet deep in water. The devastation here was not as complete. There were a lot of empty lots where Luke assumed houses must have stood, but other houses, buildings, and fast food signs stuck up out of the water like fingers. The chopper flew over a cinderblock building with a stack of cars and SUVs piled up against it. HONEST ABE'S PRE-OWNED CARS, said a sign sticking halfway out of the water. One of its support beams had caved in.

"How many dead here?" Luke said.

"Five hundred," the pilot said. "Give or take some spare change. Still a hundred or more missing. It was early morning, and there wasn't much warning. A lot of people got swept away in their homes. You're asleep in bed and the old Cold War air raid signal goes off, what do you do? Some folks apparently went downstairs to their basements. That's nowhere to be when a flood comes."

"No one expected the dam to break?" Swann said. It was the first thing he had said since they boarded the chopper.

The pilot was busy with his controls. "Why would they? The dam didn't break. That dam was built to last a thousand years."

"Okay," Luke said. "I've seen enough. Let's go talk to the prisoner."

8:30 a.m.
Chattahoochee National Forest, Georgia

The camp appeared out of the deep forest like some weird mirage.

"Pretty, it ain't," Ed Newsam said.

It sat in a perfect clear cut, one mile by one mile, a brown and gray square amidst all the dark green. As the chopper came closer, Luke could make out dozens of barracks, row upon row of them, and a large, square reservoir of water in the center of the camp. Outbuildings surrounded the reservoir, and a steel catwalk traversed it.

The chopper began to drop down, and Luke could see the helipad approaching. It was in an area in the far west corner of the camp, with a few large administration buildings, a swimming pool, and a couple of parking lots. He could now clearly make out concrete yards, an access road, streets inside the encampment, and a wall topped with barbed wire and guard towers around the perimeter. The place was an open wound in the midst of the surrounding forest.

"What is this place?" Luke said into his headset.

The chopper pilot was busy working his controls, but not too busy to talk. "I've heard it called Camp Enduring Freedom," he said. "People around here tend to call it Camp Nowhere. It's one of ours. Federal Emergency Management Agency. You won't find it on any maps. I'd guess it doesn't officially have a name."

"Does it exist?" Luke said.

The chopper was low now, the grim gray buildings of the camp rising up all around them. Luke noticed glass reinforced by steel wires on the closest buildings.

The pilot shook his head. "Does what exist? This is uninhabited wilderness. There's nothing out here as far as I know."

A signalman in a yellow vest and holding bright orange wands stood to the side of the helipad and guided the chopper in. The pilot set the bird down perfectly in the middle of the pad. He killed the engine and the rotors immediately began to slow. There was a whine as they powered down.

"When you see that Chinaman," the pilot said, "give him a couple of knocks for me."

"We don't do that kind of thing," Luke said.

The pilot turned around and smiled. "Sure you don't. Son, I fly people in and out of places like this all the time. I know who does what just by looking, believe me. One glance at you guys and I know they've decided to turn up the heat a few notches."

He, Swann, and Ed exited the chopper, heads ducked low. A man was already waiting on the pad to greet them. He wore a gray business suit and a blue tie. His hair was blown about by the slowing blades of the helicopter. The fabric of his suit rippled from it. His black shoes were polished to a bright sheen. He looked as if he had just stepped off a commuter train in Manhattan. He was about as out of place as a man could possibly be.

As Luke came closer, the man's face took form. He appeared ageless—not old, not young, some indeterminate place in between. He extended a hand. Luke shook it.

"Agent Stone? I'm Pete Winn. They told me the President sent you. Thanks for coming down to see us."

"Thanks, Pete. Please call me Luke."

Luke, Ed, and Swann followed Pete Winn away from the chopper and toward a corrugated aluminum hut at the far side of the pad. Even the chopper pad was surrounded by barbed wire fencing. The only way in or out of the helipad was through that building. The doors to the building were operated by a seeing-eye device. They opened automatically as the men approached.

"What is this place?" Luke said.

"This?" Winn said. "You mean the camp?"

"Yes."

"Ah, well, I'll give you the thirty-second elevator pitch. It's basically a detention camp. We've got just over two hundred and fifty detainees at the moment, including more than seventy children. Mostly, they're illegal aliens from Mexico and Central America whose lives would be at risk from the drug cartels or criminal gangs if they were sent back home. They haven't been granted asylum, so they stay here with their families until such time as the Immigration and Naturalization Service can decide what to do with them. Their immigration status is officially undetermined. Meanwhile, since this place is invisible, the gangs have no idea where they are."

They passed through the building quickly. It was basically a hangout for flight controllers, helipad signalers, and pilots. There were a few desks and chairs, some radio and video monitoring equipment, a radar screen, a coffee maker, and an old box of stale donuts on a table.

"So they sit here endlessly?" Swann said.

29

"Well, endlessly is a long time," Winn said. "The family that's spent the most time with us has been here seven years."

Winn must have seen the looks on their faces.

"It's not as bad as it sounds. Really. All the children go to school five days a week. The school is right here on the grounds. There are enrichment activities, including two first-run movies each weekend, shown in both English and Spanish. There's soccer and basketball, and the adults are able to take language classes and job skills training, including training with master carpenters we bring in here."

"Sounds great," Swann said. "You guys mind if I spend my vacation here?"

"You might be surprised," Winn said. "People like it here. It's a lot better than going home and getting murdered."

A black SUV waited for them outside the hut. As the car drove through the camp, they passed another fence topped with looping razor wire. A handful of men sat on benches on the other side of the fence. Four or five of them were white men. A couple of them were black. They all wore bright yellow jumpsuits. They stared through the fence at the passing car.

"Those guys don't look like Mexicans," Ed Newsam said.

Pete Winn's face began to change. Earlier it had been friendly, maybe even a touch nervous to meet Luke and his team. Now it seemed almost dismissive.

"No, they don't," he said. "We've got some home-growns in here, too."

"Are they hiding out from the cartels?" Swann said.

Winn stared straight ahead. "Gentlemen, I'm sure there are aspects of your work that you aren't at liberty to discuss. The same holds true for me."

After a few minutes they had traveled to the far side of the camp from the helipad and administration buildings. The car stopped. There was no one around—no prisoners, no workers, no one at all. A small cabin sat by itself on a desultory dirt lot.

The men stepped out. The lot was barren, hard-packed earth. Any sense of camp activity, or even life itself, was far away from here.

Pete Winn handed Luke a key ring. There was only one key on it. Winn's face was hard now. His eyes were steely and cold. His demeanor had completed its drastic change from the uncertain functionary who had greeted them on the helicopter pad, to whatever it was now.

"The existence of this cabin is classified. Officially, it doesn't exist, nor does this prisoner. Your visit here does not exist. The Chinese government has made no inquiries, official or backdoor, into the whereabouts of a man named Li Quiangguo. My understanding is the Chinese have acted like they have nothing to hide or to be concerned about, and have even offered assistance in finding the source of the hack into the dam operating system."

He gestured with his head toward the cabin.

"The walls of the cabin are soundproof. The key opens an equipment cabinet in the back room. If you feel you need equipment to facilitate your interrogation, you may find what you're looking for in that cabinet."

Luke nodded, but didn't say anything. He didn't like the assumption these people all seemed to make that he had been called in here to torture the prisoner.

Had he tortured people before? He supposed he had, depending on the definition of that word. But no one had ever called him into a situation with the idea that he was going to torture a suspect. If they did, they'd be pretty foolish—there were people far more versed at it than Luke. When he had done it in the past, it was on the fly and he was improvising, almost always because a subject had critical information and Luke needed that information now.

Pete Winn went on, but now his manner was more relaxed, and his words were mundane.

"If you need anything, lunch, beer, dinner, or you want the car to return you to the helipad, just pick up the telephone in the cabin and dial zero. We'll send you what you need. We can put you up on the base for the night if you like, and provide any kind of toiletries or personal items. Soap, shampoo, shavers—we have all that stuff. We can also get you a change of clothes, within reason."

"Thank you," Luke said.

"I'm going to leave you to it," Winn said. "Good luck."

When the man was gone, Luke stopped to talk with his men outside the cabin. Green mountains towered around them outside the camp fence. The camp seemed to be built inside a bowl.

"Swann, how many years were you in China?"

"Six."

"In what part?"

"All around. I lived in Beijing mostly, but I spent a lot of time in Shanghai and Chongqing, also a little bit in the south, in Guangzhou and Hong Kong."

31

"Okay, I want you to watch this guy closely, get any indications from him that you can. Anything at all. Where you think he might be from. How old he might be. His level of education. His level of computer know-how. Is he even from China at all? Susan Hopkins's people told me the guy is perfectly fluent in English. What are the chances he was born here in the States, or in Canada, or Hong Kong? Or anywhere at all, really. There are Chinese people everywhere."

Swann shook his head. "If the guy's an operative, I'm not going to know that stuff. He'll be too good at hiding his origins."

"Guess," Luke said. "It's not a math problem. There are no right or wrong answers. I just want to get your sense."

Swann nodded. "Got it."

Now Luke looked at him closely. "How squeamish are you?"

He had never worried about Swann's personality before, but it occurred to him now that Swann could be something of a weak link in there.

"Squeamish? Squeamish, like how?"

"Ed and I may need to get serious in there."

"Well, give me a heads-up and I'll go for a little walk around these beautiful grounds."

"If you do, make sure you wave to the snipers," Ed Newsam said.

About a hundred yards away was a three-story guard tower. Luke and Swann glanced at it. A man with a rifle stood in the tower, apparently targeting them. From this distance, it looked like he had the rifle pointed right at them, and he was sighting down the scope.

"Can he hit us from there?" Swann said.

"With his eyes closed," Luke said.

"He's just practicing though," Ed said. "Relieving a little boredom."

They went inside.

*

The man wore a bright yellow jumpsuit. He sat on a metal folding chair in the middle of an empty room. He was large, with broad shoulders, thick arms and legs, and a prominent stomach.

He wore a black hood over his head. His wrists were cuffed behind his back. His legs were cuffed together at the ankles. He was slumped forward, as if sleeping. With the hood over his head, it was impossible to tell.

Luke pulled the hood from the man's head. The man jerked in seeming surprise, and sat up. His jet black hair was mussed—it stood up in tufts in a few places, was flattened down in others. Even with the hood removed, he still wore airplane blinders—the kind people put over their faces to sleep on long flights.

He yawned as if waking from an afternoon nap.

"Li Quiangguo," Luke said. "*Ni hui shuo yingyu ma?*"

In Mandarin Chinese, his words translated to *Do you speak English?*

The man smiled broadly. "Call me Johnny," he said. "Please. It's what I use here in the West. And let's speak English. It makes it easier for everybody, especially me."

The man's English was the American version, certainly, but with no accent or regional flavor of any kind. Luke might have said he sounded like he was from the Midwest. But really, he didn't sound like he was from anywhere. He could have been beamed down from a spaceship.

"Why is it easier for you?" Luke said.

"It's easier on my ears. It means I don't have to listen to people like you butcher the beautiful Chinese language."

Now Luke smiled. "Tell me, Li. Why didn't you kill yourself when you had the chance?"

Li made a face of exaggerated surprise, even disgust. "Why would I do that? I like America. And I've been treated pretty well so far."

It was an interesting thing to say, considering that it came from a man who had been manacled to a metal chair overnight, with a black hood and airplane blinders on his head, in a detention center that didn't exist, and with no way to contact the outside world. He was not technically under arrest and he hadn't seen a lawyer. A lot of people might not agree that his arrangements constituted being treated well. Some might say he had been disappeared. Yes, he hadn't been tortured, but for most people, lack of torture was a pretty low threshold.

Li almost seemed to read Luke's mind. "I heard birds chirping outside this morning. That's how I knew it was a new day."

Luke reached with one hand and pulled off the man's airplane blinders. "Birds at sunrise. That's very nice. I'm glad to hear you've enjoyed your stay so far. Unfortunately, things are about to change."

"Ah." The man's eyes squinted in the sudden brightness. He scanned the room, took in Swann and Ed Newsam. The eyes settled on Ed.

Ed was leaned up against one wall. He seemed very relaxed, and at the same time, menacing. His body barely moved. There was so much potential energy stored inside of it, he was like a storm about to happen. His eyes never left the Chinese man's eyes.

"I see," Li said.

Luke nodded. "Yes. You do."

Li's face hardened. "I'm a tourist. This is all a case of mistaken identity."

"If you're a tourist," Ed said, "maybe you'd like to give us the names and contact information of your family, so we can let them know where you are. You know, and tell them that you're doing fine."

Li shook his head. "I would like to contact the Chinese embassy."

"Our superiors have already done that for you," Luke said. It wasn't true, as far he knew. He began to inch out on a limb, but a limb he felt would hold his weight.

"It was a backchannel conversation, as you might imagine, given the sensitivity of the situation," he said. "You may be disturbed to know that the Chinese government says you aren't real. There are no school records, no job records, no hometown or family background. They've seen a scan of your passport, and they've determined that it's a clever forgery."

Li stared straight ahead. He didn't respond.

Luke let the moment draw out. There was no reason to fill it with more talk. He had seen subjects break as soon as they realized their handlers had disavowed them. Break wasn't even the right word. Sometimes, when they suddenly found themselves without a country, they simply switched sides.

"Li, did you hear me? They're not going to protect you. You're not going to get away from this. You didn't take your pill when you could have, and now you're here. There is no way out. As far as your people are concerned, you don't exist, and you never existed. The facility you're in right now doesn't exist. You could end up stuffed inside a fifty-five-gallon drum at the bottom of the ocean, or in a shallow ditch in the wilderness, with crows picking out your eyes… No one will care. No one will even know."

The man still didn't say a word. He just stared straight ahead.

"Li, what do you know about the Black Rock Dam, and how the floodgates opened?"

"I don't know anything."

Luke waited a few beats, then went on. "Well, let me tell you what I know. At last count, more than a thousand people have died. Do you have any idea how upset that makes me? It makes me want to take revenge for their deaths. It makes me want to find a scapegoat, and make that person pay. You're a convenient scapegoat, aren't you, Li? A man that nobody cares about, nobody remembers, and no one will miss. I'll tell you something else. I know you've been trained to resist interrogation. That only makes me happier. It means I can take my time. We can stay here for days, or even weeks. We have people working on that dam problem. They'll figure out what happened. We don't need whatever pitiful information you might have. I don't even want it, to be honest. I just want to hurt you. The more you just sit there, the more I want to do it."

Now Luke squatted down on his haunches near Li's face. He was inches away, so close that his breath exhaled on Li's cheeks. "We're going to get to know each other pretty well in here, okay, Li? Eventually, I'm going to know everything about you."

Luke glanced at Swann. Swann stood in a corner by the steel-barred window. He hadn't said a word since they walked in here. He looked out at the concrete compound and the lush green hillsides surrounding it. Swann was an analyst, a data guy. Luke imagined he might never have thought about how data was sometimes extracted. Death threats were just the beginning.

"Li, the man's talking to you," Ed said.

Li managed a smile then. It was a sickly smile, and there was no humor in it at all. "Please," he said. "Call me Johnny."

* * *

An hour passed. Luke and Ed had taken turns talking to Li, but with no real effect. If anything, Li was becoming more confident. He had evidently decided that a few hard smacks from Ed were the most he was going to get.

Now Luke was watching Swann again.

"Okay, Swann," he said. "Now is a good time to take that walk around the camp."

A few minutes before, Luke had opened the cabinet with the key Pete Winn had given him. The cabinet was more of a utility closet than an actual cabinet. Inside was a fold-out table, a little bit like an ironing board, but wider, lower to the ground, and much more sturdy. It was about seven feet long and four feet wide.

When Luke and Ed set it up, the table had a noticeable incline. On the higher side, there were manacles for the subject's ankles. In the middle were leather straps for tying down the subject's wrists, and a large one in the center for the subject's waist. At the lower end was a metal ring for securing the subject's head to the table.

It was a platform for water torture.

When they brought the table out, Li became visibly agitated. He knew what it was right away. Of course he did. He was an intelligence agent, a field operative, and they had all seen it as part of their training. Americans, Chinese, whoever. Luke had watched a live demonstration of the technique once upon a time. A hardened CIA agent, a man who had come to the agency out of the Navy SEALs, who had been in-country in numerous hotspots, was the test subject.

How they convinced this man to volunteer was something Luke never found out. Maybe he got a bonus. It should have been a big one. The agent seemed relaxed before the demonstration. He was laughing and joking with his soon-to-be tormentors. Once the procedure started, he transformed instantly. He lasted twenty-four seconds before he used the safe word to make it stop. They timed it.

"You have to know that this is against the Geneva Conventions," Li said, his voice shaking just a little. "It's against…"

"Last I checked, we're not in Geneva," Luke said. "In fact, we aren't anywhere at all. As I mentioned earlier, this facility doesn't exist, and neither does anyone named Li Quiangguo."

Luke busied himself with the other implements he had taken out of the closet. They included two large watering cans, like the kind a nice older lady would use to water her gardens. There were also locks for the manacles and leather straps on the board. And finally there were a number of medium-sized heavy cloth towels and a roll of cellophane. If the towels didn't work, they could always move on to the cellophane. Luke happened to know that the CIA didn't bother with cloth towels.

"Man," Ed said. "I haven't done anything like this since Afghanistan. It's been at least five years."

"Then your experience is more recent than mine," Luke said. "So we'll let you do the honors. How'd it go when you did it?"

36

Ed shrugged. "Scary. We had a couple of them die on us. It's not like some of the other methods I've seen. You can electrocute people all day, as long as the current is right. It hurts but it doesn't kill them. People do die from this. They drown. They get brain damage. They have heart attacks. This is real."

"Listen," Li said. His entire body was trembling now. "Waterboarding is against all the laws of war. It is recognized as torture by every international body. You are committing a human rights violation."

"Man, you're all about rules and regulations all of a sudden," Ed said. "My way of thinking, someone deliberately floods out thousands of people, I'm not dealing with a human at that point. I'd say you forfeited your human rights."

"Guys," Swann said. "I don't feel right about this."

Luke glanced at him. "Swann, I told you it was a good time for you to leave. Take about twenty minutes. That should be plenty."

Swann's face turned red. "Luke, everything I've read says that this won't even give you decent intelligence. He'll just lie to make it stop."

Luke couldn't remember a single time when Swann had questioned his actions before. He'd be curious to know if Swann was questioning his actions now. Either way, he just shook his head.

"Swann, you can't believe everything you read. I've seen this get actionable, accurate intelligence from people in a matter of minutes. And because Mr. Li is our guest here, we'll be able to quickly verify any claims he makes. We can also revisit those claims with him if they turn out to be inaccurate. The truth is they don't want people to do this because as Li so accurately points out, it qualifies as torture. But it works, and in the right circumstances, it works really, really well."

Luke gestured around the empty room. "And these are the right circumstances."

Swann was staring now. "Luke…"

Luke raised a hand. "Swann. Out. Please." He gestured at the door.

Swann shook his head. His face was very red now. He seemed on the verge of trembling himself. "Why did you even call me in for this?" he said. "I don't work for the FBI anymore, and neither do you."

Luke almost smiled. He didn't know how Swann really felt, but he couldn't have scripted this better than it was turning out. This was good cop, bad cop on steroids.

"By the end of this day, I'm going to need your skills," Luke said. "But not for this. Now get lost. Please. And notice how polite I've been so far. In a minute I'm going to lose my temper."

"I'm going to lodge a formal complaint," Swann said.

"Please do. You know who I work for. Your complaint will get as far as the office shredder. It will go right down the memory hole. But do it anyway, as an intellectual exercise."

"I plan to," Swann said. With that, he went out the door. He pulled it tight behind him, but did not slam it.

Luke exhaled. He looked at Ed. "Ed, can you please fill up these watering cans at the kitchen sink? We're going to need them in a minute."

Ed gave a devilish half-smile. "With pleasure."

As he picked up the watering cans, he stared at Li. He showed Li the crazy giant eyeball look that he sometimes used on people. It was a look that gave even Luke the willies. It made Ed seem psychotic. It made him look like a man who found sadism pleasurable. Luke wasn't sure where that look came from, or what it meant. He didn't really want to know.

"Brother," Ed said to Li. "Your day is about to get a lot longer."

As Ed busied himself in the cabin's tiny kitchen, Luke looked closely at Li. The man was quaking now. His entire body vibrated as if some low current of electricity was running through it. His eyes had become wide and scared.

"You've seen this before, haven't you?" Luke said.

Li nodded. "Yes."

"On prisoners?"

"Yes."

"It's bad," Luke said. "It's very bad. No one holds up against it."

"I know," Li said.

Luke glanced at the kitchen. Ed was taking his sweet time in there. "And Ed... you must know how he is. He enjoys this kind of thing."

Li didn't say anything to that. His face turned bright red, and then gradually morphed to dark red. It seemed like there was an explosion going on inside him, and he was trying to contain it. He squeezed his eyes shut. His teeth clenched, then started chattering. His whole body began to shudder.

"I'm cold," he said. "I can't do this."

Just then, something occurred to Luke.

"They've done it to you," he said. "Your own people." It wasn't a question. He knew it like he knew his own name. Li had been waterboarded before now, and in all likelihood, it was the Chinese government that had done it.

Suddenly Li's mouth opened in a scream. It was a silent scream, his jaws opened to their full extension. It somehow reminded Luke of a werewolf howling in agony during the bone-breaking transition from human to canine form. Except there was no sound. Almost nothing came out of Li, just a low gagging sort of noise deep in his throat.

His entire body was stiff now, every muscle tensed as if the electrical current had just gone up ten notches.

"You were a traitor," Luke said. "An enemy of the state. But you were rehabilitated in prison. Torture was part of the process. They made you into an agent, but not a valuable one. You're one of the expendables. That's why you were out here in the field, and that's why you had cyanide pills. If you got caught, you were supposed to kill yourself. There was almost no way you wouldn't get caught, right? But you didn't do it, Li. You didn't kill yourself, and now we're the only hope you've got."

"Please!" Li shouted. "Please don't do it!"

The man's body shook uncontrollably. More than that. A smell started to come from him, the thick humid smell of feces.

"Oh my God," he said. "Oh my God. Help me. Help me."

"What's going on here?" Ed said as he returned with the watering cans. He made a face as the smell hit his nose. "Oh, man."

Luke raised his eyebrows. He almost felt sympathy for this man. Then he thought of the more than a thousand dead, and the many thousands who had lost their homes. Nothing, no negative life experience, could justify doing that.

"Yeah, Li's a mess," he said. "He's a trauma case. Looks like this isn't his first time around with waterboarding."

Ed nodded. "Good. So he knows the drill already." He looked down at Li. "We're gonna do it anyway, you hear me, girly boy? We don't care about the smell, so if that's your game, it didn't work." Ed glanced at Luke. "I've seen this before. People try it because they think that the smell is so rank we won't want to go forward. Or maybe we'll take pity on them. Or whatever." He shook his head. "The smell is nasty, but I've never seen it work. We wouldn't be here if we were the sensitive type, Li. I've smelled men after they've been disemboweled. Believe me, it's worse than anything you can push out the regular way."

"Please," Li said again. He said it quietly now, almost a whisper. His body was shaking out of control. He hung his head and stared at the floor. "Please don't do it. I can't take it."

"Give me something," Luke said. "Give me something good, and then we'll see. Look at me, Li."

Li's head hung even lower. He shook it. "I cannot look at you now." His face made a grimace, a mask of humiliation. Then he started crying.

"Help me. Please help me."

"You better give me something," Luke said. "Or we're going to get started."

Luke stood ten feet away and watched him. Li was slumped over in the chair, his head low, his arms tight behind his broad back, his entire body trembling. There was no organization to it—every part seemed to be doing something different and unrelated to every other part. Luke noticed now that the crotch of Li's jumpsuit was wet. He had also pissed himself.

Luke took a deep breath. They'd have to get somebody in here to clean this guy up.

"Li?" he said.

Li was still facing the ground. His voice sounded like it was coming from the bottom of a well. "There is a warehouse. It's a small warehouse, with an office. An importer of Chinese goods. In the office, everything is explained."

"Whose office is it?" Luke said.

"Mine."

"It's a front?" Ed said.

Li tried to shrug. His body jittered and jived. His teeth chattered as he talked. "Mostly. It had to be somewhat functional, or else there is no cover story."

"Where is it?"

Li mumbled something.

"What?" Luke said. "I don't hear you. If you play with me, we're going to do this the hard way. You think Ed wants you off the hook? Think again."

"It's in Atlanta," Li said, clear and firm now, as if telling it was a relief. "The warehouse is in Atlanta. That's where I was based."

Luke smiled.

"Well, you can give us the address, and we can fly down to Atlanta. We'll be right back in a few hours." He put his hand on Li's shoulder. "God help you if we find out you're lying."

*

"Nice job, Swann," Luke said. "I couldn't have asked for better if I had written the script myself."

"Did I ever mention I was in the theater club in high school? I played Mack the Knife one year."

"You missed your calling," Luke said. "You could've gone to Hollywood based on what I saw in there."

They moved down the concrete walkway toward the waiting black SUV. Two men in FEMA jumpsuits had just exited the SUV and gone into the cabin. Luke glanced at the surroundings. All around them were fences and razor wire. Behind the closest guard tower, a steep green hillside rose up toward the northern mountains of Georgia.

Swann smiled. "I tried to put just the right note of moral indignation into it."

"You had me fooled," Ed said.

"Well, it was real. I didn't have to act. I'm really not for torturing people."

"Neither are we," Ed said. "At least, not all the time."

"Did you do it?" Swann said.

Luke smiled. "What do you think?"

Swann shook his head. "I was gone only ten minutes before you came out, so I'm guessing that you didn't."

Ed clapped him on the back. "Keep guessing, data analyst."

"Well, did you or didn't you?" Swann said. "Guys?"

Within minutes, the three of them were back on the helicopter, rising over the dense forest and headed south to Atlanta.

CHAPTER SIX

"Congressman, thank you for coming."

Susan Hopkins reached out to shake the hand of the tall man in the sharp blue suit. He was United States Representative from Ohio, Michael Parowski. He had prematurely white hair and squinty pale blue eyes. Fifty-five years old, he was handsome in a rugged, Marlboro man sort of way. Blue-collar born and bred, he had the big stone hands and the broad shoulders of a man who started his career as an iron worker.

Susan knew his story. H was a lifelong bachelor. He grew up in Akron, the son of immigrants from Poland. As a teenager, he was a Golden Gloves fighter. The industrial cities of the north, Youngstown, Akron, Cleveland, were his stronghold. His support up there was unshakeable. More than that, it was mythic, the stuff of legend. He was on his ninth term in the House, and his reelections were a breeze, an afterthought.

Would Michael Parowski get reelected in northern Ohio? Would the sun come up again tomorrow? Would the Earth continue to spin on its axis? If you dropped an egg, would it fall to the kitchen floor? He was as inevitable as the laws of physics. He wasn't going anywhere.

Susan had seen the videos of him wading into the crowds at union rallies, holidays, and ethnic festivals (where he did not discriminate—Polish, Greek, Puerto Rican, Italian, African-American, Irish, Mexican, Vietnamese—if you had an ethnicity, he was your man). He was a hand-shaker, a back-slapper, a high-fiver, and a hugger. His signature move was the whisper.

In the midst of mayhem and chaos, dozens or even hundreds of people pressing close to him, he would invariably take some older woman one step aside and whisper something in her ear. Sometimes the women would laugh, sometimes they would blush, sometimes they would wag a finger at him. The crowds adored it, and none of the women ever repeated what he said. It was political theatre of the highest order, the kind that Susan, frankly, loved.

Here in DC, he was a union man all the way—the AFL-CIO gave him a 100 percent rating. He was one of labor's best friends on Capitol Hill. He was more wobbly on some of Susan's other issues:

women's rights, gay rights, the environment. But not so much that it was a deal breaker, and in a sense, his strengths complemented hers. She could speak with passion about clean water and clean air, and about women's health, and he could equal her passion when he talked about the plight of the American worker.

Even so, Susan wasn't sure he was the perfect fit, but the Party elders assured her he was. They wanted him on board more than anything. Truth be told, they had practically made the decision for her. And what they really wanted from him, besides his popularity, was his toughness. He was the baddest man in the room. He didn't drink, he didn't smoke, and it at least appeared that he didn't sleep. He lived on airplanes, bouncing back and forth to his district like a ping-pong ball. He would be on the Hill for committee meetings and votes at all hours, at a cemetery in Youngstown in the morning six hours later, fresh and alert, tears in his eyes, wrapping his big strong arms around the mother of a dead serviceman as she melted against his chest.

If his enemies claimed that he had quietly remained friends with a couple of the mobsters who he spent his childhood with in the old neighborhood... well, that only added to the image. He was soft, he was hard, he was loyal, and he was no one to mess with.

He gave her a bright smile. "Madam President, to what do I owe this honor?"

"Please, Michael. It's still Susan."

"Okay. Susan."

She led him back into her study. As Vice President, she had long ago dispensed with holding important meetings in her office. She preferred the somewhat informal feel, and the beautiful surroundings, of the study. When they walked in, Kat Lopez was already there and waiting.

"Do you know my chief-of-staff, Kat Lopez?"

"I haven't had the pleasure."

The two shook hands. Kat gave him one of her rare smiles. "Congressman, I've been a big fan of yours since I was in college."

"When was that, last year?"

Kat did something out of character then. She blushed. It was fast, disappearing almost as soon as it arrived, but it was there. The man had an effect on people.

Susan offered Parowski a chair. "Shall we sit down?"

Parowski settled into one of the comfortable armchairs. Susan sat facing him. Kat stood behind her.

"Mike, we've known each other a long time. So I'm not going to dance around. As you know, I abruptly became President when Thomas Hayes died. It took me this long to get my wheels under me. And I delayed picking my Vice President until the crisis seemed like it was over."

"I've heard some rumblings about what happened yesterday," Parowski said.

Susan nodded. "It's true. We believe it was a terror attack. But we'll survive it like we did the others, and we're going to move forward even stronger and more resilient than before. And one way we're going to do that is with a strong Vice President."

Parowski stared at her.

Susan nodded. "You."

He glanced up at Kat Lopez, then back at Susan. He smiled. Then he laughed.

"I thought you were going to ask me to herd some votes for you on the Hill."

"I am," she said. "I'm going to ask you to do that. But as the Vice President and the President of the Senate, not as the Congressman from Ohio."

She raised her hands. "I know. It feels like I'm throwing this is in your lap, and I am. But I've been putting feelers out, and holding little hush-hush secretive meetings for the past six weeks. You're the name that comes up again and again. You're the one with massive popularity in your own district, and broad appeal across the entire northern tier of the United States, and even in conservative working class districts across the south. And you're the tireless campaigner who can ride hard with me when the time comes to run for reelection."

"I'll do it," he said.

"Take your time," Susan said. "I don't want to rush you."

His smile became broader. Now he raised his hands, almost as if imploring the heavens. "What can I say? It's a dream come true. I love what you're doing. You held this country together at a time when it could have splintered apart. You were a lot tougher than anyone gave you credit for."

"Thank you," Susan said. If he could have seen her in the early days, weeping alone in this very room when she thought ninety thousand people were going to die from the Ebola attack, would he still think that?

She nodded to herself. Probably more than ever.

He pointed at her with his thick index finger. "I'll tell you something else. I always knew that about you. I can read people with the best of them. I learned it as a kid, and I saw it in you years ago, when you first came to DC. Ask anybody. When June sixth came, I told people don't worry, we're in good hands. I told that to the people who were still alive on the Hill, I told it to the TV shows, and I told it personally to at least ten thousand people in my district."

Susan nodded. "I know that." And she did know it. That little fact had come up again and again in her meetings. *Michael Parowski has your back.*

"You need to know something about me, though," he said. "I'm big. Physically I'm big, and I have a big personality. If you're looking for someone to stand in the back and fade into the wallpaper, then I'm probably not your guy."

"Michael, we vetted you eight ways to Sunday. We know everything about you. We don't want you to stand in the background. We want you upfront, being yourself. We want your strength. We're rebuilding a government here, and in a sense, we're rebuilding people's faith in America. It's hard work, and it's a lot of heavy lifting. That's why we picked you."

He gave her a sidelong look. "You know everything about me, huh?"

She smiled. "Well, almost everything. There's still one mystery I'd like to solve."

"Okay, I'll bite," he said. "What is it?"

"When you pull the old ladies aside at events, what do you whisper to them?"

He grunted. A funny look came into his face. It nearly transformed, decades of wear and tear dropping from it. For a few seconds, he looked almost (but not quite) innocent, like the hardscrabble child he must once have been.

"I tell them how beautiful they look today," he said. "Then I say, 'Don't tell nobody. It's our little secret.' And I mean it, every word of it."

He shook his head, and Susan thought it was almost with wonder—at people, at politics, at the sheer magnitude and audacity of what people like he and Susan did every single day of their lives.

"It works every time," he said.

CHAPTER SEVEN

11:45 a.m.
Atlanta, Georgia

"Is Mr. Li okay? I haven't seen him here in quite a while."

The man was small and thin, with a narrow and hunched back. He wore a gray uniform with the name *Sal* stitched over one breast. He kept a cigarette lit and in his mouth at all times. He talked with it in his mouth. He never seemed to see any need to take it out until it was finished. Then he lit another one. In one hand, he carried a heavy pair of bolt cutters.

"Oh, he's fine," Luke said.

They walked down a long, wide cinderblock corridor. It was lit by sputtering overhead fluorescents. As they walked, a small rat darted in front of them, then scurried along the bottom corner of the wall. Sal didn't seem to feel the rat was worth commenting on, so Luke kept his mouth shut. He glanced at Ed. Ed smiled and said nothing. Trailing behind them, Swann coughed.

Li's space was in a large old warehouse building which had been subdivided over the years into many smaller spaces. Dozens of tiny companies rented spaces here. There was a loading dock at the far end of the corridor, and the corridor itself was perfect for loading up dollies and rolling product in and out.

Sal seemed to work as some kind of manager or custodian of the place. He had initially been hesitant to cooperate. But when Ed showed him his FBI identification, and Swann showed him his new NSA badge, Sal became eager to please. Luke didn't show his badge. It was his old Special Response Team ID, and the SRT didn't exist anymore.

"What kind of trouble might he be in?" Sal said.

Luke shrugged. "Nothing too major. Tax trouble, trouble with trademark and patent infringements. About what you'd expect from a guy bringing stuff in from China. You must see it all the time, am I right? I was in Chongking a few years ago. You can go into the warehouses along the waterfront there and buy new iPhones for fifty bucks, and Breitling watches for a hundred and fifty. They're not real, of course. But you wouldn't know the difference to look at them."

Sal nodded. "You wouldn't believe the stuff I see come in and out of here." He stopped in front of a corrugated steel door, the kind

46

that slides up from the bottom. "Anyway, Li seems like a very nice man. He doesn't speak much English, but I'd say he gets by on what little he has. And he's very polite. Always bowing and smiling. Not sure how much business he does, though."

The metal door had a clasp with a heavy lock. Sal lifted the bolt cutter and with one quick snap, chopped the lock right off.

"You're in," he said. "I hope you find what you're looking for."

He was already moving down the hall toward his office.

"Thanks for your help," Ed called to his back.

Sal raised one hand. "I'm an American." He didn't turn around.

Ed bent over and pulled up the door. They observed what was visible before going in. Ed stuck his hand inside and slowly waved it side to side, up and down, looking for trip wires.

It wasn't necessary. Li's warehouse was unprotected by booby traps. More than that, it seemed long abandoned. When Luke flipped the switch, half the overhead lights didn't work. Plastic-wrapped pallets of cheap toys were stacked in rows in the gloom, and covered with green tarps. Boxes of generic, no-name household cleaning products, the kind that would turn up in dollar stores and odd lot outlets, were piled in one corner, nearly to the ceiling. Everything was blanketed in a thin film of dust. The stuff had been sitting here for a while.

Li seemed to have imported a shipment of junk to keep up appearances, then never bothered with it again.

"The office is over there," Swann said.

In the far corner of the warehouse was the door to the small office. The door was wood, with a frosted glass window for the top panel. Luke tried the knob. Locked. He glanced at Ed and Swann.

"Either of you guys have a pick on you? Otherwise, we have to go back down there and explain to Sal about how organized crime has cornered the market on year-old discount store crap."

Ed shrugged and took his keys out of the pocket of his jeans. The key ring had a small black flashlight on it. Ed held the flashlight like the world's smallest night stick, and smacked it against the window, smashing the glass in. He reached through the hole and unlocked the door from the inside. He held up the flashlight for Luke's inspection.

"It's like a pick, only more direct."

They went in. The office was bleak, but tidy. There was no window. There was a three-drawer filing cabinet, which was mostly empty. The bottom drawers each had a few folders with shipping manifests and receipts. The top drawer had a few power bars and small bags of pretzels and potato chips, plus a couple bottles of spring water.

There was a long wooden desk, with an old desktop computer on it. On one side of the desk were the kind of deep drawers where people often kept files on hangars. These drawers were locked.

"Ed?" Luke said.

Ed walked over, grabbed the handle of the top drawer, and wrenched it open with brute force—to the naked eye, it looked like a parlor trick, one deft snap of the wrist breaking the lock. Luke knew better. Then Ed proceeded to open each drawer in turn using the exact same technique.

"Like a pick," he said.

Luke nodded. "Yes, but more direct."

There was nothing much in the drawers. Pencils, pens, faded pieces of stationery. An unopened pack of Wrigley chewing gum. An old Texas Instruments calculator. In one of the drawers, on the bottom, were three CD-ROMs in dirty plastic cases. The cases were marked with letters A, B, and C, written in magic marker on scraps of masking tape. The case with the letter B on it was cracked.

Swann sat down to the computer and booted it up. "Pretty low-tech," he said. "This thing is probably twenty years old. I'll bet it's not even hooked to the internet. Sure. Look at this. It's from a time before cable hookups, and from way before wireless. There's nowhere to plug in a Cat 5 cable. You want an internet connection on this thing? Anybody here remember dial-up?"

To Luke, it didn't make sense.

"Why would an advance man from a country known for sophisticated hacking have a computer that isn't even on the internet, and almost couldn't be on it, even if he wanted it to be?"

Swann shrugged. "I have a couple guesses."

"Do you care to share them?"

"The first is that he's not Chinese at all. He's not part of any sophisticated anything. The hack that took the dam out wasn't particularly advanced. That dam's system was ripe for the plucking. He may be part of a group with no government backing."

"If he's not Chinese, then what is he?" Luke said.

Swann shrugged. "He could be American. He could be Canadian. He has high cheekbones and flat facial features, which could mean he's Thai. He's a big guy, which could mean northern Chinese. He could be an American of Asian descent. I didn't get

48

anything from being in that room with him that indicated any nationality. But I wouldn't peg him as Chinese just because he has a Chinese passport."

"Okay, what's your second guess?" Luke said.

"My second guess is they went low tech so no prying eyes can see what they're doing. You can't hack into something that isn't connected. If Li is not on the internet, no one can read his files. The only way to access them is to come here to this godforsaken warehouse in a crummy industrial district on the outskirts of Atlanta. The only way to find out this warehouse even exists is to torture Li, or in your case, threaten to torture him. And that's something which never should have happened in the first place, because Li was supposed to kill himself before he was caught. The people who were supposed to find this computer were Li's handlers, or in a worst-case scenario, Sal would find it when the rent money ran out. Then he would either toss this old computer in the trash, or sell it for ten bucks."

The computer screen came on and asked for a login code.

Swann gestured at the screen. "And that, right there, would have been enough to stop Sal in his tracks."

"Can you beat it?" Ed said.

Swann almost smiled. "Are you kidding? These circa 1994 encryptions are a joke. I was breaking these things when I was thirteen years old."

He typed in a command, and an old black MS-DOS screen appeared in the top left corner. He typed in a few more commands, hesitated for a moment, typed in a few more, and Windows returned, no longer asking for a password.

When the desktop loaded, Swann clicked around for a few moments. It didn't take long. "There are no files on here," he said. "No word processing documents, no spreadsheets, no photographs, nothing."

He glanced at Luke over his shoulder.

"This computer's been wiped clean. The hard drive is still here, and it functions, but there's no evidence of anything. I think our friend Mr. Li might have pulled a fast one."

"Can you get the files back that were deleted?" Luke said.

Swann shrugged. "Maybe, but I can't do it here. Could be there were never any files to begin with. We'll have to remove the hard drive and bring it back with us to NSA to know for sure."

Luke sagged the slightest amount. Generally, he had a lot of confidence in his ability to read people. But maybe Swann was right. Maybe Li had pulled a fast one. His terror seemed real enough, but maybe he had faked it. Why would he do that? He had to know that Luke was coming right back for him. There was nowhere to run.

"What about the CDs?" he said. "Let's check those."

Swann picked up the first one, marked A. He held it between two fingers as if it had something contagious on it. "Sure, why not?"

He slid the CD into its slot. The computer suddenly began to rev like an airplane preparing for takeoff. A moment passed, and then a window opened. It was a list of word processing files. The files had names that followed sequential patterns, most often with a word and then a number. There were dozens and dozens of files.

The first word in the list was "air," and it went from "air1" through "air27." A later word that seemed interesting was "grid," which went from "grid1" to "grid9." In between those two on the list was the word "dam." It went from "dam1" to "dam39." Much later, there was "rig1" to "rig19." Also, "train1" to "train21."

"Should I start with air?" Swann said.

"Okay."

Swann pulled up air1. The words at the top served as a title of sorts. *John F. Kennedy International Airport, New York City.*

"Uh-oh," Swann said.

There was a brief description of the airport, including opening date, its location by latitude and longitude, the number of flights and passengers per year, major airlines it served, and more. Then there were several pages of photographs of the terminal, a New York City map with the airport indicated, and then several maps of the terminals. Past that, things became technical—long lists of data appeared, a blur of numbers and letters. Swann went quiet as he pored over it.

"Houston, we have a problem," he said finally.

*

The black SUV raced through city streets, headed for the highway.

Luke was on hold, trying to reach the President. In the background, he could hear both Ed and Swann working their own telephones.

"I'm going to need a team of analysts to dive into this stuff," Swann said. "That's right, as soon as I can get it all uploaded. No, it's all on CD-ROM. I can't do it right now. I'm in a car. Yes. There's a base just outside of town here, Naval Air Station Atlanta, and we'll be there in a little while. I assume somebody will lend me a system with a CD slot. Why do *you* think he put it on CD? So nobody could hack it, that's why. It was in a drawer in a locked office in a locked warehouse that nobody knew about."

Ed was nearly talking over Swann. "I need you to put me through to the FEMA camp in Chattahoochee National Forest," he said. He paused for a moment, listened to what was said on the other end.

"I promise you, it exists. Try Camp Enduring Freedom, or Camp Nowhere. I was there this morning. There's a guy named Pete Winn. I don't know what his title is. Camp director, maybe. Swimming instructor, I don't know. Yes, I know there's no listing for the camp. I need this guy Winn anyway. He has a prisoner. He will know the one. We have confirmed information that we received from that prisoner. Yes, I repeat that. The prisoner is now a high-value prisoner, highest possible value. We are en route to that location. We need that prisoner prepped for further interrogation. I want a twenty-four-hour guard on him, and video surveillance. Prisoner is a flight risk and suicide risk."

Ed paused again. "Lady, just find the camp! Ask your superior for clearance. I'm telling you, I was there."

Luke listened to dead air. He was a little surprised at himself. They had left the FEMA camp without considering how they would contact it again. Luke had just assumed he could get back in touch through normal channels. It was interesting how quickly the rust built up after two months away. Would he have made that assumption if he were doing this all the time? Probably not.

After another moment, there was a click and the dead air over the phone changed. It became a wide open space, with some chatter in the background.

"Kat Lopez," came the voice over the line.

"Hi, Kat. It's Luke Stone. I need to talk to Susan."

"Hi, Luke. Susan is in a meeting right now. I can take a message for her."

"I'd like to speak to her directly, if you don't mind."

"Luke, I'm her chief-of-staff. I'm empowered to listen for her. You can trust me to take the message correctly and get it to her."

"Time is of the essence here, Kat."

Kat's voice was firm. "So if we stop jousting over whether you'd like to leave a message with me or not, I think we'll make better use of everyone's time."

Luke sighed. This was how it went. They brought you in, they sent you on a mission, and everything had to be done as soon as possible. Then, when you came to them with the intel, they were in meeting. Leave a message and we'll call you back.

"Okay, Kat, you got a pen?"

"Very funny," she said. Of course she was a tablet person. Luke had never quite adapted himself to the latest and greatest technology. He still had a tendency to scribble notes down on scraps of paper.

"We interrogated Li Quiangguo this morning. Based on a lead he gave us, we have uncovered a list, and possibly more than one list, of dozens of facilities that are likely targets of terrorist attacks. Our tech guy believes these are probably cyber attacks, like the one that opened the floodgates on the Black Rock Dam. Each target facility has its own document. The documents describe technology in use, network technology specs including data limits, size of backbone, processing speed, also age of the tech they're using, and its known vulnerabilities."

"What kind of facilities are these?" she said.

"Airports. Power stations. Entire electricity grids. Oil rigs. Oil refineries. Dams. Bridges. Subway and train systems. You name it, it's on there."

"Any timeframe indicated?"

"Yes. The last document in the list was called *Zero Hour*. We opened it. The date was August eighteenth, two days from now."

There was silence over the line.

Luke went on. "We are heading back to question Li again. It'll take us about ninety minutes to get up there. The target lists are on CD. My tech guy, Swann, is going to stay here in Atlanta and oversee uploading of the data so we can get it to analysts at FBI, NSA, and CIA as soon as possible. You might want to consider pulling your National Security people in now, so they're ready as soon as analysis starts to become available. And if you don't mind, pull us some strings so that we have the analysts we need. We're probably going to need a hundred people, today, this afternoon, which means we'll need cross-agency cooperation."

"You'd better talk to Susan directly," Kat said.

"Yes. I'll remind you that I asked to do that at the beginning. So that we didn't waste time."

"I understand."

The line went dead again.

Ed was staring at Luke. Ed's eyes were large, but not in his typically frightening way. His face was pained. He looked like a man who had just been given an unpleasant surprise, or a child who had been told there were no more cookies.

Behind Ed's head, buildings and billboard zoomed by. They were on a highway overpass now.

"I've got the chopper pilot on the phone. That's the best I could do."

"Okay, what does he say?"

"He's on the chopper pad here in Atlanta. And he's in touch with the FEMA facility."

"Okay, Ed, let's not play twenty questions. Give it to me."

Ed shrugged. His eyes narrowed.

"Li Quiangguo is dead."

CHAPTER EIGHT

12:30 p.m.
The Situation Room, United States Naval Observatory –
Washington, DC

"Should I be in on this?" Michael Parowski said.

Susan nodded. "I want you there."

They were on the ground floor of the New White House, walking briskly toward the Situation Room. Kat Lopez trailed two steps behind them. Two Secret Service men trailed two steps behind Kat.

"What do you want to tell people?"

Susan shrugged. "There's no need to tell anyone anything, or even announce your presence. Kurt Kimball often kicks some people out if things go to a high level, but otherwise, no one would be shocked to see a sitting Congressman in there."

"When will we tell people?"

Susan glanced back. "Kat?"

"We've got a tentative date of Wednesday, nine a.m. We're putting together a press conference. If the weather looks good, we'll do it on the back lawn. If not, we'll do it in the communications room. Does that give you enough time, Congressman?"

"Two days? You'd be surprised at the amount of stuff I get done in two days."

They passed through the open double doors of the Situation Room. Two more Secret Service men flanked the entryway. Big, bald Kurt Kimball, Susan's National Security Advisor, was already inside, standing in front of a large flat-panel screen mounted on the wall. He was talking to a young tech guy and holding a remote control in his hand.

The place was filling up. Kurt had several staff members in the room, and his two top intelligence analysts, both of whom he'd brought over from the RAND Corporation as soon as he arrived.

Trish Markle, the new Secretary of State, was in a seat facing Kurt, and talking to two of her young staff members. Trish had been in her job six weeks already. She had been an Under Secretary at the State Department when Mount Weather happened, and Susan had simply promoted her to the top slot. Trish was forty-seven years old. She had spent long years as a government bureaucrat—maybe too many. So far, she was doing an unremarkable job as Secretary.

"Kurt," Susan said, cutting through the background chatter.

He looked Susan's way, then came over. He shook hands with Congressman Parowski. "Mike, good to see you. I hear there's a big announcement coming."

Parowski glanced at Susan. "Interesting. I just heard about it myself."

Kimball smiled. "Word travels fast down these hallways."

"Kurt," Susan said, "if you're ready, I want to get started. I feel like we're already behind the eight ball on this. There are huge gaps in my knowledge."

"I'm ready. But people are going to continue to straggle in while we're talking. And the analysis we have is very, very preliminary. Mark Swann just finished uploading the last of the files to secure servers maybe twenty minutes ago."

"That's okay. I don't need all the details. Just get me, and everyone else in this room, up to speed about the overall threat."

Susan sat down at the head of the long conference table. Kat Lopez stood behind her and Mike Parowski sat to her left. For a second, Susan remembered how she used to feel in this room. In the early days, after the June sixth attacks, and during the Ebola crisis, she felt overwhelmed. Everything almost took on a surreal quality.

She had dropped into the Presidency as if from outer space. There were a lot more men around her in those days, and a lot of military men. It made her paranoid. The former President had just been assassinated, in part by military men. When the men stared at her, they looked like sharks eager to feed upon a tender morsel.

Things were different now. She was the quarterback. The people around her were her people—either hand-picked by her, or people from the previous crew chosen to stick around, in many cases vetted by Kurt Kimball personally. She liked the team she had.

"Okay," Kurt said now. He raised his hands in the air. "Okay, everybody, let's listen up. We've got a lot of ground to cover, and more is coming in all the time, so we're going to get started. Anybody who doesn't belong in here, you know where the door is."

He looked at Susan. "Madam President, thanks for coming."

She made a spinning wheel motion with her hand. *Let's go.*

Behind Kurt, a photo of the Black Rock Dam appeared. It was a giant, made of gray concrete, looming high above the camera angle.

"Okay. All of you know by now that the floodgates opened early yesterday morning at the Black Rock Dam in western North

Carolina, near Great Smoky Mountains National Park. Millions of cubic feet of water were released before workers could close the dam again, inundating a resort and several towns downriver from the dam. Preliminary estimates are that a thousand or more people died in the sudden flooding, and there was more than a billion dollars in property damage. The Black Rock resort, three miles south of the dam, was completely destroyed."

Next to the image of the dam a new photo appeared. It was of a large Asian man in an orange jumpsuit, his arms and legs shackled as he was led from the back of an SUV. "This is a man identified as thirty-two-year-old Chinese national Li Quiangguo. We have no idea if that was his real name. We suspect that it wasn't. We do suspect he was a Chinese intelligence agent."

"Was?" Susan said. "Wasn't? Why are you putting him in the past tense?"

Kimball looked at her. Then he looked at Kat Lopez. "Okay, somehow that little piece of news didn't reach you. Li Quiangguo is dead. There was an incident at the FEMA camp where Li was being held. Luke Stone and another operative were there to question him this morning, on your orders."

Susan nodded. "Yes, I'm aware of what my orders were."

"No one is quite sure what happened because we haven't talked to Stone yet, but apparently the prisoner soiled himself during the course of the interrogation."

"Wonderful," Susan said.

Susan thought of Luke Stone, and the idea of bringing him back for this operation. She wondered for a second if maybe it would have been better to let a sleeping dog lie. "How did that happen?"

Kimball shrugged. "People become afraid during aggressive interrogations. Afterwards, Stone told the camp director that the subject had been cooperative, and he and his team were going to investigate a lead Li had give them. Rather than have Li sit around with poop in his pants, the director decided to let him have a hot shower. This is also a pretty standard operating procedure. If a subject gives you something, you give them something in return. The reward makes it more likely they'll give you something else.

"Only they allowed Li into the shower by himself, with two guards standing outside the door. They also removed his manacles at the wrists and ankles. It turned out he had a powerful dose of cyanide embedded in a capsule inside a false tooth in his mouth. He pulled out the tooth and swallowed the contents of the capsule within seconds of when the water started running. He began experiencing seizures within a minute and a half. He was dead inside four minutes."

"Was he tortured?" Susan said.

"There are no marks on his body, except ones consistent with the small amount of resistance he put up when he was arrested."

"Is that what I asked you?" Susan said.

Kurt shook his head. "I think you should ask Luke Stone if the subject was tortured."

A low murmur went through the room.

"What's next?" Susan said.

Kimball moved to another slide. It showed an image of a low-slung red brick warehouse building along an industrial road. "Li Quiangguo gave Stone and his team information that led them to this warehouse. Inside the warehouse, they found evidence of the import-export business which was Li's cover story in the United States. They also found evidence that Li was compiling intelligence about a list of potential cyber attack soft targets in the United States. That list is as long as your arm. It contains extensive data about each target, and was kept on three CD-Rom disks in a locked drawer in the locked office of the warehouse. The information was kept nowhere else that we are aware."

"CD-Rom?" Mike Parowski said. "Why would he store it like that? It's twenty years out of date."

Susan was a little surprised that Mike chose to speak. She wanted him to know what was going on, but she also had expected he would keep a somewhat low profile.

Kimball pointed at him. "You win the prize. Best question so far. We're guessing right now that Li kept his files on CD so that no American government analysts, should they become suspicious of his activities, would be able to access the information. We can only access information kept on networked computer systems. We can't access information kept on a disk locked away in a drawer."

Parowski persisted. "So how does he transmit the information to his handlers, who I assume are in China?"

"He was an importer," Kimball said. "I'm sure he knew that we can intercept almost any web traffic originating from, entering, or passing through the United States. He probably also knew that with agencies like NSA, their real mandate is to analyze the web traffic of foreigners, especially questionable traffic associated with a place like China. His cover story was a good way to circumvent this.

"We've done some initial investigation and found that his company was sending packages to China on a regular basis— paperwork, manifests, payments, order forms, and the like. He had an account with DHL Worldwide, as well as a few Asia-based courier services. It's very likely he was sending the data in small batches as he acquired it, possibly on disks that were mostly full of dummy information. And it's likely he compiled the data for himself on those three CDs, more or less in one place, in case he needed to refer to the information at a later date."

"Would you say that was a lazy way to store it?" Parowski said.

Kimball shrugged. "I think it would be considered less than optimal. I'm sure his handlers wouldn't be happy to learn he was holding onto intelligence in that way. I'm sure he realized that, and it's at least part of the reason why he's dead now. Then again, I'm sure he felt the chances of someone stumbling upon that information were quite low, which they were."

Susan held up a palm.

"Do we have the names and addresses of the places he was sending courier shipments?"

"Sure. But there are about two dozen of them spread out in Hong Kong, Guangzhou, Beijing, in a few of the new industrial districts where fly-by-night manufacturers sprout up like mushrooms and disappear just as quickly, as well as in the mountainous region on the border of China and North Korea. It's anyone's guess, but probably most of his communications were with legitimate companies, as far as that goes."

"Do we know who is who?"

Kimball shook his bald head. "Our infiltration in China is not nearly as deep as we'd like. It was a closed society for a long time, and they're still suspicious of outsiders. They keep a close eye on both Chinese ex-patriots coming home from the West, and Chinese-Americans born in the United States who are visiting. It's hard to send agents that can blend into Chinese society."

"But we trust our intelligence?" Susan said. "We feel confident that China was behind the dam attack, and that Li Quiangguo was sending the information he gathered to China?"

Now Kimball nodded. "I think we can say with ninety percent certainty that China was behind the dam attack. We don't fully understand their reasons for it, and I believe the extent of lives lost and damage was likely a mistake. As everyone in this room probably recalls, five months ago an American destroyer, the USS

Angel Fernandez, was on night maneuvers in heavy weather in the Sea of Japan. It collided with a large Chinese fishing trawler. The trawler was rent in half and sank within minutes. Despite the efforts of the destroyer's crew, they were unable to rescue any of the Chinese fishermen. It's believed that twenty-seven men went down with that ship.

"The disaster was a public relations nightmare for the Communist Party. They looked weak and impotent in the face of widespread calls for war. The situation led to a shake-up in the Chinese leadership, and the installation of the new President, Xi Wengbo. Xi came in promising to check what he called American aggression in Asia. Personally, I think they opened that dam as part of Xi's new program. They were testing their ability to pierce our security and take down our infrastructure, possibly in preparation for larger attacks. I think they were doing it in retaliation for that collision at sea, and also to rebuke us for our aerial presence defending Vietnam in the South China Sea."

Kurt paused, and seemed to think about what he was saying.

"However, that's speculation on my part. What's one hundred percent clear is that Li was sending the data he gathered back to China. Who has been using the data and why, I think we still don't know for sure."

Now Susan persisted. She felt like Kurt was talking around the issue, a rare performance for him. He was usually to the point, and he took the shortest way to get there. "So we're sure it's China," Susan said.

"I'd say yes, we're sure."

Susan took a deep breath.

"Get me the Chinese President on the phone."

*

Half an hour after Susan made the decision, aides on both sides were holding the line open. Susan barely had time to eat half a turkey club sandwich and choke down a cup of coffee in her study.

"Can we please get some better coffee in this place?" she said to Kat Lopez as they descended the grand staircase. "I don't know what's happened to the coffee."

She realized she was nervous about talking to Xi Wengbo, and it was making her irritable.

"It's just logistics," Kat said. "We're feeding a lot more people here now. We brought in an industrial food vendor."

59

Susan stopped halfway down the stairs. She turned and gave Kat her hardest look. "Kat, have you read the latest edition of *Fortune* magazine? To hear them tell it, I'm currently the third most powerful person on Earth, after the Pope and Vladimir Putin. What would *Fortune* think if they found out their current number three can't get a decent cup of coffee no matter how hard she tries?"

Kat had stopped, too. She was a serious person, a literal person, and was not in the habit of answering rhetorical questions. Susan had hired her because she was ambitious, she was hard as nails, she could weather the storms that seemed to face them on a daily basis. But she did not have a flair for the finer things the way Richard Monk had. She didn't see the need for them. She and Susan had tripped over this again and again during Kat's time here. You could work hard, be tough, be in the fight, and still drink good coffee and sleep on a luxurious bed. Kat didn't seem to understand this.

They started down the stairs again. Susan was nervous. She knew that about herself. It was out of character for her to take Kat to task for something as mundane as coffee. The real issue was talking to Xi Wengbo. Susan just could not get used to making these difficult phone calls. Regardless of what *Fortune* magazine said, somewhere deep inside, Susan suspected that people like this were the real power players, and she wasn't in their league. As they moved down the hall toward the Room, she could feel her body trembling the tiniest amount.

Kurt Kimball was ready as they entered. Kurt was always ready. He was the definition of tireless. He was the poster boy for it. He worked long days, often seven days a week, but it seemed to have no effect on him. It wasn't that he got tired and somehow bulled his way through it. He never seemed tired at all. He was a great big bald-headed wall of endurance.

He stood at the front of the Room, with his pointer.

"Ready, Susan?"

The Room was packed. All eyes were on her. This was another thing she was still having trouble with. Not only did she have to talk to Xi, she had to do it in front of an audience. It wasn't as bad as it used to be, but still…

She sat down at the head of the table. The phone was in front of her.

"Ready."

"Okay," Kurt said. "Before we begin, here's the five-minute refresher course on Xi."

60

A photo of the Chinese leader appeared behind Kurt. He was a young man with prematurely thinning hair and glasses. In the photo, he wore a tan suit. He was not smiling.

"Xi Wengbo, thirty-four years old, is the President of the People's Republic of China. As I described, he was swept into power during the fallout from the USS *Fernandez* accident. He has been a member of the communist party since he was a teenager. His grandfather, Xi Ningba, was a communist revolutionary who survived the Long March in 1934 and 1935 with Mao Zedong. That pedigree has certainly fueled Xi's rise, but make no mistake. He wouldn't have reached where he is, especially this young, without being a consummate, and ruthless, political player.

"Xi plays chess at the Grandmaster level. He is fluent in English, and attended Cambridge University in England for his degree in international relations. There has been some question about his ties to construction companies that have been awarded large no-bid contracts by the Chinese government. Our data suggests that Xi is a closet billionaire, who has moved hundreds of millions of dollars in government money to offshore banks."

Kimball paused. "As you know, we have been experiencing unprecedented tension with China over their man-made islands in the South China Sea. Our view is that the islands they are building are an incursion on the territory of Vietnam. Their view, of course, is that the South China Sea, and Vietnam for that matter, has been in their sphere of influence for the past three thousand years."

Behind Kimball, a short video appeared. In it, a Vietnamese naval patrol boat rammed a Chinese fishing boat. "Just a few years ago, the Chinese were using commercial fishing vessels as their cat's paw in the region. Which led to confrontations with the Vietnamese like the one you see behind me. But now, Chinese warships have moved in, and the Vietnamese don't dare confront them. The Chinese have built an airstrip on one of the islands, and their fighter planes now routinely perform 'touch and go' exercises there. The entire sea has become militarized. Our Seventh Fleet has been parked outside the region for the past four weeks, waiting for the order to go in."

"I won't send them in without provocation," Susan said.

"You might have that provocation now," Kurt said. He wasn't countering her, Susan knew. There was no way that someone as studied and methodical as Kurt Kimball wanted to spark a war with China. He was just stating a fact.

"It would start a world war," someone behind Susan said.

"That war might have already started," Kurt responded. "It would be nice to assume otherwise, but right now we're not in a position to assume anything."

The room was quiet.

Susan took a deep breath. She had that nervous feeling, butterflies fluttering in her stomach, as if she was going on stage. That was fine. She had been on stage many, many times. Normally, she was there to whip up the crowd. Today, she was going to... what?

"Okay," she said. "Are we ready?"

"The line is open," an aide said. "We can put you on anytime."

Susan nodded. "Now is good."

She picked up the white telephone on the table in front of her. Holding the phone gave her a curious feeling. She remembered how, when she much younger, all phones were attached to something. The kitchen wall, a handset on a desk, something. People didn't put you on hold then. They simply put the phone down, went and did whatever it was they needed to do, and then came back. There was a sense of space over the line. You could hear background noise. That's how this call sounded.

"The President of the United States is on the line," a male voice said.

"Hold one moment for the President of the People's Republic of China," came another voice.

Susan rolled her eyes at Kurt. He was standing with a remote telephone to his ear. Of course, the guy was going to play the "you wait for me" game. Hopefully, he wouldn't feel the need to play too long.

Several seconds passed.

"Hello? This is Xi Wengbo."

"Mr. President," Susan said. The moment was like walking through a curtain and into the bright spotlight. "This is Susan Hopkins."

"Madam President," the Chinese leader said. "I have been eager to speak with you."

Susan let that one fall to the floor. If he was so eager to speak, then why was it that her side was the one to reach out?

"Naturally, I have learned of the problem with your dam. I want to express the condolences of the entire Chinese people for the loss of so many of your loved ones, and offer our assistance in any way you may need."

"Thank you, Mr. President. The American people appreciate that. But that's not why I called. At the moment, I would like to share with you some concerns that we have."

His voice was calm. "Of course. Please begin."

"Yesterday, we arrested a Chinese citizen named Li Quiangguo."

"Yes. We are aware of this person."

"He was photographed on top of the dam the day before the disaster. He was in contact via email with internet addresses originating inside China in the forty-eight hours before the disaster. The emails are encrypted, so at this time we do not know their contents. We should know soon. We also discovered lists of what we believe are targeted American infrastructure in Li's office in Atlanta."

"Where is Mr. Li now?" the Chinese president said.

Susan was glad he asked. "He's dead." She paused for a few seconds to let that sink in. "He committed suicide with a cyanide capsule embedded in a false tooth. We had allowed him a few unsupervised moments to take a shower, and he killed himself without hesitation."

Xi Wengbo didn't speak. Instead, he made a sound, like the low background hum of machinery. "Hmmmmm."

Susan pressed on. "The truth is, we are concerned that Li was a special operations agent. He was traveling on a Chinese passport under an alias that we must consider a *nom de guerre*."

There was no response from Xi at all.

For a moment, Susan pictured how many people were really on this phone call. There were fifteen in this room alone. Xi must have at least that many. The various spy agencies on both sides were probably plugged in. The Pentagon. Hell, the Russians were probably on here as well.

Xi was playing coy. Reserved. Very, very Chinese. So Susan decided to go full-on American.

"We want to know if Li Quiangguo was a Chinese agent, and if your country has committed an act of war against us."

Susan could almost hear the collective gasp from halfway across the world.

There was another long pause.

"It embarrasses me," Xi said, "to hear you say that."

Xi paused again, to let the full weight of his shame settle in.

"Some months ago, one of your ships destroyed a civilian vessel of ours, leaving many dead. We did not call this an act of war. Why? Because in China, we consider ourselves a great friend of the United States. Your triumphs are our triumphs. Your pain is our pain. We have our differences, of course, as all true friends do. But no, we have not committed an act of war against you. We do not want war with you—only friendship. Open trade. Mutual respect for traditional boundaries and territorial integrity. It seems to me that much like a magician performing a sleight of hand, someone is diverting your attention towards us, and away from themselves. I suggest, if you are looking for the perpetrators of this crime, there are other, more likely suspects. Taiwan comes to mind. It is a terrorist state, terrorism you have long sponsored, and they do share our ethnicity. South Korea, perhaps. Maybe even Japan. We all look alike to you, do we not? Perhaps your Mr. Li was not Chinese."

Despite the man's attempts at control, Susan could hear his voice rising. He was either quietly angry, or doing a good imitation of it.

"Perhaps he was an American," he said now. "How do you say it? Born and bred."

"Those are all good ideas," Susan said. "And believe me when I tell you we are already following up on them, and more. Also believe me when I say that if your government is somehow involved in this, you are going to be very, very sorry. We are still the most powerful country on earth, Mr. Xi, and we will not hesitate to use that power. I suggest you keep that in mind if some information about a second attack happens to cross your desk."

"Good day, Mrs. Hopkins. I was glad to speak with you and express the sincere feelings of the Chinese people to you."

"Good day, Mr. Xi."

Susan let a long breath go out of her. She hung up the phone, and watched as Kurt Kimball made a slicing motion across his throat to someone in the back of the room.

Within a few seconds, ten or twenty people around her all hung up their telephones.

"So..." she said to the crowd. "I thought that went pretty well."

CHAPTER NINE

3:15 p.m.
Women's Federal Detention Center – Randal, Maryland

The lockup was unlike other prisons Luke had visited. Luke tended to think of prison as a dreary place. This one wasn't too bad. He sat at a white table made of heavy molded plastic, bolted to the floor, in a large open waiting area. Two uniformed guards, a man and a woman, both big and burly, stood on either side of the entry door.

There were a dozen tables in the room, with three of them currently occupied, in each case a visitor sitting across the table from a woman in an orange jumpsuit. At one of them, an older women and three young children were visiting the prisoner—probably a young mom seeing her own children.

Eight-foot-high windows, embedded with metal wire, let afternoon sunlight stream in. Luke could look out the window and see basketball courts and a track painted with running lanes. A handful of heavyset women in prison jumpsuits were walking around the track, large orange dots moving at different speeds—slow, slower, and slowest.

Luke drummed his fingers on the table. He was nervous to see Trudy after two months. He hadn't visited her before now, and worse, he hadn't even known she'd been arrested.

Also, he didn't have all day. Even as he sat here, analysts from the various intelligence agencies were digesting the data from Li's office. At any minute, Luke was expecting a call from Susan. He glanced at his phone to see if he had missed anything. He had a text:

Where are you?

Ha! It was Gunner. He was serious about wanting to text. Luke felt a sudden, almost absurd swelling in his chest. He smiled and shook his head. God, he missed that kid. He pulled up the keyboard screen and started typing.

Visiting an old friend. Where are you?

He watched the screen. Dots zipped across it, indicating something was happening.

Home. I saw you were in North Carolina before. Mom and me are going to Screen on the Green tonight. It's Crouching Tiger, Hidden Dragon. I know you like that one. Wanna meet us?

Screen on the Green was a program where they showed free movies on a massive screen, right on the National Mall between the Capitol Building and the Washington Monument. They showed them only on Monday nights, and only in the summer. Thousands of people would come to the Mall with folding lawn chairs, blankets, and picnic baskets, and settle in to watch classic family-friendly movies like *North by Northwest* or *Back to the Future*. Luke and Becca had been taking Gunner to the movies there since he was three years old. They used to bring a bottle of white wine and some cheese and crackers, lay out on their old flannel blanket, all three of them in a pile, and call it date night.

The idea of meeting them there was almost too bittersweet to contemplate. Becca wouldn't want Luke there, and Gunner would be hoping this was the start of a family reboot.

Even so...

What time?

He sent it knowing that in all likelihood, it couldn't be. The reply came back very quickly. He could almost feel Gunner's enthusiasm, and longing, through the words that he typed. *Movie starts at 8. We try to get there at 7:15 to get a good spot. We ride the subway to Smithsonian. Will you do it?*

I'll try, Monster.

Luke got a sinking feeling just contemplating it. He'd love to watch a big screen outdoor movie with Gunner. He would do it every day of the week. But with Becca? He had no idea how that would go. And then there was the little issue of impending infrastructure attacks, if that was even real.

A thought came to him. It was a loud thought, almost as loud as if someone had spoken it to him.

Susan didn't ask you to stop the attacks. She asked you to interrogate the prisoner.

It was true. He did what she asked. He was free to go... anywhere.

The door opened and Trudy walked in between the two guards. She waited while the woman unshackled her wrists. Then she made a beeline toward Luke, not running, but walking fast between the tables. He stood and watched her as she came. Her long brown hair was pulled back in a ponytail. Her orange jumpsuit seemed baggy on her. Her eyes looked owlish in big red-framed glasses. There was an old shiner beneath her right eye, its last remnants a bruised purple and yellow, like overripe fruit. Even so, she was as beautiful as ever.

She walked straight into his arms. They embraced, and he held her tight. Her body pressed against his. He picked her up. She weighed less than nothing.

Luke watched the guards over Trudy's back. They stared at him, but made no move.

"Okay to touch here, huh?" he said.

Trudy held him tight, her arms around his neck, her legs wrapped around his legs. He could smell the shampoo in her hair. "Yes," she said, her voice barely above a whisper. "It's fine."

After a long moment, Luke let her slide to the floor. She looked up at him. "We can touch. I'm supposedly a murderer, but I'm a non-violent one. This is a special unit—embezzlers, art thieves, con artists, investments scammers. We're all flight risks, but we're not going to hurt anybody."

Luke gestured at the fading black eye with his chin. "Somebody around here is violent." He reached out and touched her face with his fingers.

She half-smiled. "Oh, this old thing? When I first came in, a few of the girls thought I had a hand in murdering President Hayes. It took me a little while to set them straight."

Trudy moved to the other side of the table, and they sat down. She reached her hands across and took his hands. Her hands were tiny. His were the big hands of the high school quarterback he had once been. They held hands like lovers. And they were lovers. They'd had one night together.

"I love your beard," she said.

"Thank you."

She nodded. "Very sexy. You should become an underwear model now that you're retired."

"I just came out of retirement."

Her eyes became wide. To Luke, they seemed almost frightened. "The dam?"

"You know about it?"

She shrugged. "We get television in here. What's going on?"

Luke glanced at the guards. They were scanning the room, on edge, for what Luke wasn't sure. This place was almost like the family room at a McDonald's.

"Trudy, I would love to tell. The truth is, I need your help. But with you in here… I don't know. I can't do it. The information is classified."

She nodded and cast her eyes down at the table. "Right. And I've lost my clearance."

"You have. Yes."

Her fingers traced a design on his hands. "Can't you give me a tiny piece of it? Something tantalizing, a puzzle for me to ponder over? I have nothing right now. Nothing to do, nothing to work on, nothing to think about. All anybody does around here is watch TV."

"What's your situation?" Luke said.

"My situation?"

"Yes. Do you owe anyone anything? Is anyone protecting you?" Trudy was a beautiful woman, she was small, and a little bit on the skinny side. There were probably some big girls in here.

She made a face of disgust, designed to show how appalled she was by the very thought. "It's not like that here. This is a pretty safe place."

He was close to telling her. It was the reason why he came here. Back at SRT, he had known all along, without having to be told, how much he relied on her intelligence gathering and her scenario spinning. She was the best in the business. Whatever other flaws she might have, she had a gift for spy work. But she couldn't do him any good while in jail. And if she told anyone what was going on, anyone at all...

"Trudy, I tell you, you tell one other person, then the guards know, and a short while later, the President of the United States is asking me why I'm spreading rumors in prison. Worse, it gets outside the prison and becomes common knowledge on the street. It's no good. I can't give you anything while you're locked up."

He shook his head. "You know the drill. Loose lips sink ships. It's as true now as it ever was."

"Thanks, Luke. For nothing."

"Trudy, what are you doing in here, anyway? Why didn't you call me?"

Now she looked up at him. Her eyes said she was wounded. A deer with a broken leg, helpless in front of the oncoming semi truck.

"You took off right after the Ebola crisis. Just gone, without another word. It seemed like we had something, that just for a moment, the elusive Luke Stone was pinned down... But then you were the incredible disappearing man again. Wham bam, thank you, ma'am."

It pained Luke to hear her describe it in that way. He was Luke Stone, the good guy, wasn't he?

"I couldn't imagine that you wanted to hear from me," she said now. "Before I was arrested, Ed Newsam told me that you were going to try to put your marriage back together. Did it work?"

Luke shook his head. "No."

She shook her head, just slightly. "I'm sorry."

Luke almost smiled. She was the one in prison. She was the one facing death, or a life behind bars. All he was facing was a life alone. Otherwise, he was free as a bird.

"What are you going to do now?" he said.

She tilted her chin up. "I'm going to do whatever it takes. Whatever I need to do to survive this. That's what I'm going to do. I'm not going to let them execute me, if that's what you're wondering. And I don't plan on doing life in here, either."

"Do you have anything you can give them? Something they don't already know?"

Now she smiled. "Loose lips sink ships. A very smart man once told me that."

Luke paused. He was hesitant to ask the next question. But it was the question he came here to ask. She might hate him for it, but…

"Do you have anything you can give me?" he said.

She stared at him. "About what?"

He didn't say anything.

"About the dam?" she said.

"Yes."

"Luke, how would I know anything? All I know is what I saw on TV. You won't give me the first piece of intel."

He shrugged. "Guess. Use your gut."

She shook her head. "If you won't give me anything at all…"

He took a calculated risk. "They're looking at China. I can't tell you why."

A gasp of air escaped her, almost a grunt, almost a sound of merriment. Just like that, the old Trudy was back. "I listened to the translations of intercepted Chinese telephone calls and bugged conversations for eighteen months when I came on board SRT. It was my first assignment out of school. I mean, calls between high-ranking party members. Calls from field operatives to their handlers. Meetings between men at the top of the secret police apparatus and their contacts inside the central government."

"And?"

She smiled. "The Chinese are cautious. Their time horizon is a hundred years, two hundred years. A trickle of water wearing away rock, you know what I mean? They usually don't go over the top. They want to kill you with kindness."

"Are you saying it isn't them?" he asked.

She shrugged.

"Hard to say. I think it's unlikely."

"What if it was an accident?" Luke said. "What if they were playing around and made a mistake?"

Trudy really shook her head now. "They don't make mistakes."

"Sure they make mistakes," Luke said. "They've poisoned their own water. They've poisoned their air."

"Sure," Trudy said. "But that's domestic policy. The people are powerless, and it's all part of the long-term plan. When dealing with Russia, or the United States, or India? No one is as careful as the Chinese. They push, but not hard enough to knock you over. They do not want to upset the applecart."

Just then, Luke's phone started ringing. He glanced at it.

She frowned.

"You have to go, don't you?" she asked. The sadness in her voice pained him.

He wondered if coming here had been a mistake. He was still not entirely sure why he had come. Was it because of his feelings for her? Or because he needed to solve this case? Or both?

But he had no choice. He nodded and stood.

There was one thing, at least, he could tell her.

"It's the President of the United States."

CHAPTER TEN

4:45 p.m.
The Situation Room, United States Naval Observatory –
Washington, DC

When Luke walked in, the Situation Room was in chaos.

He had never seen it this crowded. There were at least fifty people packed inside. The walls were lined with chairs, each chair with a person on it, and an aide or two aides standing nearby. The young aides were typing into their tablets, or scribbling furiously into notepads.

The conference table was littered with coffee cups and empty plastic takeout containers. It looked like a war zone. Every seat at the table was taken. Susan was at the head of the table, her chief-of-staff, Kat Lopez, crouched next to her and whispering in her ear. There was a steady hubbub of noise, the low background hum of whispered and not-so-whispered conversations.

Kurt Kimball stood in front of a screen at the other end of the table. He was in his shirt sleeves. The dress shirt was too small for his big chest and arms. He was pointing at a diagram of Gulf of Mexico oil rigs. The slide changed to a video of the BP drilling rig Deepwater Horizon on fire in 2011.

On screens all around the room, data appeared, scrolling lists. Luke glanced at one. Commuter rail systems, what cities they served, ridership numbers, known vulnerabilities. As he watched, the relevant stats scrolled by for the SEPTA light rail network whose primary center was Philadelphia, but which also served surrounding cities like the state capital of New Jersey, Trenton; Camden; and Chester, Pennsylvania. It was one random piece of infrastructure in a vast country full of easy targets. There were hundreds like it.

Kimball saw Luke standing there. He raised his hands.

"People! Can we have quiet in here for a moment?"

The place quieted down, grudgingly.

"Agent Stone, thanks for joining us," Kurt said.

Luke shrugged. "Okay."

If Kurt Kimball was looking to Luke for answers, he was looking in the wrong direction.

"You've been off radar for some time. Do you have any more intel?"

Luke shook his head. "You have everything I found—a dead prisoner, a list of targets, and a date, which you already know is two days from today. About all I can add is my systems guy spent years in China and felt that the prisoner might have been of Chinese descent, but also maybe not. And just as likely to be part of some terror cell or non-state actor as an agent of the Chinese government."

Luke was silent for a moment. "One last thing. The prisoner appeared to be terrified of waterboarding. Most people don't know what to expect, so they aren't all that afraid until after it starts happening. This suggests to me that at some time in the past, the prisoner might have been tortured, possibly by the Chinese, possibly by someone else."

A low murmur went through the crowd as soon as Luke mentioned waterboarding.

"Why do you say he *might* have been tortured?" a woman in a blue business suit said. "You don't know?"

Luke shrugged. "He could have been acting. One of my associates thought so."

"Did you torture him?" a tall, good-looking middle-aged man said from a seat along the wall. His tone indicated that he was accustomed to being answered with deference.

Luke stared at the man. "No."

"I don't understand the circumstances in which this prisoner died. Did you threaten to torture him, mock execute him, or in any other way violate the laws of war or his human rights?"

Luke smiled. "Who are you, please?"

"I'm Representative Michael Parowski of…"

"Okay, yes, I know… Ohio." Luke knew him by reputation. Long-time Congressman, tough political in-fighter, ties to labor, possible ties to the mob. He was one of the few high-level veteran politicians still around. The rest had been killed. That was probably why he was in on this meeting. The bench was not deep these days.

Luke took a deep breath. "Well, Congressman, I was brought in by the President of the United States to interrogate the prisoner. The President is familiar with my methods. If she was uncomfortable with them, I believe she wouldn't have called me."

He looked at Susan.

"Isn't that true, Madam President?"

Susan raised a hand, flapped it. She looked exasperated. She didn't say a word.

Luke went on. "The prisoner was a party to the deaths of hundreds or maybe thousands of innocent people—I'm not up to date on the current body count. He was clearly gathering intelligence on soft targets within the United States. And after he was captured, he was being held by the Federal Emergency Management Agency in a detention facility that apparently does not exist. Does that help you understand the circumstances any better?"

The murmur was louder this time. People in this room were not aware of the intelligence and prison apparatus at work in their own country. And they were the ones supposedly in charge.

Then again, maybe they were just pretending.

"The facility doesn't exist?" a heavyset woman said. "In what sense?"

Luke shrugged. "In the sense that it's not on any official list of detention facilities currently in operation. It's in the middle of the north Georgia wilderness, and is not marked on any map. There is no direct way to contact it from the outside, and it has no name that I am aware of. And hundreds of people are in fact being held there."

"Are you saying there is a black site in the United States?"

Kurt Kimball clapped his big hands together. They made a loud SMACK.

"Can we get this conversation back on track, please? Anyone with questions or concerns about domestic detention facilities, please talk to me off-line. Luke, we're trying to get a handle on where the next attack may take place, so we can forestall it. Do you have anything to add to that discussion?"

"The list of targets is too long," Luke said. "I have no idea."

A graying man in military dress blues, a general, raised a hand. "Kurt, we have to realize that there is simply no way we can know where the next attack will take place. My people have analyzed these lists eight ways to Sunday. It's raw data. There is no hierarchy at all. There is no indication anywhere of a sequence of attacks. I suggest we set a nationwide infrastructure alert—all first responders on a hair trigger and ready to go. And in the meantime, we prepare a counter-offensive. If the Chinese think they can just waltz in here and start killing people, we show them how mistaken they are. And we make them pay."

"What are your ideas, General Walters?" Kimball said.

The general referred to a single sheet of paper his aide handed him. "We have a pretty robust menu of immediate options in front of us. For example, we have more than a hundred sleeper cells embedded across China, which we could activate for our own acts of sabotage with just a few hours' notice. Some of those networks have degraded, or have been rolled up by the Chinese government, but many of them are still operational.

"And that's just one small possibility. The options become more devastating, and therefore more attractive, the longer the retaliatory time frame extends. Make no mistake. We will win any war with China. It will take some time, but we will prevail."

"Like we did in Korea?" someone said.

A ripple of laughter went around the room.

The general wasn't laughing. "Apples and oranges. In the 1950s, the two countries were somewhat evenly matched, especially in terms of a ground war. But even then, remember that we were fighting a limited war in Korea, and the Chinese mobilized four million men. Now, our weapons technology is vastly more advanced than theirs. And we won't even consider a ground war."

"I think," Michael Parowski said, "that any war with China is a nightmare scenario, and we should do whatever we can to avoid it."

"And if we're attacked again?" the general said.

"Treat it as criminal investigation," Parowski said.

"I can't even answer that," the general said. "Who are we going to bring up on charges? The President of China? Are you going to parachute in and arrest him, Congressman?"

"What about economic sanctions?" Susan said. These were the first words out of her mouth since Luke walked into the room. "Kurt, what will be the ramifications of that?"

Kurt shrugged. "Depends on what kind of teeth they have. It also depends on who else participates. As you know, we've been locked in a trade war with China for two years. They manipulate their currency to give them a favorable trade balance, and they destabilize markets by flooding the world with bottom-shelf products, many of them convincing knock-offs at a fraction of the cost of the originals. Their trading base becomes more diversified all the time.

"They've long traded with Russia, and they're opening vast markets in India. There are now more than a hundred million people in India with the means to buy consumer products, and China is wowing them with cheap thrills. Iran is a major market for them. And increasingly, so are South American countries like Brazil and Argentina. Meanwhile, China's own middle class is growing geometrically. Frankly, I don't know what effect sanctions are likely to have. This is a bad time for an economic confrontation with China. They might not need us anymore."

"So what we're saying," Parowski said, "is we have no idea where and when the next attack is likely to take place, and we have no clear way to respond, outside of an all out war, if it does happen?"

"Right now, the navy has a strike group from the Seventh Fleet in port in the Philippines," the general said. "It consists of the aircraft carrier *John C. Stennis*, two Aegis destroyers, and two cruisers. That strike group alone could destroy or significantly degrade China's naval presence in the South China Sea in twenty-four hours. We back them up with a second strike group currently on maneuvers in the ocean east of Taiwan.

"Then we fortify the whole thing with missiles locked on air force and naval bases in southern China. If another attack takes place, we seize the South China Sea, with impunity. We send Seabees ashore to dismantle the man-made islands they've been building, or better yet, plant American flags on them."

He raised a hand to stifle the growing buzz of complaints. "It's not a war. The Vietnamese want us there, and I'll bet we take the entire region without firing a shot."

He looked at his aide. The aide nodded.

"From this moment on, the next attack on American soil means we take territory. A second attack after that means we sink Chinese container ships at sea—all of them, anything in the Western Hemisphere or headed across the Pacific toward the Americas. How's that for sanctions? No more trade with us, no more trade with Brazil or Argentina."

To Luke, it was clear that the general was not speaking off the cuff. He had come to the meeting with these ideas in his pocket. And he wasn't speaking for himself. The Joint Chiefs of Staff had probably cooked up this plan years ago. Luke had to admit it had a certain grim logic.

"That's not a war, General?" Parowski said.

The general shrugged. "It's not a war if they don't fire back. Anyway, terror attacks on civilian populations constitute an act of war in my book."

"We don't even know if it's them," Parowski said. He turned to the President. "Susan?"

As Luke watched, all eyes were suddenly on her. She sat back in her seat and made a temple with her fingers on the table. She didn't hesitate. "Do it," she said. "Move the Seventh Fleet strike group you mentioned toward the South China Sea. How long will it take?"

The aide whispered into the general's ear. "They are eighteen hours from there at full steam," the general said.

Susan nodded. "Okay. We'll move them into place. Start them in that direction, but at three-quarters steam. We need the extra time. Also, lock surface to surface missiles on, let's say, fifteen container ships. Make it obvious that we're doing it."

Susan sighed, a long heavy exhalation.

"Now, I can't guarantee I'll give the order to destroy civilian vessels. I'll need more facts first. General, can your people get me data on how many ships we're talking about in total, personnel numbers aboard each ship, and known environmental hazards—including what the ships are carrying? I really don't want to put any more hazardous chemicals into the oceans than we have already."

The general almost smiled. Luke almost did, too. He'd have to talk to her about that. Chinese container ships were floating environmental disaster areas—it didn't matter what they were carrying. Bomb even one, and you were sending hundreds of thousands of gallons of oil and gasoline, and in many cases coal, plus tons of asbestos, plastic, sheet steel, electrical wiring lined with toxic poly-fluorocarbons, and God only knew what else, to the bottom of the sea. Of course, the military would be happy to gloss over that in their report to the President.

"I'm not a maritime expert," the general said. "But I can tell you this. Modern container ships are mostly automated. They run with skeleton crews. We can sink a hundred of them and probably kill fewer people than the Chinese killed here in the United States yesterday."

There was a moment when no one said anything.

"On that happy note," Susan said, "if none of you mind, I feel like now is a good time to take a short break."

People immediately began to rise from their seats. They had the air of people who had been here a long time, and had been waiting for permission to get out. A quiet, slow-motion stampede started toward the exit.

"Twenty minutes," Kurt Kimball called out. "In twenty minutes, I want essential personnel finding their way back in here."

Luke began to move through the crowd to the doors. Suddenly Susan was standing beside him. She was much shorter than he was She appeared to have given up wearing high heels. She tugged hi sleeve like a little girl.

Her face was serious. "We missed you, Luke. I kept turning toward the door, hoping you would walk in. Someone has to figure this out. We've been in here for hours, and we're no closer to knowing how to stop another attack. The more data that comes in, the wider and crazier the circles become. I don't want a war with China. No one does. But if we get attacked again today, that's where we're heading."

* * *

"Susan, can I be honest with you?"

She sat in her upstairs study with her new, soon-to-be Vice President. They were alone, eating small finger sandwiches, which weren't half bad, and drinking insipid coffee, which was terrible. It was a blessed relief to be up here, away from the Room for twenty minutes.

Kurt Kimball wasn't here. Kat Lopez wasn't here. No one was holding a computer tablet or reading from prepared notes. No aides were lingering at the edges of the conversation, waiting to be assigned a task that would send them darting toward the door, phone in hand, already dialing.

She sat back in her big comfortable chair. She crossed her legs. She quietly ran her hand along the pinstriped fabric of her suit pants. Her legs were getting flabby. She hated it. She had been a workout fiend since she retired from modeling.

Somewhere along the way, probably in a women's magazine, she had tripped over the idea that muscle was sexier than the half-alive skin and bones look favored in the fashion industry, and she never looked back after that. But now she was headed toward middle-aged spread, flabby arms and legs, no muscle tone anywhere. It was impossible to maintain a workout schedule while reeling from one crisis to the next.

Would people think that was a frivolous concern? Maybe. But shouldn't the President be healthy?

She sighed and glanced out one of the floor-to-ceiling windows. The sun was moving westward across the sky. The grounds were green and lush, rolling down to a wooded thicket near the western boundary of the Naval Observatory grounds. It was getting on toward her favorite time of day to be here in the study. The late afternoon light that came through these windows was just... fantastic. She imagined how a long-dead architect, 170 years before, had come to this spot, faced west, and designed a study room, a sanctuary, to perfectly capture the sunlight.

"Susan?"

She looked at Michael Parowski. He was wearing a blue dress shirt, sleeves rolled to three-quarters. He watched her with steely eyes. Rugged good looks... check. Charm... check. Intelligence... check. A large constituency that adored him... check. He seemed to have all the tools, but if so, then why was she suddenly feeling the slightest bit hesitant about extending the Vice Presidency to him?

Because he had stepped into those meetings downstairs, and then immediately overstepped—that's why.

"Sure, Michael. Be as honest as you like. This isn't the time to stand on ceremony."

He nodded. "Okay, good. Here it is. I don't think you should let people like that general muscle you around in meetings. Just a few months ago, people like him were plotting to..."

Susan raised a hand. "We vetted him. Everyone who comes in that room has been vetted as carefully as you were. He had nothing to do with the coup plot. General Walters is a lifetime military man, who also happens to be on our side."

Parowski shook his head. "These people are our ideological enemies, Susan. He would ramp us up into a direct confrontation with China. He wants to have a war in Asia? If I recall correctly, the last couple of times didn't go so well. I'm not ready to send the son and daughters of my constituents..."

"The entire American people are your constituents now, Michael."

He nodded. "Exactly. And I'm not prepared to send their sons and daughters to fight and die, or come back here with the most horrible injuries and disfigurements imaginable—and believe me, Susan, I've been to the military hospitals many, many times, so I've seen it, I know all about it—all for reasons that can't be adequately explained, or that make no sense."

"The attack on the dam wasn't adequately explained?" Susan said. "Do more than fifteen hundred dead at last count make sense to you?"

Parowski stopped. He took a deep breath. "Susan, do we even know it was China?"

"We have reason to believe it was."

She realized as soon as she said it how flat a statement it was. They had a pile of circumstantial evidence, at best. If it were a case that had to be tried in a court of law, no jury would convict. The

78

couldn't say for sure what the prisoner Li Quiangguo's involvement was, or who he might have been working for. They didn't even know who he really was.

"But we don't know."

"No, Michael, we don't."

"And you just sent a small armada of ships into the South China Sea."

Now Susan raised both hands. She gave him the double STOP signs. He was a bulldog, and that's what she was going to like about him, remember? But he was already going too far.

"Michael, you're the senior Congressman from Ohio. That's great, and you've done a wonderful job in that role. But you're moving up to the big leagues now. Things are done differently here. I sent ships *toward* the South China Sea. Not into it. At three-quarters steam, they will arrive there in twenty-four hours. At any moment, we can have them slow down, stop, turn around, or continue. If the Chinese are behind the dam attack, they will see we mean business. They don't want those ships in the South China Sea any more than we do. I'm sure they don't want us to destroy their navy, or cripple their trade with the West by bombing their container ships."

Parowski scowled. "What will that general do if you tell him you want the navy to turn those ships around?"

Susan smiled. It was a fake smile, and she was pretty sure it looked that way. She didn't feel it at all. "He will do exactly what I ask of him, or he will lose his access, and in all likelihood, be forced to resign his post."

"It looked like he was dominating you in there."

"Michael, you need to relax into this. It looked like he offered a good idea, and I went with it. No one else in that room had much to offer by way of concrete steps to take, and that includes you."

He shook his head, emphatically.

"It looked like you got bullied by a military officer. I was biting my tongue in there. You looked weak, and I'm not the only one who saw it. How can it be that less than three months after the military-industrial complex killed the President of the United States and half the Congress—many of whom were friends and long-time allies of mine, by the way—less than three months later, the new President is kowtowing to some..."

"Michael, I've heard enough. That isn't what happened. The fact that you think it was, or seem bent on twisting it in that direction for reasons of your own, makes me question my decision to pick you for Vice President. I think we should revisit whether this is going to be a good fit or not."

He sat way back in his chair. He took a sip of his coffee. He took a deep breath. He had been animated a moment ago, but now he was transitioning into something that looked like perfect calm. Susan couldn't tell what he was feeling.

"It's too late for that, Susan."

"Really? Why is that?"

He shrugged. "Someone leaked it. The pick was announced in the Toledo and Cleveland newspapers an hour ago. I noticed it on my phone when we were in the meeting. I'm sure it's out of Ohio by now, and I'd guess we should start hearing from the news networks any minute, if we haven't already. I didn't want to bring it up during the meeting because I didn't want to interrupt what was going on. I was planning to tell you about it once we were alone."

Susan nearly gasped. She felt a flush come to her face. She was the second woman who had turned red in his presence today.

"Did you leak it?" she said.

"No."

"Did your staff leak it?"

He half-smiled. "Not to my knowledge."

"Michael, don't make me play twenty questions. How did the information get out? If it was leaked to the Ohio newspapers, obviously that points to you and your people. If I can't trust you enough to follow the script we have in place, then I'll simply announce it was a mistake. It was a rumor. They have it wrong."

He stared at her now. His pale blue eyes did not waver at all. "How is that going to look, Susan? The country is under attack, and your poll numbers have dropped by more than twenty percent since you've been in office. You're under a fifty percent approval rating now. You've been in office since June, and you haven't even managed to pick a Vice President yet? Now you pick one, then un-pick him in less than twenty-four hours? That looks pretty indecisive to me."

She shrugged. "I'll live with low approval ratings."

"There's more to it than that," he said. "You don't think we knew this was coming, Susan? Everybody knew this was coming. I was the best pick for Vice President by a country mile. There is no one else but me. I knew about it through back channels a month ago. To be frank with you, I'm surprised it took this long. But since it did, my people had all the time in the world to do some research I'll tell you this. We vetted you as hard as you vetted me."

"What are you saying, Michael?"

"Please call me Mike. Since we're going to be working together."

Susan shook her head. She smiled. The man was a clown. It was an arranged marriage. She had been sandwiched into it by heavy hitters and fundraisers from the party. They thought it was the best ticket available to win the Presidency again in three years. Well, she had been forced into it, and she could force her way out again.

Her numbers would take a hit, certainly. She would lose some standing. She had wasted months choosing him. And she might put together a weaker reelection ticket as a result. But even so...

"Michael," she began...

"I know everything," he said. "That's what I'm trying to tell you. I know everything about you. Okay? I know about the parties in Paris and Ibiza when you were young. Hell, I have photographs, if you want to know. And that's not all. I want to be clear with you, so we understand one another. I know absolutely everything."

He emphasized the word *everything*, saying it slowly, pausing on each syllable.

Ev...er...y... thing.

"Don't you dare threaten me," Susan said.

He smiled and stood up. "I'm not threatening you, Susan. I'm just cementing our relationship. That's how we do it in the big leagues. And you just joined them." His phone beeped once, and he glanced down at it. A text came in. Susan couldn't read it from here—she could only see a block of words. Parowski read the text and grunted.

"Hey, look at that. My assistant has me booked on CNN tonight. I'd better go prepare. I guess we're done here, right?"

Susan stared at him.

"Are we done?" he said again.

She waved a hand at him.

His smiled broadened. "Good. Don't worry. I'll hint around on TV, but I won't confirm or deny anything. We'll do the formal announcement just like we agreed. And I'll see you tomorrow bright and early."

CHAPTER ELEVEN

6:35 p.m.
The Tidal Basin – Washington, DC

"They used to call them squab," the old white-haired man said.

Luke stood on the concrete path along the water's edge.

It was a lovely evening, and many people were out—joggers, strollers, families. This area of downtown was among the most scenic that DC had to offer. From where Luke was, he could see the Lincoln Memorial far ahead and a little to the left. Sharply to his left, and across the basin, was the dome of the Jefferson Memorial, already lit up in blue for the night, shimmering like a magic city above the water.

It was a nice spot to meet. It had the added benefit of being a quarter of a mile from the Smithsonian Metro station. After this, Luke could drift over there and meet Gunner and Becca. Maybe. Or maybe he would tell Gunner he couldn't make it, then watch them from afar. Then again, Gunner would know exactly where he was by checking the GPS. In truth, Luke had no idea what to do.

Silently, he cursed himself for letting Gunner know his whereabouts. It had seemed like a good idea at the time.

The old man sat slumped on a park bench, facing down the grassy hill toward the water. His voice had stopped Luke in his tracks. He was a disheveled old man, with a three-day growth of beard and hair sticking up atop his head in mad tufts. He wore a light gray trench coat, as if the warmth of the evening couldn't remove the winter chill from his rickety body.

"Squab, huh?" Luke said.

The man was covered in pigeons. He had a large plastic bag full of stale white bread on the bench next to him. He methodically broke off pieces of the bread and threw it, some down the hill from him, some right at his feet, some to his right and to his left. He even dropped some on the bench itself. At least fifty pigeons darted around, crazily feasting on the bread. They ran beneath the man's long legs. They jumped on the bench. They flapped their wings, became airborne for a few seconds, then landed on his shoulders and his arms.

Their low vocalizations filled the little area around the bench with sound.

Coo... Coo... Coo... Coo...

The man nodded. "Oh my yes, for three hundred years, they were a game bird. Now people think they're filthy, call them flying rats. Cities try to get rid of them. Why not eat them rather than exterminate them?"

He gestured with his head toward the Jefferson Memorial. "That's what our forefathers did. Never forget that they were our betters. Extraordinary men, and they relished a squab dinner. Why shouldn't we? Anyway, we need to do something with them. Pigeons breed too fast to ever fully eradicate."

"Would you eat one?" Luke said.

"Sure. I used to eat them a lot in my younger days. I still do sometimes, when the mood strikes."

Luke nearly laughed. The old man was crazy. He had always known that about him. Maybe he was getting crazier with age.

"I never see them advertised in the supermarkets. I wonder how you would get one?"

The old man shrugged. "Like this."

He dropped the remaining bread crumbs from his hands. There were pigeons everywhere. Suddenly, his hands darted to the ground like sharks. They came back with a pigeon between them. The old man pinned the pigeon's wings to its body with one hand, and stroked its back and head with the other. The pigeon had a short neck. It couldn't extend it far enough to peck the old man's hands. In any case, the bird seemed calm enough.

"That's a neat trick," Luke said.

"They trust me. And why not? Mostly, I feed them. Every once in a while, they return the favor." He opened his hands and tossed the pigeon into the air. It flew, but it didn't go far.

"What can I call you?" Luke said.

The man shrugged. "Howard will do."

That was funny. Most recently, he had been named Raymond. Today he was Howard. When Luke was young, the name had been Henry, or Hank. He was the man without a name, the man without a country. He had been CIA, probably. But what hadn't he been?

Luke had tried to put a finger on this man many times. He had put out feelers, and called in favors, all to no avail. Some people thought the man had been KGB, when that was a thing. Some said he was British Secret Service. Others said Mossad. Most people thought he was dead.

Luke knew he was alive, though. And someone else did, too. The man was a conduit for information from some very dark places.

"Quite an unfolding disaster you've got on your hands," Howard said, switching topics without any transition. "It looks like the bad guys have managed to peek under your dress."

"Do you know something about it?"

The old man shrugged. "I know what you know."

"Maybe you know something more," Luke said.

Howard leaned back. He put his hands on top of his head. He spoke in an orator's voice, quiet, but with authority. "For as the lightning cometh out of the east, and shineth even unto the west; so shall also the coming of the Son of man be."

"Very nice," Luke said. "What is it?"

"It's the Gospel according to Matthew, chapter twenty-four, verse twenty-seven. It prophesies the second coming of Christ. Judgment Day, the end of this world as we know it."

"Come on," Luke said. "The bad guys have intel on vulnerable infrastructure. Outdated technology. Glitches, loopholes. But I feel like cooler heads are going to prevail." Luke nodded, maybe just to assure himself. "I think we're going to avoid the Apocalypse on this one."

"Hmmm," the old man said. "You killed a man this morning. He appears to have been Chinese."

"Not guilty," Luke said. "He killed himself."

"After you waterboarded him."

Luke shook his head. "Rumors. It didn't happen. I've never waterboarded anyone in my life."

The old man looked directly up at Luke for the first time. There was a wild glint in his eyes. His face was lined and cracked. His eyes were deep set and piercing. He half-smiled. "If you say so."

"I do."

"Well, the man you didn't kill was an interesting person. Among other things, he was a member of a church that was banned in China because the government there says it's a cult. That isn't exactly what they believe, but that's what they say. They have worked pretty hard to stamp out the church over there, including executing many of its members, but it's a seven-headed hydra, that church, and very hard to kill."

Luke thought about that. Talking to this man was often a game of riddles. "You said the Chinese government doesn't really believe it's a cult. What do they believe?"

"Oh, they believe it's a cult, all right. But they also believe that we created the cult, and that its founder is a long-time CIA asset. They further believe that the whole project is designed to undermine the authority of the Chinese state by brainwashing thousands of people into following a bizarre form of doomsday Christianity. I wonder where they got such an idea?"

Howard took a deep breath. "The scripture I quoted you is the organizing principle for the church. Its official name is the Church of Almighty God. Eastern Lightning is what a lot of people call it. Church members believe that Christ has arisen, in the form of a Chinese woman. They believe that our time here on Earth is running out. They also believe that their own actions can bring about the Apocalypse. If your people bother to look closely at the many tattoos on your man's body, they will find the Chinese characters for *Dongfang Shandian*, or Eastern Lightning if you prefer, tattooed on his left shoulder."

Now Luke was confused. "He's one of ours?"

The old man shrugged. "I don't know who he belongs to. I'd say someone thought he was one of ours, once upon a time. Anyway, just because he believed in the teachings of a cult, if he ever really did, that we may or may not have created, doesn't necessarily make him one of ours, does it? He could have joined the church because he likes God, or maybe because someone else put him up to it."

"A double agent," Luke said.

"Or triple, or quadruple."

"You would know something about that," Luke said. "Wouldn't you?"

The man named Howard grunted. It was almost a laugh. "I'd say promiscuity can be more of a virtue than the slavish form of monogamy some people practice. It all depends on if you're doing it right."

"Okay," Luke said. "And this is important because…"

The old man looked at him sharply. "You're a bright boy. Connect the dots. Round about five or six years ago, someone in the intelligence community here thought it would be fun if Eastern Lightning started playing around with computers. Maybe some of the brighter ones could be trained for easy infrastructure takedowns inside China—remote hacking of railway switches, say, or electricity grids, or even…"

"Dams," Luke said.

The old man paused. He seemed thoughtful. "Sure. Dams are easy enough, I guess. I can't believe they ever meant to go through with it. It was just one of those funny ideas people get. But I also don't think they anticipated that Eastern Lightning branches would start popping up here in America, or that…"

"We would lose control of them," Luke said.

"Sure. Or that people with mixed loyalties might join the church, like the man you didn't kill."

Luke felt a familiar sensation begin to sink into his stomach. It was the feeling of dread. "Who was he?"

"I don't know. No one seems to know. From what I hear, ten years ago, people thought he was a peasant, a lower-caste country bumpkin from northern China, who was smuggled into the United States inside a shipping container by human traffickers. Although that may be how he arrived here, the bumpkin part no longer seems to apply."

"He spoke perfect, unaccented English," Luke said.

"I've been told, by people who would prefer to remain nameless, and therefore blameless, that your unknown man was among a group of six who spent a year on a CIA compound in Taiwan, learning the rudiments of computer systems. They set him loose in China, and a short time later he disappeared. Now…"

"You're saying the Chinese attacked us?" Luke said. He thought back to his earlier conversation with Trudy. "It doesn't fit the suit."

"You're right about that," the old man said. "It certainly doesn't. The Chinese tend to take the long view of things. They avoid direct confrontations. They're everybody's favorite trading partner, and everybody's best friend. Until they aren't."

"We would annihilate them," Luke said. "Our missile capabilities are a hundred times what theirs are. We could knock their missiles out of the sky and have ten thousand left to destroy their cities."

Luke heard how breathless he suddenly sounded. He stopped talking.

The man named Howard chuckled. "Quite a tempest you've cooked up in your little teapot. For a moment there, you sounded like the ten-year-old boy I once knew. A few minutes ago, you told me we were going to avoid the Apocalypse on this one. Now you're launching it. Anyway, there's a new leader in China, as you know. He's young, he's under pressure, and he wants to make a statement. But even so, I doubt this is the kind of statement he wants to make. Of course, China isn't the only tough kid on that block."

"What should I do?" Luke said.

"One place to start might be by shutting down the church. They're here. Here in DC, up in New Jersey, out in Chicago, and on the west coast. Seize their assets, and any real estate they might have. Check out their computer systems. People don't do a lot of hacking on the Dell they bought at Best Buy, if you follow me. Detain the members, and see if any of them have a background in computer science, or better yet, are former CIA assets who have wandered off the farm."

"It would take days to get the required permissions to do that. I don't have that kind of time. I'm not even sure I could get anyone to believe it. We created a Chinese cult, and then taught them how to attack our own infrastructure? Come on. Who's going to buy that?"

The old man shrugged. "I've never known you to ask for permission."

* * *

Luke walked back along the path.

It was almost full dark now. He was on the phone with Swann. Swann had just returned to his office at NSA. Luke didn't know where Ed Newsam was. Ed wasn't answering his phone at the moment.

"We need to do a takedown of a church," Luke said. "A Chinese Christian denomination called the Church of Almighty God. It's also known as Eastern Lightning. I need you to find and freeze their assets. Any named bank accounts, offshore accounts, investments. Freeze the personal accounts of the church leaders as well. I also need you to find any warehouses or other commercial-type facilities belonging to them, then get me those locations. Any real estate at all. We need to find their servers and examine the technology they have. Also, we should take their websites and social media accounts down, and seize their email accounts."

Swann grunted. "Luke, do you realize what you're asking? It's against the law. I don't work at the Special Response Team anymore. Here at NSA, things are done a little differently."

Luke rolled his eyes. "Sure they are, Swann. They do everything by the book over there. That's what I read in the newspapers, anyway."

"I'm all by myself on this," Swann said. "I would need an entire team to do what you're talking about. Either that, or a solid week to work. I'll assume you don't have a week."

Luke thought about that. He thought about the meeting earlier today. There was no consensus of any kind. There was no one with a path forward that others would agree to. Susan seemed frustrated at that meeting, and unable to force control. Would she give him a team to do an extra-judicial takedown of a church? He couldn't imagine it.

"Okay, Swann, let me think on that. But you're open to doing it, if I can get you the resources?"

"You know me, Luke," Swann said.

"I do."

Another call was coming through Luke's phone. There were only two other people on the planet who had this number.

"Swann? I have to take another call."

"Fine. Let me know what you come up with."

Luke clicked through to the next caller.

"Stone."

"Luke." It was Susan, calling him directly. She almost never did that. Usually some aide made the initial call.

"Susan. Just the person I want to talk with."

"What have you come up with?" she said.

"I have a pretty solid lead."

Now came the hard part—asking her for the resources to help Swann take down the church. Hell, while he was at it, he might as well ask her for a SWAT team so he and Ed could raid the church headquarters.

"I hope so," she said. "Five minutes ago, the computer system governing the entire DC Metro subway system started shutting itself down. The grid is going down sector by sector. Trains are stalled everywhere. Others are still in motion. Central control is without power. Hundreds of people are stranded in tunnels all over town. Thousands of people are piling into the stations with no trains coming to pick them up."

Luke stopped walking.

It's too soon. The target list said we had forty-eight hours.

For a moment, he was frozen in place. The moment went on and on, and briefly he worried that he might never take another step. All around him, it was a quiet evening along the lovely tidal basin. People were walking hand in hand. Lights glinted on the water. The Jefferson Memorial shimmered in the distance.

He looked back to where he had talked with the old man five minutes before. He could still see the bench from here. There was no one on it.

Gunner and Becca are underground.
"Luke?"

The Smithsonian Metro station was two hundred yards ahead. Luke could see the black obelisk and the clear awning that marked the escalator down to the station from the street. He hung up the telephone and started running.

7:11 p.m.
The DC Metro Subway System – Washington, DC

Gunner nearly fell down when the train stopped.

There had been one seat left when they boarded the train, so he gave it to his mom. She sat and he stood over her, holding the metal pole with one hand while he surfed the web on his phone. At each stop, the train had gotten more and more crowded, until Gunner was surrounded by a forest of arms and legs, briefcases, and backpacks. He could barely see his mom anymore.

He didn't mind. He knew she was there. And they had great cell and wireless internet aboard the Metro. Gunner knew that most cities didn't have any—the Metro had done an overhaul, wiring the whole system, to offer riders the internet and texting. Other cities were way behind.

Gunner knew things like that. He was always interested in why Washington, DC, was the best city in America. It had the best subway system, and the newest one. It had the most spies per square mile of anywhere on Earth. It was the best-designed city—and unlike most cities, it really was designed ahead of time. It had the best museum system in the world, which was totally free for everybody—the Smithsonian. Also, the President lived here.

Gunner checked the GPS app to spot his dad's location. Almost right above them. That was good. Dad was coming to meet them. It made Gunner's chest swell with a feeling he couldn't describe when he thought about his folks getting back together again. He couldn't breathe. It made no sense at all that Dad wasn't living with them. He didn't work for the government anymore. 'ell, he had gone back just this once, but... did it even matter?

89

Gunner looked at his mom. She was very pretty, wearing a summer outfit of a T-shirt and jeans shorts. She had a big colorful canvas bag filled with a blanket, cheese and crackers, a Coke for Gunner, and a tiny bottle of red wine for herself, like the kind she sometimes got when they rode on airplanes.

She should be happy they were going to a movie, but she wasn't. She was never happy anymore. She always looked sad, or angry. And Gunner knew it was because Dad wasn't with them. But he was going to be soon. Maybe just for the movie, but maybe longer. Gunner was going to figure this out. He was going to get them all back together again, whether his parents liked it or not. He was doing it for their own good.

And then the lights on the train went out.

Suddenly, they were in total darkness. Even the lights they had been passing in the tunnel were gone. The train lurched violently. People shouted and fell all over each other. A few fell all the way to the floor, but not Gunner. He held on tightly and kept his balance. In an instant, it was going much slower than just a few seconds before. But it didn't stop. Not yet. Gunner could feel it rolling along, slower and slower, gradually coming to a stop.

"Gunner? Gunner!" He could make out his Mom's voice.

"I'm here, Mom. I'm okay."

Her voice was raised, thin, frightened. "Honey, come closer."

There was no way to come closer. There were too many people in the way. The dark was almost total. The only thing lit up were the phones all around him. They gave off a weird glow, like something from a movie about aliens visiting Earth.

Gunner glanced at his own phone. The internet was still on. "My phone still works," he said, mostly to himself.

A tall black man stood high above him. He looked like a tree. "They run on a different system," the man said. "The Metro power is out, but the phones are independent of that."

Gunner stared down at his phone. Maybe there was some way to find out what was going on. As he looked, a text came through. It was from his dad.

Where are you?

Gunner glanced around. They were in a tunnel somewhere, under the ground. He had been thinking the train was about to enter their station, Smithsonian, but he wasn't sure if that was right. He looked out the windows into the pitch blackness. It was dark on this train, but it was a lot darker in those tunnels.

Another text came in.

Gunner?

* * *

The motorman was not at fault.

He was awake, alert, and not under the influence of any substance except coffee. He was a little distracted—his wife was out of work, his oldest girl was entering her junior year in high school this year, and money for college was tight. Tight? Try nonexistent.

He sat in the train cab, pondering his troubles and watching the tracks and the tunnel ahead of him. The signals went by—green light, green light, green light...

He was on the approach to Smithsonian. He had done this route one million times. There was a track switch ahead here, one he needed to slow down for. He began to brake, barely glancing at his speed.

The entire route was in his body. It was all muscle memory.

Up ahead, the lights went out.

Suddenly, the entire tunnel was dark. His train lights were on, though. He could still see. He pressed on the brake harder. He'd better stop until he could radio the command center.

The train was not slowing down. He felt that in his body, too.

He glanced at his speed. Just over forty miles per hour. Out his front window, there was another train ahead, stopped on the tracks.

His own systems went dead now. Dead, but still moving. The train's momentum carried it forward. There were no lights on in the cab. His headlights were out. He had no brakes.

He looked up again. The other train was RIGHT THERE.

* * *

Luke sprinted, the station just ahead.

The entryway to the station was crowded. Hundreds of people were streaming out onto the street and the sidewalks. Luke slowed. How was he going to push downstairs through these crowds?

He spotted two DC police officers. One was directing people to keep moving as they came out of the station. One stood in the street, white gloves on, diverting car traffic around the growing logjam of people. People milled around, some looking concerned, some laughing. There was no panic.

Then everything changed.

91

There was a sound. It came from deep below the Earth. It was like an explosion, only worse. Explosions only last a second or two. This sound went on and on, ear-splitting, shrieking, the rip and tear of metal grinding metal.

A moment later, smoke began to billow out of the subway entrance.

People were still streaming out, panicked now, a mob, a rampaging herd. The escalators were stopped, people trudging up both sides, falling all over each other. There was no way down. It was dark down there. A cloud continued to rise—not smoke, Luke realized, but soot, heavy air dirty with grit and grime.

He leapt onto the silver metal barrier between sides of the escalator. It was like a long, steep, crazy slide, except for the round discs protruding from it every ten feet—designed to stop people from using it for exactly that purpose.

He headed down, lost his footing almost immediately, fell and slid. He banged off one of the discs and gritted his teeth against the pain. He jumped up, started down again, fell again. He lay on his side and slid down. He pressed himself up at the next landing and started down again, lost his balance, and fell onto the crowd of people climbing the escalator. People fell backwards and Luke climbed over them.

He bulled his way down the escalators into the blackness—sliding, falling, rolling, knocking people over. People threw themselves to the floor when they saw him coming, gun and flashlight in hand. He walked across their backs.

It seemed to take forever to reach the bottom.

At the bottom, there were hundreds more people, pushing and shoving, trying to move through the turnstiles, trying to get upstairs and out. There was a police window here, no one inside it.

Luke pushed his way through the surging crowd. He shined the light in people's faces. Blank, panic-stricken eyes appeared out of the darkness. They were trying to get away from something. He was trying to reach it. "Police!" he screamed. "Let me through! Out of the way! Police!"

A man in a jacket and tie, looking confused, his face bloodied: "They're dying back there."

Luke kept pushing through. *Gunner,* he thought. And then: *Becca.*

People were running towards him now, terrified faces. A man crashed into him, and they both tumbled to the concrete. Luke hi his head on the platform. His flashlight rolled away. He reached f it, and another person stepped on his arm. People were stepping on him, blindly running.

He grabbed the flashlight and lurched to his feet, running along with the momentum of the surging crowd. Everywhere, people were falling down and being stepped on. Twenty yards away, a woman fell. A man stopped to help her and was knocked down himself. More people tried to climb over them and fell. Within seconds, the pile became a writhing mass of human flesh, all being crushed by the next people in line.

This was his nightmare. Desperate people, injured, dying, and Luke helpless to stop it. He backed to the wall and pressed himself against it. The people streamed by him. He took a moment to catch his breath. Deep, slow huffs, one, two, three... four... five. He let the last one very slowly. He could still breathe—the air right here was still okay.

He moved forward along the wall now, stuck to it, glued to it. Where was it? Where was the nightmare? He inched forward, scanning with the flashlight.

He had no time.

He had to find Gunner and Becca. They would have come in on the Orange Line. The crowd thinned out the slightest amount. He abandoned the wall now and raced through the blackened tunnels, down empty escalators, jumping over the bodies of people who had fallen in the mad rush of people. Horrible images scrolled through his mind.

Gunner and Becca at the bottom of a pile of dying people, people who were dead, people who were crushed by the crowds. Gunner with the blue face of someone who had died from oxygen deprivation.

Luke took a last flight of stairs, three at a time. He was on a train platform.

Dust and soot were still billowing out from a tunnel. Maybe fifty feet down from the station, the first car of a train was turned nearly sideways in the tunnel. The car was on fire. It was sandwiched between the walls, the silver steel of the car shredded apart like aluminum foil, its windows shattered. Flames and black smoke poured from it.

Luke raced through the acrid smoke toward the train. Here and there, bodies that had been thrown from the car littered the track. Luke flashed his light on them. He saw a woman without a head wearing a flowery summer dress. He saw a dead man in a suit impaled on an iron bar. Another man had been smashed against a concrete pillar. He was barely recognizable as human.

Luke kept going.

He reached the train, the flames crackling right near him. He ripped his shirt off and held it to his face. He squeezed past the flames and climbed up onto the wreckage of the car. He pushed through a long rectangular hole where a window had been. The ceiling had caved in. The support poles were bent and broken. More dead lay in piles in this car.

Suddenly, behind him, something exploded. Luke was knocked on his face by the force of it. The fire must have reached a tank or canister of flammable gas. Behind him was an inferno—the way back to the train platform. He crawled forward into the next car.

The car was over on its side. He dropped down into it. He still had his light.

The situation was not as bad here. People lay on the floor. People were slumped on seats. People cried. People moaned in pain. A pile of bodies were moving and writhing where the car had fallen over sideways. At least they were alive. But the flames were bare feet away—the entire train was about to catch fire.

"Gunner!" he screamed. "Gunner!"

"Dad?" someone said.

Luke flashed his light into the gloom. A small body was trapped under the writhing mass. Luke saw the terrified eyes of his son.

"Dad!"

Luke waded into the pile of people. He yanked them up one by one, pulling them off the pile and pushing them toward the back of the train, away from the fire. He felt the flames on his back.

"Run!" he screamed. "Run into the tunnel!"

He yanked more people up. Suddenly here was his child. He pulled him up and hugged him. He held the kid tight. Luke's whole body was numb. He couldn't think. He didn't feel relief. He felt like he was going to pass out. They had to keep going.

"Gunner. Oh my God. Where's your mother?"

"Here," a small voice said.

She was still sitting in her seat. But the way the car had fallen, now she was on her back, her legs in the air. "Becca, you gotta get up. The fire is right behind me. Can you move?"

"I'm stuck."

Luke made his way over to her and was stunned at the sight. There, atop her, were three mangled corpses, heavyset men who had died and had somehow fallen on her.

He reached down and with all his might yanked them off her, one at a time. Finally, she breathed deep, a new glint in her eyes, free.

She crawled around in a circle and worked her way on unsteady legs to a standing position on the seat. Her face was black with soot. "Oh my God," she said.

In the first car, the flames gathered pace. Somewhere, another window shattered.

"Becca, I need you to take Gunner and get moving toward the back of the train. I have to get these people moving."

She stared at him, eyes wide.

"Now, Becca! Move it!"

"Okay, Luke," she said, with the eerie calm of someone in shock. "Okay."

She took Gunner by the hand, and together they started moving toward the back of the train.

As the flames entered the car, Luke grabbed people. He picked them up off the floor. He pushed them. He slapped them. He punched them. He gripped them by the hair and launched them forward. He rained blows and kicks on them, herding them like animals away from the fire.

"Move it!" he screamed, his voice raw now from all the shouting, and the smoke.

Car to car, back through the train, away from the flames he drove them. He had an eerie thought as he did so: he was the first responder down here. And the only one.

On and on, even as the car filled with smoke, as the heat became unbearable, he saved them, one life at a time.

CHAPTER TWELVE

7:27 p.m.
United States Naval Observatory – Washington, DC

Once upon a time, she had loved this view.

Susan had excused herself from the Situation Room and had retreated upstairs here to her study. She stood at the big bay window, staring out at the beautiful rolling lawns of the Naval Observatory campus. The afternoon sun was moving west, sinking very low now. The last of the daylight was beginning to fade.

Kat Lopez stood behind her. Susan felt her there, more than saw her. It was interesting how you could know a person just by the energy they brought with them into a room. Susan could always feel when her old chief-of-staff Richard Monk was in the room with her, and now she was starting to feel when Kat was here.

"Hi, Kat."

"Susan? Are you okay?"

She didn't turn around. "Yes."

"I've got news."

"Is it bad?"

"It's not good."

"Give it to me."

"There have been several serious train crashes and derailments citywide."

"Fatalities?" Susan said.

"Yes."

"What are the numbers?"

"We don't know yet," Kat said. "Certainly in the hundreds. There have been at least a couple thousand injuries, from minor to life-threatening."

Susan didn't say anything, so Kat rolled on. "Kurt thinks we should record a statement with you that can be released to radio and television, calling for calm, and telling people that we are working to get to the bottom of it."

Susan nodded. "That sounds like a good idea."

"Should I set it up?" Kat said.

"Sure."

When Kat left, Susan remained standing in the window. She barely moved. She watched the light change, then change again.

Pierre came in.

She turned to him. He was just himself, always Pierre, in shorts, a white T-shirt, and socks. The man had no airs at all.

"You look tired," he said.

"One of those days, I guess."

His face was concerned. "Do you want to come lie down for a little while?" He took her hand in his. "You need to take some downtime once in a while."

"People have died in the subways," she said. "I need to record a statement."

He nodded. "I know. But you can't save everyone. And if you don't have some rest time, you won't even be able to save yourself. Promise me that when the statement is done, you'll come and rest."

She looked up at him. For the first time in a long time, she felt ready to cry. She thought she had grown stronger, but this job was threatening to break her again.

"Okay," she said. "I promise."

CHAPTER THIRTEEN

8:35 a.m. (7:35 p.m. Eastern Daylight Time)
Taebaek Mountains – Gangwon Province, South Korea

The man was nearly dead.

His name was Kim Ki-nam. He was thirty-four years old, and a captain in the North Korean Army. He had been walking for days—he was no longer certain how many. At some point, he had become confused and lost track of time.

He could remember how very hungry he had been for the first day or two. The rations at the base had been poor recently, dwindling to almost nothing. When he left, his stomach was already almost empty. The country was gripped by famine again, the result of crop sabotage by spies from the United States.

At this point, he had barely eaten anything in days. Even so, he no longer felt hungry, just tired. More tired than he had ever been. He had hiked, sometimes climbed, the region's mountains, in a bid to avoid detection. It had worked, but he was subsisting on bugs and tree bark.

He drank from the streams he encountered, and the water seemed clean enough, though he'd had a serious bout with diarrhea... he couldn't remember when. He had also been caught in a cold rainstorm yesterday or the day before. He spent that night curled in a ball, shivering. He had tried to cover himself over with leaves, but it did no good. Even now, his ragged uniform was still damp from the rain.

He was in bad shape.

Late one night, four or five (or maybe six, or seven?) days ago, he had deserted his post at a North Korean listening station. The place was supposed to be high security—after all, top secret encrypted transmissions from abroad came in there, as did intercepted communications from the south.

Even so, Kim had simply walked away. It was almost too easy. There was a hole in the perimeter fence in the woods at the edge of the installation. Everyone knew about that hole—it was where the prostitutes from the local villages entered the camp. It was important that the hole stay open. Not only to meet the men's needs, but also to meet the needs of the girls.

The local people were starving. Everyone in the camp knew this, too, although it was forbidden to talk of it. The girls were becoming thinner and thinner. They only accepted payment in food now—you couldn't eat the money, so in the villages, it wasn't worth anything. Food was the most important currency there was. The girls didn't even eat the food the soldiers gave them. They carried it home to their families in their purses.

Kim left the way the prostitutes came in—right through the hole in the fence. He skirted the nearest villages, and then he walked due south. His plan, if it could be called a plan, was to simply walk into South Korea.

He was stationed in the far east of the Korean peninsula—a wild and untamed region. If he kept to the woods and the high elevations, stayed out of sight in the daytime and moved only at night, he might successfully cross the Demilitarized Zone without being seen. If he made it through, he wouldn't be the first. If he was shot dead by troops along the border, he also wouldn't be the first.

He navigated by the sun and the moon. As long as they rose on his left, and moved to his right across the sky, he knew he was going the right way.

But lately, he wasn't so sure anymore. Voices had begun to speak to him, telling him that he had mixed up his left and right. They told him confusing things, like the sun rose in the west and then moved north.

Why would it do that? Didn't it used to...

He shook his head violently to clear it. He didn't know what the sun did.

The voices openly mocked him. They called him a worthless collaborator, and told him that his mother and younger sister had been sent to a work camp, where they were being raped and tortured because of his cowardice.

He could hear the voices whispering even now.

Worthless.

Coward.

Your mother will die so slowly. She is crying out for you.

He stumbled along a wooded path. He could barely walk now. He watched his feet, tripping over each other. His boots were worn away to almost nothing. One of his bootlaces was untied. He didn't care. He didn't care if the boots just fell away and left him barefoot. He would just keep walking until he died. He should stay off the path, he knew this, but he didn't think he could go overland anymore.

He had given up his plan. He no longer moved only at night. He just walked until he collapsed. When he woke, he got up again and kept walking. Sometimes it was day, sometimes it was night. Sometimes he didn't notice what it was.

He no longer knew if he was headed south. He had no idea if he had made it across the DMZ. He had no idea if South Koreans were really devils with horns, like he was taught as a child. He didn't care if they were. All he wanted was for someone to find him, and kill him. It didn't matter who it was.

He just hoped that when the time came, they did it quickly and mercifully, with one bullet to the head.

You are weak. Your sister screams, but you cannot save her.

"Shut up!" he said. "Shut up!"

Did he really say it? Or was it in his head?

He was lying on the ground now. His skull hurt, especially in the back. He must have hit it on something hard, like a rock. He gazed up at the sky. It was pale blue, and white clouds slowly skidded across it. The sun was in the sky, but he could not tell if it was north, south, east, or west. It just was. The sun.

And it was beautiful.

A face appeared, then another, and another. Koreans, like him. They wore dark green uniforms. Two men held rifles pointed at him, while another's hands roamed his body, touching his baggy uniform, feeling his bones.

"He's so skinny!"

"He's from the North."

"He looks like a corpse."

The dialect was different from his. They spoke the low speech of the South. It sounded strange and ugly compared with the classical Korean spoke in the North.

A man looked down at him. "Do you have any weapons?"

Kim shook his head.

"Can you speak?"

Now he nodded. His throat was very dry. His lips felt parched and swollen.

"Say something, then."

It occurred to him, now that he was captured, that he might want to live.

Your mother. Your sister.

Yes, he knew that. It was horrible. It was unthinkable. A nightmare. He had run away and brought terrible things upon them. He could never be forgiven for that. And he would never forget it. But still...

"I know things," he said. His cracked voice sounded like the croak of a frog. "Important things. Secret things. There's a big attack coming. Unstoppable."

He paused to rest his throat, then spoke again. "Don't kill me."

The man above him shrugged. He glanced at the other men and then laughed. They all did. "He thinks we're going to kill him," the squad leader said. "We're not going to kill him, are we?"

He looked down at Kim again. "If only it were that easy."

CHAPTER FOURTEEN

8:45 p.m.
Queen Anne's County, Maryland – Eastern Shore of
Chesapeake Bay

Luke hadn't been to this house in two months.

The taxi pulled into the driveway of the summer cabin that had been in Becca's family for over a hundred years. Down the hill from the house, the sun had just disappeared behind the waters of Chesapeake Bay.

Luke had his phone pressed to his ear. On the other end was Kat Lopez, Susan's chief-of-staff. Maybe she was finally listening to him.

"It's a Christian-based religion," he said. "They call it the Church of Almighty God. They also call it Eastern Lightning. It's actually more of a doomsday cult than a religion. They're Chinese, but they have a headquarters in New Jersey."

"You believe they're behind the attack?" Kat said. Kat had a chief-of-staff mind. She was someone who checked things off of lists.

"No. Please be careful with that. I have no idea who was behind the attack. I'm saying that the church is a possible lead. It might have been them. They might be a cat's paw for someone else. They might have nothing to do with it. The man I interrogated and who killed himself was a member of that church at one time. It's a lead. That's all."

"Okay, Luke."

"Okay, thank you, Kat."

They hung up and Luke gave the driver two hundred-dollar bills. He had no idea what the fare was to get out here. The driver seemed to think it was enough. He started pulling smaller bills out of his billfold.

"Keep the change."

On the way over here, the driver had the radio tuned to news reports from the Metro attack. More than a dozen crashes and derailments had happened system-wide. The death toll was three hundred and growing. The subway system itself was shut down citywide. At least a hundred thousand people were still looking for alternative transportation. The entire area around the National Mall and the Capitol building was restricted.

Luke had forced at least a hundred people back through the tunnels to an emergency exit. In one case, a woman's legs had been broken—he slung her over his shoulder and carried her. He thought of the chaos those people had seen when they climbed to street level through the emergency exit. Bodies were piling up at the Metro entrance a hundred yards from them. People were running everywhere. People were on the sidewalks, gasping for air. Ambulances were everywhere.

Luke had flashed his Special Response Team badge and commandeered a police squad car to take him, Gunner, and Becca out of the area. The cop drove them to a taxi hangout at the train station in Georgetown, where they caught a yellow cab all the way out here to the country house.

As the taxi pulled away, Luke led his wife and son down to the house. The lights were all out. Becca didn't use this place anymore. She and Gunner had been abducted from here two months before. The kindly old couple that lived in the nearest house, the Thompsons, had been murdered by the abductors. For Becca, there were too many nightmare memories in this house now.

And yet, Luke had told the taxi driver to bring them here. He wanted his family as far as possible from the city. If any more attacks happened, this place would be safe.

He unlocked the door, reached in, and turned on the lights. Then he led them inside. They were numb. He had seen this before, many times. The horror of what had happened, and what they had seen, was settling in. They were not able to function right now. Becca's face was caked in soot. Her hair stood up in crazy tangles. She didn't even seem to realize where they were, and that she didn't want to be here.

She went to the refrigerator and took out a bottle of beer.

"Do you want a beer?" she said.

"Yes. Please."

She opened them on the old metal bottle opener built-in to the ancient fridge. Generations of her family had opened beers, root beers, and Cokes on that thing. She handed Luke his beer and sat down at the kitchen table.

Luke stood, holding Gunner's hand. He took a sip of his beer. It was cold and delicious.

He glanced down at Gunner. "Can I have a Coke, Dad?"

"Sure, Monster."

Now Gunner went over to the fridge and pulled himself out a Coke.

103

"You know," Becca said to no one, "I killed a squirrel on the highway the other day. It was an accident. The poor thing just ran out suddenly from the grass along the side. I had no time to swerve, and there was too much traffic anyway. It ran right under my wheels. I felt it. The car went over it like it was a small bump in the road."

She looked up at Luke now. There were tears in her eyes. "I went home and cried afterwards. I was so... sorry. I never meant to kill that squirrel. But this... today... it was on purpose. They killed all those people on purpose."

Luke took another sip of his beer. "Yes. They did."

"How can you stand it?"

He shook his head softly. "I can't stand it. That's why I try to stop it."

Becca started to cry at the table. She sat there, her chest heaving. Luke felt distant from her in this moment. She had hated his job for years, and she was divorcing him because of it. Now she had seen, up close, what he'd been dealing with all this time. He wasn't sure how much sympathy he could muster.

"Gunner," he said. "How are you feeling?"

Gunner shrugged. "I feel okay. Glad we didn't get killed or anything."

"Good. I want you to go upstairs, take a shower, and change into your pajamas. It's getting late and we've all had a long day. And don't make it a five-minute shower. Really get the dirt off."

"I don't have my pajamas here, Dad. All my stuff is at home."

Luke's shoulders sagged. Then he smiled the slightest bit. "I'm sure if you go upstairs and look in your dresser, you can find a pair of pajamas that you used to love, and which you can wear for one night. They might not be your favorite pajamas now, but I think you can bite the bullet this one time. Okay?"

"Okay, Dad."

"Good man. I'll be up to talk to you in a little while."

When Gunner was gone, Luke looked at Becca. Her crying had stopped almost as abruptly as it started. She stared at the table in front of her.

"I have to go out again," Luke said. "I don't know when I'll be back. I want you to know that you and Gunner are both safe here. No one is coming for you. What happened two months ago has nothing to do with what's happening now. The people who are committing these attacks don't even know who I am. Okay?"

"Okay, Luke." Her voice was not convincing.

Luke put his beer on the table, kneeled down on the floor next to her, and wrapped his arms around her. She didn't try to stop him. But she also didn't melt into his arms. She simply sat, passively, in the same pose as before.

"I love you, Becca. I love Gunner. I brought you both here because this place is safe. It's further from the city than our other house."

She shook her head.

"I can't take it anymore, Luke. All these attacks. All this terror." Now the stiffness went out of her body and she leaned into him. "It's so horrible."

She started crying again, pressing herself against him.

"I know, baby," he said. He began to rock her. "But we're okay. I promise you that. We're all okay."

"You saved our lives," Becca said.

Luke thought of that fire spreading, moving into the train car, bare feet from them. The two of them wouldn't have gone anywhere. They would have been trapped there. The thought of it brought gooseflesh to his skin.

"I don't know," he said. "I might have."

She pressed herself even tighter to him. "Thank you," she said, her body wracked by sobs now. "Thank you."

CHAPTER FIFTEEN

9:37 p.m.
Deale, Maryland

The surface of the water was shrouded in fog.

Luke pulled up quietly to the boat dock. He had put Becca and Gunner to bed, given them both a mild sedative, and piloted his Boston Whaler across Chesapeake Bay from the Eastern shore.

It was full dark now, perfect cover for the meeting he had planned. Two men stood on the dock. The area was deserted. In the small harbor, moored boats bobbed up and down in the gentle swells. Luke killed the engine, tied up, then jumped out to greet the men.

"Guys, thanks for coming out here."

"Okay, Luke," Mark Swann said.

"How are you doing, man?" Ed Newsam said.

Luke nodded. "I've been better. I thought I lost my wife and kid a few hours ago."

The three men stood on the dock. The fog had a damping effect. There was no sound anywhere. There wasn't much to see. About a hundred yards away, out on a nearby road, a pair of car headlights went by, took a curve, and were replaced by red taillights.

"So what are we doing here?" Ed said.

"I want to run an idea by you," Luke said. "I brought you out here so no one else could hear it."

Swann shook his head. "What good will that do? Either one of us could be wearing a wire."

"Exactly. So if word of this gets out, there are only two possible suspects."

"Okay, what is it?" Ed said.

It was an outside the box idea, and one that he didn't expect would meet with their approval right away. There was no sense holding back or hinting around. He might as well just say it. "I want to break Trudy out of jail."

"Luke, are you insane?" Swann said.

Ed nearly laughed. "Man, you're crazy. We'd never make it in, and we'd never make it out. And it would be a bloodbath coming and going. We'd probably just get Trudy killed, and maybe ourselves, too. There's no way to break her out of there."

Luke looked at Ed. He could barely make out his face in the darkness. This was one time he wished he could see Ed's expression.

"So we need them to transfer her," Luke said.

The two men stood quietly while this sank in. Somewhere in the night, a lone seagull called. It was hard to tell how close or far it was. The seconds ticked away. Neither man told him how impossible it was.

"I can't let these attacks keep happening," Luke said in a quiet voice. "No one seems to know what's going on. I was at the Naval Observatory earlier today. They have no idea what's going on. They're sending a navy strike group to the South China Sea. They're also planning to bomb Chinese container ships out of the water. We're looking down the barrel at World War Three. And if that isn't enough for you, they almost killed my wife and child. That makes it personal, at least for me."

"And Trudy?" Swann said. "What good can she do?"

"I want to put the available intel in her hands," Luke said. "See what she comes up with. I've worked with her for years. I think she spins the best scenarios in the business. It's a long shot, but…"

Swann shrugged. "I can probably hack into the Department of Corrections and get her transferred to another facility."

"Special transfer," Luke said. "It has to be the middle of the night, and she's the only one going. A van or a bus, it doesn't matter. But no more than a driver, and at most two guards on board. Preferably one."

"What will you do to them?" Swann said.

"I'll treat them very, very gently."

"You're asking us to put our careers on the line," Ed said. "If we get busted…"

"We won't."

"If we hurt anybody…"

Luke shook his head. "Ed, you worry too much. We're not going to hurt anybody. And we're doing a favor for an old friend. We might even save the world in the process."

Swann took a deep breath. "Okay. When do you want to do this?"

Luke waited a beat.

"How about now?"

CHAPTER SIXTEEN

9:48 p.m.
United States Naval Observatory – Washington, DC

Susan and Pierre sat in the small sitting area of their bedroom, watching Michael Parowski on TV. He was on his fourth show in the past three hours. Without confirming anything, he had easily cemented his status as the next Vice President of the United States. He was also acting as the de facto mouthpiece of the administration in the wake of the latest terror attacks.

Susan had said nothing to Pierre about the threats Michael had issued during their meeting. What she had done was ask for a meeting with some people who might counterbalance Michael's presence, or even put Michael on his heels. That meeting should take place shortly.

"This is what I can tell you," Parowski said to the pretty blonde host sitting to his left. "I was with the President earlier today. She is firm and unwavering. She wants the American people to know that we are going to find out who is behind these attacks, and we are going to make them pay."

"Do you speak for the President?"

"I do."

"What is the administration doing to protect the lives of Americans in the wake of these two devastating attacks, first on the Black Rock Dam, and then a day later in the heart of Washington, DC?"

Parowski paused for a second.

"He's just going to pull something out of his butt," Susan said. "He has no idea what we're doing."

"Are we doing anything?" Pierre said.

Susan shrugged. "What can we do? They can hit anywhere at any time. We have a list of over seven hundred possible targets. We can't close them all. It would bring the country to standstill."

"I want to make something perfectly clear," Parowski said. "The federal government, in concert with state and local authorities, is doing everything possible to protect the lives of Americans. We are increasing our police presence and our surveillance capabilities everywhere. Our intelligence agencies are working around the clock to find the perpetrators and bring them to justice. But I also want to say this."

Now he turned and faced the camera directly. He gave it his steely-eyed glare. He was looking right into the eyes of the American people.

"He's pretty good," Pierre said.

Susan nodded. "I know. That's what makes him a menace."

Parowski pointed at the camera. "The United States is an open society. It is one of the great gifts our forefathers gave us. The terrorists hate us precisely because of our freedom, and our openness. We will protect our freedoms above all else, and we will never give them away, not one ounce, because of what terrorists do. We will win this fight, and at the same time, we will preserve the very traditions that make this the greatest country on Earth."

The host almost smiled, but caught herself. Instead, she tried to match the look of resolve on Parowski's face.

"Thank you... should I call you Mr. Vice President? Or should I wait for the formal announcement?"

"Congressman is fine," Parowski said. "For now."

Susan clicked off the sound.

"Amazing," Pierre said.

She nodded. "Yeah. I don't know what we're going to do about this guy. He's stepped pretty far over the line, and we haven't even announced him as Vice President yet. I mean, take it a little slower, am I right?"

Pierre shrugged. "He seems like a go-getter. He did a pretty good job."

"Would you hire him?"

"I don't think I'd hire any politician. To do anything." He looked at her and smiled. "Present company excepted."

Susan's phone rang. She glanced at it. "Honey, I have to take this. It's Kat, probably about the last-minute meeting I asked for."

Pierre shook his head and smiled. "Knock yourself out. I'm going to bed."

Susan picked up. "Kat?"

"Hi, Susan," Kat said. "They're here, and they're ready to meet."

* * *

Susan stood with Kat Lopez as the three men entered her upstairs study. They couldn't use the Situation Room for this meeting—it was still full of people. Intelligence was coming in day and night.

Susan almost couldn't believe she was doing this. The first man through the door was Senator Edward Graves of Kansas. He was seventy-two years old, and seemed even older than his years. His back was hunched. He walked with a limp. His gnarled and liver-spotted right hand gripped the knob at the top of a wooden cane. His face was craggy and lined. His nose was bulbous, and crisscrossed with broken blood vessels.

Only two parts of him in any way suggested youth or vitality. For one, there were his eyes, which were as sharp and alert as twin laser beams, and for another there was his hair, which was as black as coal, probably from twice-weekly applications of Just for Men. It was either that, or shoe polish.

In the madness after the June 6 attacks, as President Pro Tempore of the Senate, Ed Graves had briefly become Vice President of the United States. He was implicated in the plot to topple Thomas Hayes, and in fact was arrested along with the conspirators. But, and here was the key, there was no evidence he had known anything about the coup plot.

Ed Graves was so old, he didn't use computers. Naturally, he had an email address associated with his office, but he never opened it. He didn't text or use a cell phone. In fact, he rarely talked on a telephone at all. There was no data trail of any kind that suggested he was involved. If he knew there was a plot to kill the President, he found out about it in a face-to-face meeting, one that was far away from any listening devices.

Susan didn't believe it. She knew he was involved. She could see it in his eyes. If Thomas Hayes's body had remained intact in the Mount Weather disaster, right now he would be rolling over in his grave.

Thomas used to say that Ed Graves was as dumb as a dead tree stump.

And that may be true, but here was wily old Ed in the flesh, still alive, and not even in jail. The Chairman of the Congressional Armed Forces Committee since Susan was a teenager, Ed was as hawkish as hawks came.

"He never met a war he didn't like." That was another of Thomas's sayings about Ed.

Following Ed Graves into the room was Martin Binkle, the owner of War Junkie, a conservative website with often outrageous commentary that was nevertheless popular among high-level members of the military and the intelligence communities. It was rumored to be a CIA-funded front organization, and Susan imagined it probably was.

Binkle himself was a thin, balding man whose fashion sense made him an outlier amidst conservative Washington—he favored bizarre-themed bow ties with matching suspenders, often over pink dress shirts. His boyish appearance had stayed with him into early middle-age, and then did a rapid fade in the past few years. For a long time, he looked like a young fool. Now he looked like an old one.

After Binkle came Haley Lawrence, who was really the focus of Susan's interest. Lawrence's trajectory was firmly on the right side of the political cosmos. His father had been a general. Haley had played football in high school, had gone to Yale as an undergrad, and was recruited directly into the CIA from there. In the last Republican administration, he had risen as high as the agency's Deputy Director. When Thomas Hayes came in and tried to clean house, he had moved to Stanford University, where he lectured on Foreign Policy and International Affairs. He was a board member of the Heritage Foundation.

At the same time, Haley Lawrence was clean as a whistle. He had also been investigated in relation to the coup plot. He did use email, he texted, and he blogged. His blog was thought to have a quarter million visits a month. He was in contact with many people, and they with him. In none of those thousands of emails, texts, and online conversations was there any hint he knew the coup was coming. The plotters hadn't included him. They knew that he was a reasonable man and would never agree to such a thing. He'd probably even turn them in.

"Gentlemen," Susan said. "Thank you for coming at this late hour."

"Susan," Ed Graves said, "we have a good idea why you called us. This is a very difficult time for everyone, and we might as well try to put aside our differences. You did the right thing by calling us. And we're willing to hear you out."

Susan gestured at the high-backed chairs. "Won't you sit down?"

The three men took seats, Edward Graves sinking slowly into his chair, as if sitting too fast would break him like glass. Susan sat across from them. Kat Lopez stood, as usual. Susan had rarely seen Kat take a seat during their time together.

"I gather you've all seen Michael Parowski on television tonight?" Susan said.

"He put on quite a display," Martin Binkle said. In addition to the clown costume he wore, he had a strange, high-pitched voice. "I find him an embarrassing choice for Vice President, to be honest with you."

Susan shrugged. "Some will like him, some won't. He has his fans."

"Yes," Edward Graves said. "But not among us."

"Well, I guess it's good that I don't have to ask the Senate for his confirmation then," Susan said.

"No, you don't. But you do have to ask the Senate for confirmation of your nominee for Secretary of Defense. I assume that's why you called us in. Things are spiraling out of control, and you can't wait any longer to nominate someone. Here's what I know, Susan. You're going to want my help getting your person through the Senate, and you're going to want the help of these two gentlemen in shaping the public opinion around your pick."

"I wouldn't say things are spiraling out of control," Susan said. "Until you've been blown up, then handcuffed to a man's waist on a motorcycle in the middle of the night while assassins try to kill you… well, that's spiraling out of control. Otherwise, I'd say you're very prescient, Senator."

Edward Graves laughed. It sounded like he had a bag of marbles deep in his throat. "Hardly. I've been around Washington so long at this point, I don't think there's a single gambit I haven't seen. You need a Secretary of Defense. We all do. With that in mind, we've brought a list of moderate liberals that we might be willing to get behind, given the right circumstances."

The Senator made a show of slowly removing a folded piece of white paper from his pocket. Susan imagined the names were scribbled on there in his infamous chicken scratch handwriting.

Kat Lopez made a move to take the paper from the Senator, but Susan stopped her with a hand.

"I don't need to see that list," Susan said.

"I think you should look at it," Graves said. "Now isn't the time for a long, contentious, and tedious confirmation process."

Susan nodded. "Right. But the person we have in mind isn't on your list."

"Then we'll fight you tooth and nail," Martin Binkle said.

"There's no need for you to do that," Susan said.

"You'll give us no choice."

Susan smiled. She disliked Martin Binkle immensely. She disliked Edward Graves. The thought of making them happy gave

112

her a sick feeling in the pit of her stomach. "I don't know if you've noticed, but I am slowly rebuilding the government of this country. And I'm doing it in such a way to ensure that the regrettable events of June never happen again. I'm moving away from polarization, and building a team of rivals."

Edward Graves was beginning to look bored. Of course he would grow bored. He had no imagination. He had nothing to occupy or spark his mind.

"What are you saying, Susan?"

"I'm saying the next Secretary of Defense is in this room."

The three men stared at her. Haley Lawrence, the only one of the three with a brain, seemed to get it right away. His face took on a look of consternation, then curiosity.

Martin Binkle seemed to get it next. Susan watched him. He did it by a slow process of elimination. He looked first at Kurt Kimball. No, he was already the National Security Advisor. Next, at Susan—she wasn't about to demote herself to Defense Secretary, was she? Kat Lopez was out—too young, too Hispanic, too female to ever make it through the gauntlet of conservative senators.

Now Binkle seemed to consider himself. He got trapped there for a moment, before he realized the implausibility of it. Ed Graves? Too old, too unwilling to work beneath a woman, and already entrenched in a power base that he wouldn't leave until he reached his deathbed. That left only…

Haley Lawrence. Binkle turned and looked at him. Of course. It was a lightning strike of a choice. A conservative, with intelligence and military credentials. An academic. A scholar. He would sail through the confirmation process. And he would join a liberal administration, counterbalancing the weight of that union-backed gangster of a Vice President.

"What are you talking about, Susan?" Ed Graves said.

"I'm going to nominate Haley as my Secretary of Defense," Susan said. She turned to him. Big, blond, his former athlete's body spreading out toward fat in late middle age. "If you want it, that is."

He seemed thoughtful. He almost smiled. He narrowed his eyes at her, as if trying to read her mind. "I'm honored," he said finally, the first words he had uttered during the entire meeting. "I would like to talk with my wife first, and then take a night to sleep on it. In the morning, I think I'll know more about where I am on this."

Susan raised her hand, the famous STOP sign that was becoming her trademark. "Please know that I'd love to have you.

But before I can offer it to you formally, I need something from the three of you."

"A little horse trading?" Ed Graves said. "Nothing less than I'd expect from you."

"We're in a time of crisis, Ed. We can't have any more of our people die in these attacks. It's not a political issue. I don't care if it makes me look bad. It's a humanitarian issue. We have to make the attacks stop. Meanwhile, the intelligence I'm getting right now is not worth much. I believe the agencies are holding out on me. I need you guys to crack the whip and bring people into line. It's either that or I'll be forced to clean house, up and down the entire dial. And I'll do it, too. I don't care. I'll install someone from NYU or the New School as the head of the NSA. I'll bring someone down from the People's Republic of Vermont to run the CIA. Is that what you want from me?"

"So we bring the intelligence people into line, and Haley becomes the new Defense Secretary?" Ed Graves said.

Susan shrugged. "That, along with a turn toward positive coverage of this administration in Martin's online rags and newspapers, and I think we'd have a deal."

Graves smiled, his old face crumpling into lines that most people rarely saw.

"You surprise me, President Hopkins. You're stronger than your predecessor, do you know that? You're smarter, craftier, and a much better chess player than he ever was. This is a move that could only be made by a big person. A selfless person, willing to take flak from her own side. Someone who really cares about our country, and not her own political side. I'm impressed by this move, to be honest, and I think the men with me are, as well."

"Hear, hear," Martin Binkle said.

Susan stared back, quiet, but feeling gratified.

"Martin, do you think we can get the President that press coverage she's looking for?"

Binkle nodded. "I think we can manage it."

Susan looked at Haley Lawrence again. When Parowski got wind of this, he was going to have a cerebral hemorrhage. That filled Susan with a sense of delight. She wasn't about to let Michael push her around. Not only was she installing a conservative in a more powerful position than Michael's, just wait until Michael got a look at his own travel itinerary for the next few months.

Michael was going to spend some time mending fences and greeting the tribes in sub-Saharan Africa, and then as the cold weather came in, there was some work for him to do among the Aleut and Eskimo peoples up in Alaska. All of this had come to her while they were sitting here. If she could manage it, she'd have him visiting American scientists testing ice core samples on the melting glaciers up in Greenland.

"If you like that move, then I think you'll adore the next one," Susan said.

"And what is that move?" Ed Graves said.

"I've summoned the Chinese ambassador, and I'm about to throw her, and her entire embassy, out of the country."

They stared back, silent, clearly stunned.

"What do your people think of that?" Haley Lawrence said.

Susan shook her head. "I haven't told them. But I don't think they'd be pleased."

The three men laughed. "My God," Martin Binkle said. "President Hopkins, for a woman, you have quite a pair of balls."

Susan stood up, and the men across from her did likewise.

"Gentlemen," she said, "I feel like this has been a very productive meeting."

CHAPTER SEVENTEEN

10:35 p.m.
Women's Federal Detention Center – Randal, Maryland

"Wellington! Wake up!"

Trudy had been dreaming. It was a dream she had often had throughout her life. She was on a high green plateau above a shimmering sea. Far away, a herd of wild horses were running, coming her way. The lead horse was white. She could not hear them yet, but she could feel their thundering hoof beats through the ground.

"Wellington!"

She opened her eyes.

She was on her cot in her ten-foot-by-twelve-foot cell. Everything in the room was white, and bare. The walls were bare. The little table bolted to the cell floor was bare. She hadn't done much to personalize the place. She was never someone who had a lot of personal interests. She had no keepsakes. Her life was inside her mind.

The things that seemed to excite the other women in here—celebrities, television shows, music, and movies—held no interest for her. Give her a mystery to work through and passwords to a few databases, and she could be happy for days. Since she had no access to such things in here, she spent a lot of her time remembering the details of old cases. And she spent as much time sleeping as she could, which wasn't much.

She tried not to think about what might happen next.

She looked at the door. It was open. Two guards stood there, one woman and one man, which seemed to be the standard operating protocol around here. They were both heavyset, bulging out of their uniforms. They wore blue plastic gloves on their hands. The woman had dirty blonde hair, pulled back tightly to her scalp, and some kind of skin condition that made her face red and raw.

Trudy glanced at the nameplate on the woman's breast.

FIGDOR.

All the girls dreaded Officer Figdor. She might be a lesbian. She was definitely a sadist. Her favorite part of the job was body cavity searches for contraband. Her second favorite part was overturning cells in a search for contraband, leaving the small totems and personal items that so many women clung to broken and

116

on the floor. Her third favorite part was verbal abuse and threats. She was a piece of work.

The magnitude of everything Trudy had lost hit her in a wave. She had been a high-level analyst for an elite intelligence agency a short time ago. She had worked with the best—the best covert operatives, the best analysts, the best technology people, possibly in the world. And she was among them, and accepted by them as also the best. At a moment's notice, she might have to fly out anywhere in the country to work a case or neutralize a threat.

Now she was trapped in here, and at the mercy of this ogre. The thought of it made Trudy feel like she might vomit. It was nauseating.

"Sleeping already?" Figdor said. "It's not even lights out yet."

"I was just dozing," Trudy said.

Figdor shrugged. "I think if I was facing the death penalty, I'd try to stay awake all the time. There's going to be plenty of time to sleep after they give you the needle."

"Can I help you, Officer?"

Figdor laughed. "Honey, you can help me by getting down on your knees in front of me and showing me how you lick a sweet, yummy ice cream cone. If you know what I'm saying."

The other guard laughed now. He hadn't said a word. People, including other guards, tended to be silent around Figdor.

The sick feeling in Trudy's belly deepened. If they tried anything, she was just going to vomit all over Figdor's lap.

"No, I'm sorry to say, I'm just here to tell you to get yourself ready. New orders have come through, and you're being transferred. You're leaving our happy little home and heading down to the municipal lockup in DC."

Trudy's heart skipped a beat in her chest. Suddenly, the bully Figdor was the least of her worries. "What? When?"

"Forty-five minutes. You're out of here."

"Why? It's the middle of the night."

Figdor shrugged. "I don't make the orders, girlfriend. I just enforce them. They tell me to get you ready, so that's what I'm doing. I would guess you have a court appearance coming up."

Figdor smiled, a grin bordering on evil.

"Confidentially, just between you and me, you're going to hell on Earth. No more individual cell for you. You'll have to learn to share. And the girls down there? Not exactly the refined, educated types we have up here. They're a little more... physical, shall we say? I don't think you'll be getting a lot of nap time. Personally, I'd like to see what happens when a weakling like you gets dropped in there. Maybe I'll hear about it through the grapevine."

Trudy stared at her. Just when things didn't seem like they could get any worse... they were getting worse.

"You heard me, Wellington. Get yourself together. We'll be back for you in twenty minutes."

CHAPTER EIGHTEEN

10:47 p.m.
Prime Auto Mall –McLaren, Maryland

Luke and Ed wore black.

They cruised slowly around the perimeter of the giant car dealership. They rode in a black Saab 9000 turbo, Luke at the wheel. It was an old car. They had taken it off the lot of a Saab mechanic two towns over. The mechanic apparently fixed these things up, then turned around and sold them. When he and Ed found this one, it had a sign in the windshield, listing it at $8,999.

Free was better.

In his younger days, Luke used to drag race along Route 1 down near the King's Dominion amusement park in southern Virginia late at night. It wasn't anything organized. It was just a long empty road, where a restless adrenaline junkie might happen upon other sleepless vampires just like him.

In those days, he drove a Saab 900 turbo, a convertible, an earlier model than the one he was driving right now. It was a very fast car. Even with the wind drag when the top was down, he blew almost anything else off the line. New Corvettes, Porsches, Mustang GTs, even a Lotus one time. That Saab had an analog speedometer that topped out at 155 miles per hour. Luke could pin that needle to the floor. This car was newer, and had a digital readout, so it was harder to tell where it would top out. But Luke figured it was just about as fast.

Now they were cruising the edges of a giant car dealership. The place was lit up like a Christmas display. In fact, they were advertising Christmas in August. Ed's eyes scanned the car lot, looking for the one he wanted. They were rolling toward the Hummer section now.

"Swann?" Luke said into his telephone. "How's it coming?"

Swann had set himself up in the parking lot of a Little League field twenty miles away. When Luke and Ed left him, he had three laptops going on the hood of his car, all with satellite links. He was busy concealing his identity and whereabouts, routing his communications traffic down to Brazil, across the Atlantic Ocean to Bulgaria, then back through Western Europe to the United States.

"It's coming good. Looks like you've got about ten seconds."

"Ten seconds," Luke said to Ed.

119

Ed just nodded.

"You see one you like?"

"Yeah."

A few more seconds passed. Suddenly, the lights went out. The lights at the dealership went dark, certainly. But the long industrial road they were on went dark as well. Security lights and yellow sodium arcs above parking lots all went out at the same time. Somewhere, perhaps three miles away, a glow against the night sky showed Luke where the blackout ended.

"Go!" he said.

Ed's door was already open. A second later he was out on the tarmac, moving fast and low with a blue canvas bag in one hand. A second after that, he had disappeared. Black skin, black clothes, against a black night. Ed was gone.

Luke cut off his headlights and rolled on. The car was hotwired. There was no key. Luke wouldn't turn this car off again until he was ready to dump it.

"Swann, what's the prisoner status?" he said.

"Uh... it looks pretty smooth. The transfer went through. Prisoner is being prepared for departure. A van has been assigned from the Department of Corrections motor pool and is en route to the Randal facility."

"Staffing?"

"Two officers. Both men. The driver is forty-three-year-old Robert Lynn. Riding shotgun is twenty-eight-year-old David William Fortgang. Both are armed with service pistols, Glock 9 millimeters in this case. Also, they have tasers, and the van is equipped with a shotgun bolted to the dash on the passenger side."

"What else?" Luke said.

"Ah, let me see here. Fortgang, the younger guy, is an ex-Marine, did eight years, and has combat experience in Iraq and Afghanistan."

Luke pictured a gung-ho kid with a flat-top haircut, who still worked hard to keep his military physique. When trouble came down, the driver would probably just raise his hands and surrender, but that kid was going to tumble at it head-first.

"Terrific," he said. "Couldn't you have gotten me a couple of old-timers watching the clock until retirement?"

"I got you the prisoner transfer, Luke. I couldn't control the officer assignment. It has a lot to do with who's on duty."

Nearby, an engine roared into life. Headlights came on. A moment later, a giant black Hummer H3 rolled up next to Luke. Ed pulled up driver's side to driver's side. His window powered down.

"How is it?" Luke said.

Ed smiled. He patted the steering wheel. "Real nice. Better than yours."

"There's an ex-Marine riding shotgun in the prison van. Young guy, just got recycled back to the real world."

Ed's face was hard already. It grew harder instantly. "Okay."

"Let's try not to hurt him."

Ed looked at Luke. His eyes were serious. There was very little compromise in Ed.

"Luke, you got me out here doing some very raw shit. I could lose my job. I could lose my life. I could go to jail. You got me firing dum-dum bullets, which ain't gonna hurt anybody anyway. It's for Trudy, otherwise I would never consider it. But now you want me to take it easy on an ex-Marine? Sorry. That'll be up to him. He takes it easy, he lays down, he'll be all right. He takes it hard... Well, I'm not going in the casket for him. And I can't imagine that's what you're asking me to do. Right?"

Briefly, it occurred to Luke how many times he asked people to put everything on the line, to do the nearly impossible, to possibly sacrifice themselves. He thought back to the kid, Sommelier, the Army Ranger who had died on that yacht in Cuba. Luke had thought up the operation, and had put it together on the fly. He was trying to extract an Arab terrorist from Cuban waters. They had given him three grizzled Navy SEALs who had seen and done everything, and four green Rangers, the whole lot of them practically right out of high school. Luke was so focused on the goal, he hadn't given much thought to the dangers, or the disparities in experience on his team. The operation was a total bust. The kid came back dead, and Luke came back empty-handed. Ed had been furious with Luke after that.

"Luke?" Ed said.

As far as anyone knew, Luke was working directly for the President of the United States. Ed Newsam and Mark Swann were high-level operatives, on loan to Luke from the agencies where they worked. He had convinced them to help him break an inmate out of federal prison, a person implicated in the assassination of the previous President.

Luke nodded without hesitation. "Of course you're right. If he plays it that way, we have to stop him."

121

And now, he had just given Ed the green light to murder an ex-Marine and current Department of Corrections officer, an American citizen. Luke was all the way out there, outside the law, outside of any boundaries that made sense.

Ed nodded in kind. "Good. Then let's go do this thing."

* * *

The inmate transfer area was inside the gates of the prison.

They brought Trudy out into the warm night. The parking area was a concrete canyon, surrounded by the prison building on three sides, and a guard gate topped with razor wire on the fourth. Harsh lights shone down from all sides. A black van waited, its headlights on, its engine running.

Trudy wore her orange prison jumpsuit. Her hair was pulled into a tight braid, and her wrists were shackled behind her back. She wore slippers with no shoelaces. She was so limp, she nearly had to be supported by the guards who moved her along. They were moving her to the DC Municipal lockup? She would never survive in there.

At first, Trudy thought the transfer had to be a mistake. Why would they transfer her from a federal detention facility to a poorly run and dangerous city one? In the past twenty minutes, she had gradually become aware of an idea. At first, she rejected it, but now she recognized it as the truth. They weren't moving her because of a court appearance. They were moving her to punish her, to break her once and for all. But they didn't have to break her. She was already broken.

She felt feverish, delirious. Goose bumps popped up on her skin.

She wasn't cut out for this! She wasn't a prisoner! She was an intelligence analyst. She worked for a secret arm of the Federal Bureau of Investigation. She had gone to MIT, for God's sake.

Figdor was one of the guards bringing her out. Figdor had been in on the contraband search as Trudy passed out of the prison. Figdor was enjoying this, on the one hand. On the other hand, maybe Figdor was sorry to see Trudy go.

Trudy had an idea, one last-ditch chance to save herself. She addressed the guard by her first name.

"Emma," she said, her voice shaking.

Figdor's eyebrows raised. "What did you just call me?"

"Emma," Trudy said again. "They want me to talk. That's why they're doing this. They're trying to break me. I'll talk. I'll tell them everything. But I only want to talk to you. They can videotape it."

Figdor's head shook. "Well, that's flattering, but I'm afraid it's too late. Orders are orders. You're going to go to hell for a little while, and then maybe if you're lucky, you'll come on back here. Then we'll talk all you want. You'll be a changed woman by then, maybe not quite so stuck up."

A guard came around from the front of the van. He was tall and broad. He wore a different uniform from the prison guards. He looked more like a police officer or a US marshal than a guard. Also unlike the guards, he stood ramrod straight, with military bearing, the way Don Morris used to stand every moment of his life.

A brief image of Don flitted across Trudy's mind. Why was she protecting him? He had brought her to this, with no concern for her welfare, and besides, he was already a dead man. A dead man walking.

"I'll talk!" Trudy shouted. "I'll talk!"

The van guard took her from the prison guards. He guided her to the back steps of the van.

"Duck your head," he said.

"I'll talk!" she screamed.

Behind her, she heard Figdor laughing. "The girl's gone insane, I guess."

The guard sat her down on a bench along one wall of the van. He quickly looped a chain around her wrist shackles and secured her to the bench. Then he bent and shackled her ankles to the bottom. He pulled a shoulder strap from the wall and pulled it tight around her, just like the seatbelt in a car. Unlike Figdor, he was all business.

When he stood, she saw the name on his breast. FORTGANG.

"We've got a thirty-minute ride," he said. "Maybe forty minutes. We're going to go real gentle, and if you relax, you should be comfortable back here. We've got a listening device in here and speaker up front, so if you have any trouble, give us a shout and we'll do what we can. In most cases, the best thing we can do is get you to the next facility as quickly as possible. Do you understand?"

"Am I going to be alone back here?"

"Yes."

She didn't want him to leave. She didn't want to be alone in the back of this van, shackled to this bench, in the dark.

"Fortgang, I'm willing to talk."

He shook his head. "I don't know anything about that. I'm not authorized to accept any information from you. I'm just here to get you safely to your destination."

Trudy watched as the man exited the van, then slammed the door behind him, leaving her in near total darkness. As she sat, she heard the lock slide home on the outside of the door. She began to cry silently, tears streaming down her face.

A moment later, the van started moving.

* * *

"Where are they?" Luke said.

Swann's voice came over the three-way network he had set up for them. Luke had him in the Bluetooth device tucked behind his ear. It was funny. When it was just Luke and Swann, the sound was perfect. Now that it was a three-way, it sounded like Swann was speaking from the bottom of a tin can.

"They just left the prison. I have them on satellite. I'm getting a lag between the video and the GPS. The camera is four or five seconds behind."

"Can you fix it?" Luke said.

"I can improve it, but I'd have to simplify my location. Right now this signal is bouncing all over the world before it gets to me. But I'm not going to reveal myself on this satellite. No, thank you."

"Okay, okay. Where are they now?"

"They're moving southwest toward the highway, parallel to you and three blocks to your left. Ed?"

"I'm here."

"They're coming your way. They're about to enter the feeder road that goes to the highway. If they get past you, then they're up the ramp and headed toward the city. Everything becomes a whole lot harder then."

Luke could almost feel Ed's smirk over the cell network. "They won't get past me, Swann. I wouldn't worry yourself about that."

Swann ignored him. "Luke, if you're planning to join this party, you want to cut east at the next intersection. That's a left, if you're wondering."

"I know where east is," Luke said.

"You want to do it in a hurry. Go three long blocks and fall in behind them. Fast. They're already past you."

"Past me?" Luke got a sinking feeling. How did they get past him?

"It's the delay. It's hard to reconcile. Uh... go fast. Now!"

Luke was driving down a long industrial road with warehouses, junkyards, and parking lots of various kinds. There was no one out here with him. He pressed the accelerator, slowly but firmly. The car took off down the straightaway.

He screamed left at the next red light, tires shrieking across the pavement. He floored the pedal now, the car feeling right for the first time. He checked the speedometer. 100... 110... 125.

This was a car that wanted to go.

A black police cruiser was parked behind a billboard, crouched quietly like a spider waiting for its prey. It was the kind of fast car police forces confiscated in drug busts, then kept for their own use. It had a smoked windshield. Smoked side windows. It had speed trap written all over it.

Luke blew past it, saw it there out of the corner of his eye.

He waited a beat, hoping against hope that what he knew was about to happen, wasn't about to happen.

Luke took another turn, a screaming right.

Behind him, the police interceptor lurched into the roadway, turned left, hit its sirens and its flashers, and accelerated into pursuit.

"Damn it!"

"What is it, Luke?"

"Swann, I've got a police car behind me. What can you do about that?"

"What can I do about it?"

"Yes."

"Like what, you want me to launch a missile at it?"

Luke shook his head. The cop was his problem, not Swann's. "How far is the van?"

"You are eight blocks behind them. They're moving about forty-five miles per hour. At your speed, you'll be on them in about one minute. Which is about when they're going to cross paths with Ed."

"Ed?" Luke said.

"I'm here, man."

"All systems go. Let me worry about the cop."

"I wasn't planning to worry."

"Good."

125

Luke had the accelerator floored. There was nowhere else to go with it. The Saab zoomed along like a rocket—140... 145 now. The double yellow line was a blur. Buildings zipped by. He could see the van up ahead. Its taillights shone bright as it stopped briefly for a blinking red light.

Luke glanced in his mirror. This car was fast. The cop was faster. Even at these speeds, the cop was gaining on him.

What to do, what to do?

* * *

Robert Lynn was tired. He was just concentrating, trying to keep his eyes open at this point.

Working the overnight shift didn't agree with him. All these weird little last-minute inmate transfers—they happened every night. It found him driving long distances on dark highways, often with dangerous felons in the back. He always had someone riding shotgun with him, but still... a lot of these bad guys had friends out in the world. What if those friends somehow got the news that their buddy was out of jail and lightly guarded?

Robert heard the sirens behind him and checked the rearview.

"What is it?" Fortgang said. He didn't bother to turn around. The highway entrance ramp was just up ahead. Robert started to accelerate toward it.

He took one last look at the scene behind them. "I don't know. Two cars coming fast. Looks like a cop in pursuit of a late-night speed demon."

There was something mesmerizing about how fast those cars were coming. He almost couldn't take his eyes off them.

"Robert!" Fortgang shouted. "Watch where you're going!"

Robert looked ahead. A big black Hummer rolled out right in front of them. There was no way to avoid it. He tried to slam on the brakes, but there was no time.

"Robert!"

They crashed hard into the side of the Hummer. Hard. Heavy metal crunch at nearly fifty miles per hour. The windshield caved in, shattering glass all over them. Robert's air bag deployed in front of him, forcing his hands off the steering wheel and into the air. He smacked himself in the head with his right hand.

A long moment passed. It could have been a minute. It could have been an hour.

It could have been a week.

126

Robert had a ringing sound in his ears. White talcum dust lingered in the air from the air bags. The air bags themselves had deflated. Robert glanced over at Fortgang. Fortgang was slumped in his seat, unconscious. He hadn't been wearing his seat belt. Robert had told him about that... he'd lost track of how many times.

A black car zipped by, barely a blur. The wind from its passing shook the van. A split second later a police car flew past, lights flashing, siren howling.

Robert stared at the big Hummer he had crashed into. The entire side of it was dented in. Crushed.

He reached for his radio. He'd better call this in. Hmmm. Maybe he'd better go check the status of that other driver first. Or of the prisoner. He realized he wasn't thinking clearly. People often became confused after car wrecks. He was one of them. Confused.

He wished that cop had stopped. Well, maybe the cop had called it in.

He turned to open his door. A black man with a closely cropped beard stood there at the window. He was broad and muscular. His eyes were cold and heartless. He held a shotgun, the barrel pointed at Robert's head. Robert had never looked down the barrel of a shotgun before. He could see the shells mounted inside the barrel.

"Keys," the man said.

"What?"

"Keys to open the back of the van. Give them to me, or you're a dead man. You have three seconds."

"I..."

"Two seconds."

Robert reached for the key chain hanging from the ignition. He didn't even feel frightened. He didn't feel anything, except it was better to comply. He pulled the keys out of the ignition, picked through them, and found the key that locked the back. He held it out to the man.

The man took the keys.

"Thank you."

In one fluid movement, the man reversed the shotgun. Now the butt end of the gun, the stock, faced Robert. He stared at it curiously.

BAM.

It came fast, smashing into his forehead. His head lolled for a moment. Darkness moved in from the edges of his vision. The gun butt was still there, hovering in front of him. Here it came again.

127

BAM.

Robert saw no more.

* * *

Ed took the keys and limped around with his heavy kit bag to the back of the van.

That crash kind of hurt.

It wasn't supposed to go that way. The original scenario was that the prison van would stop when it saw the Hummer. Then Luke would sneak up behind in the fast car, they'd throw down on the guards, grab Trudy, and take off.

Ed shook his head. It was rare when anything went exactly according to plan.

"Swann, you still with me?" he said into his headset.

"I'm here. What happened down there?"

"The whole thing is one hundred percent FUBAR. We had a pretty nasty crash. My car is toast. Luke is off getting chased by a cop. Can you see him?"

"Wait a minute."

Ed didn't wait. He unlocked the back door of the van, undid the clasp, and opened the doors.

"Yeah, I've got him on satellite video. If that's him, he's out on the highway. He's got two police cars on him now. There's not much traffic this time of night, and they are whipping."

"Terrific," Ed said. "Listen, I need some wheels."

"Where are the guards?"

"Knocked out. Out of commission, but I think okay. The driver's gonna need some Tylenol tomorrow. I lumped him pretty good."

"Why don't you just put them out and take the van? Zip-tie them and dump them in the bushes somewhere? Somebody will find them in the morning. Drive the van until you see a spot to dump it. I have you on the GPS. I can direct Luke to you."

"If he makes it," Ed said.

"He'll make it."

Ed nodded. It was a good improv. Ed was on the ground here. He couldn't think of everything. And Swann was a smart dude.

"Okay. That's what we'll do."

Ed climbed into the back of the van. Trudy was here. She was slumped in her seat, her head hanging down. The guards had strapped her in tight, though. It looked like the crash didn't do much to her.

Trudy wore the orange jumpsuit of a federal prisoner. It looked like she had lost some weight while inside, but even so, she could make anything look good. He knelt down in front of her and undid the leather straps at her ankles. He felt tender toward her, and gentle. He rarely felt that way toward anyone.

He had visited her in jail exactly once. He felt bad about that, but in a way, it was also the life. People died. People disappeared. When he visited her, there wasn't much to talk about. She wished him luck. He did the same. Anyway, she had brought this upon herself, hadn't she?

Now he stood and moved to the straps at her back. He freed her, though it was going to take the bolt cutters in his bag to break those handcuffs.

He shook his head. Luke Stone and his ideas.

Trudy groaned. Her head lolled to the side for a few seconds. Then her eyes opened. It took another few seconds for them to focus.

"Ed?" she said. "What are you doing here?"

He smiled. "I've come to rescue you, Princess."

She blinked her eyes. "I think I have whiplash."

Ed heard a sound then. It was a sound he didn't usually mind. Only, in this context, it wasn't a good sound to hear. It was the metallic slide and crunch of someone chambering a round in a pump shotgun.

He turned and there was the guard at the door, the young ex-Marine. He was a flat-topped, healthy eating, weight lifting, by the book kind of guy. He was an American hero, at least in his mind. And he was groggy, but awake. He leveled the gun at Ed.

"Hands up where I can see them!" he shouted.

Ed slowly raised his hands. "Brother, let's take it easy with that thing."

"Hands up! Now get on the floor!"

Ed moved very slowly and carefully. This was the dangerous part, where overzealous, nervous types blew holes in people by accident.

"I'm going," he said. "Real slow."

"On the floor before I blow your brains out!"

Ed sighed. This was turning into a long night.

CHAPTER NINETEEN

11:01 p.m.
United States Naval Observatory – Washington, DC

The next meeting would be short and sweet.

Li Ning, the Chinese ambassador, had just arrived at the house. Susan stood in the study with Kat Lopez.

Ning came in. She was a well-dressed, pretty woman of indeterminate age. Susan knew she was forty-five, but would never guess otherwise. She wore a business suit and her makeup was perfect. Not a hair was out of place. She was very petite, several inches shorter than Susan herself. She gave no indication that Susan had awakened her from her sleep, or that she had even been unwinding at the end of a long, hard day.

No. Eleven o'clock at night was a perfectly normal time for a meeting.

It was a plum assignment, being the ambassador to the United States. Susan also knew that Li Ning's husband was a much older Communist party official. He had been the mayor of Chongqing for many years. For Li Ning, this was a patronage job. Well, not anymore.

"Madam President," the woman said once an aide had shown her in. She offered a small bow of respect. She smiled. She didn't seem nervous in the least. She spoke perfect English. "It's a pleasure to meet you."

Luke Stone's idea about the cult hadn't panned out. SWAT teams had raided their headquarters in New Jersey, as well as churches, offices, homes, and warehouses they had in six different states. There was no evidence of advanced computer equipment, there were no stockpiled weapons, and no indication that anyone with the church had ever been in the CIA. All the SWAT had done was corral a group of terrified people, who really did think the world was ending when the big American policemen stormed into their churches and houses.

If it wasn't the church, then who was it? It was China. It had to be.

"Ambassador," Susan said, "I'm going to be very clear with you. We are very upset about the terror attacks of the past two days. We want them to stop, and we want the perpetrators identified, and surrendered to us immediately."

130

The ambassador shook her pretty head. "I don't know anything about this."

"I imagined you'd say that," Susan said. "In that case, please relay this message to your President and Party leaders."

The ambassador nodded. "Yes, of course."

"If these attacks continue, if any more Americans are harmed, we will be forced to bring the perpetrators to justice ourselves. We will not stop until we do, even if this means we must find them inside your country, and extract them."

The ambassador's soft face hardened. "We have no control over this situation," she said. "You cannot make these threats."

Susan was already done with her. She waved her hand as if to make the woman go away. "I want you out," she said. "You, your staff, your entire embassy, cleared and vacated by the morning. We will have airplanes ready at nine a.m. to take your entire staff, and any family members, to Beijing. Anyone attached to your embassy operations must be on those planes. Shuttle buses will arrive at the embassy beginning at seven a.m."

"Madam President, I don't understand."

"Well, Professor Li, it's simple. We're severing diplomatic ties. You are being ousted. We consider today's attacks an act of war."

The woman shook her head. "As I've said, I don't know anything about this. We are not involved in these attacks. It must be terrorists, of course."

Susan shook her head. "Have you understood everything I've said?"

"Yes," the ambassador said. "You called it an act of war from China. This is incorrect. Surely you do not want war with the most powerful country on Earth?"

"That's funny," Susan said. "I was just about to ask you the same question."

CHAPTER TWENTY

10:12 a.m. (11:12 p.m. Eastern Time in the United States)
The Skies Above the South China Sea

From 30,000 feet, the island didn't look like much.

It was a small scrap of muted colors—tan, gray, and brown—surrounded by the vast turquoise waters of the ocean. The United States Navy P8-A Poseidon spy plane did a fly-by well to their north. At this height, and from this distance, the activity around the islands didn't look like much—some ships anchored near a reef or shoal.

"Let's bring it around," said Lieutenant Commander Edwin Russell, the plane's pilot. "We'll drop it to twenty thousand, take a closer look."

The plane was big, built on the same frame as the old Boeing 737. But that's where the similarities ended. The P8-A was the most advanced surveillance aircraft in the American arsenal. Behind Russell and his co-pilot, in what would have once been the passenger cabin on a 737, ten men sat at computer workstations mounted along the walls of the aircraft. They had access to powerful radio and radar antennae, satellite transmissions, and sophisticated long-range still and video cameras, much of it mounted beneath the plane's fuselage. Russell had heard one TV reporter refer to it as a "CIA listening station in the sky."

The plane banked, dropped altitude, slowed, and approached the reef from the west, much lower and closer than before.

"Mischief Reef," said Russell's co-pilot. "Fast becoming Mischief Island."

Russell stared at it, impressed by the pace of the work. Dozens of rusty Chinese dredging ships surrounded what only recently had been about a hundred narrow yards of sand and rock, a spit of land six hundred miles from the Chinese coast. The dredgers pumped sand from the ocean floor, spraying it high into the air and onto the surface of the reef. They were building an island out of thin air.

Further out from the dredgers, half a dozen Chinese warships were parked, lending protection to the construction project.

"I've been flying this stretch of water for eighteen months," Russell said to the co-pilot, a young guy just out of flight school named Montgomery. "There was nothing here a year ago. Nothing."

Russell thought of Fiery Cross Reef, just a few minutes to the south. It had started from nothing, too. Just a tiny spot of nowhere, surrounded by water more than three hundred feet deep. Now it was a large military installation with a runway, control tower, barracks, and a deep water harbor.

The Chinese had long laid claim to these reefs, which once upon a time barely peeked over the waves. Suddenly they were expanding them. These waters were Chinese territory now, according to them, as were the oil and natural gas deposits beneath them. More to the point, these were nifty little spots from which to dominate the whole region.

The radio crackled. A male voice spoke slowly in heavily accented and carefully enunciated English: "This is the Chinese navy. This is the Chinese navy. All aircraft in this sector, please leave immediately to avoid misunderstanding."

Russell smiled at Montgomery. "You think he's talking to us?" The kid shrugged. He seemed a little nervous for this type of assignment. Well, he'd either learn to man up, or he wouldn't.

Russell picked up his radio mic. "Chinese navy, this is a United States navy aircraft on a routine flight in international airspace."

A moment of quiet passed. Russell waited. He didn't feel much about it one way or another. His mission was to fly above these waters. That's what he was going to do.

"United States navy, these are restricted airspace," came the reply. "Please leave immediately."

"Uh... negative, Chinese navy. This is open airspace above international waters."

More time passed. The plane flew over the construction site. Russell glanced at it. It wasn't his job to look, of course. That's what all the camera equipment, and all those intelligence men, in the back were for. But it was almost too mesmerizing not to look. These Chinese projects took place on a scale you just never saw in the United States. From zero, Mischief Reef was now twenty or thirty football fields long.

"American navy," said the voice on the radio. From its earlier calm, it had quickly become agitated. The man was no longer speaking slowly. His voice was rising and speeding up, making it more difficult to understand. His English was beginning to deteriorate. "You please leave."

Russell rolled his eyes. After a few times, he got tired of responding to these challenges.

133

"Negative, Chinese navy."

This time, the reply was immediate.

"American, you go now! Last warning."

That was new. In all the pointless challenges he had received from the Chinese navy during his assignment here, it was the first time they had ever referred to it as a warning, and damn sure the first time they had ever called it the last one. That wouldn't stand.

"Chinese navy. Repeat. This is an American navy aircraft, on a routine…"

The flight intercom interrupted him. Russell sighed. It was Smiley, his radar man in the back.

"Lieutenant, can you read me?"

"Yeah, Smiley, what can I do for you?"

"We've got two bogeys just took off from Fiery Cross. Number one headed west, number two on an intercept heading and closing."

"What?" Russell said. No one told him the runway at Fiery Cross was operational, or that the Chinese had fighter planes stationed there.

"Intercept heading with what?"

"With us, sir."

Russell glanced over at his co-pilot Montgomery. Young, crew-cutted Monty looked like he was ready to puke.

"Keep your chin up, Montgomery. That's what they send us out here for. To be the guinea pigs."

"Sir?" Smiley said over the intercom.

"What's the distance on that bogey?" Russell said.

"Six miles and closing."

"Can we outrun him?" Montgomery said.

Russell nearly laughed. It was becoming a comedy show out here today.

"In this thing? We're flying a bubble-butt. We can't outrun your grandmother. Not that we would want to anyway. Cheer up, son. This is the United States Navy. We don't run from people."

He glanced at the readouts in front of him.

"Arm torpedoes," he said to the intercom. "If we get so much as a scratch from that guy, we're lighting up this island. Prepare to hit them with everything you got. We're not going to get a second chance."

"Yes, sir."

Russell held the mic to his mouth. "Chinese navy. Stand down."

134

"American navy…"

"Listen to me, you punk. This is the United States navy calling, and this is your last warning."

The Chinese man shouted over him. "No!"

Russell shook his head.

"Smiley, where's that bogey?"

"He has us on his nose. Collision course. Three miles out now. Uh… two miles."

Russell took a deep breath. This was going to happen fast.

"Acquire surface targets."

"Targets acquired and locked on."

"One mile sir," Smiley said. "Here… he… comes."

Russell looked to his right. Through the window, he got a visual on the Chinese plane. It was dark gray, coming almost too fast to see. He tried for an ID on it. The sharp lines and single cockpit told him it was probably a J-11 Shenyang—lightning-fast, super-maneuverable. It had better be. Otherwise there was going to be a mid-air crash.

His heart skipped in his chest.

"Steady!" he heard himself shout. "Prepare to fire."

The fighter zipped past just over their heads, way too close.

An instant later, the turbulence hit them and the big P8 shuddered. The P8 rode the unsettled air, then simmered down.

"Smiley?" Russell said.

"Copy," came a shaken voice.

"Status?"

"Still here, sir."

"Status on that bogey, Smiley. Not you."

"Uh… three miles out, showing us his tail. Four miles. Five."

Russell let out a long breath. He felt his heart now, thumping steadily, thumping hard, but almost like normal.

"Bogey on a heading change now, sir. On a western track, giving us his left flank. Looks like he's going to link up with his buddy to the west."

Russell looked over at Montgomery. The kid's face was positively green.

"Montgomery," Russell said. "I think you're going to like this job."

CHAPTER TWENTY ONE

11:17 p.m.
Streets of Randal, Maryland

The cop car was fast.

Luke was faster.

He came tearing around a corner, driving effortlessly now, one with the machine. The car skidded, leaving rubber on the asphalt. He straightened it out and tore down the long, empty industrial parkway.

He had left the cops several streets back. But it was only a matter of time before they found him again. His eyes scanned the streets ahead of him, both hands on the wheel. He glanced at the speed: 130.

He blew through a red light. There was no one coming. There was no one out here at all.

Up ahead, he saw the prison van and the Hummer. He was coming like a missile, listening to the voices in his Bluetooth headset.

"Stay down!" the guard screamed. "Don't you move a muscle. Don't you even twitch. I've got backup coming and we're going to wait right here, you and me."

He was talking to Ed Newsam.

"Swann?"

"Yes, Luke."

"How do we look on satellite?"

"Flashing lights converging from the south and the west. It's going to get very hot in a matter of minutes."

"Okay."

It was all coming toward him, like a big package on a fast-moving conveyor belt. He could see the van clearly now. He could see the broad back of the young ex-marine, the man in a stiff ready pose, pointing something into the doorway. That guy wasn't going to risk trying to cuff Ed for anything. He was going to wait until he had four or five guys with him. The danger here was Ed would blink wrong, or sneeze, and the jumpy guard would give him a blast of lead.

Luke was close now. Too close.

He slammed on the brakes, the car going into another skid. He steered with his left hand and picked up his dum-dum shotgun off the seat next to him with his right.

The skid was loud, and long. He steered into it, sliding sideways, showing the kid the driver's side. He rested the shotgun across his left arm and poked the snout out the window.

Here he came, sideways, sideways... Too fast, he was going to crush the kid against the van. At the last second, the kid turned to face him, all big eyes, terror in those eyes, his mouth a big round O of surprise. The last thing he would ever see, a black car coming at him broadside. He didn't even move.

The car stopped three feet short of the kid.

Luke had the drop on him, the muzzle of his shotgun bare feet from the kid's belly. "Put the gun down, kid. Drop it! Right now."

Something in Luke's eyes said he meant business. The kid dropped his gun. It clattered to the pavement. He stood, staring at Luke's gun, trying to make sense of what was happening, trying to decide if he was going to die right here.

Ed appeared behind and above him, on the lip of the van. He dropped down to the ground, punched the kid in the back of the head, then guided his body gently to the roadway.

Behind Ed, Trudy appeared in the doorway.

Luke shook his head at the sight of her.

"Luke?" Swann said inside the headset. "About to get very hot where you are."

"Okay, kids," Luke called. "We have to move right now."

They piled into the car, Trudy in the back, Ed into the shotgun seat. He dropped his gun and his big blue kit bag in the well at his feet.

Luke peeled off onto the road again.

Far behind him, in the rearview mirror, he could see the approaching flashers. He could hear the sirens. He smiled.

"Is this a family reunion or what?"

*

August 17th, 1:15 a.m.
Ocean City, Maryland

The parking lot was on the ground-floor level of the luxury apartment building. There were no basements near the beach.

"Welcome to paradise, gentlemen," Swann said.

He parked the car, a big white Range Rover that Luke had never seen before tonight. They climbed out into the empty garage. Luke wore a New York Yankees baseball cap, cut-off shorts, a T-shirt and flip-flops. Ed Newsam wore a Miami Heat basketball jersey, blue jeans, and sneakers. He carried a giant hockey equipment bag slung over his shoulder. It had a Washington Capitals logo on it. He bent from the weight, but to the naked eye, didn't seem to struggle with it.

The elevator was all carpeting and glass walls. A long double line of buttons ran along a metal panel. At the top of the buttons was a key slot. Swann stuck a key into the slot and turned. The elevator doors closed and the chamber lurched skyward.

"It's a nice town," Swann said. "You guys ever spend much time here?"

"I go to Virginia Beach," Ed said.

Swann shrugged, then nodded. "Yeah. I probably should have guessed. Virginia Beach is good. This is better. I think you're going to enjoy it here."

Luke was silent. Swann still hadn't explained what they were doing here. All Luke knew was that they needed somewhere to hide out, and Swann thought this would be a good place. Luke was reluctant to say anything in the elevator. He would wait to see once they got inside.

The elevator climbed to the top of the building. It opened directly into the foyer of an apartment. There was no hallway. There were no other doors except the tripled-locked double doors in front of them. Swann opened those with an eight- or ten-digit code he punched from memory into a keypad on the wall.

They went in.

The apartment was big. In the darkness, Swann took a remote control off the table and used it to turn on a few lights throughout the place. There were two floors. A steel and cable staircase went up to the second floor, where it connected with a catwalk. There was a living room here in front of them with a large white sectional couch. A modern art piece hung behind it, the canvas four feet wide and ten feet long, the painting a crazy horizontal blood-red scrape, like a person scratching at the walls of their prison cell with the last of their fingernails.

To their left, sliding glass doors opened to what appeared to be a deck.

Ed gingerly put his equipment bag down on the couch. He pulled the zipper along the length of it. Trudy's head popped out, hair mussed, eyes wide and blind. Her hand came up, slid her red glasses on, and she focused. She still wore her orange prison jumpsuit.

"Are we there yet?" she said.

"We are there," Swann said. "Come on out and make yourself at home."

"That begs the question, Swann," Luke said. "Where are we?"

They were in a penthouse apparently, at the top floor of a thirty-story oceanfront building. Whoever owned the apartment was rich. But it was important to know: how did Swann have access to this place?

Swann shrugged. "Does it matter?"

Luke stared at him. "You bet it matters. It's not going to take long for them to figure out who took Trudy. When they do..."

"They won't find us here, Luke."

Luke soaked in the sight of Swann. Tall and thin, with long sandy hair and aviator glasses. His hair was pulled into a ponytail. Unlike a lot of desk jockeys, he seemed reasonably fit. He wore a black T-shirt with the words BLACK FLAG in white across the front. He wore faded jeans and red Converse All-Star sneakers.

"How can you be sure?"

"No one knows about this place. It's owned by a guy named Albert Helu. He keeps a low profile. He doesn't bother anybody. No one bothers him."

"Who is he?" Ed said.

Swann didn't answer.

"Swann..." Luke said.

"He's me."

Swann paused, then saw that it probably wasn't good enough. He was going to have to give them more.

"Listen, there's a lot you guys don't know about me. I was arrested twelve years ago. That's how I got into government work. I was a twenty-three-year-old kid. Hacking. I was hitting investment firms. Transferring money from large institutional brokerage accounts to accounts owned by me. I hit big companies because nobody got hurt that way. But I got caught. I was looking at a lot of time, but when they saw what I could do, they offered me a job instead. Provided I stopped doing the other. Who could argue with a deal like that one?"

"And Albert Helu?"

Swann raised his eyebrows. "I had about a dozen aliases at the time, and they rolled up most of them. But not all. I kept Albert

139

compartmentalized and they never found him. I know this because I started using his accounts and his property again within a year or two, after I figured they weren't watching me anymore."

Swann stood, looking at them. Then he put his hands up.

"I know what you're thinking, but it's not true. They might be watching me, but they're not watching Albert. I never come here straight from being Mark Swann. I've had carte blanche access to worldwide criminal databases, satellite surveillance, email, and web traffic servers for years. No one is looking for Albert. He is on no one's radar. No one knows he's here except the staff, and mostly I steer clear of them. When they do see me, they call me Mr. Helu. I tell them to call me Al."

"So you own this place?" Ed said. He walked around the living room. He looked up at the catwalk above his head. "Not bad."

"Well, Albert owns it. But I can use it anytime I want. You should check out the deck. There's a hot tub out there."

"If you have all this money, why even bother working for the government?" Ed said.

Swann shrugged. "Why does anybody do it? The benefits are good. And if I hang around long enough, I'll get a pension. Listen, you guys want a beer?"

Trudy had climbed all the way out of the bag now. She sat on the white couch. She looked like a tiny orange spot in the giant apartment.

She looked at Luke and Ed. "Thank you for rescuing me."

Luke smiled. "You're welcome, Trudy."

Ed shrugged. "It was the least we could do."

Trudy shook her head. "No, I mean thank you for rescuing me. I am very glad to be out of there. There was a guard… she was about as mean as it gets."

I have a funny feeling," Ed said, "that I've met meaner people."

"Ones that were in charge of de-lousing you, and checking you for contraband? You know, really checking you?"

Ed grimaced. "Ah," he said.

"That's right," Trudy said. "That's the look I had on my face, too. She looked around. "So what am I even doing here? If they catch me again…"

"You tell them we took you against your will," Luke said.

"But why? Why did you do it?"

"I don't know. I figured we'd get the band back together, take a little vacation together, and hang out here in Swann's fabulous apartment. You know, relive the good old days a little."

"I don't remember those days," Ed said.

Trudy shook her head. "That's funny. Me neither."

"Well," Luke said. "In that case, I must be thinking of somebody else. Oh, right. You're Trudy. You're the one who's going to help us figure out who is carrying out these cyber attacks."

She heaved a heavy sigh.

"That's why you broke me out?"

"Yes. Sound fun?"

"Better than jail," she said. "So how do I do that from here?"

Swann came back through a tall swinging door with four beer bottles in his hands.

"Oh, let me show you," he said.

He put the bottles down on the glass coffee table in front of the couch. He picked up the remote control again and hit a button. To their right, spotlights came on in an area of the room that was in darkness a moment before. A glass partition automatically slid away into the wall. A big leather chair sat at a desk with three tower hard drives on the floor beneath it, and two flat-panel screens on top of it. Wires ran all over the floor.

"Encrypted super high-speed internet," Swann said. "Masking programs that run the data all over the world before it comes here through a secure portal. Untraceable. Access to hundreds of cable and satellite television stations throughout the world. Access to communications satellites, surveillance satellites, thousands of databases through pirated subscription services, hijacked network traffic, email servers, you name it. You need information? This is where you will find it."

Trudy stared at Swann's computer setup. "I'm really tired," she said. "I've been through the wringer these past several weeks. When do you want me to start?"

Luke picked up a beer and took a long sip. It was cold and delicious. He gestured at Swann's command center.

"This thing is operational?" he said.

Swann grunted. "Operational? It's ready to rock."

Luke knocked back another swig of the beer. "Well, in that case, I guess we start right now."

CHAPTER TWENTY TWO

7:07 a.m.
United States Naval Observatory – Washington, DC

"How's the atmosphere?" Susan said.

She and Kat Lopez were descending the main staircase together, coming down from Susan's study. Two big Secret Service officers led them down. Another one brought up the rear behind them.

Susan hadn't gotten much sleep. But today, at least, when she came out of the shower and into her private kitchen, she found a bag of Peet's Dark Roast Coffee on the counter. That was almost enough to make her day.

Kat looked the worse for wear. By the time she reached home last night, tumbled into bed, woke up, and came back here, she'd be lucky if she got three hours sleep.

"In the Situation Room?" Kat said.

"Yes."

"It's bad, Susan. I need to tell you something about it."

Susan shook her head. She tried on a smile. It didn't fit. Smiles weren't going to work today. She was looking for someplace inside of herself, some island of calm. She wasn't finding one.

"Don't worry about it, Kat. I can handle these people."

"I've got more bad news besides that," Kat said.

Susan stopped. Could things get any worse? Could there really be more bad news?

"Hit me," she said. "If I'm still standing after all this, I doubt there's much that can knock me down now."

"Trudy Wellington broke out of prison last night."

Susan nearly grabbed the hand railing for support. How could that be? Trudy Wellington, who knew about the assassination and coup plot? She wasn't a major player. She was Don Morris's mistress. Heck, they were keeping her in jail to squeeze her for information, not because they thought she had done anything.

Don Morris was in a SuperMax in Colorado. He didn't have the reach to get Wellington out. He didn't even have access to the outside world. And no one else on his side would care enough to...

She stopped.

"Luke Stone."

142

Kat nodded. "We think so. He visited her yesterday afternoon. Then late last night, someone hacked into the Bureau of Prisons database and got her transferred from the detention facility up in Randal, to the DC municipal lockup. It was an uncommon transfer, but not unprecedented. No one caught it. Two men hijacked the transfer van and freed her."

"A white man and a black man."

Kat nodded again. "Bingo."

"Was anyone hurt?"

Kat shrugged. "Some scratches, a few lumps on the head. Not really."

Now Susan really did smile. "Okay. I'm sure the police are looking for them. We don't need to contribute any of our own people. Let's just keep any eye on the situation, all right?"

"All right, Susan."

They walked down the hallway toward the Situation Room. The double doors were open, with a Secret Service officer on either side of the doorway. They had ramped up security again. After the subway attacks, it seemed to make sense. But if they were just going to attack computer systems…

Susan walked into the Room.

Kurt Kimball was there, standing as always. He wore a dress shirt and slacks, both clean and starched. His posture was upright and erect, energetic as always, but his face looked tired. There were black rings under his eyes. It was starting to get to him. For a second, Susan wondered if he had even gone home last night.

Sitting among the small crowd was Michael Parowski, looking alert and refreshed. He seemed mighty pleased with himself after his television news show tour-de-force the night before. She had to hand it to him. He was built for this. Crisis. Turmoil. In-fighting. She'd be curious to see how well he was built for the African desert.

She glanced around the room. The faces were out of place, so much so that it took Susan a moment to recognize them. Here was Brent Staples, a long-time party campaign strategist. He had been instrumental, in fact, in getting Thomas Hayes and herself elected. There, in another corner of the room, was William Ackland, a major party fundraiser. He was as far from Brent Staples as possible while still being in the room with him. Susan knew that the two men hated each other.

"I'm sorry," Susan said. "Did I call this meeting?"

"No," a voice said. "I did."

143

On Susan's left, a man pushed up out of his chair. He had once been a very good-looking man, and he had retained some of that into his old age. His name was Ronald "Dutch" Evans, and he was the godfather of the party. A long-time Senator from California in the 1970s and 1980s, in 1992 he seemed like a shoo-in to become President. Then he was photographed by a newsstand tabloid with his young, bikini-clad mistress on a fishing boat aptly, if unfortunately, named *Hanky Panky*. His mistress was barely older than his daughters.

Even after that debacle, he had gone on and become the Chairman of the Party for nearly a decade. He had built a gigantic fundraising machine that included people like William Ackland, and a political machine that won dozens of state legislatures and governorships, courtesy of people like Brent Staples. Whatever his flaws, Dutch Evans was a powerful man.

"Hi, Dutch," Susan said.

"Hi, Susan." He gestured at her chair. "Won't you sit down?"

"Dutch," she said, "I'd like to remind you that this is my venue. You're the visitor."

"Susan, I was sleeping in the Lincoln Bedroom back when you were running for Prom Queen. You're just a renter here. I own the place."

Susan shook her head. She had never liked Dutch. It was galling, the amount of arrogance he could display.

"The Lincoln Bedroom is for special guests," she said. "When we get the White House rebuilt, I'll consider inviting you to sleep there again. Personally, I'll be sleeping in the President's quarters."

She shrugged and smiled. This time, the smile felt genuine. "That's where the President of the United States sleeps. Now how can I help you, Dutch?"

Dutch Evans sat back down. Only then did Susan find her own chair.

"Susan," Brent Staples said, "we're very concerned about what's going on here. You might not feel like you owe Dutch anything. I believe you owe him a debt of gratitude for the way he has built this party, but you may not agree. That's fine. But you know what I did for you and Thomas Hayes. Arguably, you wouldn't be here if not for me."

Susan stared at Brent. He was a weak-looking middle-aged man with thinning hair. He had a long nose and no chin to speak of. His body was thin and utterly without muscle tone. He wore ill-fitting suits that he seemed to swim inside of. And all of this belied

144

the truth: he was one of the shrewdest political consultants alive. On the campaign trail, he was a warrior. He was vicious, relentless, and without remorse. He had personally engineered the strategies that made Thomas Hayes President, while at the same time demolishing the opposition.

"What are you telling me, Brent?"

"I'm telling you that you're out on a limb right now. You are all by yourself. I'm telling you that you don't hold secret midnight meetings where you appoint a member of the opposition as Secretary of Defense. We know that Ed Graves was here last night. Forget what you think you know about Ed. He tried to kill you a couple of months ago. He was successful in killing Thomas. The only reason he's not in prison right now is he's too dumb to learn how to use the internet. And his fingers are too fat to press the buttons on a keyboard."

Dutch Evans raised a hand. "You also don't simply throw the Chinese ambassador out of the country on your own initiative. Overnight, the Chinese expelled our ambassador to Beijing, and all of our embassy staff, including the United States Marines who guard the place. They have twelve hours to leave. Once the last of our people are out of there, the Chinese special police will have free run of the place. If we can't get all of our computers out, and it's really up to the Chinese whether we can or not, then the entire system will have to be destroyed. I hope I don't have to tell you the kind of secrets housed inside that embassy."

Susan stared at them. She was having trouble thinking of a rebuttal.

"All Americans in Hong Kong have been placed under curfew," said William Ackland. He had white hair, bleary eyes, a thick nose lined with burst blood vessels, and a frame that people used to call "husky." He wore a three-thousand-dollar suit, but he looked more like an alcoholic movie detective than the high-level fundraiser he was.

"After ten p.m., they can't be on the streets. They've been told that their residence status will be reviewed with seventy-two hours. People are scared, Susan. We're talking about friends of ours in the banking industry. People who helped you get elected, and who may or may not help you again. People who could help build a supermajority for you in the House of Representatives."

Susan had walked into a trap. She had no friends in this room. That much was clear. She glanced at Kat Lopez. Kat's eyes were on the floor. Kat was Susan's chief-of-staff, but the party had brought

145

Kat to her. She looked at Kurt Kimball, normally so confident, looking sheepish and hangdog now.

"Kurt?" she said.

He shrugged. "Susan, I wish we could have talked about this before you went and did it. You've brought the real war hawks on board, the worst of them, and I feel like I was boxed out of this decision."

Susan shook her head.

She took a deep breath. "I don't make my decisions," she said, "based on the needs or the fears of rich bankers in Hong Kong. I also don't base my decisions on what campaign consultants and fundraisers think."

"Careful," Dutch Evans said. "There are people in this room who made your career, and who can just as easily unmake it."

"Don't threaten me, Dutch. I'm not here to be threatened by you."

"I'm curious," Brent Staples said. "What do you base your decisions upon?"

She stared at Brent. "I base them on what I believe the American people want."

Brent shook his head slowly, as if speaking to a small child, or maybe an imbecile. "Susan," he said, and now his eyes were on fire. His eyes bore no relationship to his infirm body. His eyes were strong and fierce. "I decide what the American people want. I tell them what they want. I do it. Me. I *am* the American people."

Now Susan shook her head. She almost laughed. "Men! Oh my God. You guys are so full of yourselves. Brent, you're not the American people. Look at you. You don't represent the hopes and dreams of millions. You're a huckster in a traveling medicine show, right down to the bad suit."

She looked at Dutch Evans now. "Okay Dutch, you're the man behind the curtain, right? The Wizard of Oz. But why are you behind the curtain? Because the American people didn't want you up front, that's why. Once they got a real good look at you, and your boat, and your girlfriend, not even people like Bill Ackland and Brent Staples could save you. Am I right? Am I right?"

Dutch Evans shook his head. "We're your friends, Susan. We're trying to help you. The last thing you want is to find yourself without friends. Bad things could start to happen."

"There you go again, threatening me," Susan said.

146

Evans stood. He was just the slightest bit shaky on his feet. Susan noticed that he carried a cane with him. It was a handsome cane of polished wood.

"I don't want to see your approval rating tank any further than it already has," Evans said. "And I definitely don't want to see you get impeached. You might want to consider resigning before such a thing can happen."

"Resigning?" Susan said. "Dutch, you're out of your mind."

"Think about it, Susan. It wouldn't be the worst thing that can happen."

With that, he limped out of the room. Brent Staples followed him with two aides. After a moment, William Ackland packed up and left by himself. One by one, people were leaving the Situation Room. They were all party insiders. Outside of Kurt Kimball, there wasn't a foreign policy person to be seen.

The last person to leave was Michael Parowski. He smiled at her. He looked like the cat who had just swallowed the family bird. Susan gazed at him in astonishment. They had pushed him on her. His formal announcement as Vice President was tomorrow morning. And already they were talking about impeachment, or resignation. They were moving him in, and moving her out.

She shook her head. She wouldn't let it happen.

"You're done, Susan," he said quietly. "You know that, right?"

"Mister, you don't know what done looks like."

The room was empty now, except for Susan, Kat Lopez, and Kurt Kimball. Neither Kat nor Kurt would look directly at her.

"If we're going to continue," she said, "I need to know something from you two. Are you on my side, or aren't you? We're coming to find out that everyone is expendable around here. Kat, I shit-canned my last chief-of-staff with five minutes' notice. Kurt, I'm sure the RAND Corporation has a pretty deep bench. I'm sure Jane's does, too. My point being you're not the only national security expert on the planet."

They both looked up and stared at her now.

"If you're on my team, you're on my team." She gestured at the men who had just gone out the door. "Not theirs. And I need you to say so."

"I'm here to help you, Susan," Kurt said. "But you have to let me do that."

Coming from Kurt, that was good enough. Susan looked at Kat.

"I'm on your side, Susan."

Susan smiled. "Good. Kat, the primary order of business for you today is to arrange Michael Parowski's first trip abroad as Vice President. Thursday afternoon, I want him out of here. A good place for him to start will be Ethiopia. They have a tribe there, the women wear these giant plate things pierced through their lips..."

She glanced at Kurt.

"The Mursi," he said. "They're a desert tribe."

Now Susan's smile was broader than ever. "Yes. The Mursi tribe. We haven't engaged in any diplomacy with them in a long while. They're important friends of ours, and I want them to know that. Arrange for Michael to spend a week or so with them. Make sure we send a good photographer. I don't want to miss a moment of it."

CHAPTER TWENTY THREE

7:21 a.m.
Ocean City, Maryland

"Luke? Luke, we might have something."

Sometime before, the sun had risen in yellow and pink over the Atlantic Ocean. Luke had taken his T-shirt off and wrapped it over his eyes. He lay across a lounge chair on the roof deck of Swann's penthouse.

He felt the early morning sun warming the skin of his upper body. He enjoyed the feeling. For the moment, he didn't want to know anything but this feeling. He didn't want to open his eyes. He didn't want to think about yesterday, or about what might happen today. He just wanted to stay here, feel the sun, listen to the call of the gulls, and smell the sea breeze.

Was that too much to ask?

"Luke?"

"Yeah, Swann. I'm awake. What is it?"

"We might have something for you."

Luke took the shirt off his head. The sky was bright—almost too bright to look at. Swann stood above him. He wore all the same clothes as last night. Same BLACK FLAG T-shirt, same aviator glasses, same jeans. His feet were now bare. He smiled. It was a sickly, wan smile. Swann looked like hell.

Behind Swann, the ocean stretched from left to right, a 180-degree panoramic view.

"Have you been up all night?" Luke said.

"Yes. Me and Trudy. We've been working."

"Where's Ed?"

"Here," came a voice from behind Luke. Luke turned just slightly, and there was big Ed about ten feet away, bare-chested, sitting in Swann's hot tub. The hot tub was embedded into the roof. Three shallow steps led up to the lip of it. Luke realized he had been listening to the sound of the tub's water jets for a while now. It had been so subtle that he barely noticed it—he might have been dreaming it.

"You want to see what we dug up?" Swann asked.

Luke sighed heavily. He was more tired than he had been in a while. It surprised him a little that he was the last one to wake up, and that Swann and Trudy hadn't slept at all. "Sure," he said.

149

He pulled his T-shirt on and followed Swann through the open sliding glass doors.

Trudy sat in Swann's little command center. At some point in the night, she had ditched the orange jumpsuit. Now she was wearing cast-off clothes from Swann. She had a pair of faded jeans on, the cuffs rolled up to a ridiculous point, the waistband cinched tight with what looked like a length of Cat-5 computer cable. She also wore an old Cincinnati Bengals T-shirt. She had apparently washed her hair as well—the ponytail was gone, and her hair hung down in curls.

She looked stunning. Exhausted, but beautiful.

"Does that T-shirt belong to Swann?" Luke said. "How does it even fit you?"

"I've had that shirt since high school," Swann said. "It's one of those shirts where the bottom is cut off to show people your tight abs. If it was a normal length, it would be down to her knees."

Luke looked at Swann.

"Good morning to you, too," Trudy said.

Luke shook his head. "Good morning, Trudy. Good morning, Swann. Let's see what you guys have for me."

Luke sat in a rolling office chair that Swann pushed toward him. He pulled up next to Trudy at the desk. She had both computer monitors going, stacks of windows open on each one. Swann disappeared into the kitchen for a moment, then reappeared carrying another coffee cup, steam rising from it. He handed it to Luke.

"Okay, Luke?" Trudy said. "Ready? I'm going to assume no prior knowledge."

Luke nodded. "Fair enough."

"Swann pulled me down intel from everywhere. People have been poring over massive amounts of data from the target lists you guys found in Atlanta, as well as the attacks themselves. There's an effort underway to link the style of these attacks to known cyber-war and hacking tendencies. A major problem here is neither of the hacks were terribly sophisticated. They were both low-hanging fruit, although the DC Metro hack was a bit more advanced than the dam."

"The dam was child's play," Swann said. "Quite literally, a couple of smart twelve-year-olds could have done it."

Trudy raised one finger. "Except that the hackers masked their location by bouncing their signal all around the world, through a long series of both real and fake IP addresses."

"True," Swann said.

Trudy went on. "I spent most of the night coming up to speed on the case as the analysts understand it so far. The government has people from NSA, FBI, CIA, and Naval intelligence digging into this. Because of the capture of Li Quiangguo, it seems that most analyses start from the assumption that the Chinese are behind this. Either the Chinese government, Chinese criminal gangs, or maybe the Chinese doomsday cult that you uncovered. Since those bases are well covered, I decided to come at it from a different direction."

"That's why we hired you," Luke said.

"I assumed that the Chinese didn't do it, and began by looking for evidence that might confirm this. I didn't have to look too far."

"Show me," Luke said.

Trudy clicked on the screen. An image appeared of a thick male body lying face down on some wet tiles. The man's entire upper body was a mad tangle of ink.

"This is Li Quiangguo, moments after he was found dead in the shower. As you can see, he is covered in tattoos."

"Yes," Luke said. "Somewhere on there he has a tattoo indicating he's a member of the Eastern Lightning cult."

"Yes he does," Trudy said. "It's on his left shoulder. Who told you that?"

Luke smiled. "I'm not at liberty to discuss everything. Let's just say someone I spoke to was familiar with this case."

"Well, the guy has tattoos all over his body. He has his life story inscribed on his skin. I'm guessing someone was assigned to decipher all these messages, but I haven't seen that analysis. So I did some myself. And here's what I came up with. Li Quiangguo wasn't Chinese. He was Korean, and specifically, he was North Korean. If there was the time, or the inclination, I'd bet a thousand dollars that DNA testing would confirm this. Koreans, generally speaking, were isolated on the peninsula for a long time. Despite their close proximity to both the Japanese and the Chinese, they have a very unique DNA signature that makes them distinct from other groups."

"Okay," Luke said. "But since we're not going to do a DNA sample, how do you know he's North Korean?"

Trudy made an open hand gesture. "As I mentioned to you, I spent eighteen months listening to Chinese transmissions after I got out of school. When that was over, I spent nearly a year monitoring transmissions from the North Koreans. That... was a grim year."

"So you're an expert," Luke said.

She shook her head. "I know a little bit. Enough to see that our man Li has his North Korean pride all over his body. A lot of it is mixed up with the two dozen other tattoos he has, but there's enough here to make sense of it. For example…"

She clicked on the image, and the screen zoomed in on Li's upper back. He had an image there of a blue lake surrounded by craggy, snow-capped peaks. It was a well-done, highly professional tattoo. Beneath it were some Asian characters.

백두산

"The body of water is called Heaven's Lake. It's at the top of Mount Baektu, which is an active volcano on the border of China and North Korea. The hills you see surrounding it are actually the rim of the volcano. The mountain has been disputed territory between the Chinese and Koreans since the dawn of time. Mount Baektu is also the legendary birthplace of Kim Jong-il, former Supreme Leader of North Korea."

"Okay, but if both countries claim the mountain, why does that make him Korean?"

Trudy shrugged. "The script below the mountain uses the Korean alphabet. It says Mount Baektu. In English, it means *Whitehead Mountain*. The Chinese don't even call it that. They call it Mount Changbai, which means *Ever White Mountain*. It's a subtle distinction, but I think one that stands. By his use of the Korean alphabet and the Korean name, you can see which side of that debate he comes down on."

"All right," Luke said. "That's one point for Korean."

"And here's another," Trudy said. She flipped through various images until she found one of Li on his back. The crazy surreal landscape of tattoos continued on this side. Just above his heart was another scrap of calligraphy. Trudy zoomed in on it.

主體

"These are hanja characters," Trudy said. "They are basically the Korean usage of the Chinese alphabet. It's not to be confused with Chinese, though. The Koreans use the Chinese characters, but they retain their intricate classical pen strokes. Modern Chinese characters, as used by the Chinese themselves, tend to be simplified."

Ed had joined them. He had one of Swann's plush towels wrapped around his waist. "What does it say?"

"It says Juche," Trudy said. She pronounced it like "Choocheh."

"What is it?"

152

"It's the political ideology of North Korea. It technically means 'self-reliance,' which is part of why the North isolates itself from the rest of the world. But it's also a control mechanism, and the foundation of the cult of personality surrounding the Kim family. Juche is basically the religion for a country of godless communists. It helps them overlook the fact that in a nominally socialist country with no class distinctions, there is in fact a carefully stratified and rigidly enforced system of hierarchy, partially a holdover from the medieval caste system, but mostly just the Kim family and their friends at the top, and everyone else beneath them."

"People believe in this?" Ed said.

Trudy shrugged. "It's a religion. People will believe anything, if you start them young enough."

"Anything else?" Luke said.

"Oh yeah," Trudy said. "There's more. Here's a rising sun, and not the Japanese version. A rising sun in Korea is the symbol of Kim il-Sung, the first Supreme Leader. And here's a symbol that refers to Arirang. Arirang is an ancient Korean folk song about two young lovers who have been separated, and who can only reunite in the afterlife. It is the unofficial anthem of both Koreas. In the modern North Korean version of the story, the young lovers are kept apart by an evil landlord. I'm sure you can guess who that is. This story is so important in North Korea that they hold an Arirang Festival every year for weeks on end. It's going on right now."

Trudy looked at Luke. "And those are just the tattoos I can see in these photos. If we had the body, I'm sure I could find more."

Luke thought about what she was saying. It seemed, at first blush... interesting. But it wasn't proof of anything. No one knew quite who or what Li Quiangguo was. Luke was now convinced he had duped them into believing he was terrified of waterboarding just so he could kill himself. A guy who could do that...

"You think the North Koreans are behind these attacks."

Trudy raised a finger like a schoolteacher. "I think Li Quiangguo was North Korean. That's all I said."

Luke thought about it. "You told me at the prison that the Chinese are too cautious for something like this."

"The Chinese are too cautious to do something like this directly. That much is true, and I stand by it. But they've been known to use the North Koreans as their cat's paw before."

Luke pondered this, a thought coming to him, one he wished he'd never had.

"What if it's the reverse?" Luke asked. "The North Koreans are the desperate ones here. They've been threatening to attack the US for years. They are more desperate than they've ever been. What if they're really doing it this time? What if those first cyber attacks were just a test, a warm-up to something bigger? And what if they are using Chinese plants to throw us off course, to make us think it's China? And to simultaneously spark a war between us and China that will lead to further damage for us?"

"That would damage China, too," Swann added. "Why would they bite the hand that feeds them?"

Luke gave him a look.

"Do you know how many times they have defied China?" he asked.

A long silence fell over the room as they all pondered it. To Luke, it seemed to make awful sense.

"I want to show you one more thing, Luke," Trudy added.

She tapped through a couple of screens. In a moment, she arrived at a still from a grainy black-and-white surveillance video. She pressed the horizontal triangle in the middle, which started the video. It was shot from the upper corner of a room. A very thin Asian man sat at a metal table, smoking a cigarette. He wore a prison jumpsuit. His entire body was shaking.

Someone off screen was speaking to him, and in between inhalations from the cigarette, he replied. English captions appeared at the bottom of the screen.

You say a big attack is coming?

Arirang is coming. The end of the story. Reunification.

What does that mean to you?

The people are going hungry. We must reunite, if we are brothers.

It can't happen now.

All the same, it will happen now. The border will be dissolved. The Americans can't stop it. They will be helpless soon.

The video ended.

"What is it?" Luke said.

Trudy closed it with a tap of her finger. "Swann pulled that brief segment off a South Korean intelligence data server, and had a friend of his translate it last night. He was searching for any South Korean intel on Li Quiangguo, and he found that instead. It's a snippet of footage of a North Korean deserter who apparently walked across the border sometime in the past few days. They found him yesterday, wandering in the Gangwon Province

154

wilderness. He managed to evade both North Korean and South Korean forces until he was ten miles into South Korea. He claims that an attack is coming. He appears to be convinced of it. He crossed the border into South Korea to warn them."

"There's always an attack coming from North Korea. That's part of the fun of dealing with them."

Trudy shook her head. "I wouldn't write this off, Luke. With tensions ramping up between us and China, the Chinese may have promised the North Koreans that if a war starts, the North Koreans can attack the South. They might even let them attack preemptively, as a way of commencing a war without actually involving China."

Luke let that one sink in. He had seen the estimated casualties if a new war started on the Korean peninsula. North Korea was bristling with weapons. They were, per capita, the most thoroughly armed nation on Earth. Seoul, South Korea, was a city of ten million people, and it was only forty miles from the DMZ. It had been utterly destroyed in the first war. More than that, there were about 30,000 American servicemen and women stationed in South Korea, almost all of them within a few miles of the DMZ.

They were the most vulnerable American troops on Earth. All scenario planning suggested that if a war started, more than ninety percent of them would be dead within a few hours.

"The Chinese, or the North Koreans, or both, are testing our infrastructure," Luke said, trying out Trudy's theory. "Probing it. They want to see if they can degrade our response capabilities ahead of a new war on the Korean peninsula."

"It's not that far-fetched," Trudy said, as if Luke was the one pitching the idea and she was merely agreeing with it.

Luke looked at his team.

"We're never going to get to the bottom of this," he said. "The only way is…" An idea began to form, one so crazy that he didn't even know if he should say it. Then, finally, he did:

"We need to talk to that deserter ourselves."

They stared back at him.

"How do we manage that?" Swann said. "I pulled that video off a secure server. No one in the West even knows that guy exists."

Luke shrugged. "We know."

"Right, but we're a band of desperados right now," Ed said. "Nobody's gonna give us access to their prisoner. We'll be lucky we're not all in jail ourselves by the end of the day, never mind doing a teleconference with some guy who jumped the fence from

North Korea. We can't even show our faces anywhere. The minute we surface…"

Luke shook his head. "We're not going to surface. Don't worry about that." He looked at Swann. "Can I borrow a secure phone line?"

* * *

Luke stood in the morning sun on Swann's deck, a black satellite phone pressed to his ear. The line was blank. While he waited for something to happen, he soaked in the view. It was glorious out here. Far out on the sun-dappled ocean, he watched a big sailboat pass from left to right.

In some strange way, it delighted him that Swann owned this place from long ago criminal activity, and had never mentioned it. His people, even though they were no longer his people, really were the best. What other secrets were they sitting on?

He glanced over at them, the three of them standing there in a row, ten feet away, near the sliding glass doors. They were staring at him.

Far away, on the other side of the world, the phone started ringing.

"Luke, who are you calling?" Trudy said.

He raised a hand. He mouthed the words: "Hold on a minute."

A female voice answered. He didn't quite catch what she said to him. The words went by in a blur.

"*Yeoboseyo*," Luke said. "*Nan e mun-ui hal su issseubnida Park Jae-kyu?*" Hello, may I speak to Park Jae-kyu?

Luke watched his team watching him. Trudy's shoulders dropped. All the air seemed to go out of her body. Ed just shook his head. Swann nodded, like he knew it all along.

"*Je ireum-eun* Luke Stone *imnida.*" My name is Luke Stone.

"*Naneun olaen chingu.*" I am an old friend.

The woman's voice went away. Luke turned from his team and gazed out at the ocean again. In his mind, he pictured the man he was calling. Park Jae-kyu. About his age, good-looking guy, phenomenal athlete, maybe five feet, four inches tall. In high heels. Luke nearly laughed to think of him.

Luke had spent eight months in South Korea when he was in the 75th Army Rangers. He had done most of that time along the DMZ, staring across barbed wire fences and small green hills at heavily armed North Koreans. It was a bleak place and a lousy

156

assignment. Except that he was buddied up with a member of the South Korean 9th Special Forces Ghost Brigade.

That buddy was tiny Park Jae-kyu, 5th Dan Tae Kwon Do Master. A guy who could do 200 pushups without stopping, then go out at night while on R and R and knock back twenty drinks. He and Luke used to spar on their off-hours. Man, would they go at it. Their fights were the stuff of legend. Park's highly trained, ballerina-like striking attacks against Luke's highly improvisational blocking and counter-punch boxing style. They were like chess matches at warp speed. Beautiful.

Luke sighed. To be young again.

The deep, stern, no-nonsense voice came on the line. It already sounded like an admonishment. Or an accusation.

"*Yeoboseyo.* Park-Jae-kyu."

Luke grinned. "What's up, Gangnam style?"

"Stone?"

"Affirmative."

"When my secretary said your name, I thought it was a hoax. I figured you must be dead by now."

"Nine lives," Luke said. "I've got three left."

Luke had kept an eye on Park from afar. After his military service, Park had joined NIS, the Korean National Intelligence Service. They were an outfit with a bad reputation. So bad, in fact, that they had to change their name. Up until recently, they had been called the Korean Central Intelligence Agency, the KCIA.

Their fingers were crusted with every kind of dirt imaginable. Assassinations. Kidnapping. Torture. Bribery. Blackmail. Manipulation of election outcomes. You name it, they were into it. But Park was a good guy. That was how Luke thought of him. He was NIS, and NIS was bad news. But South Korea was firmly in the gun sights of the North, and maybe even China. And sometimes, when in a position like that, you did what you had to do. Isn't that what everybody in this secret world told themselves?

Park got right down to business. He had always been that way. A sparring session, a drinking session, a firefight on a hillside— they were all the same to him. What are we waiting for?

"You're calling for a reason," Park said. "And it isn't nostalgia for old times."

"True enough," Luke said. "You've got a prisoner, a North Korean deserter. He came over the border at Gangwon."

"I have no idea what you're talking about, Stone."

"Skinny guy, came in about half-dead. He's probably gone up to three-quarters dead since your boys have started talking to him. I'm hoping to get a word in with him before they finish him off."

"Skinny guy from North Korea?" Park said. "It doesn't—how do you say it?—ring a bell. The people in the North are starving, Stone. You might as well tell me you're looking for a fat guy from America."

Luke nodded. Now he remembered why he used to spar with Park so much. Sometimes he just wanted to punch that mouth of his.

"I know you have him, Park. I've seen video of his interrogation."

There was silence over the line. Luke waited a moment to let the statement sink in. This was the deal. We're friends, but we spy on each other. It was easy to forget sometimes. And it hurt to be reminded of it.

Luke went on. "There's no reason to play around, that's all I'm saying. I know you have him, and I know he has a lot to say. I need the information he's sitting on. I'm asking you for a favor. Yes, for old times' sake. We've got big problems over here."

"I have a hunch," Park said, "that we have bigger problems than you do."

"That may be," Luke said. He thought of the bristling North Korean arsenal, a monstrous cache of weaponry, missiles, tanks, mortars, most of it pointed directly at Seoul, a hyper-modern city of ten million civilians, well within range.

"If that's the case, then let me help you."

"Stone, what can you possibly do?"

Luke stared out to sea. The big sailboat was just dropping over the horizon. "You might be surprised."

Park's voice dropped almost to a whisper, as if whispering would somehow help. As if whispering would stop someone from overhearing you in an era when any phone call on Earth could be collected, digitally enhanced, copied a thousand times in half an hour, and listened to by operatives from two dozen countries.

"I can't talk about this over the phone," Park fairly hissed. "I can't confirm or deny anything you've said to me."

"Is it bad?" Luke said.

"Bad? I wish it was bad. It's the worst thing I've ever known."

"Listen, I need to talk to this guy."

"It's not possible," Park said. Luke knew that Park had shaken his head. NO. From half a world away, through the phone lines of

158

suburban Seoul, bounced into space from one black satellite to another, then back down to this oceanfront rooftop, Luke could almost see him do it. The movement was sudden, fast, spare, over before it started. It was a head shake that cut off any further discussion.

"Park…"

"He is the highest-value prisoner alive."

"I need him," Luke said.

A long moment passed. Neither man said a word. It went on long enough that Luke began to think Park had hung up. But then his voice came back on the line, softer now, his English less clipped.

"You have to come here," Park said.

CHAPTER TWENTY FOUR

8:15 a.m.
Newark International Airport – Newark, New Jersey

"Next up, we've got a breaking story with possible bombshell news about the husband of the President of the United States."

The woman sat slumped on a bench near the gate, staring mindlessly up at the overhead TV set. Her flight was already delayed half an hour, and it could only get worse from here.

She was a young mother with two young children. She was tired, and this was not her idea of fun. She had awakened at 3 a.m. in her home in Burlington, Vermont. Without waking her husband (who had to work today), she had climbed out of bed, gotten the girls ready, packed up and taken the cab to the airport. They caught the 6:15 flight down here to Newark, then raced through the airport to their next gate.

This gate. Only to find out that the next flight was delayed. The girls were already agitated and irascible. The next flight was a long one, from here to Phoenix, Arizona. They were going to visit her parents, who for some unknown reason had moved to Arizona when they retired. The young woman shook her head at the thought of it. Vermont was beautiful. It was a rolling green paradise. Arizona was a blazing, highway-choked hell on Earth.

It was going to be a long day.

The news came back on. They were going to talk about the President. The young woman perked up just the slightest amount. Despite everything that had happened, she still liked the President. More than that—she looked up to her. It was amazing to have a woman President. It was amazing for the girls to be growing up while a woman was Commander in Chief. It meant anything was possible. You couldn't blame Susan Hopkins for the terrorist attacks. That could happen to anybody.

A female newscaster's head filled the TV screen. She was a beautiful mixed race woman, the races mixed in such a way that it was impossible to say exactly what she was. Maybe she was Hispanic, or Asian, or black, or some combination of all of them. Her name was Audrey. That didn't help much.

"Chuck, we've got a breaking story with possible earth-shattering implications. It's about high-tech billionaire Pierre

Michaud. Most of you know him as Mr. Susan Hopkins, husband of the President of the United States, and father to the President's twin daughters. But for much of his life, he's also been known as a computer pioneer. In the early 1990s, he was among the first to see the profit potential in something that folks used to call the information superhighway, known to us today, of course, as the internet.

"For many years, they've been the ultimate power couple—one of the world's richest men and one of the world's most beautiful women. A captain of industry turned philanthropist, and a supermodel turned Senator from California, then Vice President, then President of the United States."

A photo of a young Pierre Michaud and Susan Hopkins hand-in-hand on a beach somewhere appeared on the screen, then faded into a newer one of the couple standing on a stage with their two young daughters, and waving to an audience.

Then the picture slowly faded to black.

"A series of photographs were leaked today that many people are going to find simply shocking. They appear to show Pierre Michaud lounging on a secluded pool deck with a much younger man. The two men are in various stages of undress, appear to caress each other at times, and to rub tanning oil or perhaps sunblock on each other's bodies."

The young woman stared at the TV screen. A feeling began to well up inside of her. She wanted to scream at it. She wanted it to make it stop. She wanted to break it with a rock before it could say another word.

It had been too much. These last months were just... too much to deal with. The President assassinated, the White House destroyed, all the dead people.

Now this.

The TV scrolled slowly, lovingly, through the photos of the two men. The President's husband was clearly visible, thin with dark graying hair, and wearing French-style Speedo briefs. The younger man was blond, with a muscular body. His face was blurred to block his identity. Meanwhile, in the upper left-hand corner was a portrait of a smiling Pierre Michaud, so viewers could have no doubt that they had the right man.

"In this next group of photos, if there was any doubt left about the nature of the relationship, you will see the two men kissing passionately."

161

The young woman turned away from the TV. She covered her ears with her hands to block out the eagerness of the newscaster's voice. On the bench across from her, her youngest daughter suddenly smiled. Mommy was playing a game!

The girl covered her ears, too.

CHAPTER TWENTY FIVE

8:21 a.m.
United States Naval Observatory – Washington, DC

"Oh no," Susan said.

Kat Lopez nodded solemnly. "Yes. Susan, I'm so sorry. It just started to hit the TV stations about ten minutes ago, but it's already everywhere. I thought you should know."

"Okay, thank you. Please give me some time."

"Okay, Susan."

Susan watched Kat walk through the open door of the study. A Secret Service man loomed there, three feet inside the door. Susan looked at him.

"Alone, please. With the door shut."

The officer nodded silently, went out, and pulled the door closed behind him. For a moment, she simply stood quietly in the center of the room. Her study. Her beautiful sanctuary. She stood just a few feet from the little sitting area with its deep high-backed chairs, its coffee table, and its circular rug with the Seal of the President. She remembered how when she was Vice President, she would sometimes sit in one of those chairs in the late afternoon and curl up with a good book. It was a nice memory. She couldn't remember the last time she had even tried to read a book. There was no time. There was no space in her mind for it.

She looked around. The rug was the only thing inside this room that had changed since then. Maybe it was the rug's fault. It had brought in all the toxic faults of the world. All the hate, all the envy, all the greed for power. The drumbeat for war. The death and destruction. Now it had brought an attack upon her family, the people she loved, the man she had loved almost her entire adult life.

The rug! The rug had invited these ills in here like a demon being invited into a victim's soul. It would take an exorcism to get them out again.

It was too late, she realized. In the old days, when an image crisis arose, one of the first people President Thomas Hayes would call (long before he called Susan, if he ever did) was Brent Staples. Brent Staples would set his spin-meisters to work, changing the narrative, turning it back on whoever launched the attack. Brent

Staples would not only save and protect us, he would smite our enemies.

But Brent Staples had done this to her. That's what the meeting this morning had been about. Dutch Evans. Bill Ackland. Michael Parowski. No, forget about Michael. He was their tool, their puppet. They were installing him to replace her. The old guard of the party was yanking her off the stage.

She could see the whole thing now very clearly. An embarrassment like this would be hard to come back from. Along with the sinking poll numbers, the terrorist attacks, and the criticism about the delays in appointing her cabinet... She looked ineffectual, like someone in over her head.

Now her husband had been caught... doing what? Cheating on her, she supposed. With a man. She shook her head and almost laughed. How could she explain to people that those were their judgments, not hers? She didn't care who Pierre slept with. She didn't come from that world. Good Lord, she had been on her own at the age of fifteen, in the fashion industry in Paris, and in New York, and Milan.

A man, who was married to a woman, slept with another man? In the world of fashion designers and models, and the various celebrities who were never far away, that was a boring Wednesday afternoon.

She sighed. She might as well inspect the damage.

She picked up the remote and clicked on the TV mounted on the far wall. She flicked through to CNN. She did not turn up the sound. There was a photo, clearly of Pierre, on the pool deck at the Malibu house, with a young blond guy. The guy was probably early to mid-twenties. Strong-looking, muscular, self-assured. Not a skinny twink trying to present himself as under-aged. That was a small piece of good news.

She flipped over to Fox News. A red-faced male newscaster was jabbing his index finger at the camera, spouting some vitriol. Superimposed behind him was a photo of Pierre and the blond again, a different shot from the one from CNN. There must be a whole series of them. From the angle, she guessed the photos were taken from a helicopter, using a high-powered telephoto lens. Or maybe they used a drone. She supposed that was possible nowadays.

Behind her, the door to her private quarters opened. She turned, and Pierre walked in. He wore a blue dress shirt and slacks.

His feet were bare on the polished wood of the study. His eyes were wide. His mouth was slack. He looked like a man in shock.

"Oh God, babe," he said. "I'm so sorry."

Susan shook her head. "It's okay. It was bound to happen sooner or later."

"How bad is it?" he said.

"Hard to say right now. It looks pretty bad, but I don't know. Who is he?"

Pierre's dark face was flushed red.

"Pierre. It's all going to come out. We need to know if he's solid."

Pierre shrugged. "It's Brian. I've told you about him. He's my personal trainer. I've had him with me, what, three years? He's a good kid. Smart. Knows everything about fitness and eating right. About a year ago... I don't know. One thing led to another. It was over before it started. I didn't even know he was gay, to be honest with you. He still works for me to this day."

"So this all happened a year ago?"

"Sure. A year ago, maybe more. You were Vice President. The world was a simpler place then. You were traveling all the time. I was busy. We had weekly check-ins over the phone. I had no reason to believe you were going to become President."

"How old is he?" Susan said.

"I'm not sure. Maybe twenty-nine, maybe thirty-one. In there somewhere. He looks younger than he is. He's a grown man, if that's what you mean."

Susan looked at Pierre. It seemed almost that she was looking through him, back in the past, to the early times she spent with him. She had already done *Vogue, Cosmo, Mademoiselle, Victoria's Secret,* even the *Sports Illustrated* swimsuit issue. But she was starting to age out. She could feel it. The covers had stopped coming. She was twenty-four.

Then she met Pierre. He was twenty-nine, and his start-up company's initial public offering had just turned him into an instant billionaire. He had grown up in San Francisco, but his family was from France. He was beautiful, with a skinny body and big brown eyes. He looked like a deer in the headlights. His dark hair always flopped down in front of his face. He was hiding in there. It was unbearably cute.

She had made a lot of money in her career, several million dollars. Financially, she had been very, very comfortable. But suddenly money was no object at all. They traveled the world together. Paris, Madrid, Hong Kong, London… they always stayed in five-star hotels, and always in the most expensive suite. Astonishing views became the backdrop to her life, even more so than before. They married, and they had children, wonderful twin girls. Then the years began to pass, and slowly they grew apart.

Susan became bored. She looked for something to do. She got into politics. Eventually, she ran for United States Senator from California. After she won, she spent much of her time in Washington, sometimes with the girls, sometimes not. Pierre managed his businesses, and increasingly, his charitable efforts in the Third World. Sometimes they didn't see each other for months.

About seven years ago, Pierre called her late one night and confessed something she supposed she already knew. He was gay, and he was in a relationship.

They stayed married anyway. It was mostly for the girls, but for other reasons as well. For one thing, they were best friends. For another, it was better for both of them if the world thought they were still a couple. They cut a media-friendly image together. And it was comfortable.

The truth was, Pierre was the deep relationship of her life. She loved him totally. What was wrong with that? He was her partner. And she was his. He was a wonderful father. He was caring. He was in touch with his emotions. He was probably the smartest man she had ever met. There was nothing about their relationship that concerned her.

His boyfriends came and went. He was discreet about it, and apparently they were too. She never even knew about them.

She sighed again.

This was one of those secrets the American people were never supposed to uncover. This wasn't Europe, where people were more relaxed about sexuality, and about relationships. Americans, for all their many good points, just didn't understand this sort of thing.

"Should you call this media guy, Brett… or Brent?"

Susan shook her head. "He did this. He and Mike Parowski and the party elders. They're trying to take me out."

"Oh, no."

She looked into Pierre's eyes now. All the way in there.

"Yeah. It's true. They basically warned me this morning."

Pierre just stared at her for a long moment.

"What do you want to do?"

She thought about it, but not for very long. She supposed she knew what she was planning from the first moment she heard of this.

"I want to fight," she said. "You, me, and the girls. If you're comfortable with that. Us against the world, if need be."

Pierre smiled. "I have the best public relations people on Earth. Maybe even better than your man Brent."

Susan almost smiled herself.

They might take her out, but they weren't going to break her. She was going to go down swinging.

CHAPTER TWENTY SIX

10:17 a.m.
Over the Atlantic Ocean

Luke pulled down his window shade.

The Learjet went east, out over international waters, and then turned south. Eventually, just past Florida, it would turn west and head across the Gulf of Mexico to Guatemala, where it would stop and pick up fuel. It was a long, roundabout way to go, and it would add hours to an already long trip.

Luke looked at Trudy, who was still wearing the bizarre makeshift outfit that Swann had given her. Trudy had a tablet computer on her lap, and she was poring over data she had downloaded before they left Swann's.

Behind her, Swann lay curled in ball across two seats. He was fast asleep. Somewhere behind Swann, Ed Newsam was probably doing the same thing. Luke was the only one who slept last night.

"Aren't you tired?" Luke said.

She looked up from her tablet. "I'm exhausted."

"Why don't you sleep?"

She shook her head. "I can't. I was so wired inside that prison for so long, I just can't seem to let my guard down. I barely slept the whole time I was there. I'd doze off for twenty minutes, wake up with a start, then doze off again half an hour later. The past month has been a blur."

"Well," Luke said, "you're out of the country. You're a free woman."

"Am I?"

He shrugged. "Sure seems like it."

They had borrowed this plane, complete with two pilots and a snack bar, from an old acquaintance of his, a businessman who franchised sandwich shops, hundreds of them, but had run into trouble with the protection rackets. Luke had stopped into an Italian restaurant in Providence, Rhode Island, one day a few years ago, and cleared up the misunderstanding for him. He hadn't had any trouble since, and was always eager to show his appreciation.

"We took off from an unregulated private airstrip. We didn't file a flight plan with anyone. No one knows who is on this plane, and that includes the man who lent it to me. And beyond

168

Guatemala, no one knows where we're going, not even the pilots. I'd say you're about as home free as any jailbird I've ever met."

Trudy looked at Luke seriously. "Thank you for rescuing me, if that's what you're fishing for. I am very glad to be out of prison, even if it's only temporary."

"I'm not fishing for anything. Certainly not applause. And there's no reason why this has to be temporary."

"Luke, I'm a fugitive. I'm charged with conspiracy to assassinate the President of the United States, and about three hundred counts of murder. I have no access to money. I have no identification I can use. At this point, every police organization in the world probably has my picture, including all the big ones. I'm not like you. I can't survive in the wilderness somewhere until this all blows over. I've never been camping in my life. I like a big, soft, comfortable bed. I like fuzzy blankets. I like fancy restaurants. I'm not going to make it on the run. I will get cold, and hungry, and scared, and lonely."

Luke imagined what he would do if he were in her shoes. Disappear into the Canadian Rockies for a couple of years, he supposed. Build a hut deep in the woods and live off fish and deer and wild berries. Or go to Nepal, buy some forged ID, and become a Himalayan mountain guide. Anything, really. He could do anything.

She was right. That wasn't her. It was him.

"Okay," he said.

"I know why you broke me out," she said. "I know you want me to help you crack this case. That's fine. It's nice to be out of jail. It's beautiful. I appreciate these moments more than I've ever appreciated anything before. And I enjoy doing the work. But I know that in the long run, this is a little fantasy escape. I've got some very hard days, and some very tough decisions, ahead of me."

Luke thought of the conversation he'd had with Park Jae-kyu. This was the worst thing Park had ever known. That was bad. There could be some hard days ahead, but not for the reasons Trudy believed.

Luke gestured at the tablet. He might as well change the subject.

"What do you have there?"

She seemed happy enough to move on. She tapped the tablet. "I'm looking at the situation in North Korea."

Luke smiled. "How's it look?"

169

She didn't smile. "Dire. I'm looking, in particular, at the effects of UN Security Council Resolution 2270. These are sanctions the Security Council put in place a few years ago, after a couple of the North's nuclear test launches. There is a lot to these sanctions, but the worst of it is its effect on trade. The resolution bans the North from exporting minerals like gold, titanium, and vanadium, as well as coal. These are resources North Korea actually has in abundance, and before the sanctions started, they made up more than half of their exports, with coal alone accounting for nearly forty percent."

"What's the fallout?" Luke said.

She glanced down at her screen. "Starvation. That tends to be what happens when half a country's export revenue dries up overnight. The economy, such as it was, has collapsed. To their credit, they are trying to feed the children through school programs, but average adult calorie intake is estimated to have dropped by more than a third. Vitamin deficiencies are rampant. All of this was apparently intended to force them to the bargaining table, but it hasn't worked. They've doubled down on weapons testing instead."

"So they're getting desperate."

She nodded. "They're teetering on the verge of a famine. They just had one fifteen years ago that killed over a million people. People remember it. Incidents of unrest are the highest they've been in over a decade, and recall that this is a totalitarian police state designed to quash unrest before it happens. Our spy satellites are picking up evidence of public protests. That's unusual. Group gatherings not organized by the government are generally against the law, and are broken up almost instantly. If we're seeing them, that's really something. Things are so bad at the moment that the RAND Corporation now categorizes North Korea as a failing or eroding totalitarian system. That might seem like a good thing, but it isn't. They've got nukes, making a collapse very, very dangerous."

"And China?"

Trudy shook her head. "The Chinese are not helping them, beyond modest aid. The Chinese signed off on the Security Council resolution. What I am working on here is a theory that the Chinese are deliberately pushing the North Koreans into desperation. With no food and no international aid, the abundance of food and resources in the South has to look pretty appetizing to the North Koreans right about now.

"Meanwhile, the Chinese want us to allow them to build their little islands in the South China Sea, then they want to claim the entire area as Chinese territorial waters. If we get tied up in a war with the North Koreans, they probably hope we won't have the stomach to open a second front."

Luke thought back to that general in the Situation Room. He seemed to have plenty of stomach for it. He seemed like a guy who'd be disappointed if it somehow didn't happen. But that didn't necessarily mean Trudy's scenario about China was wrong. It might mean the Chinese were wrong in their assessment of American willingness to fight.

"A war on the Korean peninsula would be bad," Luke said.

Trudy nodded. "More than bad. An apocalypse. I have a breakdown of the total conventional military hardware they have lined up on the border, most of it targeting Seoul, but a lot of it targeting American bases and positions in the South. It's staggering. Want to hear it?"

Luke slid open his window shade again. Bright sunlight streamed in. He looked out. There was nothing but sky everywhere. They were high above a white cloudbank.

He shook his head. "Not really."

"Okay," Trudy said. "Suffice to say that it's large, and it's devastating. We would of course gain the upper hand within a day or two, and we could probably destroy their entire antiquated air force in a few hours. Most of it wouldn't even get off the ground. But here's the bad part."

Luke looked at Trudy again. He wasn't sure what the point of all this was. He didn't want to hear the bad part.

"The North Korean rocket corps still communicate by runners and couriers. They move under cover of darkness. It's very low-tech. What this means is they can deliver the order to commence firing in a way that's impossible for our intercept software to detect. An attack could start, and the first thing our people in South Korea would notice is thousands of incoming missiles, mortars, and artillery rounds."

An image flashed in Luke's mind of Li Quiangguo in a dusty warehouse, sitting quietly at a computer with no internet access, putting lists of cyber targets on CD-ROM. It was a low tech approach, with no way for a technologically superior opponent to intercept it.

He shook that thought away for the moment.

"That sounds like fun, Trudy," he said. "We'll be there in about twelve hours."

"Let's hope they delay the attack until we leave," she said.

CHAPTER TWENTY SEVEN

01:05 p.m.
United States Naval Observatory – Washington, DC

Kat Lopez felt stupid. She wasn't young anymore, but she felt young, and incompetent, and thrown into the deep end, way over her head.

"Thirty seconds, Susan," a male voice from the control booth said. "Watch for my light. When the light goes red, you are live."

Kat stood at the back of the small amphitheater in the New White House, watching the action unfold.

Susan and Pierre were up on the stage at the front, dressed to the nines. Susan wore a blue dress. Her hair was done in a coif on top of her head. Her makeup screamed Hollywood. She was glittering, she was beautiful. Her look was a radical departure from the deliberately dour, serious, conservative image the public relations handlers had been building for her these past months.

Pierre stood next to her in an expensive, dark blue three-piece suit. He looked somewhat presidential himself. On the other hand, he was standing next to Susan, which also made him look invisible.

The room itself was packed. It had at most a hundred seats. It had a gradual slope, upward from the front, as though it doubled as a movie theater. Every seat was taken. Every space along the back wall was taken. All of it was a fake.

At 9:30 this morning, a little more than an hour after the photos of Pierre first hit the airwaves, a TV producer had rolled up in a black limousine. He was a young guy, thin, with a crazy nest of black hair and a long goatee. Two young guys and a young woman climbed out of the limo with him. Clearly, they were not from politics.

"Michael Parowksi's access to this building has been rescinded," Susan told her five minutes later. "He left in a car with Dutch Evans this morning, but if he tries to come back here, he can't come in. His name popped up on a security watch list. I'm sure it's a computer glitch. We'll have to get it worked out before tomorrow. Okay?"

Kat looked into Susan's eyes and saw the lie there. A good liar was one thing Susan was not.

"Okay, Susan."

"Also, Dutch Evans himself. Brent Staples. Bill Ackland. Any of that crew who was here this morning. They're barred from the building."

Kat nodded. "What's going on?"

Susan smiled. "We're going to change the narrative. Or die trying."

Actors and actresses had begun appearing moments later, dressed in various styles, of varying ages, all of them carrying wardrobe satchels. They had access to the building, but not the new Vice President?

"How do we look?" Susan said now, from the stage. To Kat's eyes, she looked stunning. The two of them looked like a red carpet couple. Throughout the amphitheater, the actors and actresses had transformed themselves in something that looked very much like the Washington, DC, press corps.

"You both look beautiful," the voice from the booth said. It was the weird TV producer speaking. He had an informal style that was jarring in this environment. "Calm. Steady. At the helm. This is your world. The rest of us are just visiting. Ten seconds. Camelot, part two. Pedal to the metal. Own this moment."

Kat took a deep breath.

She was pulling for Susan, she really was. Susan had grown on her these past couple of months. She would almost say she… loved Susan.

The thing that Susan didn't know was Dutch Evans was behind Kat being hired here. She and Dutch went back a long way. She had dated him for more than a year after she arrived here in Washington. Yes, Dutch was married, so they weren't really "dating." It was just how you moved up in this town. Kat knew it instinctively when she hit the ground here. And move up was what she had done. She and Dutch hadn't been together in a long time, but he still took care of her, and she took care of him.

Kat had been dropped in here as a spy. That was the painful truth. And Kat didn't want it to be the truth anymore. What Dutch and Brent did today was beyond the pale. It was ugly, it was unfair, it was…

"Five seconds," the producer's voice said. "Good luck, kids."

There was the slightest pause.

Near the podium, Susan and Pierre whispered some last words to each other.

A new voice came on. "We are live in four… three…"

174

Susan smiled. For a split second, the smile looked sickly, like death itself. Then it changed. Then it was gone altogether.

"Two…"

"Calm," the producer said. "Rock solid. Like gods."

The look on Susan's face became a look of authority.

"One."

Susan stepped up to the podium. Now her eyes were somehow both stern and soft. As she had been her entire life, she was the most beautiful woman in the room. But there was more to it. She wasn't just beautiful. She was substantial. There was a weight to her that Kat didn't remember her having when she was Vice President.

And Kat realized: Susan had grown and matured. She really had guided this country when it was at its most vulnerable. She really had stood up to terrorists. She really had given the American people something to believe in. She was a leader.

Kat hated Dutch in that moment. *Hated him.* He was a string-puller and a manipulator and a behind-the-scenes wheeler-dealer. She knew that about him. But what did he think he was doing this time? He would destroy two people's lives, and add more turmoil to the country, because he felt he couldn't control Susan? Because he wanted to install Michael Parowski instead? How dare he do that? Dutch wasn't the king maker, and he wasn't the king.

Susan was surrounded by bulletproof glass panels. Four Secret Service agents stood on the stage with her. The crowd of fake reporters, or whatever they were supposed to be, cheered and clapped for her.

"My fellow Americans, you already know the story," Susan said, utterly without preamble.

"You already know what's going on here."

A few people in the crowd murmured their assent.

"You know what happened this morning, and why it happened."

"Yes, we do!" someone shouted.

"I was attacked," Susan said. "They attacked me, by attacking my husband, Pierre. Now, until a moment ago, I was planning to come up here and defend Pierre. I was going to tell you that Pierre Michaud, through his technology businesses, has done more for this country, and for our shared future, than the next hundred people combined.

"I was going to tell you that this man"—she pointed an arm back toward Pierre, who stood behind her and to the right—"employs more than a hundred thousand people in the United States alone. And I was going to tell you that he has contributed more than a billion dollars to clean water, basic healthcare, and peace initiatives in the Third World. Three million people, mostly women and their children, have benefited from his work."

The crowd continued to clap and cheer. They didn't go crazy for Pierre, they just gave him long, sustained applause. You could feel the meaning of it. They respected him. He had done a lot for people. It was true.

"But you know what?" Susan said. "I'm not going to tell you any of that."

Now a ripple of laughter went through the room. She wasn't going to tell them what she had already told them.

"Pierre doesn't need me to defend him. You know who he is, and what he's done."

She paused now, waiting until she had quiet.

"This is what I am going to tell you. They attacked me, and they attacked Pierre, because they want you to judge us. And they want you to judge us because they want to weaken this country and destroy our resolve at a difficult time. They want us to be fractured and in disarray. They want us to lose faith."

Now a murmur of anger seemed to rise in the room. Susan raised a hand to quell it.

"But we're not going to lose faith. We're going to stand together, despite our differences. Listen, if your neighbor has a different view on abortion, gay marriage, stem cell research, any of those things, you are still both Americans. Neither one of you is more patriotic than the other. Neither loves their country any more than the other one. Differences of opinion don't mean that we can't stand together.

"And I want to tell you this. Together, you and I will succeed in building a better country, and a better world, through understanding and love. And what is love? It's acceptance. It's commitment. It's allowing a person to grow and change. That's what real love amounts to—letting a person be what he really is.

"I believe that this is a country where we accept each other, and we love each other. I met Pierre more than twenty years ago. He is among the greatest men I have ever met. He is a wonderful father to our children. He is smart, he works hard, he does the right thing. He is my best friend in this world. I love him more than I have ever loved another person. And he happens to be gay. I don't have a problem with that, and I don't see why you should."

The crowd erupted into cheers.

Susan pointed at someone in the audience. "Do you have a problem with it?"

The person shook their head.

Susan picked another one. "Do you?... Do you?"

Now Susan shook her head. "Of course you don't. You know that we need to live together, and we need to work together, to continue to make this the greatest country on Earth. Is it any of my business what you do in the privacy of your home, if you're not hurting anyone?"

The crowd gave her a resounding "NO!"

Kat smiled. She had no idea how this little dog-and-pony show was going to play in the so-called flyover territory, the middle of the country where people tended to more conservative, but it was sure to be a winner on the coasts.

"America is more than just a country," Susan said. "It's an idea. It's a promise."

The crowd clapped and cheered at each new applause line, and now Kat found herself clapping along.

"And the promise is if I'm a good person, if I work hard, there's going to be a place for me."

Kat, almost swept up in the enthusiasm that she herself knew was manufactured, could see how clever the move was. Don't deny what's undeniable. Don't defend what isn't to be defended. Appeal to their better angels instead. Remind them that they loved you in the past, and make them love you again.

She was asking the American people to accept her arrangement with Pierre. She was asking millions of people to step outside their comfort zone for her. It was bold, it was daring, and it was strange. It just might work.

CHAPTER TWENTY EIGHT

2:01 a.m. Indochina Time, August 18 (3:01 p.m. Eastern Time, August 17)
South China Sea

"We've got problems."

The submarine lurked a hundred feet below the surface.

It was the USS *Lewiston*, a Los Angeles class fast-attack sub, moving alone, deep inside the South China Sea. Its captain, Commander Patrick Vitale, stood in the close confines of the control room. He was listening to his situation deteriorate.

He had been awakened only five minutes before by the Messenger of the Watch, a young kid whose name he hadn't caught yet. They had been stalking a Chinese destroyer for the better part of a day, cruising silently in its wake. The wake, or baffles, was the area right behind the ship—where the motion of the water confuses the ship's sonar.

In this case, maybe not enough.

Vitale looked at his Officer of the Watch, a man named Chipman. Chipman still carried scars on his face where he must have had severe acne as a teenager.

"What are we hearing, Chip?"

"We've picked up at least three ships in the vicinity. We've got the destroyer on our nose. Nothing's changed there. But in the past ten minutes, we've picked up two more."

"Bearing and distance?"

"Port side. We're listening, but we're running silent, so we can't ping them. The data we have is limited. We don't know their headings or distances. But they just appeared there, both at once."

"What are they?" Vitale said.

"At a guess? A battle cruiser and a sub. Which means a carrier probably isn't too far behind them."

Vitale felt his shoulders sag before he caught himself, and stood tall again. The men would pick up on the slightest body language change from him.

"Any chance they're friendlies?"

Chipman did a quick head shake. "No. We're on a limb out here, all by ourselves."

Vitale stood quietly for a moment, processing the information—or rather, the lack of information. No one in the control room said a word. Stalking that destroyer meant the *Lewiston* had to be as quiet as possible. And that meant they were using passive sonar, which gave them the bearings and sizes of nearby ships, but no idea of their heading or speed. They were blind down here, and hiding. And suddenly, it seemed like someone knew exactly where they were.

"I don't like it, Cap," Chipman said. "That's why I sent for you."

Vitale took a deep breath. The men sat at their stations, their backs to him, silent, waiting, the control arrays spread out in front of them. The scene took on an almost surreal tone. These men were hanging on his next words. Behind him, most of the crew were asleep in their berths. There were 134 men aboard this sub.

"Take us up to periscope depth," Vitale said.

"Captain?" Chipman said.

"You heard me. We need to see who's here."

"We'll be naked up there."

Vitale nodded. "I know it. But I have a hunch we're already naked."

Chipman nodded. "Quiet in Control," he said to the men in the room. "Helm, take us to periscope depth."

The control room was tense as the sub ascended. Vitale could feel it. The men were afraid. He wasn't immune to it himself. They thought they had been hunting that destroyer, but now it looked very possible she was leading them on the whole time. And her friends had just joined the party.

In a few moments, they reached periscope depth, about sixty feet from the surface. At this depth, they were vulnerable. Aircraft could spot them from the sky. Worse, they were about to become even more vulnerable. The Chinese had technology almost as sophisticated as the United States these days. Once the periscope broke the surface, the *Lewiston* was going to become visible on radar. If they wanted to remain hidden, the periscope could only stay up there for a few second.

Well, hell.

"Up periscope," Vitale said. "We'll make it quick."

After a few minutes, the periscope reached the service.

Then:

"Large ship off port. Large ship dead ahead."

And a few seconds later, "Radio transmission coming in."

Vitale gritted his teeth. He knew it. The periscope had a radio antenna on top of it, and the bad guys were waiting for it to appear.

"What's the transmission?"

There was a delay while the radio man listened to his headset.

"Submarine, this is the Chinese Navy. We have you targeted and locked on. Surface and prepare for boarding."

CHAPTER TWENTY NINE

10:24 a.m. August 17 (4:24 p.m., Eastern Daylight Time, August 17)
Over the Pacific Ocean

It was crazy going all this way just to interrogate a prisoner.

Luke stared out the window at the vastness of blue ocean around them. They'd been flying for hours, and they had hours more to go. It occurred to him that in Korea, it was already August 18. August 18 was zero hour.

He looked across the aisle from him. Trudy had been asleep for a long while, curled into a ball. Now she was awake again, looking out her window. He glanced in the back. Ed and Swann were both dozing.

"Why do you suppose," he said, "the Koreans didn't tell us they had this prisoner?"

Trudy shrugged. "A lot of reasons. They've only had the guy a day. The North Koreans are always crying wolf, like you said before. There's always a big attack coming, which never comes. And the South Koreans are trying to get out of our shadow a little bit. They had that rape case two years ago, and my understanding was that intel sharing dropped away to nothing after that. It's barely come back since."

Luke remembered the case. Three drunk Marines had raped an eleven-year-old girl while on leave from their base. Months of massive protests had followed the case. The South Koreans demanded the soldiers be turned over to the local authorities.

Instead, the Americans sent them home to be tried in a military court. They were all doing twenty years in Leavenworth. That didn't satisfy the South Koreans, who probably wanted to drop the soldiers into hell with the worst, most violent criminals their society had to offer.

He and Trudy lapsed into silence. The plane bounced over some turbulence. For a couple of seconds, the ride felt like a rollercoaster. Luke barely noticed it. He stared at Trudy for a long minute. She was just gazing out that window, her eyes far away.

"A lot of water out there," Luke said.

She nodded. "Yes."

"It's a big world."

She sighed, her entire chest heaving. She turned to him. "I need to disappear."

He nodded. "For a little while, probably."

"Will you help me? I'm going to need a new identity. A place where I can live, and hold a job. I need a whole new life."

"I'll help you. I know a lot about that kind of thing."

She took another deep breath. Her voice shook. "I may never see my parents or my brother again."

Luke almost went to her. But he didn't. He didn't know why he held back, except that what was between them didn't seem to be part of this team. Ed and Swann were not involved, and he didn't want to put them in the middle of it.

"That's not how these things go, Trudy."

"Okay," she said. "So tell me how they go."

He thought for a minute about the people he had known who were in hiding. He thought about the bittersweet meetings they would have with their loved ones, in out of the way places, under false names, under cover of darkness. He'd like to tell her something positive, so…

"You will see your family. At first, maybe not for a year. And never as often as you like. But once you learn the ropes, you can see them from time to time. They can travel outside the United States. We have Swann make sure they're not being monitored. They're eating in a café in Rome one day. A woman with blonde hair and sunglasses is passing by on the street and sits with them at their table. They have a nice long meal, maybe drinks. Maybe it lasts an hour. Then the woman gets up and walks away."

Trudy shook her head. "Gee, Stone, that sounds romantic."

"It's better than the alternative, which, by the way, is always available to you."

"Prison?" she said.

Luke shrugged. "They can visit you every week."

She almost laughed. "I don't know which would be worse. Never seeing them, or seeing them all the time."

CHAPTER THIRTY

05:45 p.m.
United States Naval Observatory – Washington, DC

"How are we doing?" Susan said.

She and Pierre sat in the study together, holding hands. They hadn't watched any of the TV coverage of the simulated news conference they had given earlier. Pierre was willing to turn it on, but Susan couldn't bear it.

Kat stood in front of them, wielding her tablet. She had just come into the room.

Kat nodded. "Things look good. Our early telephone polling suggests the response has been very favorable."

"Give us the highlights," Susan said.

"Well, overall, the speech has a seventy-one percent favorability rating, with just sixteen percent unfavorable, and thirteen percent undecided. Your physical appearance had far and away the highest rating."

"We asked questions about my physical appearance?" Susan said.

Kat nodded. "The wisdom nowadays is that appearance sways opinion. We've always known it, since Kennedy beat Nixon in that first televised debate. Now we measure it. People like to look at beautiful people. And they like beautiful people more than they like unattractive people. Human nature, I guess."

"So hit me with it," Susan said.

"Okay. A full ninety-three percent of respondents said your appearance was attractive or very attractive. Five percent couldn't decide, probably people with vision impairments. And then, you know, a handful of haters rated you unattractive or very unattractive."

"I'm not sure what show they were watching," Pierre said.

"I'm not, either," Kat said. "But the strength of that rating seems to have driven the results in other areas. In terms of the content of the speech, sixty-eight percent of those polled said they agreed with the message of your speech, twenty-one percent disagreed, and eleven percent were undecided. Our pollsters tell me those are much higher positives than they would have expected."

"A lot of Americans still don't like gay people," Pierre said.

"That's right," Kat said. "Even with the attractiveness factor, we would expect to see agreement with the content at below fifty percent, neck and neck with disagreement, and with a significant number of people on the fence. One caveat is that the pollsters feel that the surprising positive effect will wear off with time."

"What else?" Susan said.

"Your overall favorability rating is back over fifty percent for the first time in a month, and the pollsters suggest that during the next twenty-four hours, it may climb over sixty percent. That's not bad. The key will be to sustain it. These numbers tend to peak within a few days after the event, then gradually drift downward again. But the good news is the leak seems to have backfired."

"What's the response on TV?" Susan said.

"Also somewhat surprising. Martin Binkle has been on FOX for the past half hour, defending you. He's taking the libertarian tack that no one has the right to infringe on the personal liberties of another. You're the President, but you also have a private life, and you're entitled to it. Amazingly, much of the conservative chatter-sphere is falling into line behind him."

Susan almost laughed. Martin Binkle was on television defending her. Would wonders never cease? All she had asked was for positive coverage on his websites. Now he was going the extra mile. It was as if the world had been turned inside out and stood on its head.

"What else?"

"Well, Michael Parowski's office has requested a sit-down between you and Michael. He tried to come back here earlier this afternoon, but was stopped at the gatehouse. He hasn't been able to get on the grounds."

Susan shrugged. "Michael is done. I'm happy to meet with him, but not today. In the meantime, I want to relaunch the search for Vice President. And I mean from scratch."

Kat looked up from her tablet. Susan watched her closely. Was she the slightest bit disappointed that Michael wasn't coming on board?

Susan went on: "We didn't look terribly hard at women last time, supposedly because it would overload the ticket. But you know what? We had male Presidents and Vice Presidents for two hundred years, and nobody ever worried about that overload."

Kat nodded, suppressed a slight smile. "Okay, Susan, I'll have a broad list of possibles in twenty-four hours, with complete vitaes, and vetted for skeletons and security risks."

Susan nodded. "Thank you. That sounds good."

Just then, the door opened and a Secret Serviceman let Kurt Kimball in. Kurt looked like he still hadn't gotten any sleep. His shirt, normally tight to his broad chest, was rumpled and saggy. The beginnings of a beard were growing along the bottom of his face. It was startling to see hair growing anywhere on that cue ball head of his. The tiny slip in discipline gave Susan the impression of a man in the grips of a sudden and unexpected downward slide.

"We just got word from the Pentagon," he said, without any introduction. "Maybe ninety minutes ago, the Chinese captured one of our submarines in the South China Sea. That carrier strike force we have en route? They're demanding that we turn it around."

* * *

"General, what in God's name was that submarine doing there?"

The Situation Room was packed, as usual. Susan sat in her customary spot, at one head of the conference table. Big Haley Lawrence, her incoming Defense Secretary, sat on her right hand, and Kat Lopez hovered behind her. At the far end of the table, Kurt Kimball stood. Behind him was a large flat-screen, with a map of the South China Sea.

General Walters looked just a bit uncomfortable. Haley Lawrence had asked the question, and Walters's normal condescending calm was starting to show cracks. Susan noted this, but didn't feel strongly about it either way. Maybe Michael Parowski was right—maybe the general had been bowling her over a little bit. And maybe it was a gender thing.

"Haley," General Walters said, deliberately not calling him by his title. "You're new, so let me give you a little bit of background. We have an extensive naval surveillance program throughout the world. Submarines track the ships of other countries as part of that program. We do it to the Chinese and the Russians. We do it to the Iranians. We do it to the Indians. Hell, we even do it to the French and the Israelis."

"I'm aware of the surveillance program, General. And I've spent much of the past twenty-four hours reading classified intelligence reports. Kurt, where was that sub intercepted?"

At the end of the table, Kurt indicated a spot on the map. A red pin appeared between a large island shaded the color of China, and the country of Vietnam. The region was a kidney-shaped gulf, almost entirely surrounded by Chinese landmass.

"About thirty nautical miles west-northwest of Hainan Island, and a hundred miles east of Halong Bay. Eighteen miles outside of what we would call Chinese territorial waters, but a very deep penetration inside what the Chinese would consider their sphere of influence."

"And the name and class of the sub?" Lawrence said.

"USS *Lewiston*," Kurt said. "Los Angeles class nuclear sub, what we used to call a hunter-killer. Capable of running silently. Armed with torpedoes and surface to air missiles."

Haley Lawrence addressed the general again. "So the *Lewiston*, a hunter-killer sub, was trailing a Chinese destroyer, very close to the Chinese mainland. Would you call that a provocation, General?"

General Walters cleared his throat. Even his aides were starting to look worried.

"I would call it part of routine surveillance activities."

Haley lifted a sheaf of paperwork from the table in front of him. "Yet nowhere in this stack of intelligence reports is there any mention of the USS *Lewiston*, its whereabouts, or its activities."

"Uh, the *Lewiston*'s activities are top secret," Walters said.

"These are classified reports, General. And I am the Secretary of Defense."

"I beg your pardon, sir. You are not the Secretary of Defense. The Secretary of Defense is the title of a person who has been confirmed by a vote in the United States Senate. You are the current nominee for Secretary of Defense."

Haley Lawrence smiled. He seemed almost ready to laugh. "General," he said, "do you suppose there's any doubt that I will be confirmed by a majority vote in a Senate dominated by Republicans? And after I am confirmed, do you suppose I'll have forgotten your reluctance to bring me up to speed as quickly as possible?"

The general shrugged. It was a strangely ineffectual gesture, coming from a member of the Joint Chiefs of Staff. "Top secret activities are a higher clearance level than classified."

"So let me get this straight," Haley said, changing the subject. "We have submarine activities that are simultaneously top secret *and* routine, and those activities aren't included in briefings provided to the Secretary of Defense?"

Susan watched as General Walters searched for an answer that made any logical sense. None seemed forthcoming. She had to admit she was enjoying this show the tiniest amount. She should have hired Haley a month ago.

"You're not currently the Secretary of Defense," the general said finally. "You're a professor at Stanford University. We don't have top secret clearances for college professors."

Haley Lawrence shook his large head. He seemed to dismiss the general for the time being. "Kurt, if you don't mind, where is that naval strike force?"

A new red pin appeared on the map. Kurt indicated it. "Our lead strike force is now located about a hundred nautical miles northeast of the Paracel Islands. We have a second strike force just entering the region. Our latest data has them passing between Taiwan and the Philippines as we speak."

"Too far from the *Lewiston* to help them?" Haley said.

"Nowhere near the *Lewiston*," Kurt said. "As a practical matter, the *Lewiston* and its men are well out of our reach. Our intelligence suggests most of the men have already been taken aboard a Chinese tanker, leaving just a skeleton crew to pilot the *Lewiston*. We believe the *Lewiston* will be escorted to the Chinese harbor of Beihai."

"Where the Chinese will pull it apart and reverse-engineer it," Haley said.

Kurt seemed to almost cringe. "Los Angeles class subs have been in use for quite some time. It's not our most advanced system. That said, you never want technology to fall intact into the hands of your enemies."

Susan stepped in. She was beginning to see how she could work with Haley. He was detail-oriented to an extreme. She was a big picture person. His job was to pick apart the details. Hers was to get a clear sense of what the implications were.

"Kurt, what is your assessment of the overall situation?" she said.

"Well, it's not ideal. Technically, even though its actions could be considered provocative, the *Lewiston* was in international waters, and had every right to be there. The strike force that the Chinese want us to turn around is clearly in international waters. If the Chinese are able to blackmail us into leaving the South China Sea, it sets a bad precedent. Nearly half the shipping trade in the world passes through there at some point in its journey, so it's critically important that the South China Sea not become a Chinese

187

lake. As for the sub, the *Lewiston*'s men are protected by numerous treaties, to which China is a signatory. They must be treated as guests, and not as prisoners. We can insist on their release, and we will be in the right. It's simply illegal for China to use them as a bargaining chip, or to imply that any harm might come to them."

"So what do you suggest we do with that strike force?" Susan said.

"I think it's clear," Kurt said. "The strike force continues deeper into the South China Sea, as allowed under international law. If the force comes under fire, they destroy any and all attackers. If *Lewiston* crew members are harmed in any way, it's a clear act of aggression by China, and grounds for a full-scale military intervention."

Susan took a deep breath. They were inching closer and closer to war.

"Haley?" she said.

He nodded. "That sounds about right. I would add that we increase exercises by bomber and fighter squadrons in that region, filing flight paths ahead of time with the Chinese, so there are no surprise interactions. We want to show them that we're the biggest kid on the block."

"General?"

General Walters was playing with a pen on the table in front of him. He looked up and stared directly at Susan. His eyes were so bloodshot that they seemed to glow red. No one was getting any sleep, Susan realized, and that was becoming a problem. Executive function eroded with lack of sleep.

Walters shook his head. "I say we start bombing Chinese container ships."

CHAPTER THIRTY ONE

11:02 a.m. Korea Time, August 18 (10:02 p.m. Eastern Daylight Time, August 17)
Headquarters of the National Intelligence Service – Seoul, South Korea

The headquarters, in a suburb south of the city proper, were sprawling. The place probably didn't employ as many people as the Pentagon, but the grounds seemed larger. Buildings fanned out from the central building like spokes on a wheel.

They were met at the airstrip and brought by limousine to the main building. Luke, Ed, and Swann were all still dressed like they were on summer vacation. Trudy was dressed in Swann's cast-off clothing—she looked like something out of a story about a young homeless waif who steals her clothes from people's backyard clotheslines.

None of them spoke. Although they had all dozed on and off, the twelve-hour flight would take the vinegar out of anyone.

A young woman in a blue military uniform walked them down several gleaming corridors to a security checkpoint. A man in a pin-striped suit stood at the checkpoint with four guards. He had salt and pepper hair, and was just a touch overweight. Paunchy, even. Nevertheless, he was very handsome, in a middle-aged sort of way.

He was also very short.

His sharp eyes and stern face followed Luke's movements the whole way down the hall. He didn't smile.

Luke watched him as well.

"Stone?" the man said.

"Park?"

The man shook his head. "Stone, what are you wearing?"

Luke looked down at his own cut-off shorts, T-shirt, and sneakers. "You know?" he said. "I was thinking I might go to the beach while I was here."

Park smiled. He faced Luke. It had been a long, long time.

Suddenly, Park put his hands across his stomach, left hand over the right. He bent his knees and slowly dropped to the floor. He put his hands on the ground in front of him and crossed them. In the same movement, he crossed his feet and then touched his forehead to his hands. It was the *keun jeol*, the so-called "big bow,"

189

the sign of utmost respect and reverence. Park held the bow way too long.

They stood in the hallway of the NIS headquarters, this man prostrated before Luke. Luke glanced around. Little knots of people here and there watched them.

Get up, Park, he wanted to say. But didn't.

When Park stood again, Luke turned to his team. "This is Park Jae-kyu. I don't know if you can tell, but we used to know each other.

"Park, this is Trudy Wellington, my science and intelligence officer. This is Mark Swann, information systems. And the big man is Ed Newsam, weapons and tactics. These people are the best in the business."

Park did a normal bow from the waist to each of them in turn. Afterwards, he looked them over. He sucked his teeth and almost smiled again.

"My secretary will take your sizes and order you guys some clothes."

* * *

They rode an elevator deep into the bowels of the building. A hallway light flashed into the chamber as they passed each floor.

"This man is considered our most important prisoner. He has talked a lot about what he claims to believe is an impending attack, which we have no way of verifying at this time. However, his testimony confirms many things from inside the North which we have believed to be true for some time."

"For example?" Luke said.

"He says the economy has completely collapsed. He believes it's from sabotage, but of course we know the minimal extent of the sabotage possible. North Korea is a police state and a closed society. Neighbors spy on neighbors. Family turn in family. Strangers are watched closely by everyone. It's almost impossible to keep our sleepers alive long enough to commit acts of sabotage. Naturally, we know it's the UN Security Council sanctions, combined with the brittleness of the North's command economy, that has caused the collapse."

"What else?" Ed said.

Park went on. "A famine has begun. The villages are low on food. The elders, because they have already enjoyed long lives, are

190

being allowed to starve to death so that the children and young parents may eat. They are protecting the future, so to speak.

"Morale is low. The will of frontline troops to fight is nearly gone. Anger among the ordinary people is high, and growing all the time. The regime itself may be on the verge of collapse. They no longer have anything to lose."

The fast-moving elevator slowed to a stop.

"And that, my friends, is the problem."

The door opened.

"Let's go see our man."

* * *

They were deep underground.

They sat in an observation room, watching the man through a one-way mirror. Large speakers were mounted just above the glass. Six people were in the observation room— the four from Luke's team, Park, and a young woman who was simultaneous translator from Korean to English.

Through the window, the prisoner sat at a long wooden table. He wore a white smock. He didn't appear to have any clothes on underneath it.

He had probably just eaten a meal, since there was a tray with two empty plates in front of him on the table. He took a long gulp of what appeared to be water. He was leaning back, smoking a cigarette. There was a half-empty pack and a lighter on the table near his left hand. He seemed relaxed enough, maybe because he could smoke as much as he wanted.

"What's his name?" Trudy said.

"It doesn't matter," Park said, then caught himself. He was being too harsh. "When they come across from the North, we have to eye everything they say with skepticism. He may have given us his real name, he may not have. Almost everything he says is impossible to verify."

"Why is he the most important prisoner alive?" Luke said.

Park gestured at the window. "Listen."

Two men stood across the small room from the prisoner. They were sharp dressers, business suits, slicked back hair, expensive leather shoes. They looked more like young investment bankers than secret police.

One of the interrogators said something, too fast for Luke to understand.

191

"Tell me," the young translator said. "When will the North invade the South?"

The prisoner shrugged and said something.

"Tonight, tomorrow. I don't know. Very soon. I lost track of days in the wilderness. I don't remember. When the Great Leader attends the Arirang Festival, an aide will whisper in his ear—the bombing has begun. It has been planned that way, and it will happen exactly that way."

"And when the invasion comes, why won't the Americans respond?"

"I told you a hundred times," said the translator.

"Tell me again."

On the other side of the window, the prisoner paused and took a long drag of his cigarette. He coughed slightly.

"We have nuclear warheads ready to launch. San Francisco, Los Angeles, Seattle, and Portland will all be destroyed. Honolulu will be destroyed. Japan will be totally destroyed."

"You don't think the Americans can stop this?" the young sharpie in the suit said. "The Americans have missiles that can knock your warheads from the sky."

The prisoner shook his head. "No. They will be unable to launch. Their communications will not function. Their network systems will not function. They will be helpless to stop it. No communications, and in many places, no electricity. Their warheads will sit useless on the launch pads."

Luke was interested. "Ask him how this…"

Park raised a hand.

"How can this be?" the sharpie said.

The prisoner exhaled air. It was almost a laugh. Then he started speaking.

"The Americans have lied," the young translator said. "They have a…" Now the woman hesitated. She looked at the assembled Americans. "I have trouble with this concept. He says you have a control of death, or lever of death. It is something for the communications networks. It closes down all communications, and many of the power grids."

Park stared at the woman, evidently not pleased with her translating ability. He barked something at her in Korean.

Luke didn't understand what Park said. Luke's rudimentary Korean moved in slow motion. When Koreans talked among themselves, especially in anger, he could not catch the words. Inside

192

the interrogation room, the men were asking more questions. The observers were missing the interrogation now.

The translator stared at the floor in shame. Her face turned crimson.

"The direct translation is kill switch," she said. "I think this must be a slang term. He says the Americans have one. It is hidden, but the North Korean government hackers have located it. They can control it now."

"A kill switch?" Luke said. He looked at Swann. In fact, both Trudy and Ed were looking at Swann as well.

Swann eyes became very wide. He raised his hands and shook his head. Then he stared at the man inside the window with something like awe.

"We need to talk about this," he said. "Stop the interview."

Ten minutes later, Park had found them a conference room to use. He stood with them listening to their conversation, but not speaking. They were just down the hall from the observation room. The room was oval, with a rounded ceiling. That gave Luke the sense of it being hardened against bombing. Luke could sense the weight of the building above them. He had counted twenty-eight stories on their way down from the surface.

"It's impossible," Swann said.

"Impossible?" Luke said. "How so?"

"It just is."

"It's not impossible," Trudy said. "Egypt had one during the Arab Spring. When the protests became outright rebellion, the government killed the internet, network communications throughout the country, and half the power grid. It happened very quickly. It can be done."

"Trudy," Swann said, "with all respect due, do you have any idea how vast, how complex, and how advanced the information systems are in the United States compared to Egypt? The American internet is the most intricate machine ever built. The intricacy is what makes it robust. No one entity controls it. No one entity *can* control it. No one entity can pull the plug on it.

"Look, there are countless nodes in the system. There are nearly an infinite number of paths information flow can follow. Take thirty percent of it out, which is a tall order in itself, and within seconds, the data will reroute itself. End users will experience this as systems being down for a minute or two, and maybe a couple of vulnerable ones being down for a few hours. The

193

Egyptians could knock out their own communications all at once, sure. Their networks are less than one percent the size of ours."

"So that makes it impossible?" Luke said.

Swann paused. He stared at the table in front of him. His hands rested on the table, folded lightly. Luke watched him as he almost seemed to go into a trance. His eyes looked up and to the right. Several minutes passed.

"Not impossible," he announced at last. "Not easy, but not out of the question. It would take a lot of people working on it to develop it. I feel like something on that scale, it would be hard to keep it secret. And in addition to being able to shut down government networks, you could only build it with the compliance of at least a dozen major companies that control internet traffic."

Luke gently shook his head at that. Keeping secrets was what the government did. It was entirely possible that at an agency with a black budget, like the CIA or the Pentagon, there could be an entire department dedicated to this sort of thing. No one outside the department might know of its existence, including the people at the agency tasked with overseeing it. Outside the agency? No one would know about it at all.

"But if they managed it, it could shut down communications?" Luke said.

Swann did a sort of head shimmy, his head bouncing side to side at the top of his long neck. "If you could block network traffic, the rest is less complicated. Compared to that, cell phone systems are easy to take down. Power grids communicate internally, and with outside grids and large-scale users, by way of computer networks. So take out the information flow, and sure... you could theoretically take out cell communications, electricity systems, even weapons systems. You could lose communication with missile sites. Air traffic control would go haywire."

"Everything would go down?" Ed said.

Swann raised a finger. "No. You'll never take everything out. Land-line telephones would likely still work. You might have satellite communications using battery-operated, hand-held technology."

"A satellite phone?"

Swann nodded. "Possible. As long as the satellites were still up and functioning, and there's no reason they shouldn't be. Once they're in the sky, many of them are not dependent on Earth-based systems to maintain their orbits."

"What else?" Luke said.

Swann shrugged. "Hard to say. I mean, it's never been done before, so this is all speculation."

"Okay," Luke said. "I guess the thing to do is find out if the kill switch really exists, and if so, who has it, and how secure it is. We should probably call the President and tell her where we are."

Trudy looked stricken at the thought of calling the President. It would mean telling her where they were. Which meant giving Trudy up to be arrested again.

"Luke?" she said.

He raised a hand. "Trudy, this has to be done. I promise to protect you the best I can, okay? You just have to trust me."

Luke glanced at Swann again. "North Korean hackers? Penetrating American computer networks? Are these the cyber-terrorists?"

Swann shrugged. "I never would have guessed that. I would still bet that the Chinese are feeding them the code, or providing them with the hackers. When I picture North Korean information systems, I think of pneumatic tubes."

Luke and Swann stared at each other. Luke made no move to pick up the telephone. Calling the United States seemed like a dangerous move. By now, they must have figured out that he, Ed, and Swann were the ones who busted Trudy out of jail. Susan and her people couldn't be too happy about that. Luke had masterminded the breakout, thinking that the end game was they would pick up a piece of valuable intel, then trade it for Trudy's freedom.

But what was he really offering Susan? A North Korean defector who thought the world was about to end. A man who believed that North Korean hackers would take down not only American missile defense systems, but the entire internet. Luke could almost buy that the North Korean hackers opened a simple dam, or disrupted a subway system. But wipe out whole communications networks?

Come on.

"You probably want to hurry," Park said. They were the first words he had said in a while.

"Why's that?" Luke said.

"The prisoner says the attack will start when Kim Song-Il attends the Arirang Festival. Our intelligence reports suggest that's going to happen tonight."

CHAPTER THIRTY TWO

10:47 p.m.
The Atlantic Ocean, near the coast of Maryland

At night, the ocean changed.

The diver was among the best his country had ever trained. He had been below the sea hundreds of times. And night dives were his favorite.

He worked with a team of three others. Twenty minutes before, they had dropped into a vast sea of bioluminescence, a billion white and blue shining lights, sketching the line between black water and black sky. The boat they dropped from was disguised as a fishing trawler. Its rusty hull hid the fact that it was a scientific vessel, with sensitive detection equipment trained on the bottom of the ocean.

The four men used their weight belts to quickly sink to the bottom—this close to the shore, the water was only about forty feet deep. They waited until they were nearly halfway down before turning on their lamps. Then the pitch darkness was lit up, casting an eerie glow. A bull shark passed like a white ghost.

For the man, there was no sound but his own breathing, loud in his ears.

The man was proud of what he was about to do. He felt close to these men with him—they had trained as a unit for more than a year. And he felt close, in a different way, to the men in the other dive teams. They were brothers, united by patriotism and a feeling of pride in belonging to such an elite group. Ten groups of four—forty soldiers unequaled in the world.

Even so, there was also a melancholy feeling, knowing that a war was about to start, one his country could not win. He was not supposed to believe that, but he did. His people likely faced annihilation in the coming days, and he would never make it back in time to die with them.

He reached the soft sandy floor of the ocean. His flippers touched bottom, scaring an octopus. The octopus swam away, spraying a jet of black ink that the man lit up with his lamp. He smiled. How he would like to follow the octopus, but there was no time.

Now, all four men scanned the sea floor, looking for what they knew must be right here. They were at exactly the right coordinates. It took five minutes or longer, but eventually he found what he was looking for. He reached down with a gloved hand and swept sand away. Of course. Here it was. It was like a snake, laying in a few inches of sand, just beneath the surface. He pulled it up. It was a wire.

He almost laughed. This wire was no wider than a fat sausage. Inside of it were terabytes of data, the internet, rushing past, between the United States and Europe. There would be more just like this one. The wires lay on the sea floor, very much in the same place people had been laying electricity and telephone cables since the 1850s. Unprotected, unsecured, simply lying here.

Near him, one of his team had discovered another wire. There were several here, at a choke point near where they entered the United States, and before they spread out to cross the ocean toward different countries far away.

The man pulled a knife from his diving sheath. The knife itself had been invented for the role it was about to play. It was designed to cut easily through the many layers protecting the sensitive information passing through. There was the outer covering of rubberized plastic. There were several layers of insulation and steel mesh. There was a soft buffer to keep the steel away from the cables, and finally, deep in the heart of the sausage, were the internet cables themselves.

The sharp, serrated knife glimmered in the light of his headlamp.

With one deft movement, he cut deep into the wire. He was halfway in before he even tried to exert any force. He grunted, unleashing a storm of bubbles around him. He finished the job with the sawing motion of a man cutting a log.

He let the two halves drop to the sea bed, as above him, vast swaths of international communications suddenly went dead.

CHAPTER THIRTY THREE

11:15 p.m.
**The Situation Room, United States Naval Observatory –
Washington, DC**

Susan was ready to adjourn the meeting.

Really, she was ready for bed. It had been a long day, topping off a whole series of exhausting and wrenching days. There seemed to be no end to it on the horizon. She looked around the Situation Room. The faces of her staff were desultory, to say the least. Tired, tired people, reaching a place where they were no longer capable of making smart decisions.

That was when the first reports came in.

Kurt Kimball took a telephone call at the head of the room. An aide brought him the phone, and Kurt listened with a quizzical look on his face. After a short while, he hung up. He faced Susan across the table.

"That looked like good news," Susan said, sarcastically.

Kurt stared at her in a way she had never seen before. Kurt Kimball was a former elite college basketball player, a man who was built for contention and competition, a man who had been the Rock of Gibraltar during her entire early tenure as President. But now he looked utterly spent. He looked shell-shocked, the victim of a natural disaster.

"The internet and telephone connections to Europe have just gone dead."

"Where?" General Walters said. "From this building?"

Kurt shook his head. "No. From everywhere."

"What does everywhere mean?" Haley Lawrence said. Haley, just one day into the job, was the freshest face in the room.

Kurt shrugged, a jerky motion that suggested someone with Tourette Syndrome, rather than simple frustration. "Everywhere. The entire Eastern seaboard of the United States and Canada seems to have lost contact with all of Europe. Our people are in touch with the telecommunications companies. There are apparently work-arounds that will take some time to implement, rerouting traffic and calls through South America."

"What about the West Coast?"

"The West Coast is still functioning. But their contact with Europe is routed through Asia. The guess is that the undersea internet and phone wires on the Atlantic side have been cut. The wires tend to be more spread out the further out in the ocean you get. But closer to shore, there are apparently choke points that could potentially be hit by divers."

"How many divers would it take?" Haley Lawrence said.

Susan raised her hand. "Let's not worry about that for the minute. I'm sure there will be data available soon enough. Right now, let's make sure that any choke points like that on the Pacific side are being protected."

"Good point," Kurt said.

Suddenly Kat Lopez was at Susan's ear. She spoke very quietly.

"Susan, a call just came in. I think you probably want to take it."

Susan looked up at her Chief-of-Staff. "Who is it?"

"It's Luke Stone. Calling from Korea."

* * *

"Luke, what are you doing?"

Susan sat alone in her upstairs study. Pierre had come in a moment ago and kissed her good night. The night of their great victory on the domestic front was slipping away on the international front. She longed to just go to bed and lie with him.

The room was dim—yellow light came from one solitary desk lamp. Things were out of control, but she felt like she could fall asleep any second. Her head felt like it was stuffed with cotton. Her eyes wanted to close.

"Susan, I'm in South Korea, with my old team from the SRT."

"Yes, I heard."

"I broke Trudy Wellington out of jail."

Was this the confession hour? "I figured as much. I wish you wouldn't do things like that, Luke."

"I had no choice, Susan. Trudy is the best, and you wouldn't give her to me, so I had to take her."

Susan rubbed her eyes. "Okay. Is that what you're calling halfway around the world to tell me? That you committed multiple felonies while aiding and abetting the escape of a woman who is both a mass murderer and a traitor?"

"I want you to pardon her."

199

"Luke, I'm sure you know that's impossible. Please don't waste my time. We are teetering on the verge of war with China. They just seized one of our submarines in the South China Sea. I don't have a lot of extra energy for games right now. I was hoping you would participate in this situation; instead, you broke your old girlfriend out of jail and fled the country."

Susan sighed heavily. Maybe she was going too far, but she was beginning to wonder why she had even taken this call. Luke Stone had been an exceptional agent once upon a time, maybe the best there was, but he had drifted off into his own world. He had become a distraction at best, and at worst, a... what?

A blind alley. Yesterday, he thought a doomsday cult was behind the attacks. Then he engineered a prison break. Now he believed it was the North Koreans. Why couldn't he just accept what was plain as day to everyone else? It was China. After decades of gradually growing in power and prominence, the Chinese were ready to directly challenge the United States. War was coming.

There was a long pause over the line.

"We can talk about Trudy later," Stone said. "Please listen to me. I have evidence that the cyber attacks were not carried out by the Chinese, but by the North Koreans."

"Luke, please."

"There's an internet kill switch," Stone said. "It can take out American computer networks, telecommunication networks, even power grids. Someone... maybe the CIA, maybe the NSA, maybe the Pentagon, developed it. It was probably built by a skunk works—a totally compartmentalized group, secret, cut off from everything, paid for from a black budget that no one ever sees. You don't know about it, Congress doesn't know about it, it's very likely the bigwigs inside the agency where it was created don't even know about it."

"Luke, this is crazy talk," Susan said. "Why would someone do that?"

"Control," Stone said. "If there were an insurrection, you could just shut down communications nationwide. Or perhaps you could hold the country hostage yourself."

Now Susan was beginning to wonder about his sanity. "Luke, don't make me regret calling you in on this case. Listen, you interrogated Li Quiangguo. You found the list of targets. That was all very helpful, but this is going too far."

"Susan. The North Koreans have found the kill switch. They've taken control of it. Their plan is to cut off communications.

200

They're going to take down our missile response, then launch simultaneous attacks. Nuclear attacks on our West Coast and Japan, and a conventional attack on South Korea, followed by an invasion. They're desperate. The country is in a famine. They have nothing more to lose."

Susan let the words wash over her. It was impossible.

"We need to coordinate with China," Luke said. "The last thing either country wants is…"

The line went dead.

For a moment, Susan thought she had drifted off and come back during a pause in Stone's little soliloquy. She stared at the phone. "Stone?"

Nothing. Just blank air.

So what? It didn't mean anything. It was a call from 12,000 miles away, and it got cut off. That wasn't unusual. These things happened. She returned the phone receiver to its cradle.

She sat in the almost dark room for a long moment. She gazed into the shadows. Everything was vague, ethereal. It was time for bed.

The phone rang again. She picked it up before the second ring. "Stone?"

"Susan, it's Kurt Kimball. Now the phone and the internet lines between here and Asia are down. It's clear that we're under attack again."

"Okay," Susan said. "I'll be down in five minutes."

CHAPTER THIRTY FOUR

Timeless (1:45 a.m. Eastern Daylight Time, August 18)
Cyberspace

The bot was not alive. It did not think.

It had no history. It did not know who developed it, and it did not know how it came to be released. It did not know that for more than two years, it had been sitting dormant and sequestered on a secure network server in the sub-basement of a drab office building in suburban Virginia. It did not know the cost involved in creating itself—more than twenty million dollars. It did not know the building where it was housed was owned by the CIA, or that it was mostly empty now, and no one except low-paid security guards ever entered the place anymore.

The bot did not think of itself as bad or good. It did not wonder about the task it was performing—it simply did the task. The bot was an automated network process, nothing more than a small software program released into a network of computers. Its job was to crawl the network, find a way out, and move on to a new network. Once it entered a new network, or a new device, its job changed. It new job was to send a message back to its server.

The message: *Here I am.*

The bot would then receive a message in return.

Shut down that system.

The bot replicated itself, and doubled its own numbers, once every second.

One second after its release, there were two bots in existence.

Ten seconds after its release, there were more than a thousand.

Thirty seconds later, there were more than a billion.

And counting.

Within two minutes, the number of bots was beyond the comprehension of most people on Earth. A handful of scientists and mathematicians could understand the number, but the vast majority of the human race, if confronted by it, would simply stare at it, turn away in confusion and irritation, or say, "Infinity."

And still counting.

The bots swarmed through networks like red ants racing along tree limbs, replicating out of control. System after system, network

202

after network, device after device after device, were shut down by the ever-growing swarm of bots.

At a hospital less than a mile from the server where the bots originated, a floor nurse was entering patient record updates on the computer at the nursing station. She took a sip of coffee—it had gone lukewarm—and when she looked back at her screen, it was frozen. A few seconds later, she heard a familiar cry:

"Code Blue... Code Blue..." However, this time the emergency call was different. Every single life support machine in the twenty-person Intensive Care Unit had suddenly shut itself down.

Half a mile further on, a cell phone tower was swarmed by bots. It shut down within seconds, dropping more than seven hundred late-night calls as it did so.

Two miles down the road, a cable television transmitting station shut itself down. In an instant, more than a quarter million TV sets went dark.

Onward the bots went, network to network, swarming everything, shutting down everything.

And doubling in number every second.

CHAPTER THIRTY FIVE

3:16 p.m. Korea Time, August 18 (2:16 a.m. Eastern Daylight Time, August 18)
Headquarters of the National Intelligence Service – Seoul, South Korea

"Okay, kids, I'm up for grabs," Luke said. "What do we do?"

He had called Susan three more times. Then he tried his former house in the Virginia suburbs, hoping to reach the answering machine. Then he tried Ed Newsam's house, and Swann's fancy apartment.

Nothing. No calls were going through to the United States.

They sat in the small conference room—Luke, Ed, Swann, Trudy, and Park Jae-kyu. Swann and Trudy were in front of laptops.

"It's started," he said.

"I think we get that," Luke said.

Swann shook his head. "I don't mean just the telephones. Systems are crashing. It's all over the intelligence chat rooms. The shutdown started on the East Coast, near Washington, DC, but it's spreading rapidly throughout the country. It's moving through network connections. It seems random because it's popping up everywhere, but it's probably just following direct lines through network infrastructure. Systems administrators who experienced it are saying it's a denial-of-service attack, trillions of self-replicating bots invading networks and clogging them in seconds."

"How long before it shuts everything down?"

Swann shrugged. "It'll probably have most systems in the country down in a few minutes. There could be isolated networks still functioning twenty-four hours from now."

"Missile defense systems?" Luke said.

"I don't know."

Trudy spoke up. "It just took down a vulnerable electric grid. Most of northern Maine and New Hampshire, plus southern parts of the Canadian Maritimes and Quebec are now without power."

"Ugh," Swann said. "When the larger grids start to go…"

Luke looked at Park. Park was on the telephone, speaking rapidly in Korean. After a moment, he hung up. He was calm.

"Communications are shutting down across the United States. We've lost contact with our embassies in Washington, DC, and

204

New York. Our government has lost contact with Korean companies operating inside the United States. Everything is consistent with what the defector tells us. We can only assume that he has good intelligence, and the attack is coming. Kim Song-Il will give the launch order during the climax of the Arirang Festival."

A realization had been growing in Luke's mind for sometime.

"It was never the Chinese," he said.

Park shook his head. "No."

Luke looked at Trudy. She shook her head as well.

"There is no way the Chinese would push North Korea into a nuclear war. It would be a disaster for the entire region, and the world. No logical actor wants that, and the Chinese, while not always reasonable, are always logical. My guess is the North Koreans have kept this thing a secret from the beginning. I'll bet the Chinese know nothing about it. We were led astray all this time. The North Koreans led the world astray. And they setup the Chinese. The one nation on earth that feeds them, that protects them."

"Isn't it always that way?" Park said.

Luke and Park stared at one another.

"Kim is a madman," Luke said.

Park nodded. "The Kim family have always been madmen. Since you and I were young soldiers, and before. I've lived in the shadow of these men my entire life."

In his mind, Luke began to run down options. As invasion of the North? There were tens of thousands of American troops here, but it would be the next thing to impossible to get them across the DMZ. By the time they did, Kim would have given the order. Surgical airstrikes? Not a chance. There were too many missile silos, many were hidden, and deep underground.

Pre-emptive nuclear attack?

The nightmare option. No one, in good faith, could take that path.

Ed Newsam spoke for the first time in a long while. He was leaning back in his chair at the far end of the table from the rest of the group. His workboot-clad feet were on the table. He didn't have a laptop or a tablet in front of him. He wasn't trying to make telephone calls or research possible solutions. It wasn't his style.

"What if Kim never gives the order?" he asked.

"What if he never gives..." Park began, confused.

Ed directed his attention to Luke. "You've been running around, calling people, trying to sleuth this thing. You also seem to be hoping that somebody—the President, maybe—is going to take this off your plate."

Ed shook his head slowly.

"Ain't gonna happen. Anyway, you don't need to get it off your plate. You just need to focus on eating it. If all this intelligence is correct, the man you want to see is just across the border from here. Are they gonna launch those missiles if the fearless leader has a gun pressed to his head? Will he give the order if he knows that he dies in the next second? I don't think so."

Luke stopped. It was a moment of clarity like no other. What Ed was suggesting was so audacious that no one, least of all the North Koreans, would ever expect it.

Park flushed, seeming outraged by such an audacious idea, looking at Ed as if a madman had snuck into his house.

"It's impossible," Park said. "Kim is surrounded by bodyguards at all times. Security will be tight at the event. The North is a police state. There is very little freedom of movement. The crowds at these events are vetted beforehand. Only the Communist Party faithful…"

Luke stopped listening as Park recounted all the reasons why it couldn't be done. He found himself in a silent place, as a picture began to form in his mind. He could see it, just how it would go. No one had ever done it before. It would take a miracle to pull it off.

And that's why it would work.

"Trudy." He turned to look at her. Her eyes were wide behind her big red glasses. She looked afraid. He would need to push her past that.

"Luke?" she said, concern in her voice. "It's crazy. Do you realize what you're thinking about? You can't infiltrate North Korea. If you go, there's no way you will ever come back."

"It's suicide," Swann added.

Luke paused. Everyone in the room seemed to be staring at him. Then they stared at each other. Then they turned back to him.

Luke watched as the realization sunk in with all of them. It was as audacious a plan as had ever been conceived. It was outrageous. You don't just go into North Korea and take its leader hostage.

Even so, they would do it.

They had to do it. America was going to be hit by nukes in a few hours, and its defenses were down.

There was no other way.

Luke watched Ed, Ed watched Luke.

Finally, Ed smiled when he saw Luke had come to a decision. He laughed. "Aw, man. Here we go."

"I need a history and description of this festival," Luke said to Trudy. "I need to know everything about the specific event Kim is attending. I need whatever intel is available on the bodyguards he keeps around him. Size, training, age, skills, years of service. I need to know how he travels—how many vehicles, what kind... Are they armored? Are there decoy vehicles? Are there body doubles?"

She shook her head. "I don't believe this."

"Trudy, I'm going. With or without your help. Your help makes it a lot more likely that I come back. Okay?"

She couldn't raise her eyes to look at him. "Okay, Luke."

"You are madmen!" Park said, increasingly outraged.

"Swann," Luke said, ignoring him.

"Yeah, Luke?"

He glanced at Swann. Swann was calm. That was good. Swann was able to separate himself from these situations. He had no reason to be afraid. It wasn't like he was going to drop into North Korea.

"I need satellite imagery of the stadium I'll be going to. I need a map of the stadium, including basements and sub-basements. I need a layout of the electrical system if possible. I also want to see old clips of Kim's motorcades in motion. I want to see how they move, how they operate, especially when they're in transition. Arrival, departure, moving him in and out of venues. I want vulnerabilities. I want holes in their thinking. Don't assume they follow Secret Service–style protocols. Look for mistakes that are badly out of whack with what we do."

Swann nodded. "All right. Easy enough."

"I also want your eyes on me when I'm in country."

Swann took a breath, held it, exhaled. "Not as easy."

"Why?"

Swann shrugged. "Any drone I might use, even a high altitude one, is liable to get shot down and alert them to something unusual going on. Satellites won't necessarily give you the detail you're looking for, and are subject to being blocked by weather patterns. Also, they move fast, and I would need to hop from one to the next. If the Koreans are good enough, they might spot me doing that."

Swann always had too much information. Too many mitigating factors. Too much to think about. "Is it doable?" Luke said.

"Sure, it's doable, but..."

"Then do it. Don't tell me about all the difficulties. You'll be sitting at a desk. People are going to be shooting at me, but I'm not telling you how tricky that is. See what I mean?"

Swann raised his hands. "Okay, Luke. I'm just trying to keep you alive."

Luke nodded. "I appreciate that." He turned to Park.

"Park, do you have someone inside North Korea, someone reliable who can meet a drop team and drive them into the capital? Preferably inside a truck of some kind?"

Park sat there, silent for a long time, shaking his head over and over.

Finally, Park sighed. He nodded. "Yes."

"Then I'll need a squad of paratroopers, commandos, the best your country has."

Park had given up trying to derail the idea. "Ghost Brigade is still the best," he said, his pride showing. "I can get you a dozen men who all train together. High altitude jumps, extractions, hostage resolution."

"This will be a hostage resolution in reverse," Ed said.

Luke shook his head. "Too many men. We won't be able to slip in unnoticed with a team that size. And we won't be able to move. Get me your five best, and I'll round out the group to six. Five men who are ready to die, please."

"Make it four," Ed said.

Luke looked at him. Ed was still lounging there, his big feet on the desk. He was built like a brick wall. He was fearless, athletic, and immensely strong. He was highly skilled in all the arts— weapons, fighting, demolition, skydiving, you name it. But he didn't fit the suit on this mission.

"Ed, we're dropping into North Korea. You're hardly going to blend in up there."

Ed smiled. "And you will, white man?"

Luke shook his head. "You don't speak Korean. You won't be able to communicate with your own team. You won't be able to make demands of our opponents or give orders to any prisoners we take. If you get separated, or the team gets destroyed, you won't be able to speak to civilians while you try to escape."

Ed's smile broadened. "I speak with my guns," he said. After a second, he held up his big fists. "And I speak with these. You need me, man. There's no way you can go in there without me. You know it, and I know, so let's not waste time arguing about it."

Luke turned back to Park.

208

"Give me your four best men. We'll go in with a squad of six."

"I'll get you three men," Park said.

Luke stared at Park. Park was not obese, he was not really even overweight, but he clearly had let himself go in recent years. His lines were not sharp—he was not living the lifestyle of a special operator. To look at Park, and then at Ed, was to look at two different species of animal. As a result, Luke dreaded the next words out of Park's mouth:

"I'm coming with you."

CHAPTER THIRTY SIX

2:45 a.m.
The Situation Room, United States Naval Observatory –
Washington, DC

"Communications are dropping everywhere," an analyst said. "We've lost contact with Alaska missile defense."

"Central Command in Florida is still reporting," another voice said. "Predator drone program is becoming non-responsive. One by one, we are going blind across the Middle East, the Persian Gulf, and the southern Arabian peninsula."

A female voice: "Santee Cooper power grid throughout South Carolina and northern Georgia is down."

"Fort Benning is non-responsive as of thirty seconds ago."

One entire wall of the Situation Room was dominated by a line of young analysts and aides at laptops and on telephones, touching base with command centers across the country, reporting a litany of failed and failing networks.

It was all very exciting to hear. But Susan didn't see how it was helping matters. They needed a response, not a scorecard of disaster. Everywhere in the room, people were tapping information into tablets and laptops, and talking on telephones. Systems were still working here. For now, the security firewall had kept this place functioning, even if everywhere else was falling apart. But let's not waste that functionality writing the postmortem.

"Kurt," she called over the din of voices.

Kurt Kimball was at the front, in his customary place, talking with an aide. If he had seemed tired before, he seemed very awake now. The alarming implications of what was happening had snapped him out of his stupor. Even so, he didn't seem to notice Susan or hear her.

"Kurt," she said again, louder this time.

"KURT!"

He stopped. Everyone stopped. All eyes were on her.

"Can you please call a meeting to order here?"

"Of course."

Kurt clapped his hands, twice. The sound was loud. "Okay, people. Here's what I want. I want this room cleared of all but decision-makers. Aides, analysts, continue to gather information, but be nearby, prepared to implement policy at a moment's notice. Thank you. We will overcome this. So let's move."

The young people began to file out. Susan looked around the room. Haley Lawrence was still here, as was General Walters from the Pentagon. Kat Lopez was here, giving instructions to a couple of aides as they were leaving. A half a dozen others were here. It was good.

Susan took a deep breath. She slid into her chair. "Kurt, give me the quick and dirty."

"Our software people are calling it a denial-of-service cyber attack, the largest and fastest moving they've ever seen. It started sometime in the last ten or twenty minutes, and may be unrelated to our losing communications with Europe and Asia."

"Unrelated?" she said.

Kurt made a gesture with his hands, almost as though he was throwing sand into the air. He seemed unaware of it. Between facial tics and bizarre and sudden movements, Kurt seemed to be losing control of his body.

"Unrelated is a strong word," he said. "Of course they're related. But they are likely separate, coordinated attacks. The overseas phone and internet cables were probably cut manually by saboteurs. What we're facing right now is an out of control piece of malware which is rapidly infecting information systems across the country."

"Did we make it?" Susan said.

"Did we make what?"

"The malware."

Kurt looked around the room. "I'm under the impression that this is a cyber attack by a foreign country, most likely China. I believe it's in retaliation for what they see as an incursion by the USS *Lewiston*, and our refusal to…"

"Come off it, Kurt," General Walters said. "It's part of a pattern of unchecked aggression from them. First the dam, then the subway, now this. We're getting hammered, and no one has even fired a shot."

"Can I put forward a theory?" Susan said.

"Of course," Kurt said. "This is your show."

"I was speaking to Agent Luke Stone just before the phone lines to Asia went down."

"Is Agent Stone in Asia?"

"Yes. He's in South Korea. He told me he believes these attacks are being carried out by the North Koreans. He said that one

211

of our intelligence agencies has developed what he called a kill switch, which could take out information systems across the country. And he said that the North Korean hackers had found it."

"Susan, with all due respect," General Walters said, "is this the same Agent Stone who believed a Chinese cult was behind the attacks? The same man who engineered a prison break within the past twenty-four hours?"

"He never said it was the cult," she corrected. "He just offered it up as one of many potential leads."

Walters shook his head.

"He doesn't have much credibility left, does he?"

"Kurt?" Susan said.

"I like Agent Stone," Kurt said. "But I've studied North Korea for years. They are bristling with weaponry, certainly, but at the cost of all else. They are a low-tech society, decades behind most of the world. Their basic infrastructure—roads, trains, air transport—is all failing or in serious disrepair. They are subject to repeated crop failures, which keep their population struggling to maintain sufficient calorie and vitamin intake. Hacking into American intelligence networks to release a doomsday virus, or activate a kill switch that we ourselves created? I don't know about that. It seems well beyond their capabilities."

"Wouldn't we know if we had created a kill switch?" Haley Lawrence said. It was the first time he had spoken.

Kurt smiled. Haley was clearly new here. "Not necessarily. The left hand doesn't always know what the right hand is doing."

"It's a fantasy," the general said. "Luke Stone is out of his mind. We need to deal with the reality in front of us. Our missile defenses are going down. We don't know when we'll get them back up again. That's fine. We can go to old-school radio contact with our bases throughout the world. Hell, we can use hand-crank or solar radios if we need to. Our ships and planes are independent of domestic communications networks. We have conventional missiles ready to launch from sites in the Philippines and Japan. We can put bombers in the air whenever and wherever we want. We can give China the spanking they well deserve, and will never forget, and I suggest we do that, starting this minute."

"Kurt?" Susan said.

He nodded. "The general has a point."

"Haley?"

"We've been hit by them repeatedly," he said. "And we haven't even offered token resistance yet. I would say a show of force is in order."

They were talking about war, possibly the start of World War Three.

"Okay," she said. "How do we begin?"

The general leaned back in his chair. The aide to his left slipped a single sheet of paper in front of him. "All along, I've been saying hit their container ships. But after this? I say we strike right in the heart of the Chinese mainland. Somewhere away from the major cities, but close enough to show them we mean business."

The general picked up the piece of paper and referred to it for a moment. "We've studied this eventuality for years, and we have contingency plans ready to go. There are targets immediately available to us, which we can reach with conventional missile systems, and which puts none of our own personnel at risk. I'm talking about a menu of options that include food and coal stockpiles, military bases, and research facilities, just to name a few. We can also take out power stations and water supplies. We can see how they like drinking out of the toilet."

As the general spoke, Haley Lawrence looked at Susan. He didn't seem angry. There was no fire in his eyes. Instead, he seemed relaxed, like a man choosing what was appetizing from the general's buffet.

"Haley?" Susan said.

"I like what the general is offering, Susan. So here's my recommendation. Go for the jugular. A knockout punch. Pick a city or region, and knock out its supply of clean water."

CHAPTER THIRTY SEVEN

8:07 p.m. Korea Time (7:07 a.m. Eastern Daylight Time)
The Skies Above the Sea of Japan – Near the North Korean Coast

Ed Newsam breathed pure oxygen through a mask affixed to his face.

He sat alone on a bench inside the plane. His giant combat pack was belted to the front of him, his legs spread out around it. He had a submachine gun belted to one side of him. It was a Korean Daewoo K7, a cheaper knockoff of the Heckler and Koch MP-5 that Ed had always loved so well. He had a stack of loaded thirty-round magazines for the gun, stuffed in various pockets of his jumpsuit.

Strapped to his other side was his favorite weapon—the M79 grenade launcher. He had a dozen grenades for it. If the world was his canvas, the M79 was his paintbrush. There were also handguns mounted to his waist, and tiny .25 caliber pocket pistols taped to each one of his calves. He was strapped with guns, just how he liked it.

The jump door was open. He guessed they were at altitude now, between 25,000 and 27,000 feet. It was cold in here, despite the special polypropylene jumpsuit that covered him nearly head to toe. Outside the door, he could see the last of the day's sunlight fading far to the west.

Luke came by and squatted in front of him.

"Ed," Luke said from inside his own oxygen mask. Ed could barely see his face. "These guys can't speak to you, so I'm going to serve as your jump master. Got it?"

"Yeah."

"Okay, let's run your checklist." Luke took out a small piece of paper and held it in his thick gloved hands.

"Altimeter?" Luke said.

Ed patted the fat watch on his wrist, tapped a button on it, and got the reading: 26,738.

"Check."

"Automatic parachute activation device."

"Check."

"Parachute."

Ed touched the parachute on his back. "Check."

"Knife?"

"Check."

"Helmet."

Ed tapped himself on his hard, molded-plastic head. "Check."

Luke went through the list, thorough as always. Water, bailout oxygen, combat pack, gloves, freefall boots. It was all here.

"How's your breathing?" Luke said.

"Feels good."

"Dizzy, any nausea or tingling sensations?"

"No, man. I'm good."

"This is a HAHO jump. High altitude, high opening. You comfortable with that?"

"You know I am."

"When we jump, as soon as we're clear of the plane, we're going to pull cords immediately. They can't bring this thing into North Korean airspace, so we're out over the ocean, as you know. Note that we are far out over the ocean. Note that it is deep water, and you don't want to be in it. We're going to steer due west, horizontal as we can, for thirty-five miles. No lights, no sound. No radio contact. We're just playing follow the leader. It's going to be dark out there, so stay sharp. I've got a landing site picked out in Mount Kumgang National Park. Should be far enough away from any prying eyes. Park knows the way, and that's where we pick up our ride. Got it?"

Ed nodded. "Got it."

Luke looked at him closely. "Last chance to back out. Last chance to tell me you've never done one of these."

"Luke, you were Seventy-Fifth Rangers before you joined Delta Force. You boys used to fall out of helicopters for a living. But before I was Delta, I was Eighty-Second Airborne. I can do this thing in my sleep."

Luke patted him on the helmet and smiled. "All right, brother. You're good to go. But stay awake for it, if you don't mind. I'll see you on the ground."

Several more minutes passed. Soon, on a signal Ed didn't understand, the men began to stand and waddle like penguins toward the open doorway, their big combat packs strapped between their legs. Ed was last in line. Before him, each of the men waddled to the line, paused for a second, then jumped. No hesitation. They just went.

Ed always hesitated, or felt that he did. Maybe every man did. Maybe it just wasn't visible to others. When he reached the open

215

door, there was nothing but darkness and open space, and wind. He couldn't see anything out there. It was all hope. He wanted it to be smooth, like the others had done. But there was that moment, that split second, when his entire body, his entire being, rebelled against it.

On the threshold, that's when the doubts came to him, and the fears.

He had two young daughters, and he had been estranged from their mother for years. He could see them, four-year-old Serenity and five-year-old Diana, close enough in age to look like twins, with brightly colored plastic barrettes in their hair, beautiful like their mother. He sent money like clockwork, but the girls were growing up without him in their lives. And he could die. He took on missions, like this one, where the chances of dying were probably higher than the chances of living.

Maybe, if he survived this, he would just walk away. Walk away and watch his daughters grow from little girls to young women.

In the night sky, the others were falling far ahead of him. He had to go NOW. He had lost his momentum, so he pushed hard with his legs.

He was out.

He fell away, and the plane was gone in an instant. For a few seconds, all of life was falling, a rushing sensation, upside down, wind against his face. When the chute opened, it opened for real. He was jerked back violently, the jolt like a car crash, one he knew he'd be feeling for days.

Then he was riding in the darkness. Far to the south, the bright lights of Seoul lit up the night. The lights marched right up to the straight line of the DMZ, where everything went black. Far, far to the west, there was still the tiniest sliver of sunlight, disappearing any second.

Now, Ed didn't think about what they were planning to do. He stopped thinking about his past life or his future. He didn't think about how cold he was. He didn't consciously control his chute—the control was in muscle memory.

All he did was stare out at the dark coming in around him, and think:

Beautiful.

CHAPTER THIRTY EIGHT

9:05 p.m. Korea Time (8:05 a.m. Eastern Daylight Time)
An Underground Bunker – Near Chongjin, North Korea

The order would come tonight.

Deep underground, in their tiny living quarters, the four men knew it now. The rumors had been circulating for weeks, but now they knew it was real. A young courier had reached them just moments ago, climbing down the long metal stairwell to their position. He gave them a packet of orders without comment.

The packet said to prepare for radio contact. The contact was not a drill. It was not a hoax. It was not a mistake. Everything had been prepared in advance. The timing was perfect. When the orders came by radio, sometime in the next hours, initiate your launch sequence.

The men were nervous, but upbeat. The Supreme Leader was finally going to war against the Americans, and their vicious stooges, the Japanese. There were two nuclear missiles controlled from this bunker. One, a twenty-megaton device, was a long-range missile targeted to the city of Portland, Oregon. The other, a ten-megaton medium-range missile, was targeted to the outlying suburbs of Tokyo. Both would wreak havoc on their target zones, raining death and destruction upon their enemies.

The men tried not to think about the consequences of their actions. They tried not to consider the many children who would die in the attack, innocent even if their parents were not. They tried not to think about their own families, or how well this bunker would withstand the storm of bombs likely to come in response. They tried not to notice they had less than a week's worth of food and water rations on hand.

Although these many things were hard to ignore, as each man looked at his comrades he knew: the time had come to be brave. The missiles were targeted and armed. When the order arrived to launch, they would be patriots, and they would answer the call.

CHAPTER THIRTY NINE

8:15 a.m.

The Situation Room, United States Naval Observatory – Washington, DC

"Susan?" someone said.

"Susan."

She had been lost in thought. She rarely thought of her childhood in suburban Ohio. Her father had died when she was in the sixth grade. Her mother, without the man she loved, became a shell of herself. Depressed, a drinker, and chronically unemployed. In the middle of the tenth grade, Susan, who was already modeling locally, decided to light out for the territories. The territories, in this case, being New York City.

The memory in question was of a time when she was very young. There had been a snowstorm, and her father was pulling her along on a Flexible Flyer sled. She was laughing because it was so much fun.

"Susan, please."

She looked up. It was Kurt Kimball, staring at her. Man, she was tired. She didn't remember ever being this tired.

"Susan, the electricity grid serving Greater Los Angeles has gone down. There are early reports of looting and fires. It will get worse as the day goes on. Hospital staff are manually pumping the hearts and lungs of people on life support."

"Okay," Susan said.

"The general has a report for you."

She turned to General Walters. His eyes were narrow and eager. Susan, in contrast, felt numb.

The general held a single piece of paper in front of him. The general always seemed to be holding a piece of paper—one that controlled the fate of countless people. "Susan, we have missiles locked onto the reservoirs serving the city of Shanghai on the central east coast, as well as the city of Guangzhou, formerly known as Canton, which is in the south. We can commence firing whenever you're ready."

"Haley?" Susan said.

"I've reviewed the targets the general has put on the table, and I agree that they are excellent options, given the circumstances."

"What happens when they start shooting back?" Susan said.

"Obviously, the hope is that they come to their senses."

"And if they don't?"

The general conferred with an aide to his left. The aide handed him a second piece of paper. The general scanned the page, then spoke:

"In the event a shooting war breaks out, we have an immediate list of nearly one hundred targets, which include military, research, as well as civilian infrastructure. Hitting these should bring much of Chinese domestic commerce, and many day-to-day activities, to a standstill. If they persist after that, we have an additional list of six hundred targets. Hitting that list will set Chinese society back to a pre-modern era, from which it will likely take decades to emerge. When it comes to that list, all of the options we choose will include a mixed use of land and sea-based conventional and nuclear weapons."

"You're describing a nuclear war, General."

"Limited in scope, however. So limited that I don't think it could really be considered a nuclear war, at least not in the way the public imagines one."

"Cost in lives?" Susan said.

The general shook his head. "Impossible to guess. I don't see that as our problem. All we're doing at this moment is hitting a few reservoirs and some water tunnels. The rest is up to them."

"They'll hit us back," Susan said.

"They might. If they do, I assure you they will be very, very sorry."

Susan looked around the room. Faces stared back at her, pinched, confused, anxious faces. The general thought he was offering clear-eyed leadership. It was possible he was offering the Apocalypse instead.

"We will destroy them, Susan," he said. "Utterly, totally, completely."

Susan was so tired, for some reason she focused on his mouth while he spoke. To Susan's eyes, the general's teeth resembled the razor-sharp teeth of a shark.

CHAPTER FORTY

9:30 p.m. Korea Time (8:30 a.m. Eastern Daylight Time)
Rungrado 1st of May Stadium – Pyongyang, North Korea

It was the largest stadium in the world.

Except for photos Trudy had shown him before he left, and maps Swann had downloaded for him, Luke didn't have much idea what the stadium looked like. He did know that it had numerous arches, and was open to the air. Beyond that, he didn't have much.

After the six commandos reached their landing site on a hillside in Mount Kumgang National Park, they had been met by an old Soviet-style military truck driven by two stern-faced young women. Park Jae-kyu had spoken with the women briefly, then the men had all climbed into the back.

They rumbled over rutted and pitted roads, the men hidden in the gloom behind crates and what seemed to be large iron radiators. The Koreans sat on the floor, leaning against their packs. A few of them took out energy bars and small bottles of water and had a snack. There wasn't much talking.

What little was done, was done in whispers.

"The stadium is very large," Park told Luke. "We will come in from underneath it. A military parking garage. We may have to secure that area. If so, we must do it as quietly as possible. Sometimes, during the Arirang games, there is absolute silence. It will be bad if that happens when there is shooting going on."

"What will the games look like?" Luke said.

"Impossible to describe. You must see it for yourself."

"Where will Kim's box be?"

"Second tier," Park said. "High, but not at the top of the stadium. It will be hardened, difficult to penetrate. I hope so. The glass in front will be bulletproof, possibly so thick that it's impossible to shoot through. So thick that it warps the vision of people behind it."

"How does he watch the games in that case?"

Park shrugged. "I don't think he cares. I think we ignore the glass. We may be able to blow the entry doors with C4. If not, this is going to be a short trip."

Luke knew the whole story—they had gone over it before leaving on the plane. Park was going over it again, probably just to

220

work off nerves. Luke also knew, from Trudy's research, that they would be unlikely to catch Kim coming or going from the games. The North Koreans employed body doubles and entire decoy entourages, sometimes a bewildering array of them. Three or four different motorcades would leave the stadium at the end of the night—making it a long shot that six men would pick the right one.

In any event, they couldn't wait until the games were over. They had to take Kim while he was in his viewing box. And they had to hope it was really him.

Luke's eyes were getting used to the gloom. He looked at Park again, the man's forty-year-old belly protruding over his waistband. Park looked like what he had become—a desk jockey, and a man who ran spies. Not a spy himself, and definitely not a commando. Luke worked constantly to keep himself fit. And often enough, he felt it starting to slip away. Park's fitness had slipped away some time ago. Now it was off, running away down the block.

"Park," he said. "Are you really up for this?"

"I did the jump, Stone. Didn't I?"

Luke had to admit Park had done fine. He had guided them perfectly to the landing site, even in pitch darkness. But jumping from a plane, even a jump as strenuous as one from high altitude, was one thing. Facing a shootout, possible hand-to-hand combat, and acquiring a target in a fast-moving, unpredictable environment—that was another thing entirely.

"I don't want to worry about you out there," Stone said. "And I'm not going to carry you. Every man has to pull his weight."

"Stone, do you know I was the best paratrooper in South Korea at one time?"

Luke shrugged. "I don't doubt that. But it's not true anymore. And these kids you picked for us are fifteen years younger than you. If there's any chance you're going to put them in jeopardy when the truck pulls in, I want you to walk away. You've been in country before. I'm sure you'll make it back home. We can manage with five."

Park's bright eyes flashed anger. In a long ago time, Luke's words would have been grounds for a sparring session. "Stone, I want you to understand something. This is my country. All of it. These are my people. Not just the people from the South, but the people from the North as well. It's my job to free them. It's my job to reunite them. We are one nation, and rebuilding it has been my life's work. You think I've gotten old and fat. You think I can't fight anymore. Whether that's true or not doesn't matter. This place, tonight, is my destiny."

One of the young commandos hissed something urgently in Korean. Park instantly shut his mouth. He put a finger to his lips to quiet Luke.

Outside, the truck entered a lighted area. None of the men spoke. None of them even moved. The truck idled at some kind of checkpoint. A man's voice spoke. A few words were passed between the female driver and the man. Luke couldn't make out what was said.

After a moment, the truck rolled on again, much slower now. A few minutes later, it rolled to a stop.

Up front in the cab, one of the women said something loud enough for them to hear.

The men began to gather their packs and their weapons.

"Okay," Park said. "We've arrived."

* * *

They were in a vast underground chamber. About a hundred military trucks were parked down here, and hundreds of old buses. Luke didn't see any cars. The women had parked the truck in a far corner of the chamber, in the shadows, among the rusted hulks of vehicles that hadn't been used in a long time.

Luke and Ed were the last men to climb out, after Park let them know the coast was clear. In the yellow light of the dim overhead lamps, Luke looked at the military women who had driven them here. They were young and pretty, but also thin and severe. They looked very nervous.

One of them looked at Luke. She gestured at him and Ed.

"You have made a mistake," she said. "You will die here."

"It's okay," he said. "We do this a lot. We've never died before."

"Our people are dying," she said simply.

The women turned and walked away from the truck. Within a minute, they had disappeared entirely. Behind the truck, the three young commandos were gearing up, checking weapons, and discarding unnecessary items. The uniforms they wore marked them as North Korean soldiers.

Above his head, Luke could hear music blasting, and at times, people cheering.

"I need to get upstairs," he said to Park. "I have a satellite phone. If I can get some open air, I'll see if I can pick up Swann."

"The women left you both these," Park said. He held out black uniforms and helmets with visors. "They are riot police uniforms. Before we left the South, I asked the women to provide these if they could, and somehow they managed it. I don't know where they got them. The smoked visors will buy you a few extra seconds before people see you are not Korean."

Ed and Luke changed into the uniforms quickly. They almost fit. Ed's uniform wasn't broad enough, and Luke's was too short. They looked at each other and laughed.

"Oh, man," Ed said. "I feel like the Incredible Hulk in this thing."

"You are the Incredible Hulk," Luke said.

Luke's heart was beating very fast. His mind raced.

Calm, he told himself. *Calm.*

A few hundred yards away was an old stairwell. Two of the commandos went to it and disappeared up the stairs to the stadium, to scope out their position relative to Kim's skybox. Several moments later, they were back. Their eyes were wide and frightened. They spoke rapidly to Park.

"They say we are very close," Park said. "From that stairwell, Kim's box is no more than another hundred meters. They say it is impossible to reach it. More than a hundred armed guards stand between the stairwell and the entryway, with barricades erected behind them. They say it is the same story on the other side."

"Luke, I got an M79," Ed said. "If these boys can snake me around to the side, I'll take down a chunk of those guards with just a couple shots. Should create a panic, depending on how disciplined they are. I might be able to take that glass partition out too, or maybe the doorway."

"It will have to happen fast," Park said. "Once a disturbance occurs, his close guards will rush to get him out the secret emergency exit."

"If it's secret, how do you know about it?" Luke said.

"I know it exists. I don't know where it goes. We have struggled with this for years. Intelligence in North Korea is a black hole."

"How's the crowd?" Luke said.

Park said something to the two men.

"*Keun,*" one of them said.

Luke knew the word. It meant "Big."

He turned to Ed. "I like it. Just go easy on civilians, all right?"

Ed shrugged, didn't commit to that idea one way or the other.

"Ed?"

Ed nearly laughed. "You're crazy, man. You know that? You put me in these impossible situations every single time, and then you tell me to take it easy on people. I don't get off on icing noncombatants. I don't. But geez... you know? Sometimes people get in the way."

"I know it," Luke said. "And when they do, let's try not to kill them."

Ed shook his head. "Okay, Luke. I'll mow down the soldiers for you. At the same time, I'll hand out ice cream cones to the kids, and flowers to the ladies."

"Sounds good," Luke said. "In that case, let's rock this."

He turned to Park. "Can one of your men get Ed a clean shot? He can clear out a lot of that trouble for us."

Park barked something to one of the men. The guy gestured at Ed, and off they went through the dim, cavernous parking lot. "Five minutes, Ed," Luke said. "Watch for my signal. I'll fire a flare where I need a path cleared."

Ed didn't turn around.

"How many hits you need?"

"Two. And then run like hell."

Ed raised a hand in response.

Luke looked at Park. "Okay. Let's go."

* * *

For a moment, Luke entertained the idea that he was invisible. He stood near the top of the stairwell, gazing out from his helmet visor at the Arirang Festival. The thing was so majestic, why would anyone look at him? More than that, in a country that had *this,* why was everything else so horribly wrong?

The stadium was dark. Down on the field, hundreds of ballet dancers flowed through precision movements, all of them in synch with the others, all of them seemingly lit up in green, and then red, and then gold, from within their own costumes.

Suddenly, there was a flash, and across the stadium from him, in the crowd, the gigantic image of an old man in an army uniform appeared, pointing his arm toward the sky. A second later, the image instantly morphed into a lake surrounded by snow-capped crags, the same one Trudy showed him tattooed on the back of Li Quiangguo.

It took Luke a few seconds to realize how they were projecting those images onto the crowd. They weren't projecting them at all. Thousands of people were holding up placards, together creating one image, then flipping them to instantly create the second image.

A muscular man with a sledgehammer appeared, driving a railroad spike. A symbol of the workers, of course. Then suddenly, fighter planes streaking across the sky.

Meanwhile, on the floor of the stadium, the dancers had turned into winged blue and white butterflies.

It was amazing.

"I told you it was impossible to describe," Park said. "You have to see it for yourself."

Luke shook his head clear of it. This wasn't the time for distractions.

"How long has it been?" he said.

Park nodded. "Just about five minutes."

Luke shook his head. "Well, I hate to spoil the show, but..."

He glanced over at the guards. They were tall, thin, stern-faced young men. They blocked a wide stairway that rose to what must be Kim's private viewing box. From the outside, the box was like a cement bunker or machine gun nest. The double doors to the box were closed.

"This has to happen fast," Luke said.

"Very fast," Park said.

The two commandos with them gazed anxiously at the guards, then back at the festival. At the guards, then the festival. The guards...

Luke didn't like it. "If we hang around here much longer, we're going to draw attention to ourselves."

"Yes."

"Are you and your men ready?" Luke said.

"Yes."

Luke glanced at Park. Park stared at Luke. They both laughed. "Well, old buddy," Luke said. "If one of us doesn't make it, and one of us does, I guess we'll connect again on the other side."

"Of course," Park said.

Luke ducked down into the stairwell and took out his flare gun. He was going to get one shot at this, so it better be a good one. He loaded the flare and counted slowly to ten, imagining Ed growing impatient on the other side of the stadium.

225

Okay, this was it. Luke popped up and fired.

The white flare arced low across the sky and landed in the midst of the guards ten feet in front of the barricades. Luke ducked down again, as did Park's men. Air expelled from Luke like from a punctured tire. That was a good shot. He couldn't have asked for much better. Now it was on Ed. He had better hurry.

No one in the crowd had responded to the flare. They probably thought it was part of the show. But the guards? That would be a different story. Park glanced through a crack in the cement top of the stairwell.

"Uh-oh," he said. "Here they come."

From far off to the right, nearly on the other side of the stadium, Luke saw a brief flash. In his imagination, he could almost hear the hollow sound of the M79, a sound that was all out of proportion to the type of havoc that weapon could wreak.

Doonk.

A trail fizzled across the sky. Luke didn't see the grenade itself.

"Down!" he shouted.

A second later: Kaa-POW!

The metal stairwell shook from the explosion.

"Wait," Luke said, his hand on the back of the young commando ahead of him. "One more."

The crowd started to scream. It was dawning on them that this wasn't part of the show. Suddenly, the music stopped. In a moment, it would be chaos.

Luke watched another trail fizzle.

He crouched again.

BOOOM! This time, with no competing sounds, it was an eruption.

"GO!" Luke shouted. "GO! GO! GO!"

He popped up, the MP-5 out ahead of him. He balanced it on the cement entry to the stairwell and opened fire. The guards had been blown into a wide circle. A few were getting up. He fired the submachine gun, mowing them back down again.

Then he was out and running.

Park and his men were out in front. Luke ran to catch up. Everywhere in the stadium, the crowd surged, desperate to get away from the attack. He couldn't think about that now.

Up ahead, Park leapt the fallen barricades and climbed the short flight of wide steps to the double doors. He squatted. One of his commandos was there half a second later. Park put his hand ou

The commando placed a C4 charge in his hand. Park stuck it to the door, then held his hand out again. The commando gave him another, and Park placed that one. He lit the fuses, then stood to duck away.

Suddenly there was a barrage of machine gun fire from Luke's left. He hit the ground, but the bullets weren't meant for him. As he watched, Park and the young commando did a crazy dance as the bullets pierced them.

"Ah," Luke said. "Oh, God."

He rolled onto his right shoulder, found the shooter fifty feet away, and blew him down with a double burst from the MP-5.

He looked back at Park. Park stumbled a step, then another. He didn't seem to know where he was. He gazed up at the sky. His commando was dead on the ground behind him.

"Park!" Luke screamed. "Get out of there!"

The C4 blew. The first charge, then an instant later, the second.

The light from it was blinding, the sound deafening. Luke ducked and covered his helmeted head with his arms. When he looked up again, the doors were gone and the doorway itself was on fire.

There was no sign of Park at all.

The MP-5 was empty. Luke chucked it and pulled both his handguns. He jumped up and ran screaming toward the doorway. From the corner of his eye, he saw motion to his right and behind him. He glanced, and the other young commando was still with him, running for the door. He still had his machine gun.

They pounded up the steps and blasted through the flaming doorway.

The skybox was crowded with men. Someone had pulled open a trapdoor from the floor. People pushed and shoved to get through it. A couple of bodyguards were trying to knock people out of the way, so that a small fat man in a tan suit could go through.

Luke fired both guns at once, killing the two men.

The young commando ripped up the bottleneck at the top of the trapdoor. Five bodies fell in different directions. Then the young man went over, kicked the bodies out of the way, slammed the door closed, and locked it.

And then, as the smoke settled, a small man emerged, standing there, frozen, facing him.

Luke could hardly believe it. There, before him, he held the Supreme Leader of North Korea in his gun sights.

"*Nan dangsin eul jug-il geos-ida!*" Luke shouted at him.

He had forgotten that he even knew that one. It meant *I will kill you.*

The commando had Kim in his sights now, too.

Kim stared impassively at the young commando. The Supreme Leader hadn't tried to move, or speak, or do anything. He didn't seem surprised that his entire bodyguard had just been wiped out, or even concerned.

Luke took stock. They had captured the man they came to see, but it was only a start. With no way out, the question became: *How to hold him?* The doors were blown open, leaving them exposed, and the military units were moving closer, facing the skybox, and taking up firing positions.

The North Koreans were gathering themselves for the counter attack. That was about to become a bigger problem.

Luke crouched below the window, out of the line of fire.

He took a second to think. Then it came to him. He still had the satellite phone. He glanced up at the open roof of the stadium.

Swann.

He pulled the phone out of his vest. It was worth a try. He glanced at the readout. He had a signal. That was good. Swann had rigged this so that a single touch would make the call. Luke pressed the green button. A moment later, the phone started to beep.

The call picked up. "Swann," came the voice.

Luke almost dropped to the floor in relief.

"Swann, it's Luke."

"Hey, Luke, how's it going in there?"

"Uh, we're in trouble, Swann. We've got Kim, but Park is dead and the team is split up. I don't have Ed with me. I'm trapped in the skybox."

"You've got bigger trouble than that," Swann said.

"Yeah? What is it?"

"I've got the stadium on satellite. People are streaming out by the thousands. But I've got about ten military convoys incoming, complete with troop transports and tanks."

Luke didn't have time to think about that. They weren't about to fire tank shells in here, not with Kim at gunpoint. "All right," he said. "I need you to find me a way out of here. Tunnels under the stadium, maybe. There's a trapdoor here. I don't know where it goes. But maybe there's a chance..."

Luke stared at the phone. It had dropped the call. Swann was gone.

From outside, someone strafed the open doorway with machine gun fire. The cinderblock wall crumbled into a thousand pieces. Luke hit the deck. So did the young South Korean. Lying on the ground, Luke covered the doorway with his gun. Cement dust hung in the air. Luke could taste it on his tongue. A North Korean darted by just outside. Luke fired.

Missed.

He reached for the satellite phone again, just feet away. He snatched it, but it didn't feel the same as before. It had been hit. A third of its plastic casing was just gone—blown away. He pressed buttons, hoping for a read out. Nothing. The phone was junk. There was no other way to call out of here.

A tear gas canister bounced in through the doorway, trailing smoke. The young South Korean caught it one-handed, in mid-bounce, and tossed it back out again.

Luke heard a noise then, one so totally out of place with the surroundings, he couldn't immediately identify it. A moment passed before it resolved into something he could remember. It was the sound of laughter.

From the floor, he glanced up at Kim. The man could barely suppress his delight. The machine gun fire hadn't made him duck. He hadn't moved at all. He had one small hand covering his mouth, like a giggling little girl might do.

"Luke, you said? Luke Stone, is it? I thought it was you. I recognized you from your picture. I'm a fan of yours, did you know? Oh yes, ever since the U.S. government crisis. You were profiled on the television. The super spy, Luke Stone, who saved the Vice President and the American Republic. You're a famous man, Luke. You should have your own show."

Now Kim shook his head. He seemed sad. "But you should never grovel on the ground like this. It's unseemly for a man of your caliber."

Luke stared at Kim. The little man spoke perfect English. Gunfights and slaughter didn't bother him. He didn't even seem to notice it. Now he raised his arms in an expansive gesture, as if indicating lush green hillsides and rocky coastline, rather than a shattered, smoky, bloody skybox in a stadium overcome with panic.

"Welcome to my country, Luke Stone. It will be an honor to have you die here."

CHAPTER FORTY ONE

8:57 a.m.
United States Naval Observatory – Washington, DC

"Susan, we have to act. The only thing these people know is force."

"General Walters," Susan said. "I call you by your title as a sign of respect. I wish you would do the same for me."

Walters stared at her.

The Situation Room was silent. Susan took a deep breath. All the men in this room seemed ready for war, and she was hesitating. She was being the indecisive woman again, the one who couldn't even pick her own cabinet members, the one whose husband cheated on her with other men. The entire communications infrastructure of the country was collapsing, and she couldn't decide what to do. It was pathetic, right?

She was so tired.

"I don't want to go to war," she said. "I don't want to be responsible for the deaths of thousands, or tens of thousands, or even millions of people."

"Susan..." It was General Walters again.

Now Susan just stared at him.

Up at the front, an aide was whispering to Kurt Kimball.

"Susan, we have an incoming call," Kurt said. "Apparently, it's urgent. The man insists on speaking with you. He broke through a security firewall to call here."

"Who is it?" Susan said.

"His name is Mark Swann. He's one of the agents we gave to Luke Stone when Stone came back on board. He works as an analyst for the NSA."

Susan nodded. "Yes, I remember him. I know who he is."

Susan couldn't imagine what Swann might want, or how it could be helpful at this point. He was overreaching his authority to call her directly. She wouldn't normally take this call unless she had invited it herself. But speaking to him might just buy her a few minutes of time, and a chance to clear her head.

"Put him on speakerphone."

Kurt gave a hand signal to an aide. The aide reached for the black conference call device on the long table. He pressed a couple of buttons on it.

"Call coming through," he said.

"Hello?" a male voice said. "Where have I reached?"

"This is President Susan Hopkins." Susan almost couldn't believe it. Things had reached the point where random people could call in during the middle of national security meetings. She rolled her eyes at the people in the room.

"This is Special Agent Mark Swann with the United States National Security Agency."

"Yes, Swann. We know who you are. What can we help you with?"

"I've just hung up with Luke Stone. Our call got cut off, and I can't reach him again. He's in North Korea with a team of South Korean commandos, trying to kidnap Kim Song-Il. He believes, and I agree with him, that Kim plans to launch a nuclear war against the United States tonight."

"Stone is in..." Kurt Kimball began, eyes wide with shock.

"Yes, North Korea. And he has captured Kim."

Susan felt her heart plummet. What animal had she unleashed out of the bag? And how many crises could she withstand at once?

She stared at the others and they all stared back at her. They looked equally dumfounded. Even the general, for all his poise, looked off kilter for the first time.

Kim. Held hostage by Luke Stone. In North Korea. It was too crazy to be true. And yet, even crazier, knowing Luke, somehow it all seemed perfectly normal to her.

"He's trapped and surrounded," Swann rushed on. "He has no way out. He needs you."

Susan cleared her throat.

"Swann," Susan said, "why would we want to help Stone? If he's causing an international incident, then how does he..."

"It was the North Koreans all along," Swann said. "The Chinese had nothing to do with it. They set them up. Kim's preparing to launch nuclear missiles against the west coast and Japan. He was testing us. All those cyber attacks were just a dry run. Now he's figured it out. He's insane, and his country is starving. Do you think China wants a nuclear war with the United States? I don't think so."

Susan stared at the phone. Everyone else seemed to be doing the same thing. The magnitude of what Swann was saying, and the likely truth of it, hit her for the first time.

She glanced around the Situation Room. What were the rest of them thinking?

"Hello?" Swann said. "You still there?"

"We're here," Susan said.

"Luke needs help. He and Ed Newsam are in a bad situation. They're trapped inside the Rungrado Stadium in Pyongyang. The place is surrounded by North Korean troops, with more pouring in. We've got thirty thousand American troops here in the south, and loads of military hardware. I think you should send someone over the border to rescue them. I don't see how they come out alive otherwise. They are totally surrounded. And Kim, I'm sure, still has his fingers on the button somehow."

"We will take that under advisement," Kurt Kimball finally said.

"Well," Swann said. "Don't for too long…"

Kurt made a gesture like a hand cutting across his throat. An instant later, the call went away.

Everyone in the room turned to her.

"I want the President of China on the phone," she said.

The general shook his head. "It's too late for talking," he said.

"I agree," Haley Lawrence chimed in.

She knew how it sounded. Nothing in this room had changed. All the momentum was still for war. And calling the President of China looked like weakness.

"Direct communications have been knocked out," Kurt said.

Susan shrugged. "Swann just called here. He did it. However you can patch another call through to Asia, just do it. Satellite phone, tin cans tied with a string, walkie-talkies. I won't mind."

"Susan." The general glared at her. "You can't do this. You are making America look weak."

"If you don't like it, General," she snapped back, raising her voice for the first time, "I will accept your resignation now. I am President of the United States. I will do whatever the hell I wish."

* * *

"The line is open," an aide said. "We can put you on anytime."

Susan nodded.

General Walters sat there, arms crossed, fuming, as Susan picked up the white telephone on the table in front of her. A good old-fashioned landline, the last refuge when everything else failed.

"The President of the United States is on the line," a male voice said.

232

"The President of the People's Republic of China is on the line," came the reply.

"Hello?" Susan said.

"Hello? This is Xi Wengbo."

"Mr. President."

"Madam President, to what do I owe this honor?"

"Sir," Susan said, "I think we have a lot to talk about."

"We are aware of the very many fighter and bomber sorties you are flying," Xi said. "Many of them are dangerously close to our territory. We are showing the most restraint we can, but I admit, we are disappointed that this is your response to recent troubles. We hope that there will be no incidents of violence."

"We are under cyber attack again," Susan said. "Our entire information infrastructure, including much of our electric power, has shut down or is shutting down. This has put us in a very violent mood."

The Chinese President sighed. "I assure you it is not us. We seek friendship, coupled with respect, and nothing more."

"I believe you," Susan said.

There was a long pause.

"You believe me?" Xi said. "So..." Xi began, apparently confused.

"I believe you don't want war," she said. "We don't, either. But we may not be able to avoid it. The North Koreans are behind the cyber attacks. They are trying to take down our defenses in preparation for a missile attack. We believe Kim Song-Il is going to launch nuclear missiles at us at any time. As you know, if he does that, we will have no choice but to respond with overwhelming force. China will be in the fallout zone, and we cannot guarantee that some of the missiles themselves will not hit your territory by mistake."

"Please wait a minute," Xi said. "What proof of this is there?"

"Sir, I suggest you just take my word for it."

233

CHAPTER FORTY TWO

10:17 p.m. Korea Time (9:17 a.m. Eastern Daylight Time)
Rungrado 1st of May Stadium – Pyongyang, North Korea

"My grandfather created this world," Kim Song-Il said. "That's what people like you don't understand."

Luke lay on the floor in the shattered, bloody mess that was only recently a luxury skybox. He had a gun in each hand. One was pointed at the head of Kim, North Korea's Supreme Leader. The other gun was pointed at the blown out doorway. Bodies of North Koreans were piling up at the entrance.

Kim had done Luke a favor and was crouching next to him. To his credit, the man was not sniveling or crying. He seemed calm. He was not afraid in the least. Luke hadn't expected that from him.

The reason for it, of course, was that Kim was crazy. Being a madman had its perks.

Nearby, the young kid from Park's old Ghost Brigade was crouched down, back pressed to the wall, two handguns aimed at an angle through the same blasted opening. The kid had killed at least half a dozen Northerners who had tried to come through there, but he had also just run out of ammunition for his machine gun.

Another Northerner made a suicidal run at the doorway.

BAM! BAM! BAM! BAM!

The kid gunned him down, using four shots when only one might have done the trick. The Northerner writhed on top of the other corpses, before sliding to a place at the bottom.

Luke shook his head. They were never going to hold this place. The only reason they still held it was the North Koreans were afraid to use overwhelming force with Kim still alive in here. Which made it very important that Kim stay alive.

"My family are a race of gods," Kim said in a conversational tone. "I'm blessed by that, and it makes me greater than the others. In a nuclear war, I won't die, and my children won't die, even if all other people do. Even if the land is poisoned for a thousand years, we will continue."

Machine gun fire strafed the thick viewing window above their heads. The glass held, for the time being. When that window went, all bets were off. If a hole that big opened, the Northerners would launch tear gas after tear gas through it.

234

There came a thumping sound. Luke couldn't tell what it was.

BOOM... BOOM... BOOM.

He looked around the remains of the skybox. The bodies piled on top of the trapdoor were shuddering.

BOOM... BOOM.

Someone was under the trapdoor, hammering at it. They were probably using a battering ram, but the angle was wrong. Still, it wouldn't hold forever. Luke took his gun off the demolished entryway and pointed it at the trapdoor. When the trapdoor went, he'd get the first couple of people to come through it. Then, if he was lucky, he'd pop a grenade down there.

"The bullets can't hurt me, Luke. They pass right through my body. Look at me, I am unscathed."

Luke looked at him, and was unsettled to see that he really was unscathed.

"Do you see this, Luke?" Kim continued.

Luke followed his gaze as he held up a small device, hidden in his palm, a large red button in its center, flashing.

"When I press it, and press it I will, the order will go down to my dutiful soldiers to launch the nuclear warheads and obliterate your beautiful country."

He grinned widely, an awful sight Luke hoped he'd be able to wipe from his memory.

"You see, Luke Stone?" he continued. "Your country is finished. And there's nothing you can do to stop it."

Luke, heart pounding, watched Kim close his fingers on the device—when suddenly, another burst of gunfire hit the window. The glass cracked in a spider web pattern, and a shard of it came flying and sliced Kim's hand, making him drop the device.

Kim went for it.

Luke leapt up, grabbed Kim, and dragged him to the ground. The floor was awash in blood, and they slid in it. Luke pressed him down.

"Luke!" the South Korean shouted.

A bum rush of half a dozen Northerners came through the doorway.

Luke turned and fired both guns.

The young kid fired.

The noise was deafening.

BAM, BAM, BAM, BAM, BAM.

The Northerners dropped, nearly as a group. One held up the body of the dead man in front of him, using it as a shield. He charged Luke.

Suddenly, the South Korean commando was there, up and stabbing. Behind him, Luke saw more men running up the stairs. This was it. They were just going to throw bodies at that doorway nonstop, until sheer numbers prevailed.

A bottleneck at the doorway, Luke fired into the squirming mass.

Suddenly, he felt a sharp pain in his side. He turned, and now Kim Song-Il had a knife. He had taken it right off Luke's belt. He was stabbing at Luke, mostly hitting his body armor. One slice had slipped through a gap in plates.

Kim then beelined for the device.

Luke dropped one gun and pinned the knife hand to the ground. He clubbed Kim in the face with the other gun. Once, he hit him. Twice. Three times.

Kim's face was an instant bloody mess.

Kim lay on the floor, holding his bleeding face with both hands. It must be a shock for him to be injured by a mere mortal.

Luke rolled over. The South Korean was caught in hand-to-hand combat with three men, all of them sinking to the floor. He was done. Behind them, more men raced up the stairs. Luke fired his gun at the advancing troops.

Click.

Click... click.

Oh God.

Luke hurled his gun at the first man through the opening.

Suddenly Luke heard a rumbling in the sky. Perhaps it had been there several moments, but it hadn't dawned on him until now. He fell back, scrambling for the pistol taped to his calf. As he did, he caught a glimpse through the opening in the roof of the stadium. High above them, a horizontal line of planes went overhead. As he watched, black silhouettes fell out the back of the planes. His initial thought was that the planes were bombers, and he waited for the awful shock of the first bombs to hit.

But the bombs never fell. They became parachutes instead, and slowly drifted toward the ground. Paratroopers were coming down. Luke took a deep breath now. There were already several waves of parachutes approaching the ground.

He turned, and four North Koreans stood above him, rifles pointed down at his head. But their eyes were not on him. They were also looking at the sky.

Another line of planes went by, more paratroopers jumping. Then another, and another.

Spotlights were turned on from the ground now, and Luke stared at the planes. Under each wing, he could just make out the single round star.

The symbol of the People's Republic of China.

Luke shook his head. The irony, he thought. After all this, to be rescued by the Chinese.

Seconds later, the first paratroopers were reaching the stadium floor, gliding in through the open hole in the roof. As they landed, they shed their parachutes and drew weapons. They did it smoothly, almost in one move.

Wave after wave they landed, and the North Korean troops, recognizing who they were, began to surrender to them without firing a shot.

Suddenly, Luke sensed motion. He turned to see Kim, awake again, darting for the device.

Luke watched in horror as Kim beat him to it—and began to close his fingers on the button.

Luke knew there was no time to stop him.

With no other choice, Luke reached into his belt and extracted his final handgun. He raised it at Kim's smiling face.

And just as Kim's fingers were closing, he fired.

BOOM!

Luke sat there, stunned. The South Korean stared back at Luke, stunned, too, as if staring at a god.

There, before him, the Supreme Leader of North Korea lay dead.

The button still blinked. His fingers had not yet touched it.

Smoke rose from the muzzle of the gun.

No one said anything.

Just like that, the reign of the Kim family was over.

A moment later, half a dozen Chinese commandos raced up the stairs, vaulted the bodies at the doorway, and entered the room. Luke raised his hands. The North Koreans raised their hands. The South Korean raised his hands.

The Chinese were tall and thin, young wiry guys, strapped with guns. They stared wide-eyed at all the bodies on the ground. They didn't seem to know what to make of it. Did they know that the headless man in the tan suit was the remains of the great dictator? Luke couldn't tell.

Luke guessed the young Chinese didn't understand a word of English, but he didn't care. He lay back against the ruined wall. His entire body was shaking.

"Man," he said, "you guys are a beautiful sight."

CHAPTER FORTY THREE

10:45 pm Korea Time (9:45 am Eastern Daylight Time)
An Underground Bunker - Near Chongjin, North Korea

The order never came.

Deep underground, two men were at battle stations, two men remained behind in the living quarters. The radio was silent most of the evening. At just after 10 pm, there was a burst of static, the kind of which was sometimes followed by orders. But nothing happened.

Later, the two men in the tiny living room heard voices and footsteps descending the metal stairwell from the surface. The steps were heavy, like the boots of military men, and there were a lot of them.

A pounding came at their door.

One man briefly considered putting his service gun to his head and pulling the trigger. Before he could take action in this direction, the other man opened the door. A squad of twelve Chinese soldiers came in.

"There is no war," the squad leader told them. "The missiles will not be launched."

The four Koreans were walked to the surface by the Chinese. Technically, they had surrendered their post without firing a shot. But at the surface level, the night air was cool and refreshing. The men hadn't been above ground in more than a month. There was a Chinese military encampment not far away, where the Chinese were bringing Koreans from the missile silos in the region.

There was hot soup at the encampment, with meat and potatoes in it, and there was bread and butter. There was water in plastic bottles, and there were cots with pillows and wool blankets. The four men from the silo sat together with stern faces, eating the meal provided for them. They had a tradition among them of being stoic and brave. But nearby, some of the other Koreans wept over their food. Many hadn't eaten a full meal in weeks.

In the night, the man who had considered suicide lay awake on his cot. He stared up at the moon, riding high and round in the sky, clouds skidding across it. Not far away, there was a road that came down from the border with China. Chinese troop transports and tanks rolled south along that road the entire night. Until almost dawn, he listened to the squeaking sound of the tanks tracks, and felt the Earth rumble beneath the heavy vehicles. The Chinese had taken over the country tonight.

And this was a good thing.

CHAPTER FORTY FOUR

August 20
9:01 a.m. Korea Time (8:01 p.m. Eastern Daylight Time)
Gyeongbok Palace – Seoul, South Korea

Gunshots echoed through the vast plaza. A thousand people filled the flagstone square near the steps to the ancient palace. Behind the palace, a green hillside rose up through morning mists that were still burning off.

Honor guards from the Republic of Korea Army, Navy, Air Force, and Marines flanked the caskets, standing at attention. The traditional honor guard, in red, black, and gold medieval costume and carrying longbows, stood at attention in front of the caskets. A pipe and drum band, also in traditional dress, stood in the back and to the right.

Luke and his team occupied places of honor in the front row of the square. Luke himself was seated next to the President of the Republic of Korea, a small dapper man with graying hair.

Luke was exhausted and in pain. He could barely understand the proceedings. It turned out that Kim had stabbed him three times—sheer adrenaline was why Luke hadn't noticed at first. He had a rash all over his body from flying debris during the firefight.

He tried to put those things out of his mind. As he sat, he pictured Park as a young man, tiny, but very strong, and able to seemingly defy the laws of gravity. As a party trick, he used to shatter overhead light bulbs with spinning kicks. He would simply get airborne, keep rising, and then *stay up there.*

He remembered their fights, and how he would time his punches for when Park landed. A physics professor would never believe how long he had to wait. He remembered his drinking bouts with Park, and Park's infectious smile when he knew free time was coming.

At an appointed time that Luke didn't understand, the President touched his hand.

"We will give them both the deepest bow," the man said.

Luke nodded. "Yes."

He stood with the President and approached the casket on the left, the one with Park's photograph on it. Luke knew the casket was empty. He was there when Park died. There had been nothing

241

left of him to bury. He put his hands across his stomach, left hand over the right. He bent his knees and slowly dropped to the floor. He put his hands on the stone ground and crossed them. Then he crossed his feet and touched his forehead to his hands. To his right, the President did the same.

Luke remembered how it had embarrassed him when Park gave him this same bow, the *keun jeol,* when Luke had first arrived after so long away. Luke hadn't done anything in return. Now he was offering this bow to a dead man.

He held the bow a long time, his head pressed to his hands, his palms against the warm stone. Gradually, he moved his hands aside and pressed his forehead directly to the flagstone. He felt a tear leave his eye and roll up the side of his head into his hair. Then another came, and another. Soon, his body shook with the force of them.

He should have given the bow while Park was still alive.

CHAPTER FORTY FIVE

Commander Patrick Vitale stood with his officers on the dock, facing his opposite numbers from the ships that had captured the *Lewiston*. Behind him, his men stood in formation, American sailors, every man in formal attire, every man at attention.

The *Lewiston* itself was in a deepwater dock a hundred yards away, its bridge above the water, waiting for its crew to come aboard.

It was a hot and sticky day, getting worse all the time. It was still morning, but the sun was already like a blazing nuclear reactor in the sky. Southern China in summer was hotter than Hades.

The Chinese had organized a brief ceremony to commemorate the friendly and auspicious meeting of the USS *Lewiston* and the Chinese navy, and to celebrate the visit of the American crew to Beihai. A local troupe of children had put on a traditional dance performance. Vitale had to admit it was nice.

The captain of the destroyer Vitale had only recently stalked approached him. He took off his captain's hat and offered Vitale a bow, which Vitale returned, somewhat awkwardly.

Then the man stuck out his hand for a shake. Vitale was better at handshakes. His large paw swallowed that of the Chinese commander.

The man smiled. "We are thankful for your stay with us," he said. "We wish you, as the Americans say, fair winds and following seas."

243

CHAPTER FORTY SIX

August 21
11:05 a.m.
United States Naval Observatory – Washington, DC

"Today," Susan said, "is finally a new day."

She stood at the podium on the rolling back lawn behind the New White House. She looked out at about fifty reporters and maybe two hundred ambassadors, diplomats, American office holders, and various other dignitaries. It was a sunny morning. There was even something cheerful about it.

"The long night of terror is over. The terror we experienced at the hands of North Korea, and the terror ordinary Koreans experienced, has come to an end. The seven-decade reign of the Kim family has ended."

There was a smattering of applause. Susan glanced down at her prepared remarks. They weren't making it. She had hoped that Kim family line would have gotten wolf whistles and cheers. She soldiered on.

"But the job isn't done. That's why I'm announcing today a billion dollars in immediate emergency food, medicine and other assistance to North Korea. Now, many people might say that we shouldn't give North Korea anything. They might say we should take revenge on them instead.

"They tried to kill us, didn't they? No. I don't believe that. I don't believe the people of North Korea ever wanted to kill us. A spoiled, corrupt regime wanted to, but that regime is gone now. Its leader is dead and his henchmen are all in custody. And the people of North Korea need our help."

Susan went on, the crowd polite and respectful, but not really riding with her. People still had trouble with these concepts, she knew. Or perhaps the speech was just boring. She wasn't sure. She made her points anyway, even if not everyone was with her.

South Korea, as wealthy as it may be, was too small to absorb and pay for a basket base society like North Korea right away.

The United States, in cooperation with our friends the Chinese, would take responsibility for administering North Korea, paying for the country's needs, and allowing the necessary time for the people to gradually increase their standard of living to that of the South.

This cooperation would mark the greatest partnership yet between the great powers of China and the United States.

We had reached a time for healing, both between the two Koreas, which would one day become one Korea, but also between America and China.

It was also a time for forgiveness.

Susan thought about that, even while speaking to the assembled crowd, and by extension, to much of the world. Forgiveness.

She was still getting some blank stares, especially among the Americans in the crowd. People were not often ready to forgive so soon, even if forgiveness was the best and fastest path to rebuilding, and to stability. Even now, as her speech reached its climax, and she began to exhort them about Abraham Lincoln and the better angels of our nature, she noted the reluctance to accept it. Many people were dead, and there were people in this crowd who wanted revenge.

It didn't really matter. Those feelings would dissipate with time. The highest ideal here was to build bridges of understanding between peoples. And to Susan's way of thinking, you led from the front, not from the rear.

After the speech, there was a reception in the garden. Pierre had taken a pass on this event, and she didn't really blame him. Kat Lopez shadowed Susan as she mingled. After a moment, Haley Lawrence was there.

"Susan, I have to thank you," he said. "I was wrong. I was in over my head, and I lost my composure. You stood alone, made difficult decisions, and saved us from a possible world war. If that story is ever written…"

Susan smiled. "Thanks, Haley. Let's hope it never sees the light of day."

General Walters was just steps behind Haley. He offered his hand for a shake.

"Madam President," he said and smiled.

Susan was in a good mood today. She shook his hand and returned the smile. "General, I'd like to see your resignation on my desk tomorrow morning."

His smile faltered. "Susan?"

"Oh, don't worry," she said. "I'll give the press the usual great American stuff when I go public with it. You'll keep your rank and

245

your pay grade. It's just time for you to retire. You're a hothead, General. And you're a warmonger. I guess I never realized that before now. We can't have people like you near the levers when things start to go wrong. For the sake of our children, and our children's children."

The general had been struck dumb.

"Sound okay to you?" Susan said. Her smile never wavered.

"You'll regret this," General Walters said. "I'm a decorated general. I've spent my entire life serving this country. And you— you're just a woman."

Susan met his steely gaze. In the past, men like this had intimidated her. But no longer.

"I am President of the United States," she replied, her voice as steely as his. "And as you refuse to address me as such, you may leave these grounds right now. Or shall I have security escort you out?"

He turned beet-red, scowling, and Susan wondered if he had ever been so angry in his life. And yet, he glanced around at the Secret Service flanking her, and if he had any ideas, seemed to think better of it. Grudgingly, with no other choice, he turned and strutted away.

Susan mingled a bit longer. She was getting ready to leave when she spotted two more guests she hadn't realized would be here. Brent Staples and Michael Parowski stood near the edge of the garden, eating finger sandwiches and drinking champagne. She caught herself staring at them. Brent was as rumpled and frail-looking as ever. Michael was as virile and handsome and confident as ever.

When they noticed her stare, they approached.

"Susan," Brent said. He didn't offer his hand. "Credit where credit is due. You did a masterful job. You dodged a bullet with the sex scandal, and then saved us all from nuclear Armageddon, so I hear. All in a day's work, eh?"

She didn't give ground.

"Why are you gentlemen here?"

Michael smiled, as confident as ever.

"We're here to bury the hatchet," Michael said. "The crisis is past. It's a good time to start rebuilding party unity."

Susan wasn't sure if her mouth was hanging open or not. She closed it firmly, just in case. The gall of these people. It was outrageous. It was unbelievable. It was…

Susan smiled sweetly.

"Brent," Susan said. "Are you still on retainer here?"

"Oh yeah," Brent said. "I've been on retainer since Thomas and you were first elected. Thomas Hayes was the third President to have me on permanent retainer, and your administration has continued…"

"In that case, you're fired," Susan said.

He stared back, mouth agape.

Now she looked at Parowski.

Kimball ambled over. He was relaxed, looking well rested and sharp. His bald head gleamed in the sunlight. His body once again seemed strong and fit. It hadn't taken him long to get back to normal.

"Kurt, can you tell me, has that security clearance issue with Michael been resolved?" Susan asked.

Michael made a face of dismissal. "You know I'm not a security risk, Susan. I mean, all's fair in love and war, but for the love of God…"

Kurt raised his eyebrows. "With everything else that's been going on?" Kurt asked. "I very much doubt it."

"Good," Susan replied. "Keep it that way."

She turned to Michael.

"Michael," she said, "I have made very few bad decisions in my life, and you were one of them."

He smiled, a cold, steely smile.

"And I am the only one you can't undo," he said, smug.

"You are wrong about that," she went on. "You're fired."

His smile hardened.

"You can't do this," he said. "The flip-flop will hurt you more than me."

"I can do, and I've already done it," she replied. "As we speak a press release is hitting all media outlets, informing them you will not be my pick for vice president. I don't care if it hurts my polls. I never want to see your face again."

She turned to the Secret Service, standing close by.

She smiled wide, and for the first time, took a big breath of relief.

"Escort the congressman," she said, "from the premises."

9:05 a.m. (12:05 p.m., Eastern Daylight Time)
Over the Pacific Ocean

247

It was a long flight home.

They had been flying for six hours, and there were still five hours to go before they reached the west coast. Time, as it often did when crossing the International Date Line, had ceased to have any meaning.

In the back of the plane, Swann and Ed had been drinking beer and playing cards for hours. They had stopped making sense a long time ago. Mostly, they were just laughing now. They were blasting rap music from the 1980s and 1990s, which they had discovered was a mutual passion.

"You talked to the President?" Trudy said. She seemed a little bit tipsy herself. Luke didn't blame her. He was halfway there. He found that alcohol numbed the pain from his stab wounds. It didn't do much for the hole where Park Jae-kyu used to be, however.

"I told you five times that I talked to her."

"And she said?"

"Trudy, she said you're off the hook. You don't have to go back to jail. You won't even be questioned, unless you want to come forward and share what you know."

"So… it's like a Presidential pardon, right?"

Luke shook his head. Trudy knew better than that. She really was drunk. "It's not a pardon. To be pardoned, you first have to be convicted of something. You were never tried or convicted. In your case, the charges have been dropped for lack of evidence."

"But will I get my old job back?" she said, and here she offered him a sly smile.

"Trudy, your old job was with the SRT. There is no SRT anymore."

"That's what I mean," she said. "Is there going to be one?"

Luke looked at her. It had never even occurred to him, before this moment, that such a thing was even possible. Would Susan Hopkins offer him a small agency if he wanted one? Something specialized, only the very best analysts and operatives, an elite, hand picked by him? They would work the most challenging cases, ones other agencies were either too big or too slow to take on. It would be the kind of agency that…

He nearly laughed. He sure was a sucker for that kind of thing.

"Trudy," he said. "I'm retired, remember?"

248

CHAPTER FORTY SEVEN

August 23
3:35 pm
United States Naval Observatory - Washington DC

"This is good coffee," Luke said.

They were sitting in Susan's upstairs study, in the small living room area, with the circular Seal of the President of the United States rug under their feet. It was pleasant in that room - Luke could see why she liked it so much. The time of day was right, throwing just a perfect amount of light through the west facing windows. And it was a good time for a cup of coffee. Luke had been back in the States a couple of days now, but he still didn't feel like he had recovered from his trip. The truth was, he felt exhausted. And when he looked at her, he saw someone who looked much the way he felt. She should be careful. This job was going to run her down one day.

"So how's life, Luke Stone?"

Luke nodded. "Not bad. Glad to be home. I heard you had some controversy around this place while I was away."

She held her forefinger and her thumb about an inch apart. "Just a little, yes. But we're pushing through it."

Luke had heard something about it, how it turned out Susan's husband was... gay? That seemed crazy, but okay, that's what people told him. Really, he didn't care either way. Gossip had never been his thing. Still wasn't. He could easily picture a life where a gay man and a heterosexual woman were married, especially if they'd been together a long time. People could do what they wanted, as long as they weren't hurting anybody in the process. That's why it was a free country. And that's why he had repeatedly put his life on the line for it.

"How is your side?" Susan said.

"Where I got stabbed?"

"Yes. Where Kim Song-Il stabbed you."

Luke shrugged. "Uh, you know. It hurts. Feels sore, like... eh. I don't know. A stab wound, if you've ever had one of those."

Susan shook her head and laughed. "Can't say that I have."

"Well, they've got me on some good painkillers for the time being. He didn't hit anything too important, so the whole thing should fade with time."

"I know you were there when he…"

"Died?" Luke said.

"Yes. And I know you were debriefed about that. The report that you…" She trailed off.

"Killed him?" Luke asked.

She nodded.

"Is that true?"

He nodded.

"He was going for the button."

Susan shook her head slowly, in clear admiration.

"Can you imagine if he had pushed it?" she asked. "You saved us from a nuclear attack."

Luke shook his head.

"He was just a cog in a wheel," he replied. "If the Chinese hadn't shown up when they did, someone else would have found a way to launch them. *You* saved us."

She smiled.

"What was he like?" she asked.

Luke smiled.

"The craziest man I'd ever met," he said. "And I've met a lot."

She laughed again, and Luke joined her. It felt good to laugh about horrible things. For a second, Luke caught an image of Park Jae-kyu, stumbling and shot full of holes in the last seconds of his life, but Luke waved that away like an annoying insect.

"So here's the serious question," Susan said. "Now that we've broken the ice. Do you want to come back? We can create another Special Response team for you, if you're willing. You could cherry pick the cream of the crop from any intelligence agency or special operations branch of the military. It would be an arm of White House security, and you would report directly to me. Which also means that in the field, your orders would supersede those of any other agency. You'd be the boss out there."

Luke sighed. He'd had a feeling this was coming.

"Well, it's tempting," Luke said. "But I'm just not ready to commit right now. I've got a family I'm trying to piece back together."

Susan nodded. "I understand that. Family is important."

"Maybe more important than country," Luke said.

"Probably so."

There was a pause where neither one said a word. Luke could see where, in another minute or two, the pause might become awkward. Despite their history together, they barely knew each other.

"Will you carry a satellite phone?" Susan said. "In case I feel the need to get in touch with you?"

Luke smiled again. "I'll carry it. But I can't guarantee what I'll do if it rings."

Susan almost seemed ready to smile, but then didn't.

"Fair enough," she responded. "Fair enough."

CHAPTER FORTY EIGHT

August 28
6:45 p.m.
Queen Anne's County, Maryland – Eastern Shore of
Chesapeake Bay

The days were getting shorter. It was noticeable now, if it hadn't been before. The sun was already far to the west. It was going to be an early evening, and maybe a cool one at that.

Jacket weather was coming in.

He and Gunner were in the boat, not far from shore. In fact, Luke could see every detail of the house from here. He watched as Becca started a fire in the outdoor fireplace and set the table on the patio. Luke had been back in the house for a week. He had no idea where this was going. He was still sleeping in the guest bedroom, but...

He noticed as Becca put a bottle of white wine and two glasses on the table.

He and Gunner weren't really trying to fish, Luke knew. They were just out here, messing around with the boat, enjoying each other's company. Gunner was about to turn eleven years old. How did that happen?

Oddly, he wasn't even wearing a zombie shirt. He wore a black T-shirt with the word ZERO HOUR on it. There was also a clock striking twelve.

"So what's Zero Hour, Monster?"

"Oh, they're a rock band, Dad. You probably never heard of them."

Luke nodded. "Hmmm. Probably not. Are they good?"

Gunner smiled, barely looked at him. "They're really good."

"Maybe we should go to one of their shows if they ever come through town."

Luke noticed Gunner didn't want to touch that one with a ten-foot pole. Sure. What would be about the uncoolest thing ever? Going to a rock show with your middle-aged dad would be right up there.

Gunner nodded at the satellite phone on the bench, maybe because he was curious, maybe just to change the subject.

"What are you planning to do now that you're back?"

"What do you mean?" Luke said.

"Well, I noticed you still have that phone. That's for if the President calls, isn't it?"

Luke nodded. "I guess it is, yeah."

"Will you answer it?"

Luke thought back to his meeting with Susan, after he had returned. It had been short and sweet. She had congratulated him, had actually hugged him. She had hinted that she'd wanted him to stick around, in whatever capacity he wanted, with whatever department, whatever personnel, he wanted. He hadn't said no. And he hadn't said yes, either. There was no need to. There was no new crisis now, for the first time he could remember.

It was time to relax. He would cross that bridge when he came to it.

But one thing was clear: he had a friend in Susan. A real friend. As crazy as it was, he was one of the closest people out there, he realized, to the President of the United States. Whenever, wherever, he was, he could reach her with a single phone call—and she'd likely stop whatever she was doing to talk to him. That made him feel gratified. It made him feel that his country loved him back.

And that feeling was enough.

"I don't need to answer it, Monster," he finally replied. "It's not ringing. And I don't think it's going to ring for a long, long time."

Slowly, Gunner's smile widened, a wider smile than Luke had ever seen. He had made his son's day.

Luke glanced ashore. Becca was there, waving her arms now.

"Let's go, Monster," Luke said. "Dinner's ready."

Coming soon!

Book #4 in the Luke Stone series

BOOKS BY JACK MARS

LUKE STONE THRILLER SERIES

ANY MEANS NECESSARY (Book #1)
OATH OF OFFICE (Book #2)
SITUATION ROOM (Book #3)

Jack Mars

Jack Mars is author of the bestselling LUKE STONE thriller series, which include the suspense thrillers ANY MEANS NECESSARY (book #1), OATH OF OFFICE (book #2) and SITUATION ROOM (book #3).

Jack loves to hear from you, so please feel free to visit www.Jackmarsauthor.com to join the email list, receive a free book, receive free giveaways, connect on Facebook and Twitter, and stay in touch!